Secrets & Howls

A Wolf's Head Bay Mystery

J.J. Brown

No Problem! Press

DEDICATION

For my friends and family, for always believing and
supporting me.

For my mom, who was the first person to read the early
drafts

For Tanya Langkopf, who knows.

Secrets & Howls

TUESDAY, JUNE 6, 1978

PROLOGUE

She was being watched.

Sitting at the scratched and battered desk in her window-framed office at *The Bay News,* she could feel it in the sharp prickling on the back of her neck, as though the tiny hairs had been touched by a cool breeze.

It was not a new feeling.

Holly Prescott-Wyatt pulled the red pencil she'd been chewing on out of her mouth, the corrections for the next day's copy falling to her lap. The typed-written pages detailing the controversy over the Heights project as well as the related interview with the Wolf's Head Bay Historical Society's president were forgotten. Next to the interview were the ads slated for the Bay's anniversary in July, celebrating one hundred twenty-five years as an independent town. Her gaze both sharp and calm, Holly surveyed her surroundings, taking in movement from the newsroom just beyond her office.

Except for the old janitor, who was busy emptying the trash baskets, and herself, the room was empty.

So. It was coming from outside.

Holly put both the copy and pencil down, then casually stood, pushed her chair back and stretched languidly. The chair moved easily on its rollers, coming to stop just inches from the tall filing cabinet. Then, with an equally casual stride, she walked around the desk to the window, gazing out into the surrounding woods, adjusting the blinds open so that she could see clearly.

Something fluttered at the edge of the building's exterior light – Holly fixed on it at once, her eyes sharp, searching as she waited for it to repeat itself. Nothing but a parking lot with only a handful of cars – hers and the few belonging to the printers working the night shift to get the paper ready for pick-up at four the next morning.

She watched for few minutes more, waiting.

Nothing happened.

Pulling the blinds shut, Holly picked up her pages, gave them a final, cursory look and initialed them. Ditto the anniversary ads. Double-duty as a part-time reporter and editor had kept her excited about her job. The controversy over the Heights and the discovery of several skeletons, recently identified as being over one hundred years old, had been the scoop of a lifetime. It had brought her into contact with many of the key players, including Cecelia Tanner, the president of the historical society.

Cecelia Tanner, a part-time elementary school teacher, had thrown herself into the Society some months after her husband's peculiar death three years earlier, moving up from clerk to president. From their first meeting through her own daughter's entry into the first grade, Holly liked Cecelia Tanner and was glad that the older woman had found a new focus.

It was also a point of pride for her that she had managed to get a statement from the tall, sexy, tight-lipped FBI agent up from San Francisco, brief though it was.

Enigmatic and to the point, he gave out information in little nuggets – just the facts, ma'am. No speculation, no embroidery of the actions being taken at the site. It would only be much later back at the newspaper, as she began to put her first story together, that Holly realized he had done what Chief of Police John Dylan always did – he gave away nothing while seeming to give away everything.

Only the FBI agent was better at it than Dylan. Holly snorted, startling herself back into the present briefly.

The special agent has been at it longer than our esteemed police chief, she thought and snickered again.

Her thoughts turned back to the story at hand, her eyes falling on the stack of manila envelopes, waiting to be mailed. One of them, slightly larger, darker in color and thicker than the rest, held her attention for a long moment. Although she couldn't see the name it was addressed to, she knew immediately to whom it was for.

*****

The Historical Society had reclaimed Jonas Brye's house in the summer of 1967 – at some point, between his death in 1911 and the Society's purchase, the previous owners of 347 March Street had installed modern plumbing, rewired the entire place and remodeled the kitchen. Although it was no longer an historically accurate building when the Society took it over, the house's interior had been carefully redone to match the time-period when Jonas Brye had first moved into it in 1853 as closely as possible, taking full advantage of the updates for fire-safety.

It was into this modernized kitchen that Mrs. Tanner had gone to prepare tea, leaving Holly alone in the sitting room, surrounded by file boxes, packed bookcases and furniture that looked like they had seen better days. As the lead reporter and a close friend of the Brye family, Holly chose to cover the story and the interview the Society's staff.

While the older woman was busy getting out plates and cups, putting the kettle on for tea and rummaging for the cookies, Holly began to poke around, opening one file box after another, her reporter's nose itching, not from the dust she disturbed, but from the certainty that something wanted to be found. She took care to put things back exactly as she found them, scanning papers, old news clippings and photographs and the old, leather-bound books stacked on shelves.

All the while, Mrs. Tanner continued to talk cheerfully from the kitchen about her plans to keep the construction site closed.

Listening to her, perusing a shelf at the far end of the room, Holly had been about to make some reply when her eye caught a non-descript book in a corner on the top shelf of the bookcase. Unlike its companions, this one had no gold-embossed title stamped on its spine and it seemed to be hiding in the shadows cast by the bookcase itself.

Mrs. Tanner's voice faded into the background as Holly pulled the old book down from the shelf. A quick examination revealed that it was a leather-bound volume, worn with deep scratches in the binding. Curious, Holly carefully opened it to the first page, wincing a little when the spine cracked, and began to read.

Cramped, a little faded and not easily deciphered, the hand-written words seemed to bleed together into one long, spidery sentence. But the longer she looked at it, the more Holly realized that she was reading the first in what appeared to be a series of long letters that had been bound together to create the volume she now held. Turning back to the first page, she found the date of the first letter – June 13, 1852. It had been written more than a century ago and addressed to someone whose name began with 'M'. Skipping ahead, she came to the end, where the writer made his regards.

Silence seemed to permeate her entire being when she finally deciphered the name of the letter writer.

In the kitchen, the kettle began to whistle. Mrs. Tanner murmured something that Holly couldn't hear, but she understood that her time was growing short. Knowing who would benefit the most from the letters-turned-diary, Holly stuffed the book into her large, denim purse carefully and discreetly, then returned to her vacated chair.

Mrs. Tanner came in the room less than a minute later.

After taking in more tea in twenty minutes than she ever had in a week, Holly made her good-byes politely and managed to get out of the historical society with no one the wiser.

*****

Holly shook her head free of the memory, then stood.

Holding both the corrected copy of her interview in one hand, she gave it a final look-over. Satisfied, she decided to take it downstairs and pass it off to Max, who would make the necessary adjustments before the paper went to press. And then she would go home and have dinner with her family. At least, she and Tim would have dinner. Patty was off on vacation with both sets of her grandparents down in Arizona.

Holly glanced at her watch and grimaced. Half past eight. Make that a late dinner, then. Or, better yet, take-out from the Moonstone at the wharf. She smiled – Tim would like that. The restaurant may be tiny, little more than a one room shack with a kitchen, but the food, particularly the blackened salmon, was delicious.

She really hated this aspect of her job – granted, it was rare that she was in the office this late, but it irked her all the same. Patty was growing up so fast – it seemed that one day she had been the dark-haired little girl in pigtails and shorts asking "Why, Mommy?" and now she was entering her junior year of high school.

Where had the time gone?

In spite of the tension inspired by the sensation of being watched, Holly chuckled as she shrugged into her jacket. She gathered up a stack of manila envelopes addressed and ready to go out in the next day's mail.

Fingering her own handwriting, Holly hoped she had made the right decision.

Checking to make sure each envelope had been addressed correctly, Holly paused at the larger one bearing a familiar name and local address.

"Marty, I really hope you know what you're doing," she muttered. "Because I sure don't."

Scooping up her purse, Holly turned off her office lights and closed the door.

Twenty minutes later, the corrected copy safely in Max's hands and the thick stack of manila envelopes in the outgoing mail slot, Holly fumbled for her keys as she left the news building and crossed the parking lot to her car.

Her skin prickled again and she stopped, alert.

Whoever was watching her was back. Or he'd never left. She suspected the latter – the sensations were so strong that she instinctively knew he was still around. Gripping her keys, she turned in a slow circle, her eyes touching on every shape, muscles tense, aware of the scents carried on the ocean breeze. From the center of town, she could hear the post office tower's bell chime out the hour.

He was close – she could feel it. The question was, where would he come from?

The attack, when it came, was sudden – her body's instinctive reflexes were faster than her mind and she ducked just in time to miss the swinging, clawed fist.

He roared, furious. She leapt back, dropping her purse, her breath coming in sharp rasps.

He was new to this – it was obvious from the way he carried himself. But new or not, if she wasn't careful, he may just take her by sheer brute force.

She intended to take him down first.

They circled each other – Holly hoped that something or someone would distract him long enough so that she could gain a better advantage, but she couldn't rely on it happening. She had to rely on herself.

As she studied him, gauging his skill, her analytical mind suggesting strategies that she automatically considered or disregarded, it occurred to her reporter's mind that there were peculiarities surrounding the death of Jackson Tanner. Peculiarities that had been similar to another death.….

Her attacker growled – her eyes widened in shock as she saw him literally expand in size and knew that she was in far more danger than she had at first realized.

She had no choice now. This was a fight that would end in one way.

She roared at him until her throat was raw, her hands like claws, and she ran at him.

His first blow sliced through her shirt and opened up her belly – four neat, parallel incisions, nearly gutting her.

The next blow killed her.

Dear M.,

I am writing to thank you again for the wonderful gifts you have made of Mr. Dickens' *David Copperfield* and Mr. Melville's *Moby Dick*. It gladdens me that you remembered how much I enjoyed the shorter tales of them both. And, given the length of our tour up the California coast on our way to Washington, both novels will help make the time go by quickly, I feel. As Mr. Hawthorne's brilliant *The House of the Seven Gables* was far too short, the massive tomes you have so graciously supplied me (matched in size only by the whale one recounts within its pages) will surely satisfy. I plan to start with *David Copperfield*, as I have not read this tale since its first publication in serial form. Let us hope that it lasts beyond this voyage, and that I do not devour the story in its entirety as I did its parts.

The voyage from San Diego to Santa Barbara, our last major port until Monterey Bay and then San Francisco, has so far been quiet, almost unnaturally so.

The contrast from the crowded and busy harbor several hours behind us as we sail north is marked — a seaman for most of my nine and thirty years, I had only seen the ocean this calm once before, when I was just twelve.

The weather is benign, with a vividly blue sky, the unbearable heat of the summer sun tempered by bracing winds from the southwest, billowing the snow-white sails of my ship, the *Bonnie Jane*.

My crew, already a cheerful lot (for I find that an unhappy crew is a poison to one's confidence and can seriously affect any voyage), can be heard often to shout foul jokes while attending to their duties, though they are careful when our passengers are present, particularly the two ladies.

And I am especially pleased to note that not once have any of our passengers taken ill, either due to the food or to the ship's movements.

It is the most uneventful voyage I have ever undertaken as captain and I thank the good Lord every morning and night for keeping us in His hands.

And yet.

And yet, since this voyage began, three nights running I have awakened from a deep slumber, my bed sheets twisted and damp with sweat, my heart pounding forcefully against my ribs, stomach in knots.

And yet, while walking the decks at high noon, I sense the darkness beneath the sun's bright rays and my throat tightens involuntarily.

As I stated earlier, I had not seen such a calm day since I was a boy of twelve and serving aboard the *Lady Jane* and witnessed a battle with the pirate Druas. In that one short and brutal day, I learned that even men who make deals with the Devil can be killed and my youthful fascination for strange tales had been put to rest.

I do not believe in the supernatural – that is to say, I have never witnessed anything untoward as examined by Friedrich Anton Mesmer or the young Fox sisters my great-aunt Lavinia has written so much of in her spidery hand.

And yet, I am experiencing presentiments of unease

regarding the days ahead.

I am afraid. I, a man who has seen the ravages of war, the brutality of marauders and nary turn a hair, am afraid of the dark.

I –

Half past six.
My thoughts of the past had been interrupted by a rapping at my door. A bright youth no older than fourteen years poked his head in when I bade him entrance. My cabin boy, Billy Tanner, had joined us three years earlier, on my last voyage north. I did not know much of his past, for he kept to himself, but he brought such a vigor to his work that it amused the men and they eventually invited him to learn of their own skills.

"Captain Brye, Master Andrews said to warn you there won't be any food left if you don't come to supper." From beneath a shaggy mane of thick, brown hair, his gray-blue eyes burned anxiously into mine. I smiled.

"Andrews must learn not to worry so much. It will be the death of him," I said and, capping my inkbottle, followed the boy to the galley.

It was with relief that I sat at the table in the cramped kitchen, hoping to distract myself from my dark turn of thoughts. I was joined by Andrews, my first mate, and two of my passengers, Victor Madison, who had hired my ship, and the Reverend Jonathan Williams, whose role in this I was never quite clear on. The Reverend's appearance is one that inspires images of a friendly rotund dwarf of legend, but when his pale eyes fall on me, I can only think of the winters in my father's home state of Maine – bitingly cold and never pleasant.

Have I not gone into detail about my passengers? In looking back at your last letter, I can see that you have raised questions that I have yet to answer, even in my ramblings of the otherworldly kind. I see I did not even report to you the nature of this voyage! Nay, not simple travel, but the building of a fortune from a gold mine. Even after the first flush of fortune, one could hardly expect California to still offer up gold from her mountains to those patient enough to till from her. And yet, she seems to have an endless supply of that precious metal.

It is not even a claim-jump – according to Mr. Madison, the mine he hired me on to take him to had gone undiscovered until ten months ago. After several months of research and much negotiation, he purchased the right to excavate the mine and sought me and my ship out.

Here, I anticipate your next question – how did he come to know of and hire out my ship for passage north? On recommendation, it seems. I hardly know what to make of that, myself, but as word of mouth is excellent for the mercantile life, then so must it be for those at sea.

The Reverend Williams, as I have mentioned, is one of Mr. Madison's companions on the voyage. How they met, I confess I do not know. I did not presume to ask, as it is not the polite thing to do, but neither did they enlighten their relationship. I suspect that it is through Mr. Madison's wife, than Mr. Madison himself, though how I came to that idea is pure speculation.

The good reverend kept to himself during the voyage – at least, up until this point. If it should change, that is up to Tomorrow. As it stands, he did not invite conversation with anyone, personable or otherwise. When spoken to, a response came through gritted teeth and was kept short.

Mr. Madison, on the other hand, is quite the opposite. A congenial man who made some of his own wealth in the sunny climes of Florida, he intended to do what the other miners have done – to find some of his own gold at the end of the rainbow. If nothing else, he would have a piece of land to make his own.

Is that not a kind of gold in itself?

His wife, Agnes Madison, is a kind, gentle creature who spends most of her time with her babe and another woman, a distant cousin who helps her tend to the child.

The tenderness with which her husband bestows on her and his son stirs an unfamiliar ache in my heart and her soft voice singing lullabies ring in my ears into the night.

M., I now find myself pondering the choices I had made in my life and the choices I did not make. Had I been right, to give up the prospect of having a wife, children and a permanent home in order to pursue a life at sea?

Many men in my profession did, finding their satisfaction with prostitutes when they were in port and while I also engaged in the same activities, I have long since learned that it merely served the itch and failed to cure the longing.

Observing the intimacy between Mr. Madison and his wife brings home to me the ultimately loneliness of my profession. I suppose I ought to salute him for his courage in leaving all that is familiar and throwing one's lot in with the unknown, especially with a young wife and child in tow, for such a task is not an easy one.

But I find I cannot – any expedition that involves the Reverend is bound to come to a bad end. Why do I sense such darkness attached to this man? He has not spoken a word except in prayer since boarding my ship, but the shadows I have sensed at the start of the voyage I now associate with him. Why? I have come across several zealots in my travels, but however misguided they were, none held evil in their hearts as this man did.

How I knew this, I do not know and dare not explore. I can hear you chastise me – the only one who knows what lies in a man's heart would be our Lord and Savior. And you are quite right to correct me.

If Mr. Madison also courts evil in the company of this man, he hides it well. For his family's sake, I hope he is innocent of the Reverend.

My hand is trembling as I write this – I stare at it, half in disbelief, half in amused terror as I scratch out words on this blank page. I almost spill my inkbottle as I dip my quill, my hand is shaking so badly.

Pray for us.

I realize this sounds rather histrionic for a voyage that so far seems to be going well, but I do ask it of you, my dear, M-. Pray to God to watch over us, that if we are indeed in His hands, as we have been taught from birth, then perhaps, in His infinite wisdom, guide us away from our current path, one I sense holds great danger.

I will mail this letter when we stop next. I hold you in high esteem and look forward to the day when we can meet again in calmer times.

Yours in good health,

Jonas Brye

Captain, the Bonnie Jane

WEDNESDAY, JUNE 7, 1978

ONE

The sun had crossed behind the redwood forest and into late afternoon by the time Marita Brye passed a sign indicating distance in miles to the next three cities – Wolf's Head Bay (1 mile), Sleepy Eye Cove (17 miles) and Wickerman Falls (35 Miles). It occurred to her that she could simply keep on driving, stopping only long enough to keep the gas tank full and the occasional trip to the ladies' room.

She put more pressure on the gas.

A little more than a mile later, she turned her light blue 1968 VW bug right onto the exit from the California coast highway and onto the less commonly traveled, but more familiar, roadway. Although the Pacific was now hidden from view, she could still taste the salt in the air, even fancied that she could hear the surf pounding mercilessly against the coastal cliffs.

The radio had been on since she'd left Bodega Bay over an hour ago – the much-needed lunch break had given her a chance to slow down and breathe deep. From the first whiff, she realized how much she had missed the salty air.

Her hand hovered briefly over the knob to turn it off

– the volume was at nearly full blast and it competed with the deafening chatter of the engine. She could barely hear the d.j.'s cheerfully long and obnoxious monologue as he set up the next song.

She left it alone.

The initial excitement surrounding her move back into the area had gradually given way to a heavy sense of dread. The natural canopy created by the tall redwoods blocked the sun's golden rays effectively, leaving the road in shadow as it twisted ahead and out of sight. The greens and red-browns seemed muted now, darker than when she had left – had it only been fifteen years ago?

It had – except for that one unbearably hot week in July of '69, the summer after the twins had turned eight, Marty had not set foot in the town she'd been born and grown up in. Instead, she had purposefully invited her younger siblings down to visit her rather than make the long drive back up and face old ghosts.

And yet, here she was, in the only car she'd ever owned, driving down the two-lane paved road back to the town that haunted her.

A chill settled over her and she shivered involuntarily, wondering if it was the shade or the premonitions she now felt. Her heart thudded against her chest – the memory of the bitter and final argument with Ben before her departure from Los Angeles echoed in her mind like a black, viscous pool of tar, reminding her of another argument surrounding a similar set of circumstance. The lawyer's letter that led to her decision to make this long journey home alone had suddenly seemed like a godsend.

A deer stepped into the road without warning – she twisted the steering wheel hard to the right, slamming both feet onto the brake.

The little blue car spun wildly near the edge of the road, gravel spewing up from the tires. For one crazy moment, Marty thought it would tip over. A precious, silent pause, and then it righted itself, landing on all four wheels with a teeth-jarring jolt. The engine cut off and left her in silence, with only the sounds of crickets and the occasional cry of a hawk.

She pulled up the emergency brake with a jerk, hands shaking. After a minute, she began to struggle with her seatbelt – finally unlocking it, she got out of her car and leaned against it, trembling, her breath quick and shaky. Her heart kept pace with her breath and she closed her eyes tight to hold back the sudden flush of hot tears.

Ben's criticism of her driving whispered for attention, teasing.

She ignored it.

Taking several deep cooling breaths, Marty opened her eyes and raised her head, meeting the calm, curious gaze of the deer. It was a doe, she realized, still young and beautiful, not yet afraid of humans.

It seemed they gazed at each other for hours – then, from somewhere in the forest, a shot rang out. Startled, both woman and deer looked east – then, with a flick of her tail, the doe vanished, the only visible sign of her existence a small pile of pellets steaming in the cool air.

Feeling a little steadier, Marty circled the bug, looking for a flat tire, a leaking radiator, anything to keep from going on.

Nothing. The car was perfect. Unless the engine didn't turn over, she could get into town and take possession of her house before two, only forty-five minutes away. Coming back around the front, she stopped abruptly, her gaze fixed on the windshield on the passenger side.

A small hole, cracks spidering out from it, had appeared. It hadn't been there when she'd left Los Angeles early this morning, she knew.

Marty's fingers traced the jagged patterns as she searched her surroundings intently, seeking the shooter and finding no one but the trees, the road and the oppressive silence as her companions.

Getting back into the driver's seat, she shut the door and took a deep breath, turning the key, resisting the urge even to think that the little car wouldn't start. The engine turned over on the first try, caught and settled into its familiar rattle, the tiny car vibrating into her teeth. Satisfied, she turned the engine off and leaned back, resting her head in her hand, her elbow on the door. Her eyes slid from the hole in the window to the passenger seat beside her.

The blank manila envelope lay there, bulging from the contents inside.

She watched as her fingers caressed the worn, thick paper, tracing the outline of a bulky object inside. Underneath it was another envelope, worn and creased, written in a hand as familiar to her as her own.

Pulling it out, she smiled at Holly Prescott's handwriting, remembering that same script marking her yearbook, holiday and birthday cards and the long letters detailing her life after high school and college. Now Holly's letters detailed the tempest known as Wolf Heights and her excitement at Marty's return to the Bay, noting that with Marty's home on Fry Street, they were only a block apart, practically neighbors.

Tucking the envelope away, Marty faced forward and started the engine again, shifting into first. The radio came back to life in mid-song as the VW lurched forward and she maneuvered it down the narrow road. As she rounded a sharp curve, the song ended, but the d.j. came back on in full swing.

"That was *Rockin' Down The Highway* with the Doobie Brothers and coming up on this spectacular day are the newest hits from Donna Sommers, the Eagles and Barry White. Don't forget the recap of Casey Kasem's Top Forty Hits in thirty minutes and coming up, Warren Zevon howls out his latest."

A jingle for RC Cola came on, loud, bright and cheerful. She gave up and turned the radio off.

Moving was such a pain in the ass.

*****

Coming out of the thick gloom of the forest and into the brightness of the sun was almost like hitting a wall.

Blinking, trying to block out the sun's rays with one hand, Marty almost missed the *Welcome to Wolf's Head Bay* sign (founded July 19, 1853, pop. 9,782) – an enormous block of wood intricately carved into the shape of a howling wolf. A sign proclaiming the one hundred twenty-fifth anniversary of the Bay's founding had been put up just below it, its design matching the city logo of howling wolves.

Just beyond the sign was a small hill – coming up over it, she finally was able to get a good look at the town she'd last seen at twenty. It looked as she remembered, as she had left it – sleepy, peaceful, and dull.

She didn't find that sameness very comforting.

A mile later, the road split and she finally saw something new, something that hadn't been there when she'd left. It was the lane going to the right – freshly paved for several yards, it then became packed gravel. At the start of this fresh, new lane was another sign, this one clearly not meant to be permanent. The faded look to it gave that much away, as did the crossed out date.

In a fancy script, the sign proclaimed *Wolf Heights, to be dedicated September 15, 1978.*

Indignation at the mere thought of the hills surrounding the Bay being dotted with homes warred with anger over the cavalier attitude the city managers were taking over the recent controversy.

In the days leading up to her return, Marty had held long phone conversations with her older brother. Their mother, had she been alive, would have said that she was testing the waters. Marty preferred to think that she was gathering important information on the emotional atmosphere of her family and how she would be received. In one such call, after much griping on the influx of tourists buying up property and demanding changes on their new town, Mike mentioned that, while turning up earth on the first tract over a month ago, contractors had uncovered what appeared to be a mass grave.

Holly had confirmed this in her most recent letter, one Marty had received only two days before she left Los Angeles.

The construction workers had been given strict orders to not talk about the project in any way except as to what their specific jobs entailed. Had this rule been followed, no one would have been the wiser about what was found (or not found) while the Heights was being built.

The only reason why anyone knew about it at all was that one of the workers was pimply-faced Cory Tanner, a boy two years out of high school and one of Mike's former students. His mother, Cecelia Tanner, was the zealous president of the Bay's Historical Preservation Society, a position she'd taken over only a year after her husband had died, and it was to her that he blabbed the grisly discovery.

Mrs. Tanner immediately whipped the town's sense of civic duty up into a frenzy and questioned the mayor and his colleagues about the matter. There were town hall meetings, petitions, and, at one point, insults bordering on fisticuffs, but it wasn't until Mrs. Tanner uttered the words "burial site" that the matter took on a whole new tone.

The local sheriff called in the FBI, who, after determining that the remains had been buried for more than fifty years, brought in a team of forensic archaeologists, led by the well-known archaeologist Doctor Albert Sneldon, who then gave the mass grave a more definite age of at least one hundred to one hundred fifty years.

The construction had been shut down until further notice.

A flash of movement caught Marty's eye and she put her foot on the brake, slowing to take a longer look at the

Heights.

On a cordoned-off plot closest to the road were three men in jeans and flannel shirts, carefully digging into the dirt. Standing on the mound next to them was a tall man in a dark blue suit.

She had the briefest impressions of dark hair, a sharp gaze and a walkie-talkie before the road curved down and to the left, leading away from the Heights. With it now behind her, her attention was quickly arrested by more familiar sites as she surveyed the town and bay before her.

On a hill at the edge of the forest, four miles north of the town and two miles west of the construction site, was an old mansion. If she remembered right, it would be locked behind wrought-iron gates and its windows shuttered, the turrets barely seen through the branches and ivy covered the gates hungrily.

She looked further west, her eyes resting lightly on the old lighthouse and cottage overlooking the Bay and the ocean beyond. Ahead of her, the two-lane road stretched out through town. It disappeared into a thick grove of eucalyptus trees, she knew, leading to the tiny harbor and wharf where she had spent many childhood hours with her friends chasing the seagulls along the docks, just as she did the day before her birthday.

The day before her mother died.

She turned her attention back to the road, her hands trembling. She would not fall apart, she would not, she would not.....

Weaver's Garage came up abruptly on her right and the old Rosemont Hotel on her left. Slowing to a stop at the three-way stop intersection between the two buildings, Marty took a deep breath. It may be fun, she thought, to take the long route to her house. See how the old home town has changed in the years since her last visit.

She shook her head, amused. *Yeah, right. What changes?*

Almost of its own volition, the Beetle turned left, heading four blocks south towards Rockland Way and the tiny building that housed the mayor's office. At the stop sign, she turned left onto Chaney Road, down one block and turning right onto Talbot Street, heading towards the ocean, the afternoon sun glinting off the water in bright, blinding darts. Marty passed the post office and its tiny tower on her right, then maneuvered the car south down Main Street a block later.

She drove by Myrna's Diner, where the best dark chocolate shakes and fries in town were served. She remembered how, as a teen, she and her friends would go to the diner and have one after the matinee show at the Wolverine Theater. Across the street from the diner stood the police station and its connecting parking lot. There were only two cars parked there at the moment, she saw, which meant a couple of deputies were out on patrol somewhere. If there was anything in the Bay to be patrolling, of course. She snickered at the thought. On the next block over was the Second Time Around Bookshop, which Holly's husband co-owned and managed with his father. Beyond that, stood the library.

Turning onto Clifton Road, she passed the old mortuary and the tiny hospital on her left. It occurred to her now, as it had when she was young, the irony of having the two buildings so close to one another. The situation couldn't have been more perfect than if the school had been built right next to them.

In between were newer streets, upscale shops she didn't remember and a number of young families on bicycles.

Five blocks down, she turned south again onto Chase Avenue, passing the all-school athletic field. Next to the field stood the three-story school house, looking tired and old with its brick façade chipped in places.

Marty remembered the stories surrounding the summer fire of '28, when the original building burned to the ground. Several people had died trying to put it out, among them, her grandfather. The cause of the fire had never been explained and the sheriff's office had eventually declared it unsolved. The current building had been erected the following year and dedicated to those who had died. It opened its doors a month later, when the fall session began. Now, as it settled into its foundation and began to lose its newness, the structure seemed to hunch in on itself.

Marty looked away, feeling overwhelmed by the past.

TWO

Tavis Riley, Special Agent FBI, paused in his cursory communications over the walkie-talkie to the sheriff when the light blue VW bug rattled past. The tiny vehicle slowed, its lone occupant obviously wanting to catch a quick glimpse of the activity surrounding the housing construction site.

His nose twitched once, scenting a light floral scent that did not match any of the surrounding fauna, and smiled. Female.

Harsh static from the walkie-talkie in his hand pulled him back to the present, and he blinked. Last night's violent death of the newspaper editor had set everyone in the police department on edge. He thought of her now, recalling when he had met the woman, who was also a reporter.

Her last name was Wyatt; when he'd first arrived at the dig, she had been covering the story and tracked him down. Upon their first meeting, it was clear that his arrival back at the Bay was not a coincidence and she knew it. There was an unspoken agreement to not bring up the past. He understood her position, as she did his — it seemed to amuse her and he had hoped to talk with her more during his stay. Unfortunately, his work and her job kept them from talking as freely as he would have liked.

And now she was dead.

So, because of his respect for her and the local chief of police, he'd agreed to be on a tighter contact than he normally would have liked. Tugging at his collar, he spoke into the walkie-talkie again. "Riley. Did you copy that?"

"Copied. Keep me posted on any new developments. There are some very anxious people standing just outside my office. Over."

"Roger that." To prevent any more unexpected interruptions, Tavis Riley turned the walkie-talkie off and turned to his car, intending to leave his tie in the back seat. Raking his fingers through his thick black hair, he paused in his movements, his gaze flickering once to the view of the ocean, then faced the older black man climbing out of the trench.

It had been nearly six weeks since he had been sent up from the San Francisco office to take charge of the investigation. He had at first thought of turning the case down, not wanting to stir up old memories of his past by returning to the town of his birth, the place that had been his home for a brief time. In the end, curiosity won out and he had driven up, renting out a tiny, old cottage that was nestled up against the woods on the south-east side of town. It was an ideal home, as it had the added benefit of a long dirt drive and the nearest neighbors were more than a mile away.

If anyone thought that the handsome FBI agent was being deliberately reclusive, he'd have simply pointed out that he liked his privacy. No one had brought it up and he was left alone. Now, he was glad that he had chosen to accept the case. Once here, seeing what had been found, he knew that, logically, there could have been no one else. And found the irony both amusing and troubling.

Identifying the bones as either human or animal had become a long and tedious task, although, regardless of species, after having sent several bone samples back to the lab in the San Francisco office for testing, it had been firmly established that, in spite of the lack of weapons in the grave, the condition of the bones indicated that there had been a fierce battle and that the mass grave had been dug more than a century earlier.

So far, that had been about all that anyone could really agree on.

"Agent Riley?" the man asked. Tavis searched his memory and soon came up with a name. Albert Sneldon was one of the few leading experts contracted by the FBI when dealing with sites such as this.

"Dr. Sneldon."

Sneldon stopped just a foot or so away, staring at the fragment in his hands. It was a large piece – from where Tavis stood, he suspected it to be a part of the skull, most likely a lower jaw bone. He waited for the older man to speak.

"It's not something I've ever seen before," Sneldon said at last. "Some of the lines on the bone structure suggest that this may be a human jaw bone, but…." He trailed off, troubled.

"But?" Tavis prodded gently.

"No human ever had teeth quite like this. Not even a gorilla would have these kinds of incisors or canines. These look more like wolf teeth."

They fell silent, contemplating the strange jaw bone.

"Send it to Doctor Galloway at the lab, anyway," Tavis said at last. "That's pretty much all we can do at this point." He turned and started to walk back to his car, a dark blue sedan, then paused to ask, "What does next week look like? Will you have your team back out?"

Sneldon shook his head. "Not until later in the week. We have a two day conference over the weekend and then some of my team members need to issue final exams at the university. So it'll be a much smaller group. Maybe next Thursday."

Tavis nodded. "Sounds good. And, like the good sheriff said, keep me posted on your findings."

Sneldon gave him a tired grin. "Good luck with your anxious friends."

Tavis grinned back. "They're not my friends."

Sneldon chuckled as he started back for the dig and his crew, then turned back, digging something out of his pocket.

"Found this," he said, handing it to Tavis. "Looks like something from a woman's necklace."

Tavis took the small piece, staring at it, the rest of the world falling away as he took in the exquisite details. It was a small moonstone, its setting clearly broken from a larger piece. The setting was copper, twisted into delicate leaves spreading outward, as if the stone had fallen into a pool.

"Seen something like it before?" Sneldon was asking.

Tavis pulled himself back to the present. "Yes. A long time ago." He hesitated, his hand curling over the piece. "Do you mind if I keep this?"

Sneldon waved a hand. "It's documented, but don't go giving it to a girl."

Tavis grinned again, but it held no humor. "Don't worry. Haven't met one I wanted to give jewelry to."

Sneldon snorted. "No worries. That'll change."

Tavis waved a hand at the older man and went to his car. He was no longer needed at the site, at least for the time being. His presence only impeded their work. If Sneldon and his crew found anything, they knew how to contact him.

He turned his car around and pointed it towards town, his eyes on the small wharf and fleet of fishing vessels. He needed lunch and there was only one thing on his mind to satisfy his stomach – steak and lobster.

*****

Twenty minutes later, Marty turned the little bug south down Fry Court and parked in front of Number 17. The van had backed up into the driveway and was now parked, the movers out and lounging with a relaxed air against the van.

Marty made no move to get out of her car – instead, she sat and looked at the house, one hand playing with the moonstone pendant around her neck, her heart a dead weight in her chest. The engine chattered, ignored.

This was it – the house she'd grown up in. Was born in, actually. Lost her first tooth in the front yard, never to be seen again. She had still gotten her dime under her pillow, but it came after writing a lengthy letter of apology in red crayon to the Tooth Fairy, with Mom's help. She had kissed a boy for the first time at age thirteen on the front porch, both of them spitting afterwards. Celebrated many birthdays until the last one, the one when her mother died.

Although it had not been lived in since she had left the Bay fifteen years earlier, the quaint two-story Craftsman house had been kept clean and maintained. The lawn had obviously been mowed recently and someone had taken it upon himself to paint both the fence and house a fresh white.

Then one of the moving men – his name patch read 'Jeff' – came up and tapped on her window. She started, then rolled it down as she turned the engine off, smiling into his warm brown eyes.

"You have the key, ma'am?"

She nodded. "Yes, I do. Wait."

Marty opened the door and got out, her green skirt billowing slightly in the cool breeze.

Jeff moved aside, admiring her legs silently as she opened the manila envelope and pulled out a heavy set of keys. She took one key off the ring and handed it over to him, then watched as Jeff trotted up the walk and porch steps to unlock the front door.

The other man – Frank, she would find out later – was busily opening up the van and unloading the dolly.

She studied the bright orange California poppies that bloomed on either side of the porch steps, the porch-swing rocking gently in the sudden breeze, the woodshed almost hidden to one side, then looked back at the house itself.

She had the sudden, disconcerting feeling that the house was looking back at her, waiting for her.

Then the feeling was gone.

She grabbed her old suitcase from the trunk, the files off the front seat and her purse and hurried up the walk, shivering delightedly in the cool, sunny day.

The movers had, by this time, succeeded in maneuvering the couch from the van to the porch and were presently stuck in the front door. Smothering a loud giggle born of exhaustion and stress, Marty went around to the back, gripping the house key.

She resisted the urge to give the backyard more than a cursory glance, aware of the heavy, wooden picnic table and chairs in the far corner. They stood empty where a party had once held sway. Even more, she refused to look up at the deck that she knew was adjacent to the master bedroom.

"Mrrreow!"

Marty looked down at the orange tabby sitting at her feet. The cat was gazing up at her expectantly with intelligent gold eyes.

"Thank you, but no," she said, firmly, nudging the cat away with one foot. "I am not interested in having a cat right now. Find someone else."

She unlocked the kitchen door and was about to push it open when she saw the note taped to the window. Her name was scrawled on it in the familiar script older brother and she smiled. Taking it down, she unfolded it, reading.

Glad to have you home. The painters finished up late yesterday morning, so I left a few windows open. Out on the lake with Dad. Will be home after 5. Call me or come on by the house. We need to talk. Mike

THREE

She tore the note off the door, scowling, her mood darkening.

"Gee, Mike, I wonder what about," she muttered. Not that she couldn't figure it out for herself, given the recent and rather argumentative nature of their phone calls prior to her moving back. Grumbling under her breath, she stuffed the note into her purse and turned the key, pushing the door open. Standing in the doorway, she could smell the faint scent of new paint. The cat shot inside, brushing past her ankles. Dropping both purse and suitcase, she chased it through the kitchen, down the narrow hall and up the stairs, taking them two at a time.

She paused at the landing, awash in a sudden flood of memories, and counted the number of doors (six). Proceeding down the hall, cat forgotten, she tried each one, beginning with the one to her left. It revealed a narrow staircase that led to the attic.

Marty closed that door and continued on, rediscovering the common bathroom, the hall closet and the master bedroom. The master was spacious, open and airy, much larger than she remembered as a child. It offered huge closets and a full bath. French windows opened out onto the small deck overlooking the back yard. She stared at the French windows for a long time before stepping back into the hall.

This would be her room, she decided, quietly closing the door behind her.

Opening the remaining doors, she discovered three more bedrooms, two of which that faced the street. The third room had been Mike's, she remembered and was a good size, but it faced the woods, something she hadn't been too keen on as a kid. Storage for now, she decided. If she changed her mind, it could always be redone.

She moved on to the one next to it, a spacious, well-lit corner room that not only faced Fry Street, but the ocean beyond. This one had been hers, right up until her father had moved them out more than a year after her mother's death.

She had left for college not long after that.

Marty shook her head loose of the past firmly. She would make her old room into her office. Her desk would fit quite nicely under the window, where she could set up her typewriter to write and think and research in solitude. Plus, the porch roof extended itself right under the window and she imagined sitting on it to watch the sunsets and shooting stars like she used to before everything changed.

Thinking this, she opened the window in question to air out the room. Looking out onto the street, she breathed in the salty air before noticing the boy and girl.

They were coming out of the side-yard of the soft yellow single-story house across the street, where they had clearly dumped their bikes unceremoniously.

The boy was latching up the gate. He had red hair and fair skin that looked like it had seen too much sun and was deep in discussion with the girl, who clearly wasn't paying close attention.

The girl's skin was fair, too, but not as sun-kissed. Her own hair was as black as the clothes she wore and had been parted in the middle to make two thin braids. The braids twitched from one shoulder to the other whenever she shook her head in response to what the boy was saying. The utter flat blackness of her hair suggested that it had come from a bottle, but in spite of this, the similarity in looks and build and their camaraderie made it easy to suppose that they were siblings.

The cat jumped on the sill, climbed onto the porch roof and flopped down, purring contentedly in the sun. She sighed.

"Fine, have it your way. But don't expect me to give you a name." She looked back at the teens.

The boy was obviously upset over something, but the girl was no longer listening to him. She had caught sight of Marty and was staring back with undisguised curiosity. The boy didn't notice – he was busy scuffing the sidewalk with one shoe and almost tripped over his own feet.

Dumping her stuff in the master bedroom, she almost ran downstairs. By this time, Jeff and Frank were struggling with the dining table, once again stuck in the front door by its awkward shape. She changed course and went out the back, going through the dining room, then the kitchen and was outside, running around to the front before her thoughts could reclaim her mood.

*****

Cassie Brye watched the activity surrounding Number 17 with great interest, ignoring her brother, Peter, as he grumbled under his breath, their quest for the perfect milkshake temporarily forgotten.

Although twins, they were not identical. Despite this, they had, over the years, managed to confuse their teachers enough to make it worthwhile. At least, until Cassie decided to dye her hair. Her nose ring pinched a little and she scratched it carefully.

"What am I going to do?" Peter asked of no one. "My summer totally sucks."

She barely glanced at him. "It's your fault. You

should have been paying attention."

"But she didn't have to flunk me!"

Cassie rolled her eyes. "Ms. Brennan is the easiest teacher in the world. I don't get how you could flunk her English class."

Peter squirmed. "I got bored. I don't see why you're taking summer classes if you don't need to."

"I'll get bored. Besides, I promised Mr. Wyatt that I'd start my history paper early."

"You only need one paper for AP History."

Cassie grinned, smug. "I know. I'm doing two. One regular, one in depth. Pictures, graphs, the works."

Pete wasn't paying her any attention. He was looking across the street at the moving van. "Hey, I wonder who's moving in?" Cassie whapped him over the head. Peter yelped, glaring at her. "What'd you do that for?"

Cassie sighed. "You're such an idiot, you know that? No wonder you flunked Ms. Brennan's class."

Peter only glared at her and started grousing again, kicking at a loose pebble in the sidewalk and almost losing his balance. The right bedroom window facing Fry Street opened and a woman poked her head out.

The sun caught the muted fire in her hair when she saw them. Peter didn't see the woman, but Cassie did, recognizing her almost immediately.

The woman disappeared, only to reappear a few minutes later, emerging from behind the house at a run. She was across the street and embracing Cassie before Pete thought to look up.

"What the -?" Pete began, before he, too, was caught up in the woman's embrace. "Marty! Hey, how are you?"

Marty stood back, flushed and happy. "Doing good, monkey. How's Dad?"

Pete grinned, showing braces. "Good. Ellen's not thrilled you're back, but hey, can't have everything."

Marty thought briefly of Ellen Farley, now her brother's wife, then dismissed it. She gestured to the house they now stood in front of. "Do they live here now?"

Cassie nodded. "Yeah. They used to live on Maple Street, but Mike wanted to live here. Ellen's totally pissed."

Marty stared up at her brother's new home, thoughtful. "Is Ellen home?"

Cassie shook her head. "She's out at the lake with Mike and Dad. Another reason her knickers are in a twist. She hates fishing. I think she likes her antiques more than people. Or nature." She touched her nose suddenly. "Damn ring."

With a quick movement, she plucked the ring from her nose. Marty fully expected blood to come pouring out and screams to ensue. None did. Cassie caught her bemused stare and held the ring out for him to see. "Fake nose ring. I didn't have the guts to go all the way. I'm not into pain.

"Oh." For a minute, Marty couldn't think of anything to say. Then, eyeing her pale face, dark eye make-up and black clothes, she asked, "Who are you supposed to be this week? Wednesday Addams or Lily Munster?"

Cassie giggled. "Neither. I just like the look."

They fell silent. Then Peter broke the silence by inviting Marty to join them for a milkshake.

"Would love to, kid," she said with a sigh, "but I've got the movers to supervise and things to unpack."

"Are you going to be at Dad's Friday night?" Cassie asked. "You know, the weekly family dinner."

Marty grimaced. "I don't know. Does he even know I'm back?"

"Who knows," Pete said. "I don't think he remembers that you left." Marty laughed. "So, how about those shakes?"

Marty shook her head. "Not today. Give me a couple days and I'll treat you both."

"Hey, good deal." Pete grinned, his hazel eyes impish. "We're gonna hold you to it. Come on, Cass."

The twins started down the walk. Marty glanced

down at their bikes.

"Why not take your bikes?" she called after them.

Pete kept walking, but turned so that he was going backwards. "The chain on mine broke. Cassie won't ride double."

"Our combined weight would break it," Cassie pointed out and they broke up, laughing.

"See you at Dad's for dinner!" Pete yelled. Marty smiled, waved and started back towards her house feeling lighter in her heart than she had in days, maybe weeks.

Perhaps moving back wasn't such a bad idea, after all. And, for the first time, Marty began to look forward to re-visiting her home town.

*****

Tavis Riley sat alone at a corner table by the window overlooking the harbor, his back to the wall, a position which also afforded him an excellent view of the dining room.

While not the only restaurant on the wharf, it was certainly the least fancy of them, more for the locals than the tourists to enjoy. It was a square room, decked out in fishing gear and nets, wooden mastheads in each corner and a mounted swordfish on one wall. The Moonstone Tavern had been recommended to him his first night in town ten weeks earlier by the real estate agent who had found him the small cottage on the south-west side of town that met his requirements.

The same real estate agent, an attractive, dark-haired woman in her forties, had also suggested mutual exchanges of the personal kind. He had politely declined. As a thank-you for her hard work in finding his home, however, he took her out to dinner, to the Moonstone, and had become a regular patron ever since. Only a few minutes earlier, he had put in his order to the waitress. Now, he was enjoying dark ale, the glass cold to the touch, his eyes sweeping the dining area and the outside views periodically.

At the bar, two men in their seventies were debating over what time to go fishing the next day, their tones low and amiable. Nathan Copes, the man standing behind the bar and wiping down glasses before putting them away, was younger than his customers by at least two decades. Nate picked up the lease from the previous owner three years earlier, made a few changes and reopened under its current name, intent on owning the building.

The first year, so Tavis was made to understand, had been rough, but Copes was determined not to give up. In fact, the real estate agent had confirmed that the building was now in Copes' name. Now, while Tavis watched, the new owner straightened the framed deed and business license, all the while observing the two older men at his bar with a studied casualness. Occasionally, Copes threw a word in here and there to redirect the flow of conversation when it seemed to get a little heated.

Tavis smiled to himself as he observed the scene, reminded of another man from his youth who would do much the same thing.

His gaze drifted to the window and the town east of the harbor. He could barely make out the Heights and the road going back to the highway, as trees partially obscured the view. The town center was too close and up-hill to see clearly, but the lighthouse was visible to the north. His eyes followed the line of the treetops, traveling up until he saw the snowy mountain peaks that gave the town its name.

"Or so some believe," he muttered under his breath.

"Excuse me, sir?"

Tavis looked up at the waitress, his dinner steaming from the plate in her hand. Her name tag, he saw now, read 'Jesse'. She was looking at him curiously. He smiled and leaned back, allowing her to place it on the table in front of him.

As she leaned forward, her bracelet slipped forward on her wrist. Tavis recognized the gems as moonstone.

"Lovely bracelet," he said, picking up his fork.

The waitress — she couldn't have been more than twenty-one, he thought — beamed with pride as she held it up. "It belonged to my great-grandmother. My mother gave it to me when I turned sixteen."

Tavis complimented the treasure again, sending the girl away glowing. Chuckling to himself, he took his first bite of the medium rare steak. His taste buds erupted with saliva and he dug into it, his eyes watching the other patrons with casual curiosity.

The two men at the bar finally seemed to settle on a time, he noted. The elder of the two, a lean, silvery-gray haired gentleman, stood and shook hands with his companion and Nate before slapping an old ball cap on his head.

Just as he reached the door, his friend called out, "Five sharp, Clarke!"

The man Clarke waved a hand to show he heard and left, the door swinging shut on a gentle breeze.

Tavis stopped in mid-bite, his gaze sharp on the man as he walked easily across the parking lot to a battered truck. There had been a ring on the forefinger of his right hand, of that Tavis was sure.

He was also sure that the gem the ring held was the same as the ones in the young waitress's bracelet.

Moonstone.

FOUR

Sitting in the dark, cramped living room of his house on Oak Street, Ronald Brye lounged comfortably in front of his TV, the remote in his left hand and a half-empty bottle of soda in the other.

Next to him, resting against his left thigh, was a plain, varnished wooden box. Made of oak, it was twenty-two inches long and ten inches wide. His hand would occasionally leave the remote lying on the couch cushion and caress the box. He was not aware of his hand doing this.

The restored antique grandfather clock in the corner behind him tolled the half-hour – he glanced at his wristwatch to gauge its accuracy and noted with satisfaction that the time was seven-thirty. Ellen had been a marvel with that clock.....

A bowl of popcorn was cradled in his lap and he ate each popped kernel one by one, chewing thoughtfully. Cassie and Pete weren't home when he'd returned from his trip to the lake with Mike and Ellen twenty minutes earlier – he assumed they were either at Myrna's or with friends.

Channel 6 was airing one of his favorite movies, an

old black and white starring Gene Tierney – since he only had the aerial antenna, the picture was none too clear, but it wasn't long before he had stopped paying attention to it.

Instead, he watched the shadows playing on the walls and over his father's hunting rifle, remembering similar ones around the campfires Carl Brye would build.

The last time they had driven to the lake two hours away had been the June of '28, the month he had turned ten, the summer of the fire in Wolf's Head Bay that took not only the old school building, but his father's life.

Going to the lake had always been the highlight of his childhood, mainly because they would take the old county road instead of the newly created one, which went to the regular campgrounds. Instead, they would go to the campgrounds that had lost favor to campers when the new road went in.

The truck would bounce through ruts, over rocks and on more than one occasion, Ronald would clip his head against the door frame, sometimes hard enough to make his teeth hurt. Although secure, the old rifle Carl Brye kept clean and polished would rattle in its rack, reminding young Ronald of its deadly power even when empty.

The county road ended maybe thirty feet past the creek, a couple of fallen trees on the right going in, but was wide enough to hold the '22 Ford truck as it spewed gravel and dirt from beneath its tires.

It had been like any other camp-out with his father, Ronald remembered, but it had stopped being the same when they reached their final destination. The site looked the same – the circle of rocks coated in black soot from past fires had been covered over with leaves and twigs.

It assaulted them when they climbed out of the truck – the rank stench of unwashed fur mingled with smells too overpowering to identify.

Young Ronny Brye clamped a hand tight over his nose, but he thought he could still smell it, even through his mouth. His father was tense, alert. Ronny was reminded of his dog, Homer, who had died two years earlier. When he scented something unfamiliar in the air, Homer would grow rigid, growling softly in his throat at anyone who came near until he was sure all was safe. Carl Brye had the same attitude.

When he finally spoke, his voice was sharp, hoarse. "Get back in the truck, boy. We're going home."

"But, Dad…"

"Now." The quiet intensity in Carl Brye's voice convinced Ronny that the situation was serious and he silently climbed back in the truck, his heart beating furiously against his chest, leaking adrenaline into his body.

After what seemed like an eternity, his father climbed into the driver's side and fired it up, not even bothering to let the engine warm. Throwing the truck in gear, he wheeled the truck around and started back the way they came, hitting the brakes so hard a minute later that Ronny hit his chin on the dash, his teeth slicing his lower lip open.

One of the dead trees was lying across the road, blocking their way.

"Dad," Ronny said, his voice shaky.

"I know," came the man's grim reply. Reaching behind the seat, Carl Brye pulled out a heavy rope and left the truck, walking cautiously towards the tree. After a minute, Ronny followed and watched as his father looped the rope around the trunk a few times, then secured it in a knot he had yet to master. Something cast a shadow over them and they jumped.

Standing between them and the old truck was the tallest, strangest-looking creature Ronny had ever seen. It was also the hairiest – head to toe, long, thick hair hung from its body.

For a long moment, man, boy and legend regarded each other silently. Then, in long quick strides, the creature turned and disappeared into the darkness. When the sounds of its traversing had diminished, they bolted for the truck. Once again, gravel sprayed from the tires as the truck strained against the weight of the tree. Finally, though, it began to move and, when sufficient space had been made, they quickly undid the rope from the truck and left it with the tree, driving back to the Bay.

Ronny finally broke the silence. "Dad, what we saw…"

"We saw a bear," Carl Brye said curtly. "That's all."

Wonderingly, he said, "It let us go."

"It already had its supper." But there was no real conviction in his voice. Carl Brye was silent for a minute. "Best not to mention it to your mother. Like as not she'll worry and nothing happened anyway."

"Sure, Dad."

Half an hour later, they were at one of the newer campsites, closer to other people and the smells of hot dogs and marshmallows roasting.

Two nights later, after they came home from the camping trip, tired, sore and with enough trout to eat for a week, Ronny woke to find himself tangled in his bedsheets, his breath tight in his chest.

He had been dreaming of fire and his father's screams still echoed in his ears.

Now, decades later, his eyelids grew heavy, drifted shut his thoughts breaking up into a kaleidoscope of colors and as he passed into sleep, he thought once more about his father's old rifle. He never forgot that strange June night and he never spoke of it, not even to his father.

The empty soda bottle slipped from his right hand to the floor. His left hand rested comfortably on the wooden box. The TV played out its drama, ignored.

The shadow, an old, familiar, and welcome visitor, slipped up behind him, bent for a drink and then whispered into his ear.

FIVE

It was after seven that night when the movers finally left, happy with the generous tip she had given them and the fresh coffee that filled each of their thermoses. Marty was glad she had not taken her younger siblings up on their offer of a shake, feeling the need to just be alone for awhile, to think and organize her house.

Dressed in faded jeans, her favorite red T-shirt and sneakers, she had just finished unpacking the living room and moved on to the kitchen. She paused at the door separating it from the dining area, remembering the meals her mother had cooked in the cheerful, sunny room, the Sunday morning breakfast before the mad dash to church.

The house had been in her mother's family for over a century, starting with Cowyn Fraser, her great-grandfather. It had been a surprise to discover that Denise Fraser Brye had left it to her, Marty, upon the older woman's death fifteen years ago.

Now, as the sun moved languidly across the sky into deepening twilight, she crossed to the kitchen sink and washed the dust from her hands. Reaching for the clean blue and white checked dish towel, her eyes fell on the black telephone hanging on the wall, just below the clock.

Holly would be home by now, she mused, maybe finishing up dinner with Tim and Patty. It couldn't hurt to give her a quick call, touch base, make a lunch date with her oldest friend.

She quickly dried her hands, dropped the towel on the kitchen counter and went to the phone, picking up the receiver. Listening for the dial tone, she dialed Holly's number from memory, her fingers touching the keys lightly and quickly. Sounding far away, the phone rang ten times before Marty frowned and hung up, making a mental note to call again tomorrow.

"There are plenty of reasons why she didn't answer or have the answering machine on," Marty told herself as she made her way upstairs. "I'm just too tired to think of one right now."

She stopped at the entrance to her room, looked inside. The king-sized bed had been placed on the wall opposite the French windows that were now open, a soft, fresh breeze wafting in. She had made up the bed as soon as the movers had put the frame together and topped it with the mattress and box springs.

Now it beckoned her, cozy and comfortable. The light on the bedside table gave off a warm glow.

Marty surveyed the bed with longing, wanting nothing more than to climb in and disappear for a week, knowing that if she did, she would kick herself for neglecting the work that needed to be done.

Something brushed her ankles and she jumped, looking down. The big orange cat rubbed its head against her calf, purring.

"Where have you been hiding, cat?" she asked, stooping down to scratch behind his ears. He arched into her hand – then, with a throaty *mreow*, he trotted down the hall and into the dark.

Not wanting to have him poking around, Marty followed the cat, checking each door to make sure they were shut securely.

One door swung open silently when she touched its knob.

Marty swallowed, staring into the yawning blackness. The only thing visible was the bottom stair, its companions leading up to the attic.

"I am not going upstairs," she said out loud. Her voice startled her and she laughed. "I am going to go downstairs, fix myself some cocoa or tea and go to bed. Tomorrow, I will clean house, run errands, write what I see."

Her left hand reached out of its own accord, sliding up the wall until it had flipped the switch on. Light spilled over from the landing above, illuminating the stairwell in soft beams.

She shrugged. "At least I don't need to replace the light bulb. Now I'm going to go to bed."

She went upstairs, taking each step with caution. Her heart pounded in her ears and she felt as though a band was tightening itself around her ribs. The steps were covered in dust and creaked with her movement.

Halfway up, she stopped. "This is so stupid. It's my house and I'm acting like Vera Miles going to meet Mrs. Bates. Get a grip, Marty."

But she found she couldn't move.

What solved the matter was her uninvited guest. The orange cat, seeing a new place to explore with abandon, bounded up the stairs in a flash. Marty, not wanting to lock him in the attic, followed.

Once on the landing, she stopped and surveyed the space. Some of the toys she and Mike had played as children were still boxed and stored in the far corner by the window overlooking the backyard. Next to it, sheet-draped furniture stood guard. Unaware of the soft, nostalgic smile on her face, Marty walked over and pulled the dust sheet off the old dining table that had belonged to an uncle. Dropping the sheet to the floor, she traced the patterns of the golden wood's grain with her fingertips.

Smooth as silk, just like she remembered. She thought of the dining table downstairs – that set was not nearly as gorgeous as this one, hidden away here, in the attic. Maybe she could get Mike and Pete to help her move this downstairs and sell the other? Not a bad thought.

Turning to leave and go back downstairs to the relative safety of the kitchen and hot cocoa, Marty stopped abruptly, her eyes on the window. She hesitated, then went to it, not seeing anything but the paned glass and frame and her own reflection staring, wide-eyed, back at her.

Her eyes traveled up, imagining the rope as it was drawn tight in a sudden, quick jolt when her mother….the body fell. The support beam above Marty still bore the deep welts where the rope had been wrapped and tied.

Her eyes traveled back down the wall next to the window and the deep grooves in the wood, as if someone had tried to claw their way back in. She touched them lightly, being careful not to catch a splinter.

Something soft rubbed her calf and she looked down, smiled. "Come on cat. Let's go back downstairs."

She scooped the feline up, went back down to the second floor, turned off the attic light and shut the door securely. Putting the cat down, she went downstairs to the kitchen and got out the cocoa and a mug. The cat followed, ears pricked, hopeful that food was in its future.

Twenty minutes later, she was back in her bedroom, unpacking storage boxes and putting her clothes away. Taking some clothes on hangers out of a tall box, she went to her closet and hung up them up – some skirts, a dozen dresses, several blouses and a long coat she bought specifically for the trip home. Marty was glad to see, as she unpacked and broke them down before stowing them in the garage, that the cardboard boxes were slowly disappearing from her room. Her old tall bureau, standing just outside the closet, would be filled next with undergarments, socks and scarves.

Partially hidden under an old sweater, the unmarked

manila envelope lay in the center of her bed, its muted color bright against the whiteness of her sheets. As Marty stepped towards the back of the closet, a board creaked under her weight and she felt it shift, as if the nails holding it in place were loose.

Frowning, she put all of her weight on it, testing to see if it was just her imagination or if the board really needed fixing.

It gave easily under her weight.

Dropping to her knees, she tried to pry the board up, hoping that since it was already loose, she wouldn't have to get a hammer to pull it up. It stubbornly refused to give way, despite its looseness, but on closer examination, she saw that the nails were poking out of the wood as if the weight of someone else had pushed them up.

She sat back on her heels, fingers sore, a little breathless with exertion. Her thoughts turned to the hammer and crow bar in the black toolbox underneath the kitchen sink. Her eyes remained on the loosened board.

"After dinner," she said out loud. "I will pull that board up after dinner. Right now, I need to put food in my belly before I do anything else."

She didn't find that decision at all comforting – even saying it out loud, even though the cat was her only audience, made her feel suddenly silly, childish. Crossing the room, Marty picked up the manila envelope from the bed and headed back downstairs, thinking she would peruse the reports and avoid looking at the pictures over dinner. Or, better yet, leave the papers in the car and bring a book to read.

Well aware that she had yet to do any serious grocery shopping, she decided to go out to dinner. Myrna's had long since closed and she didn't know the other restaurants very well, but she remembered seeing a flier for the Moonstone Tavern down at the harbor as she drove through the town square. Maybe she would have dinner there.

She left the room, ignoring the insistent itch to glance back over at the closet one more time. Catching herself starting to turn at the doorway, Marty gave herself a shake and went downstairs, keenly aware that while her stomach rumbled, it was her curiosity she wanted to satisfy the most.

SIX

Up at the old lighthouse, his fishing gear set out by the front door, Denver Clarke made himself busy for the rest of the evening by polishing the brass in the tower itself, finding it a hypnotic and enjoyable chore. The moonstone ring he wore seemed to have a pale glow in the pale light, though it was partially hidden by the rag as it fell over his right hand.

On the occasion he found it hard to sleep (an occurrence that seemed to happen more often than he liked as of late), he would pull out the glass cleaner, brass polish, a few old rags and start to work. Several times, he had found himself finishing up in time to watch the sun rise over the trees in hot, blushing pinks. His cat – a moody dark gray he'd named Hard Tack – would join him, if the mood took him, purring with content in the time, the place and the man.

Hard Tack had gone missing one week earlier and Clarke wondered about it enough to file a missing pet report, but did not worry overmuch about it. At thirteen, Hard Tack was old, far older than he'd ever expected the tiny, stray kitten he'd picked up so long ago to become. Animals knew when their time was up and often had the good sense to greet it with dignity and privacy.

Pausing in his cleaning long enough to take a swallow of beer, Clarke looked out into the night, seeing nothing but the inky black of night and a few stars brave enough to shine through the growing fog.

From this vantage-point on a clear day, it was possible to see the entire town of Wolf's Head Bay and the people who walked it. Not so clear were its secrets, but they were there – he had been born in this town, as were his parents and their parents before them and he had what he liked to call an ear for rumors.

Most of what he knew was common knowledge among the Gossip Gaggle at Lida's Beauty Salon and Shop, but he was aware, as most were not, that the town's founders had done something not recorded in the local history books. He did not know what. He had an idea that his parents had known, but they would not speak of it in front of him.

Taking another swallow of beer, he thought of the fishing trip he would be making the following morning with Mole Parker, his belly rumbling softly at the thought of fresh fish frying nicely on the stove. He and Mole and Bob Palmer made it a point to go fishing early in the morning twice a week, often going out for a week every other month, leaving behind their families and responsibilities, feeling as though time had passed them by and they were still the boys cutting up in school and out.

Until Bob died. Clarke paused in mid-thought, his hand still, the cloth firmly planted on the brass handle. It had been strange, Bob's death.

In the summer of '73, he had supposedly committed suicide while out on his boat, taking it out of the Bay, alone.

Drowned, the county coroner had said. Didn't sound right to Clarke. Not like Bob Palmer, who had been a champion swimmer in high school. Who had taken the time to school both a young Mole Parker and Denver

Clarke as teens before they would go out fishing or swimming in the lake. Who had taught them how to move with the ocean's current on the off-chance one or both fell into the water from a boat or the docks, to not panic when the shore seemed to move away from them.

Didn't explain the vertical slashes found on Palmer's lower abdomen. He found that out after bribing the Payne boy with some fresh fish. Good thing, too – the kid had lost his lunch after describing the deep, vicious wounds.

Shaking his head at the memory, Denver Clarke took a breath, inhaling the cool air deeply, savoring its salty scent, then exhaled. He supposed it was the prospect of going fishing in the morning with Mole that had brought on such memories. If he didn't sleep any tonight, he figured he could drive down early and beat his friend to the wharf. Mole was less of a loner than he, having a wife and three boys to go home to.

A handsome, silver-maned man who had no trouble with the ladies, Clarke preferred solitude over the company of others, but did make time for the few friends he did have, counting among his habits fishing, playing cards (mostly poker) and running up a tab at Olson's bar. Up until eight months ago, if the night was ripe for it and he felt the urge to, he would go to the Madison place and revisit the youthful passions that had not been tempered by time.

Tonight, like most nights, he felt compelled to stay at home.

As he set his beer in his tool box by his feet, a flash of movement caught his eye – frowning, he looked down into his well-lit yard, cursing under his breath when he saw the shadow flutter past.

If it was a trespasser (and at this time of night, what else could it be?), he'd give him a what for. He left his cleaning supplies where they were and hurried down the circular staircase, his footsteps ringing in the narrow passage, his breathing harsh. He reached the door and flung it open, the hot insults dying on his lips.

The fog was growing thicker, moving in thin, wispy strips – cold, mysterious and ominous. Suddenly uneasy, he took a tentative step further into the night, aware of a vague wish for the comforting weight of his fire poker.

"Hello?" he called out, his voice sounding small and frightened. Clearing his throat, he called out again, tension filling his stomach with a sour taste. Nothing.

Relief flooded him in waves that almost sent him to his knees – he hadn't realized how scared he was and decided that it wasn't something he wanted to experience ever again. He stumbled back towards the lighthouse door, thinking he would stay upstairs in the tower for the night.

He had an old sleeping bag in a closet somewhere inside – he would use that to keep warm.

Liking the idea more and more with each passing second, he was hardly aware of the nightmare standing between him and safety, its mad-red eyes gleaming with death, drool hanging from its misshapen mouth in long, thin, shiny ropes.

He was reminded of fishing line and the fish he was hoping to catch in the morning with his best friend, Mole.

His last thought, just before the powerful clawed hand tore his head off, was that the fishing trip might not happen after all.

From its hiding place among the rock and brush, a gray cat, thin and boney with age, watched the violent end of its owner.

16 JUNE, 1852

My dear M-,
We made a brief stop in Monterey for fresh supplies and I
gave my men leave until the noon hour. I myself stayed
aboard ship with Andrews, intent on mapping out our
course and discussing any dangers from changes in the
weather to conflicts with the native people with the dock
master.

I look back at the letter I wrote you at the beginning
of this voyage some four days past and feel rather
embarrassed by my out-pouring. I hesitated to mail it, and
indeed, had not Andrews taken it along with a number of
others and a list of supplies to procure early this morning,
I would not have sent it. No matter, I suppose. We know
each other well enough to see past the faults and I daresay
that you will dismiss my fancies as simply that. But I will
hasten to assure you that nothing untoward as yet has
occurred, although I dreamt last night of a mournful
howling, unlike anything I've ever heard in the waking
world.

Strangely, it seemed to be coming from the hold.

I went to investigate, but none of the passengers were
awake and of my crew, only those working were moving

about.

Now, here I sit, at my tiny desk in my quarters, my lamp burning bright and writing to you again. The dream I had prior to waking is still with me and I am finding it difficult to shake off. If I write about it, perhaps the strength of it will lessen and I will be able to go back to sleep, eh?

I don't recall ever telling you about my first tenure as a cabin boy, aboard the *Lady Lou*. Although the job had been more my father's idea (and one I had reluctantly agreed to do), it was what set me on my path to where I am today – captain of my own ship and master of my own crew, though I find that a captain and his crew work best in symbiotic form – together, rather than separate. Yes, yes, I know – as captain, the final decision lies with me and my word, while not precisely law, is to be followed to the letter.

Still, one does not take to a life at sea and survive alone.

And I see I have yet to start on this dream I had. Well, now is the time or it may be never. I am surprised at the detail, the smells and textures within this dream. It was like I was re-living it, to what purpose, I do not know.

I was eleven years old when my father signed my life over to the captain of the *Lady Lou*. I remember that day as clearly as if it had been yesterday, but it was not the subject of my dream. No, the events I dreamt of happened one year later.....

I was twelve then and assigned to the Lady's galley. I had been given the most glorious task of peeling potatoes. However, as I was sitting next to a porthole, I freely admit to spending most of my time gazing out to sea, dreaming the grand thoughts only a boy would have, a full barrel of unpeeled potatoes to my right, the basket for the peeled potatoes holding only three.

A hardened roll cracked my skull and I looked up to see One-Eared Sam glower over at me.

The scar that had left him with only one ear traced a thick and ugly pink path across his left cheek and down below his jaw, puckering deep where the stitching had not been strong. How and where he got the wound, or even survived it, I never knew, for he was closed-mouthed regarding his past and in light of his fiercely black temper, I chose not to ask.

The portholes had been opened wide – puffs of cool air wafted in, relieving the heat from the iron stove, where Sam had stationed himself over the boiling stew.

I began peeling busily, my face burning with shame, my thoughts going to my father and his disappointment if I should be thrown off ship for being negligent in my duties. I paused only once more to glance out at the sea. On the horizon, perhaps five or six miles away, a thick bank of fog loomed heavy and dark.

Still glowering, Sam came to my side for the basket of potatoes I had already peeled and cast a glance out the porthole himself, making a sign that I recognized as one that wards off evil, something I had learned early on not to make light of, or draw attention to the fact that I had even notice.

My father would have dismissed Sam as an uneducated and superstitious fool.

Sam went back to the stove, his wiry frame tense with – what? At the time, I was too young, too naive to understand that the more time one spent in nature, the more apt one would become in reading it. This was an intelligence my father would have appreciated even as he mocked it.

I recognize now what I saw in Sam then as fear tempered by anticipation.

My bare feet planted on the wood floor, I had peeled two dozen potatoes and was beginning a third when a shout from the crow's nest arrested my hand.

Quivering with tension, Sam moved to the door as he strained to hear the cries from above deck, his nostrils flaring with each breath.

He gave me a cursory look. "Stay put, boy. Ain't no place for you up deck. You see em comin down, make scarce. Hear?"

I nodded, my heart trembling in my throat. He eyed me a moment, then slipped out the galley. When the door was secure behind him, I went back to the porthole and looked out, curious.

The fog had drawn closer and it was this I saw now. Everything was still, calm. I could not imagine what had made the watch cry out a warning.

Then I saw her and my blood ran cold. From portside aft, she slid out of the fog as a ship from hell, her sails and rigging as black as the soul who captained her. Even I, a city boy, knew this ship without having to see her firsthand, the stories about her abounded in great detail.

It was the Devil's Wolf and she was drawing closer with every swell.

I gripped my paring knife tightly and waited. I did not wait long.

The Devil's Wolf drew alongside and her men swarmed the Lady Lou like wasps. Swords clashed heavily against flesh and steel while pistols cracked the air with infrequent shots. I could smell the burn of gunpowder and in my mind's eye saw the men, friend and foe alike, discard their spent pistols and reach for fresh ones secured in their belts.

The twists of linen with measured powder and the small steel balls were harmless when separate, deadly when combined and still unreliable. The most efficient way of killing was with a sword or dagger. Even a knife, like the one I held in one sweaty hand, was better.

Booted steps thundered heavily in the corridor and I quickly ducked under the table instinctively. The stench of burning linen tickled my nose and I realized that in my haste, I had knocked an apron onto the stove. As I crept from beneath the table to the water barrel, a hand tried the door, found it locked and proceeded to try and force it open. The air was thick with smoke as I grabbed a bucket and, coughing, filled it with water.

Outside, a rough voice cursed the door and its stout refusal to be broken.

My eyes stinging with smoke and tears, I flung the liquid at the fire, its answering hiss acknowledging my mark and I turned back for more. There was a heavy splintering noise and I jumped back, dropping the wooden bucket. It landed at my feet with a hollow thud and rolled away. The galley door swung open and I felt the presence of evil in the room with me. The smoke was still thick, even with the portholes open, and I struggled against the cough that wanted to free itself from my throat and failed.

The presence walked in, emerging from the veil of smoke in garb as black as pitch, the gleam of his two pistols dull in the haze and I realized that I was staring at Captain Druas. My body was numb with terror as our eyes met — his a fathomless black, shiny like polished marble, mine, I'm sure, bugging almost out of their sockets. Thick brows arched over his eyes and a neatly trimmed beard and mustache covered his jaw and upper lip. The rest was smooth, as smooth as the ocean's flat calm.

He smiled, one as chilling as ice in a Maine winter, and approached me with slow, deliberate steps, grasping my chin with a black gloved hand and tilting my head this way and that. "A pup left to man the kitchen. Such a great weight to be put upon your thin shoulders." Releasing me, he turned his back, as if taunting me, knowing that a boy would not, could not attack someone so much more powerful.

The paring knife lay forgotten on the floor, but my fingers found a cleaver, its head buried in the wood, and gripped its handle tightly. I tried to free it, but it resisted my tugs — I would not be able to remove it without catching Druas's attention.

The Lady Lou lurched suddenly — I almost lost my footing, but Druas never missed a step, not once putting a hand out for balance. At that moment, in my feverish boy's mind, I believed every word spoken or written about him — that he had struck a bargain with the Devil. Something slimy rolled into my palm and I clutched it instinctively, recognizing it vaguely as one of my peeled potatoes.

Without thinking, I hurled it as hard as I could at the stew bubbling on the stove — its splat distracted Druas, who focused his attention on it, his sword appearing as if from nowhere. In that same instant, I yanked on the cleaver — it came out of the wood with an unwilling groan. Druas whirled again to me, his eyes creased in cold amusement as he took in my feeble weapon.

"You think you can take me?" His laugh sent chills down my spine, but I stood my ground. "I commend your courage, pup, but it *will do you no good. Men twice your age and strength have not brought me down, though they tried." He brought out one of his pistols, aiming it at me. A part of me wanted to flinch, to close my eyes against seeing the end. But another part refused to allow me such a luxury and I met his cold gaze with something akin to defiance.*

He seemed regretful as he cocked the pistol. When the shot came, I did flinch, but I did not go down. Instead, I watched, bewildered, as an expression of shock crossed his face before he tumbled to the floor. I stared at his body, utterly convinced that he was playing a trick, that he was not dead or injured, that if I tried to walk past him, he would grab my ankle and pull me down to slit my throat.

Then a hoarse voice spoke from the door, asking if I was all right. I looked up and saw Sam, a pistol smoking in his hand. Behind him, supported by the first mate, stood our captain, bloodied and exhausted. I think I may have opened my mouth to speak, but I am not sure — everything became a blur. I vaguely recall the Devil's Wolf *making her escape with a few hands, but that was all….*

I surfaced from that dream quite abruptly, M. It was one I hadn't had in nearly thirty years and I found my bed sheets had twisted round me. I sat shivering in a cold sweat, rising towards consciousness with surreal slowness, almost as if I were striving to break through to the ocean's surface. I had been aboard the *Lady Lou* again, helping in the galley with one of the meals, One-Ear Sam supervising to make sure I did it properly.

The smell of stale beer clung to my nostrils, although I kept none in my quarters.

My vision blurred suddenly and I began weeping for the man who had become my father to me in all but blood.

I do not know how much time had passed, but as my private storm passed, I was brought back to my surroundings by a knock on my door. I regained control of myself and rose, reaching for my previous day's trousers.

"Yes, what is it?" I said, my throat tight.

Through the door, came Andrews' voice, deep with

concern. "It's the Tanner boy, sir. It seems he's ill."

I bade him entrance. Andrews stepped in, his usually grave countenance creased with worry, and gave a brief, but detailed account of the boy's condition. I must confess that I, too, became concerned.

"Take me to him." I followed Andrews down to the crews' quarters, where I could hear the sharp moans of the boy almost at once. Slick with sweat, he had thrown back his blankets and was even now tossing and turning in his narrow bunk. I touched his brow with one hand, testing for fever, but in spite of his sweat, he was cool. With Andrews' help, I carried the boy to my quarters, where I made him as comfortable in my bed as I was able and roused Kelley, the ship's doctor, to look him over.

His consensus was to make sure the boy got some rest and some broth. If there were no changes, then we would have to leave him behind in the hospital, a thought that gives me the shivers, as you may remember why.

After Andrews and the doctor left, I then strung up a hammock for myself and went about preparing for sleep, but although it is now after two in the morning, I am unable to do so. I now sit at my desk, writing all that has transpired to you as I wait for the sun to rise and vanquish the not quite-full moon.

17 June 1852
Half past six AM
I brought the boy some more broth, which he ate greedily, spooning it as quickly as he could into his mouth, wiping what failed to make it into his mouth with a sleeve. His shirt sleeves had fallen back and I noticed that, despite his youth, his arms carried a great deal of hair. When I noted this, he merely shrugged.

"My da's family is hairier than any beast you'd think of meeting," he said with a grin. "Not much to worry on, sir."

I smiled back, but now, as he lies sleeping, clearly unaffected by last night's sweats, I wonder. I decided to keep him here with me for a few more days to observe him. Thank goodness Doctor Kelley's prediction for hospital has not come to pass!

The good doctor has just come to check on the boy and with some more good news, of which you would have every right to chastise me for.

It seems that Reverend Williams is being detained in his bunk due to a very uneasy and un-seaworthy stomach. I am relieved. I am also ashamed to admit that relief.

I await your chiding words with a glad heart.

Yours with much affection,
Jonas Brye

THURSDAY JUNE 8, 1978

SEVEN

She was in the backyard, laughing with friends, when she heard glass shatter. Under it, she thought she heard a howl of rage, but could not be sure — what she was sure of was the horrifying sight of her mother hanging by her neck, the rope disappearing into the broken attic window.

Then, she was in the forest, running haphazardly through the brush, barely aware of the fresh scratches left behind by the clinging branches, tears hot and scorching burning her cheeks. Hiccupping, gasping for breath, she stopped dead in her tracks, blinded by the tears.

Wiping them away, she pressed on, her surroundings a green blur as she sought to escape the shadow that refused to leave her alone. Her feet slipped out from under her suddenly and she tumbled down the slope, crying out when her elbow rapped against a rock sharply. When she finally came to earth, she just lay there, her face buried into the ground, sobbing brokenly. Time passed; the sky grew dark. She didn't know how long she lay there, only that she had stopped crying and was now breathing the moist, damp earth in long shaky breaths, slowly growing aware of her heart as it beat rhythmically against her ribs.

She closed her eyes, overwhelmed with exhaustion.

The rough tongue was what brought her back to wakefulness

and, rubbing them, she opened her eyes. The wolf's dark blue eyes gazed down at her, anxiety evident in the way his tail whipped at his haunches.

Drowsily, she hitched herself up on one elbow, knowing that she should be afraid, but finding comfort in the animal's presence. Whining, he licked her face several times, occasionally tickling her throat as he wiped the dried salt of her tears away. She found herself laughing, burying her hands in the thick black fur as he caught part of her old sweater in his teeth and pulled at it, growling playfully.

Her fingers roughed the silky fur around his ears – smoothing it, she hiccupped once more, her eyes filling with fresh tears. He licked them away as fast as they slid down her cheeks, tripping over her as she sat up, taking in her surroundings blearily.

Above them rose a gnarled tree, guardian to the hollow just below it. Crawling on her hands and knees, she curled up into it, her back pressed against the natural wall. A minute later, the wolf joined her, curling himself into her. Putting an arm around him, she closed her eyes, inhaling his wolfish, earthy scent.

Sleep claimed her in mid-breath…..

Marty opened her eyes, half-expecting to see blue patches of sky through the trees above and was, therefore, surprised to find the big orange cat staring at her instead. A sense of sorrow settled over her and she sighed. She had not dreamt about the day her mother had died in years – even now, it still felt tender.

The cat placed one large forepaw on her mouth. Spitting, she looked at her alarm clock on the nightstand to her left.

It read eight-thirty. She stretched, listening to her body pop, heard papers crackle, felt something cut into her right hand when she rolled over.

The photos.

Instantly, she was wide awake and sitting up. The cat yowled in protest and, leaping from the bed, vanished. She held the stiff black and white pictures in her hands carefully, the police photos and reports lying forgotten beside her. Staring at them, she remembered taking the hammer from the tool box under the kitchen sink when she had come home from the tavern, dropping her key ring onto the counter. She had then gone upstairs and spent the next half hour working to pry the floorboard loose.

She had been surprised to find the flat, rectangular envelope, just lying there, clearly for many years – it had been yellowed with age. She had pulled it out, climbing onto her bed to look at it, turning it over in her hands. A brief, but cursory, look had made it clear that there was something inside, and she opened it quickly, much like ripping a band aid off an old wound.

The pictures fell out in a jumble and she picked through them carefully. The photos had been taken in the backyard of this house – she'd recognized the balcony and French doors almost immediately.

Shaking herself back into the present, Marty caressed the pile of photos before she picked one up. Turning it over, she was startled to recognize many of the people in the old photographs.

They were mostly of herself, celebrating her birthday, surrounded by her friends and family – Holly Prescott frozen in laughter as she tied a red balloon onto Marty's belt, her boyfriend-now-husband Tim Wyatt looking on; Ellen Farley, now her sister-in-law, was standing apart from the group, looking uncomfortable.

There were a couple pictures of Mike trying to steal some of her birthday cake. And scattered among many others were the twins, barely a year old, clapping their hands and frozen in excited squeals.

One was of her mother, looking off towards the forest, a wistfully sad expression on her face.

Holding the photo, Marty looked at it the longest before putting it aside and getting up, intent on taking a shower. If she remembered right, there was a breakfast menu at the Moonstone Tavern, which, according to the description, served up some of the best omelets in town. It also had a perfect view of the bay, the tiny harbor filled with fishing boats and the sandbar separating it from the ocean. It was a view best appreciated in the morning, with the sun's rays warming whatever they touched.

Settling the matter of breakfast energized her and she found herself singing in the shower, her hair wet and lathered with shampoo. She laughed, her mood light and the Bay seemed to be less threatening in the bright sun of the morning than it had the day before, when she had been tired and hungry and unsure of her decision. Her reservations about moving back had vanished and she was glad to be home.

The question would goose her later. Who put the pictures under the floorboards?

EIGHT

Eddie Payne narrowed his eyes, holding the gaze of the man across from him, confident that this time, victory was within his grasp.

"You're bluffing," he said and laid down his cards. "Full house."

His opponent, Tavis Riley, laughed, his dark eyes bright with amusement. The scar over his right eye creased deeply, disappearing into his thick, black hair. "Better, Eddie, getting better. But you need to keep trying. Work on that poker face." Tavis laid down his own cards, leaned back in his chair easily, the dark brown suit jacket swinging out behind him like a flag. "Royal flush. In spades."

Eddie groaned. "Damn it, Tavis, it wouldn't kill you to at least pretend that I win once in a while." Grumbling under his breath, Eddie began reshuffling his cards.

Leaning back in his chair, Tavis's wide grin grew wider. "But then, you wouldn't be learning anything, Eddie."

In the weeks he had been back in the Bay after so many years away, Tavis Riley was surprised at how quickly and easily his friendship with Eddie had sprung up and enjoyed every minute of the younger man's company.

Now, as he began to deal the cards, Eddie's face took on a most serious expression.

Tavis held in the laughter that wanted to explode with great difficulty. "So, has the chief decided who's going to head security on the anniversary?"

Eddie shook his head. "Not yet. I think Sean Andrews is gonna do it, though. He's got the most experience. I'll probably do parking or something." He looked glum as he hunched over the cards, shuffling them.

"Hey, Eddie?" Amelia Juarez poked her head into the police department's break room, her dark eyes questioning.

Eddie stopped shuffling and looked up. "Yeah?"

"There's a woman upstairs asking for you. Says she knows you. Marty Brye?"

Eddie pushed back his chair so fast that he knocked over the light on the desk behind him. "What the hell is she doing here?"

Amelia pressed herself against the door as he rushed out. "Hey, watch it!"

"Sorry," he muttered and bolted upstairs.

Tavis looked after him, curious. "What's with him?"

Amelia shrugged, her eyes troubled. "Women. What else?"

*****

Eddie was gasping for breath by the time he reached the reception area, sweeping the area with his eyes. At first, all he saw were his co-workers, old Mrs. Thompson reporting that kids were terrorizing her poor Waldo, an over-sized mutt, yet again, and a woman dressed in a sophisticated grey suit staring out the window. Then she turned, almost as if she sensed his presence, and Eddie recognized his old school friend.

"Marty," he said, hating the weak sound of his voice. He coughed, cleared his throat, tried again. "Marty. Good to see you."

She smiled, her eyes warming. "Good to see you, too. I wanted to thank you for files you sent me….."

Eddie took her arm, led her back to the window. "Keep your voice down. No one knows about that."

She bit her lip nervously. "Sorry. I just, well, they were helpful."

"Good." Then, "Do you want to go for coffee sometime?"

Marty only half-heard the question, her gaze flitting around the front office, passing over the other officers. Her eyes stopped on the man in the brown suit as he entered the reception area, his thick black hair almost hiding the scar over his right eye.

He handed a thick sheaf of files over to a clerk and looked up, his eyes meeting hers – the look that passed between them left her flushed and trembling.

He was the same man from the Heights. Although she hadn't had a clear look, she knew without a doubt it was him.

With an effort, Marty tore her eyes away from him, tried to focus on Eddie. It wasn't easy.

"Sorry," she said. "No, I'm still getting settled in. I just came in to say thanks again for the files. They've been helpful."

"Sure," he said. "How is it, living in that house again?"

She forced herself to grin. It felt stiff. "Ask me again in a month. I've gotta go. See you." Turning on her heel, she almost ran out of the station, aware only of the roiling heat inside her…..and the dark haired man who sparked it.

Eddie frowned after her quick departure, jumping when Tavis spoke. "Is that her?"

"Huh?"

"The woman who asked you for a favor?"

Eddie blushed furiously. "Yeah. What of it?"

Tavis grinned, but his eyes were dark with an emotion Eddie could not read. "She is very beautiful."

"How'd you know…?

Tavis waved a hand. "Only a woman could twist a

man in such a way that he'd risk his job for her."

Eddie flushed crimson. "She's an old friend from high school. We were just good friends."

"But not for a lack of trying," Tavis guessed.

Eddie's color deepened. "Knock it off, Riley."

Tavis only laughed.

Eddie scowled and went back downstairs. Still chuckling, Tavis turned his gaze out the window and watched as Marty hurried across the street towards Mryna's diner, his own body flush with desire.

He was well aware of the others like him, those who had slowly returned to the Bay over the years, before and after his arrival. He was quite sure that they were aware of him, as well, but he neither sought them out nor acknowledged their true natures when their paths did cross. So far, they had respected him in the same way. He was content with that, knowing they were waiting on the return of their pack alpha, but there had been only one for whom he had long been waiting.

His heart-rate was slowing, his pulse regular again, but he could still smell her scent – fresh, female, fiery. That same flowery perfume he had scented at the Heights as the battered VW bug rattled by.

She was home again.

NINE

From the front bay window of her diner, Myrna Kowolsky watched as the young woman hurried across the street from the police station. She shook her head, *tsk*-ing to herself softly as she dressed the tables in the main dining room for lunch.

She recognized Marty Brye almost immediately, a grown-up version of the girl who would come in for a chocolate shake and fries every Saturday afternoon after the matinee or double feature at the Blackwood.

In the kitchen, her cook, Elise Mottes, burst into song, the lyrics as cheerful and bright as the morning was gloomy. Barry Willes, the diner's newest waiter, chimed in, their voices blending in perfect harmony. Annie Chapman, who claimed seniority over both after Myrna, scowled at them as she stuck three new breakfast order tickets in the turnstile and took a side of bacon to another customer.

The bell hanging over the entrance rang as the door opened.

"Mornin', Myrna Loy." Norris greeted her with his usual affectionate term. Myrna Loy was his favorite actress and the eighty-year old mailman had given her the nickname when she had opened her diner thirty years

75

before.

He handed her the day's late mail. "Here you go, have at the world."

"Thank you, Norris." She gave the old man a peck on the cheek. He went straight for the counter, plunking his mailbag in a seat next to him.

"I'll have the usual, if you'd stop that caterwauling, Barry," Norris hollered into the kitchen. Barry came out, his face flushed and smiling sheepishly as he carried a cup of coffee.

"Here you go, Mr. Norris," he said, setting it down. He ducked down, coming back up with a spoon, cream and sugar and a napkin. "Anything else?"

"That sweet roll over there is lookin' mighty tasty. Throw 'er in the oven and heat it up."

"You got it."

Barry went about his business. Myrna sat next to Norris, studying a letter that looked official. She was frowning slightly.

"Something wrong, Myrna Loy?" Norris poured a big helping of sugar in his coffee, adding some cream. "You look like the cat ate something bad."

She glanced at him sharply, then back at the letter. "It's nothing, Norris."

He shrugged. "Suit yourself."

Barry came back with the sweet roll, dripping in melted sugar, then disappeared into the kitchen. Norris dug into his roll with a satisfied grunt, the melted sugar dissolving on his tongue. Myrna put the letter in her pocket and studied her bills, the frown vanishing as if it had never been, but Norris was aware that she was angry.

He ignored it. Whatever was bothering her was none of his business – if she wanted to share it, she would when she damn well felt like it. He almost bumped into the young woman as she pushed open the door, the bell ringing away madly, tipped his hat and went out, muttering.

Myrna didn't look up from her letter. "How do, Marty. Would you like your shake?"

Marty grinned, pleased that she was remembered. "Sure, I'd love one. They taste better here."

"Won't take but a minute. Have a seat wherever you like."

Marty looked around at the empty diner and took a seat at the counter, slipping off her jacket and draping it on the back of the stool before sitting, swinging her legs freely, feeling very young, remembering the days she and Holly had spent as girls giggling over boys and sharing their favorite shakes. Resting her head on one hand, she traced a star on the counter with her finger, smiling, lost in memory.

She was almost able to forget the strong, almost visceral, attraction to the man in the brown suit she'd seen while talking to Eddie in the police station's front reception area, the invisible arc of electricity that passed between them when his eyes lit on her.

Almost.

The door swung open again, the bell ringing madly once more to announce yet more patrons. Another woman entered, her dark brown hair pulled back into a thick braid. She slipped onto a stool two over from Marty's left, her denim jeans whispering on the vinyl seat in time with her movements. She slipped off her sweater, draping it on the seat next to her, the scooped collar of her blouse revealing an old scar at the base of her neck.

"How was the morning hike, Ms. Brennan?" Myrna put a mug in front of the woman and poured out black coffee.

Ms. Brennan wrapped long, scarred fingers around the white mug, leaning forward to inhale the steam as it curled upwards. "Exhilarating, as always."

"Lunch?"

"No, just coffee." Myrna nodded and left the woman to herself. Marty tried to read the new menu, but her eyes kept straying to the vibrant blue of the woman's blouse, one that seemed to match her eyes and set off the dangling earrings she wore – tear-shaped moonstones.

Almost as if she sensed Marty's gaze, the woman looked up, met it and smiled. "I'm Daria Brennan. Are you new here?"

Marty shook her head. "No, I grew up here. I just moved back yesterday. I'm Marty Brye." She held out her hand. For a brief second, it seemed that Daria would not accept it, but then she did, in a firm grasp. "How long have you been in the Bay?"

Daria didn't reply right away. "About three, three and a half years."

"Then you must like it."

"I do, very much. It reminds me of the town I grew up in." The warmth in Daria's voice was tinged with amusement.

Marty grinned. "I know what you mean. I left fifteen years ago, but it kept pulling at me to come back. I couldn't stay away."

Daria laughed. "I felt it, too. Like the songs sirens sing to lure seamen into the watery deep."

Marty gestured to Daria's ears. "Your earrings – are those moonstones?"

She nodded, touching them lightly. "Yes. They're an heirloom from my aunt."

"They're very beautiful. Is that silver?" Marty turned a little pink at Daria's curious stare. "The metal work. Is it silver?"

Daria shrugged, her smile slow and thoughtful. "No, it's white gold. I'm allergic to silver, as was my aunt."

Marty turned even pinker. "Sorry, that was rude, wasn't it?"

Daria smiled and this time, it held warmth. "No worries."

In the kitchen, Barry and Elise started singing again.

TEN

By eleven-thirty that morning, the breakfast rush had wound down at the Moonstone and the staff began prepping for lunch. Nate took a dry cloth and, going to the chalkboard that hung just outside the door, wiped it down. He took great care to preserve the intricate and rather colorful design that his sister had drawn at the top. It incorporated the name of the tavern and his fishing boat and he again considered the idea of redoing both his fishing business and restaurant logos into one.

He wrote quickly and with a flourish the lunch specials of the day, pausing now and again to smother a yawn that threatened. Getting up at four in the morning to open up the tavern wasn't getting any easier and he sure as hell wasn't getting any younger. Shaking his head, he finished writing up the menu and recalled, with some humor how, in his days at college, he had been able to pull all-nighters that lasted five days.

Not anymore, he thought and chuckled.

Most of his daily customers that came in before dawn were fishermen, both local and tourist. Among those in the crowd would be Mole Parker and Denver Clarke, each man wearing his own favorite fishing hat or jacket for luck.

Parker had been in at four on the dot, but after waiting for an hour, his mood darkening, he left the tiny harbor on his own, keeping in radio contact with Nate.

Mole Parker had not been a happy camper about it. And as amused as he was by the older man's grumbles, Nate himself was more than a little concerned at the no-show of Denver Clarke. It was unusual for the man to make plans to go out fishing and then not get in touch or leave behind a message that those plans had changed. Now, Nate watched as Mole Parker piloted his boat back into the harbor, guiding it back into its berth with a grace that belied its size.

Nate finished the menu, then turned to watch and wait for Mole to come in. Twenty minutes later, his boat secured, the older man ambled over to the tavern. Nate noted with some amusement that Mole's mood had not improved.

"How was your morning, Mole?" he asked, wiping the chalk dust from his hands and holding the tavern door open.

Mole grunted something unintelligible as he walked in and made his way to the bar, sliding onto a stool.

Nate grinned and followed him inside, signaling to one of the waitresses to take care of Mole's order. If his demeanor was anything to go by, Mole was going to need a couple of beers to go with his fish and chips. Nate went to the kitchen, whistling softly. Maybe he would add a double portion of chips, give Mole something to chew on before he went home to sleep off the trip.

*****

After a satisfying lunch, Mole Parker kept his eyes on the road as he drove his truck back towards town. The road from the harbor wound its way up through the south end of town and over the hill. Although his home was on the south-east side, he turned north. He was headed for the lighthouse, intent on bawling out Denver Clarke for making him wait over an hour at the docks before he decided to hell with it and went out on his own. It had just gone on one before he had come back in with his catch. It was not his best haul, though Nate was fair in his trade. More so with his lunch. The over-abundance of fries with his fish and chips was telling on him – he'd been belching since he had climbed into his old truck.

Best friend or not, you just didn't leave someone hanging out to dry after making an agreement. His anger burning a hole in his heart, he jerked his truck onto the left fork, the tires spewing dirt.

Damn fool made me lose the best catch, he thought, shifting gears. There was an ugly grinding sound and he cursed vehemently. If Clarke thought he could change his mind at the last minute, he had another think coming.

Muttering under his breath, he slowed when the lighthouse and caretaker's cottage came into view. He hit the brakes, the front bumper of his truck almost kissing the white fence surrounding the back yard, and hopped out, slamming the door with more force than was necessary. Gravel crunching under his feet, he marched to the front door, not bothering with the bell or knocker. Raising his fist instead, he pounded on the door until it rattled in its frame.

"Clarke!" he shouted. "I know you're in there! Come on out and maybe I won't take some of your teeth!"

Silence. Frowning, Mole pounded on the door again, harder this time. Still, there was no answer.

"Goddamned son of a bitch," he grumbled, stepping back to look up at the windows on the second floor. Maybe he could see a light on in one of them…..

Glancing towards the lighthouse, he hesitated, squinting hard, unaware that his feet were moving slowly towards the tall building.

The door was open. Mole blinked. Clarke never left the door open, not even when he was inside, paranoid that some smart-alecky kid would come in and goof around and get hurt, maybe worse. His eyes were drawn to the pile of dark-stained rags resting on the stoop as he drew near.

"What the hell…?" His words hung on the air like a gull in a strong wind, his body numb with foreboding, his eyes never leaving the rags. Something sharp and tangy filled his nostrils, reminding him for some reason of his catch packed on ice in his truck. He knew this scent, knew it and never wanted to smell it again. He blinked once more and the rags came into focus sharply. They were not rags, he realized with dim horror, but clothes that had been ripped to shreds.

And the stains marking the torn denim and shredded checkered flannel was blood, lots of it, as if whatever had worn them had simply exploded.

He turned and ran back to his truck, throwing the old vehicle into gear and spewing dirt and rock in his rush to get away.

ELEVEN

John Dylan was in his office, sitting at his desk, studying the small, black velvet jewel box he turned over in his hands. Lying to one side on his desk was a missing pet report that Denver Clarke had filed five weeks before.

The old man had seemed inclined to think that his cat had wandered off to die in peace, but filed the report anyway.

Underneath the missing cat report lay the coroner's final report on Holly Prescott-Wyatt. Set aside to the left of both reports was the itinerary of the Wolf's Head Bay 125th Anniversary Celebration and the security plans.

He ignored all of these. Holding the jewel box, he considered long and carefully the delicate ring that rested inside. In the outer office, the phone rang shrilly.

"Eddie!" someone shouted. "Your desk is ringing!"

There was no reply. Someone else muttered something and the outer room broke up in laughter.

Dylan placed the small box carefully on top of the stackable trays and pulled out the coroner's report on Holly Prescott-Wyatt, opening the file folder. Cause of death, he read, was from loss of blood due to the deep, vertical slashes on her stomach and neck. There were four vertical cuts. It was the coroner's conclusion that the woman had died when her head had been torn off.

He frowned. Where had he read about similar cuts?

The phone stopped in mid-ring when another deputy answered.

"Wolf's Head Bay Sheriff's Department. This is Deputy Sean Andrews," he said, all business. "Uh, hold on a second." He leaned over the desk, grabbed a pad of paper and a pen. "Go ahead." Someone spoke shrilly on the other end. Andrews winced a little, but said only, "Uh-huh", among other encouraging words.

John Dylan tuned his deputy out, only vaguely aware of the one-sided conversation, even less aware that his eyes were on the black, velvet jewel box again. It therefore took him a minute to realize that Andrews was talking to him and he jumped, almost dropping the box.

"You gonna ask her tonight?"

Dylan blinked. "What?"

Andrews gestured to the jewelry box with his left hand. "Are you gonna ask her to marry you tonight?"

"I think so. I'm still trying to figure out if I should do it before dessert or somewhere private and romantic." Dylan went back to his desk and sat, picking up the paper, trying to look busy, pretending not to feel the sudden burn on his face.

Andrews grinned. "She's something, John. If I wasn't so sure she had eyes for you, I wouldn't mind courting her, myself."

"Go on with you." Dylan threw a paper ball.

Andrews ducked, grinning hugely, pausing at the window looking out at the parking lot. "I'm going across the street to get a cup of coffee and one of Myrna's sweet rolls. Want anything?"

"Just a cup of courage."

Andrews's laugh was loud, but it faded as he ambled his way out of the building, hat in hand. Dylan picked up Denver Clarke's missing cat report. Somewhere, a door opened and shut with greater force than necessary. Dylan sighed.

"What's Mole Parker tearing around town like that for?"

Dylan looked up. "What?"

Eddie Payne stood just outside his office door, holding a mug. He gestured towards the window. "Mole Parker's driving like crazy. He almost took out the stop sign on the corner. Want me to handle it?"

"Sure."

But before either man could take action, the squealing of tires and sudden roar of an engine silenced them both. Seconds later, a trembling and gray Mole Parker stumbled into the station. He gripped the front desk tightly, his knuckles white.

"I want…to report a…a….," the old man began and promptly fainted.

*****

After calling for an ambulance to take Mole Parker to the hospital, where he now resided in the ICU for a heart attack, John Dylan drove out to the lighthouse and approached the crime scene warily. Jean Fletcher, the local doctor, had been there for over an hour and was currently examining what remained of the body.

The lighthouse itself had been marked off with bright yellow tape and the tarp that covered what was left, presumably, of Denver Clarke, had been pushed aside carefully so that Fletcher could do her work.

Another of his officers was up in the lighthouse itself, searching for anything that might have led to the man's death, while Amelia searched the house.

Dylan suspected that none of them would find anything. Gazing around at the area, taking in the ocean, the crime scene and the lighthouse, he found himself looking at the officers blocking the crowd of curiosity seekers who had made the trek from town to see what all the excitement was about. It startled him anew when he realized that the face he was looking for – Holly Prescott-Wyatt of the *Bay News* – would never be there again to question and spar with him about the crime rate, the identities of the dead, the suspects, the crime itself.

Taking deep breaths with his mouth and hoping to God he didn't forget and breathe through his nose, Dylan approached the doctor. She didn't look up.

"Find anything?"

She shook her head. "All I'm able to do at this point is say absolutely for sure that this was a human before someone got pissed enough to rip him apart."

"Him? You know it's a male?"

She met his gaze and he was surprised to see the humor in them. "Considering that the pelvic bones are consistent with a male, my doctorate wouldn't be worth a dime if I said it was a woman. Besides," she picked up a bloodstained wallet with a gloved hand and gave it to him, "this was in what was left of his pocket."

Dylan took a pair of rubber gloves from a box Fletcher kept handy in her kit box and snapped them on before taking the wallet. Opening it, he saw Clarke's driver's license, a credit card and thirty dollars in cash plus change.

"Now, if I were to identify this as Denver Clarke without a complete, by the book exam with a forensics team, I'd be pushing it." She stood, pulled the tarp back over the remains and stepped over to Dylan, snapping off her gloves, wadding them into a neat ball in one hand. "But I can tell you right now, unofficially, that I'd be surprised if it was anyone else."

He nodded, putting the wallet into an evidence bag and tagging it before kneeling to place it with the other items found. About to stand, he hesitated, staring at the bloodstain on the stoop. "Hey, Jean, what's this?"

She flicked a glance at it. "Looks like blood."

Dylan sighed. In spite of the crime scene, it was going to be one of those days. "I know, but does it seem to be a shape of anything?"

She knelt beside him, being careful to touch nothing. "I'm not sure what you're asking me to see, John."

"I want your honest opinion."

She was silent, the long seconds ticking away, studying the dark stain with careful consideration while Dylan tried to conceal his impatience. After what seemed like an eternity, she answered his question. "It looks like a print of some kind. Too big to be a dog or a mountain lion."

"A bear?" Even as he said it, he knew that he was wrong.

"No." But she sounded doubtful. "I'm no expert on animal tracks, John. You might want to find someone who is, have them take a look."

Dylan looked around, shouting at Evans to bring a camera over. When the deputy arrived with it, the sheriff took it and snapped several pictures of the print. To Fletcher, he said, "You know of anyone off hand who has an interest in tracks?"

"Ronald Brye might. He's in charge of the local nature group. Or he used to be."

"Look him up and see what he says." He hesitated, toying with a point that had been bothering him for awhile, then pushed it out. "Jean, has it occurred to you that maybe Denver Clarke's death is connected to Bob Palmer and Jack Tanner?"

She frowned, shook her head. "I don't really see how. Their deaths were completely different. Bob Palmer drowned in a boating accident and Jack Tanner was killed by a rogue bear."

He stuffed his hands in his pockets. "I don't see how, either, if you want to know the truth. But....I feel it. And it bothers me."

Fletcher regarded him, curious. "It's the cuts on Bob Palmer, isn't it? The ones made by his boat propeller."

He nodded. "Could never piece together why those

cuts looked so odd. And he was a good swimmer. Why would he make such rookie mistakes?"

She smiled. "Well, you'll figure it out. That's why you got elected chief of police."

"Thanks," he said sourly.

Something rustled in the bushes closest to him – both he and Fletcher tensed, and he put his hand on the butt of his gun.

There was some more rustling in the shrubs and then the thin, mewling cry of a small animal. Dylan glanced at Fletcher, who wore an equally puzzled expression on her face. Both of them crouched down and he pushed back a branch carefully.

An old, skinny, gray cat peered out at them balefully, both ears pinned flat against its head. It hissed at them, baring toothless gums, one paw raised defensively. Then, as if to underscore the point, it growled, the sound coming from deep within its scrawny chest as it leaned back on its haunches, one paw ready to strike if necessary.

Dylan sighed with relief. "I'll leave this one for you, Jean."

She favored him with a sour look. "Thanks a lot."

A shout from one of his officers made him look up. Amelia was waving him over, a sick look on her face. Dylan approached the group with some reluctance, his soul heavy with resignation. Hidden beneath the shrubs by the lighthouse door was a human hand, severed just above the wrist. The jagged edges of flesh indicated that it had literally been torn from the arm, not sawed.

The skin was clearly tanned and weathered by the sun and the startlingly white band on one finger made it clear that the dead man had worn a ring.

And that, whoever killed him, had taken it.

TWELVE

Marty reached the front gate of her house, the paper sacks rustling loud in her ears as she walked, her belly deliciously full of chocolate ice cream. She licked her lips hopefully for imagined traces of chocolate syrup, but found none. The fog was finally breaking and she shivered delightedly in the fresh air, despite her heavy sweater.

After Myrna's, she'd gone to Wilson's General Store, the local market, picking up a few groceries so that her cupboards wouldn't look so bare. After a few days, when she felt more settled in, she would make a proper shopping list and go from there. She still needed some dishware and furniture for the house, but she didn't feel focused enough to want to deal with it.

It seems wiser, to wait, to write it down as I go, she thought, walking in the market aisles, pushing her cart forward. The aisles were shorter and narrower than she remembered and the shelves were not as tall. Shaking her head, she went forward with her grocery shopping. Almost as an afterthought, she threw in a bag of dry kitty kibble and dishes into her cart.

Now, as she trotted up the front porch steps, she found herself eager to be home for the first time, her thoughts going to Holly. The desire to see her oldest friend again in the town they grew up in mixed up with a very irreverent glee at the thought of revisiting their favorite haunts and she grinned.

She was at her door when a voice called her name and she stopped, turning. A tall man was hurrying up the walk, his stride uneven – she remembered the fall from the cliff overlooking the bay that had broken his right leg, cursing him forever with a limp and destroying any chances of a career in football. Much as she loved her older brother, she wished he had chosen another moment to appear.

He stopped at the bottom of the porch steps, stared up at her. "You never called me back." His tone was almost accusing.

"Hi, Mike," she said. "How are you?"

"I could be better," he said, his gray eyes watching her. She sensed a deep wariness in them, sighed. Except for the fiery red hair passed to them from their mother, Marty and Mike shared no other physical characteristics that would mark them as siblings.

She shrugged, resigned. "Want to come in for some coffee?"

"Sure." Mike followed her into the house, his own mind crowding with memories. "What are you doing back in the Bay?"

Marty kept her eyes forward. "I told you. I've decided, since I'm on sabbatical from teaching for a year, to live in the house Mom left me." She paused – Mike didn't answer, so she pushed on, hearing the nervous rush of her words and unable to stop them. "You remember Holly Prescott, right? My best friend from high school? She's the editor for *The Bay News* now. She always liked my short stories and thought I could write a book, that it would be good for me to go somewhere quiet to do it." Marty gave her brother a cheeky grin. "So, here I am."

They entered the kitchen, both ignoring the bright

color scheme. Mike cleared his throat. "Listen, there's something you need to know….."

Marty glanced at him, amused, as she set the grocery bag on the counter. "Are you still mad Mom left it to me and not you?"

Mike shook his head, his face finally relaxing into a grin. "Naw, that's Ellen. I just think you're here for reasons other than the one you just said."

She sighed. "Why else would I be here, Mike?"

He gazed at her, his expression thoughtful. "I think you came back to find out why Mom killed herself."

"I see." She began to put things away, absently choosing the cupboards their mother had used so long ago to store her food.

"Leave it alone, Marty. You won't bring her back."

She opened another cupboard, pulled out a mug. "I'm not looking to bring her back, Mike. She's dead and I don't believe in zombies. I just….I really don't think she killed herself. I've been looking at the pictures and her autopsy and…." She stopped abruptly, aware she had said too much.

Mike stared at her, disbelieving. "You have *what?*"

"Read Mom's autopsy report."

"Who did you bribe to get them?"

"No one." Filling the kettle with water, she put it on the stove, turned the burner on, and went to the cupboard. It wasn't the first lie she'd ever told her brother, but it wouldn't be the last. "Look, it's just something I have to do, so that I can…."

She groped for words.

"Get some sleep at night?" he prodded gently when she didn't go on. "I know you had nightmares after she died. And I'm guessing that you're still having them."

"But…?" She tried to smile, but her face felt stiff, wooden, as if unused to such an action.

"But you need to let it go. Let her go."

"I can't. I wish I could, I wish I could make you

understand why I can't, but I don't know how. I don't have the words. It feels too….big, somehow. Huge." She shrugged, one corner of her mouth quirking into the awkward smile he remembered. "What do you remember? About the day she died."

Mike looked away, his gaze settling on the view of the backyard from the kitchen window, resting his left hip against the counter opposite the sink. "Not much. I remember grabbing some cake, I remember the twins crying in the crib near the kitchen while Mrs. Farley was changing their diapers. Angie Blake was making eyes at me and Ellie – Ellen – was trying to sneak out the back gate with Jimmy." He paused. "Then glass shattered and you screamed and ran and Mom was hanging from the attic window over the master bedroom. That's all." He finally noticed what his sister had bought and picked up the bag of dry kibble. "When did you get a cat?"

"I didn't. It got me."

Mike gazed at his sister, worry evident in his eyes. "Who is he, Marty?"

"Who is who?" She spoke lightly, but didn't look at him.

"The man who hurt you."

She bit her lip. "His name was Ben and he turned out not to be the guy I thought he was." Marty looked over at her brother. "But he's not why I came back, Mike. It truly isn't. I just need to put Mom behind me."

Mike nodded, as if expecting this. "Then I hope you find whatever it is you need." He coughed. "Look, about Holly….."

"What about her?"

"There's no easy way to say this." Mike scowled. "She was late for dinner, always working on a story. Tim found her, in the parking lot of the newspaper, the night before you left Los Angeles. She'd been murdered."

A cup fell from Marty's hand, shattered on contact with the floor; she stared at her brother, numb. "What?

How?"

He shook his head. "The police aren't saying and now rumor has it that Denver Clarke was killed last night."

"Oh, my God, Holly." Marty covered her face, tears stinging her eyes. Then Mike's words penetrated her shock and she looked at him. "Two deaths in three days? That's not the Bay, that's crazy."

"I know."

"That must be why no one's been answering their phone….." Marty wiped angrily at the tears escaping her eyes. Mike reached over and pulled her into an embrace, hugging her hard. They were silent for a long while, the only sound their breathing and the muted crash of waves on the rocky shore of the bay.

"There's going to be a prayer service for Holly on Sunday," he said roughly. "If the rumors are true, then for Denver Clarke, too."

"That'll be good, for Tim." Marty pulled back and went to the pantry, grabbed the broom and dust pan and began to clean up. "So." She cleared her throat. "How's the teaching gig going?"

"Not so bad." Mike studied his hands. "Beats playing college football." He flashed her a crooked grin. "They must really like me at the high school. I'm teaching a couple of history classes this summer. Cassie and Pete are in one."

Marty quirked a brow. "Isn't there a rule about teaching one's relatives?"

"Naw. Only if they're my kids." He started down the hall. "Look, I've gotta go. See you around?"

She nodded. "Sure."

Mike paused at the front door. "Will you be at Dad's tomorrow night for dinner?"

"Wouldn't miss it," she called back and waited.

"I'm really sorry about Holly. I know she was your best friend."

The front door opened and closed quietly.

Mike was gone.

19 JUNE, 1852

My dear M.,
We are one day closer to our destination, but we now face a heavy storm front. Clouds are boiling dark and thick to the north and, if the rocky shores of our current position are anything to judge by, we may have to go a bit further north and then work our way down once we hit dry land.

Once I approached him and explained the change of plans, Mr. Madison appeared amenable. Although he remained silent, I had the feeling that Reverend Williams disliked this unexpected detour – after sparing me a sour look, he left our company, his black coat flapping behind him like a sail. The movement stirred memories, but I pushed them back and turned again to Mr. Madison, who was now asking about transferring passengers and cargo to the shore. I took him on a minor tour, pointing out our boats lashed to both sides of the ship, explaining the plan of loading cargo in two and a small group of my crew in another to begin set-up.

He listened intently, asking brief, pointed questions about the voyage from ship to shore, the camp we would set up and the eventual hike to the original site. I answered his questions as best I could. He has an intelligence that you would appreciate greatly, I feel – he is a learned man, someone who takes time and effort to research his thoughts, plan it out accordingly and then put it into action.

Then, without any warning, he reached into his breast pocket and pulled out a tightly wound parchment. Glancing about, not wanting any others to see, he undid the string that bound it, unwinding it to reveal carefully drawn lines forming the shape of the California coast. Touching one spot that had no name with a gloved finger, he said softly, "This is it, Captain. This is the place I wish to go."

I studied the map curiously, aware of his tightly wound excitement. Words scrawled in a fine hand denoted the cities of Santa Barbara and San Francisco, the smaller towns of San Buenaventura and of villages whose names I have never heard. I took the parchment without thinking – he let it go, as if sensing I would not betray his secret. Yellowed with age, what I held in my hands was far older than the date scrawled at the bottom, next to the representation of a sea dragon eating an unfortunate seaman.

Where he wanted to set up his new life was a strange marking, one I was unfamiliar with. Next to it were the words *waya ayegali*, which had been struck out in an angry slash and the words *los lobos silenciosos* were written in – the silent wolves. I felt my brow furl in confusion and I looked up at Mr. Madison, meeting his quiet gaze.

"For the last several months," he said, in answer to my unspoken question, "I have been doing careful research, trying to find the perfect place. Nothing satisfied me – not the areas in the south, nor in the middle of the state. I was driven to find this spot."

There was an intense coldness in his eyes that stirred unease in my heart. It was with some difficulty that I maintained eye contact.

"The gold mine?" I asked. I will admit here, in the

privacy of my quarters and in this letter to you, my old friend, that I was both surprised and equally gratified to hear that my voice sounded calm and steady.

My companion and charge nodded with enthusiasm. The strange light in his eyes did not diminish. "I would pray, quite often, in my study, asking for guidance from the good Lord above. And one day, He showed me the way." Madison tapped the parchment. "I found this while going through old documents in a San Diego courthouse, hidden away behind some old folios. It was providence."

It was theft, I thought, but did not say. I handed him back the parchment. He took it, rolling it back up and securing it tightly. Placing it back in his breast pocket, he nodded and turned away to study the California coast, his expression thoughtful. I hesitated, not quite ready to part from his company, my mind half on the parchment.

It was on the tip of my tongue to ask why he had allowed the unpleasant Reverend into his company, but one of my men ran up, requesting my presence below to inspect the cargo which would accompany us on tomorrow's sailing.

I bade the gentleman good morning, which he acknowledged with a nod, and took my leave.

Noon

I took Billy his lunch of broth, bread and a chunk of cheese and am pleased to note that he seems to have fully recovered from his mysterious ailment. He is somewhat pleased and mightily embarrassed by my scrutiny and is anxious to return to his duties. I told him to rest for another day and then we'd see what Doctor Kelly's thoughts were. As you may have guessed, he was somewhat reluctant in his agreement.

Midnight

Something woke me from my sleep, something both familiar and unnatural. I had fallen asleep at my desk and my back muscles protested painfully as I straightened.

Normally I sleep heavily, attuned to the ship's sounds, knowing one wrong creak would rouse me instantly.

But this sound was different, closer. As I stood and went to the porthole, I heard it three times more, as mournful as the wind that carried it.

Glancing over at my bunk, I was surprised to see that it was empty and that Billy was nowhere to be found. Fearful for his safety, I left my cabin and made my way to the top deck, listening intently. The only sounds I heard were the complacent creaks of my ship as she crested the gently rolling swells. Bathed in the pale light of the swollen moon,
the *Bonnie Jane* took on an unsettling, eerie quality – all that was familiar in the day was now full of shadows and mystery.

I walked from bow to stern, from port to starboard, seeing nothing. A shadow rose from the steps and I recognized Billy. He was staring at the coast, his back stiff, the soft breeze lifting his hair lightly. I approached him, touching his shoulder and saying his name at the same time. He jumped, growling low in his throat and in the brightness of the moon's light I saw something glowing in his eyes. Startled, I fell back a step and then his eyes cleared and he became the boy I knew, albeit a rather bewildered one.

"Come, Billy," I said, touching his shoulder. "Let's get you back to bed."

He nodded and slipped through the door. As I turned to follow him, I glanced round and over at the coast, where he had been gazing. What I saw gave me pause and before I knew it, I was at the railing again, gripping the weathered wood so tightly it left imprints in my palms through the next afternoon.

Tiny pinpoints of light dotted the hills just to the south of our landing point. It did not flicker with life as befits a torch or fire and after my conversations with Mr.

Madison, I had been confident that the only mammals living this far north were the wildlife native to the state, such as the grizzly and wolf. He had been confident that the Indians had been pushed further north and east.

I could not make sense of what I saw and I turned away, intent on going back below and getting some semblance of rest when I heard that unearthly sound once more.

Howling.

I believe that, as unlikely as it seems, it came from the main land, near where those lights I'd seen were, when I found the boy in such a strange state. Are wolves known to live so close to human settlements? And if there is a gold mine there, how is it that it has not been claimed before, when others clearly appear to be living in this area?

I leave you with my questions that I know you may have no answers for, but perhaps I may have some in the days to come.

Always yours affectionately,
Jonas Brye

FRIDAY, JUNE 9, 1978

Less than a half mile from the wharf, Eddie Payne stood on the north side of Maple Road and stared down, one hand clamping a hanky to his mouth and nose, the other scratching his head in honest bewilderment. Behind him, his beloved cruiser was silent.

He had conducted a fruitless search yesterday for Mr. Gordon and his dog, prompted by his wife's worried call to the station. From her, Eddie took down Mr. Gordon's walking route and the length of time it took him and the dog to walk it. Then he drove it, going well below the speed limit as he scanned the sides of the road. Twice he had to park and get out of his cruiser and soon, he had ended up at the wooded stretch of Maple Road between Chaney Creek and the harbor.

Two more hours of driving, stopping and walking several yards at a time away from the roadside followed, as he looked for clues. Eddie had been on foot when he was drawn to the Chaney Creek Bridge by something that sounded mournful. Thinking that he had found the missing man, Eddie quickly scrambled down the side of the bridge.

There was no sign of Mr. Gordon that day. He did,

however, find the dog, Toad, hiding under the bridge, whining and shivering. It cowered back when Eddie tried to crawl in with him. It had taken well over an hour and a pound of hamburger before the dog allowed himself to be dragged out from beneath the bridge and put in the backseat of Eddie's cruiser. The dog was now hiding under the Gordon porch, coming out only long enough to gobble up his meals and drink slurping gulps of water, before retreating once more to the dark safety the space under the porch provided.

Today, Eddie was drawn once again to the bridge by a swarm of flies hovering above the creek. He walked over, not hurrying, expecting a dead animal – a squirrel or a blue jay, maybe even a raccoon. He found something else, instead. At the rocky bottom of the dry creek bed, the flies buzzing in low hum, was a pile of bloody rags that might have been a shirt in its previous life.

Feeling sick, Eddie went back to his cruiser and sat in the driver's seat, sinking into the hot vinyl. He thought briefly that after three years on the job, he ought to be used to seeing blood and violent ends by now, that he ought to stop feeling like losing his lunch every time he came upon one. Then again, the Bay wasn't exactly a hotbed of crime to begin with, like Chicago or New York or even San Francisco, so maybe it wasn't that surprising violent crime scenes made him sick.

He picked up the handset and radioed in. Clara Banks, the station operator for the last thirty years, spoke curtly and patched him through to the sheriff, who was still at the old lighthouse.

As he waited, he wondered idly what Clara was so snippy about.

"Dylan here. What have you got?"

"A pile of bloody rags, but no sign of Mr. Gordon. I think he met something big."

There was a short pause. "How can you tell?"

Payne swallowed, his eyes falling reluctantly on the

site where he had found the shredded shirt. After calling in at seven that morning to report that her husband hadn't come home with their dog after their nightly walk, Mrs. Gordon had personally come in to the station at noon to describe her husband's clothing.

Mr. Gordon had been wearing a dark blue plaid flannel shirt over a white tank top and jeans. According to Mrs. Gordon, she had bought it two days ago at the tiny department store. Mr. Gordon had just put it on for the first time to go on his walk, the ironed creases still sharp and new.

All Eddie had found so far in his search was the shredded flannel shirt.

Now it looked like dirt. "I found what's left of his shirt."

"Shit." Dylan's voice was soft. "Have you found Mr. Gordon?"

"Not yet, but I'm gonna take another look around. He can't be that far away. What's happening at the lighthouse? Second day up there, John. You planning to man it?"

There was a long pause that Eddie didn't like at all. Then Dylan spoke. "It's a mess, Eddie. Denver Clarke wasn't just murdered, he was slaughtered."

Eddie gave a low whistle. "What the hell's going on, John?"

Over the airwaves, Payne could hear Dylan sigh. "I'll send Fletcher down, have her deal with the mess. Amelia, too. Search the area again, see if you can find anything that you might have missed the first time around."

Eddie noticed that Dylan avoided answering the question, but didn't press it. "Yes, sir. And the Gordons?" The silence on the radio was almost palpable.

At last, Dylan spoke. "Hold off until you come up with something concrete. Then break it gently."

"Roger that. When can I expect Doctor Fletcher?"

"They just left. Give them twenty minutes."

It was closer to forty minutes, but arrive Jean Fletcher did in her specially designed station wagon that served as her mobile office and lab. Amelia was in the squad car right behind her. They pulled up single-file behind Eddie's car and parked, engines off and cooling.

Eddie had been poking around on the west-bound side of the road thirty feet away, his movements coming with great care as he looked for any sign of Mr. Gordon. When they pulled up, he started walking back.

Snapping on surgical gloves, Fletcher climbed down to the creek bed to examine the remains of the shirt, dictating to Amelia, who wrote them down dutifully on a legal pad, speaking only to clarify something said.

Then Jean Fletcher stood, walked back up to the bridge and surveyed the lonely road thoughtfully as it twisted down towards the old wharf. The watery sunlight glinted in her black, kinky hair, the dusky tones of her skin damp with air moisture.

Amelia stayed below, sketching a detailed picture the scene. Eddie made his way carefully to Fletcher.

At the moment, they were the only ones on the road – everything was quiet. Even the birds had fallen silent.

"Whoever or whatever did this sure wasn't shy about it," she said at last. Her voice was troubled and matched the expression in her dark eyes. "What time did Mr. Gordon go out for his walk last night?"

"Eight. Every night, rain or shine, he's out. Very religious about it."

"Does everyone know about it?"

Eddie shrugged. "I don't suppose it's a state secret, so it's possible."

She leaned over the rail, frowning down at the torn and bloodied shirt. "Then where was he?"

"Don't you mean, 'Where is he'?"

She faced the deputy. "It's, what, two-thirty in the afternoon? Three? The remains of that shirt was left probably seven or eight hours ago, maybe nine, if I really wanted to stretch it and I don't. That puts it at approximately around six-thirty, maybe seven in the morning. Mr. Gordon went out for his walk at eight last night. That's a window of eleven hours unaccounted for." Fletcher made a vague gesture to the west. "This road is the only one that goes to the wharf. Knowing how religious our fishermen are about the catch of the day, this road is busier than rush hour between four and five AM."

"In which case, somebody should have seen something?"

She shrugged. "Seems likely. Any reports of suspicious activity?"

He thought about this as she pulled off the gloves, tucking them into a wastebasket in the back of her car. Until Mrs. Gordon had called the station, there had been no reports of anything unusual occurring or being sighted on Maple Road. The nightshift officer would have fielded it. He said as much to Fletcher as they walked back to her vehicle.

The older woman then snapped on a fresh pair of gloves, frowning at him briefly. "So, what or who would dump just the torn shirt and not the body? And how would they do it unnoticed?"

"I guess that's what I have to find out." He nodded to Fletcher. "Have a good day."

"You, too."

He walked back to his cruiser, passing Amelia on the way as she climbed back onto the road, her sketch finished. Jean Fletcher watched, amusement teasing a smile on her face, as the two muttered quick good-byes, their eyes averted.

Then Eddie climbed back into his cruiser and started it up, pulling onto the road and going past the bridge before pulling a u-turn to head back towards town. As he passed Jean Fletcher's wagon, his gaze flickered to the east-bound side of the bridge, his mind registering what his eyes did not – color.

He hit the brakes hard, almost clipping his chin on the steering wheel, and put the car in park, stumbling out, forgetting the engine, ignoring Amelia's startled voice. He stood at the edge of the road, barely registering what he was looking at. He could think of nothing but the dog that was probably, even now, hiding under the porch. Toad was not a small dog – he was a mix of German shepherd and Great Dane, standing just over three feet at the shoulder.

Partially hidden by the ditch and the brush growing over it lay the savaged, twisted body of Stanley Gordon. One arm lay three feet from his head, torn from the socket. His stomach had been sliced open, intestines spilling out beside his corpse. Something damp and purple-toned rested against his right shoe.

Whatever stopped Mr. Gordon had clearly been much bigger.

Trying very hard to not look too closely, Eddie turned to say something to Amelia and threw up instead.

FOURTEEN

That evening found the Bryes under the same roof at 29 Oak Street for the weekly family dinner. Normally a cheerful occasion, this particular dinner featured Bessie Mills, the housekeeper Ronald Brye had hired fifteen years ago, after the funeral of his wife. The tension among the younger Bryes was palpable.

Thin and mousy, Bessie was a widow, harboring an undying infatuation with Ronald Brye. Although she was younger than him, her make-up and thinning gray hair pulled back in a small bun made her appear ten years older. The fact that he remained continually oblivious to her attentions was lost on her. The romance novels left behind, her coy simpering and repeated, not-so-subtle hints about putting aside the past and returning to the living annoyed the four Brye siblings to the point that they would each have taken turns to cheerfully throttle the woman and have done with it.

Tactless as the widow was, Marty thought she outdid herself on this night when Bessie invited herself to their family dinner.

Even Ellen, who could be counted on to side with Bessie against Marty and Mike on most subjects, seemed to find the housekeeper's gall distasteful.

At the moment, Bessie was praising herself over the pork chops she had cooked and offering unwanted advice to Mr. Brye. "….really ought to consider dating again," she was saying, sipping daintily from her glass.

Both Ellen and Mike glowered at her, unnoticed. Marty skewered her vegetables on her fork, barely able to tolerate the atmosphere.

Ronald said nothing, chewing absently on a piece of meat.

Bessie went on, blithely. "It would do the children good, knowing you were happy."

Marty cleared her throat pointedly. "We're hardly children, Bessie. I'll be thirty-five in October."

"And I'm thirty-seven," Mike said, offering a frosty smile.

"Right," Cassie chimed in. "And Pete and I will be seventeen in July."

Bessie's eyes narrowed. "I'm only thinking of your father's best interest."

"I'm sure you are," Marty said coolly. The two women eyed each other, distrust and dislike evident. Ronald laid his fork across his plate.

"I'm finished," he said with a sigh. "I'll be in my study. I found the most unusual paw print today…."

His voice trailed off as he moved down the hall. As soon as he was gone, Bessie glared with undisguised hate at Marty, who looked back calmly.

"You are a selfish woman, Marita," she said coldly. "Why you insist on letting your father wallow in sorrow that should have been put aside years ago is beyond me."

"Number one, Bessie, she's not insisting that our father do anything," Mike said in clipped tones. "And two, he's a big boy and can figure out for himself when he's ready to let my mother go. Until then, keep your big mouth shut and don't presume on your duties here, or I'll have to ask you to find employment elsewhere."

Bessie's gray eyes flashed at him. "You can't fire me."

Mike smiled unpleasantly. "No, but I can let my father know that you've been going through some private things which are none of your business."

The older woman gaped, her cheeks flaming with indignation. "Well, I never!"

"No, you won't," Marty agreed calmly, finishing the remainder of her wine. Mike choked back laughter, his eyes sparkling merrily.

Bessie left the table in a huff and disappeared into the kitchen, where the clattering of dishes could be heard. Cassie and Pete gazed at Marty and Mike in awe.

Marty glanced at them, then away. "What?"

"Wow," Cassie said softly.

"That was great!" Pete grinned, his eyes sparkling with mischief.

Mike eyed him uneasily. "Don't go making Bessie any more miserable. Just because we don't like her doesn't mean that we have to torture her."

"Don't worry about us," Cassie said, confidently.

Marty studied the twins. "That's why Dad had to hire her in the first place."

Ellen sat in her chair, stiff. "Don't you think you were a little harsh on Mrs. Mills?"

Mike didn't look at her. "Not really. She's a nosy parker with too much time on her hands….."

"Who needed to be reminded of who signs her paychecks and why," Marty finished, stabbing at her salad with her fork.

Ellen glared at her sister-in-law. "I don't see why you have any say, Marty. It's not like you stuck around to help raise the twins."

"Ellen, please…" Mike began, but Ellen cut him off.

"No, Mike, it has to be said. After your mother died, all Marty did was moon about the Bay over some guy and her college applications and then sailed off to Los Angeles at the drop of a hat, leaving you to deal with raising the twins and cope with your father's grief —"

Mike frowned. "Ellie, she had every right to go. She'd put it off for a year. And it's not like I had any colleges beating down my door. The accident took care of that."

"Mike, the twins needed her here…."

Pete looked up from his dinner. "Hey, right here. Not deaf."

Cassie added, "We turned out fine, too."

Marty put down her napkin and stood, ending the conversation effectively. "Thanks for dinner. It was lovely."

"Marty…" Mike and the twins began, but Marty shook her head.

"I'll see you guys later." Her eyes flickered to Ellen's cold gray ones. "When the company is friendlier."

Marty left. Dinner was finished in silence.

FIFTEEN

Shortly after dinner, they went out to the porch to watch the sun set over the ocean and paint the sky in vibrant oranges and reds.

Without speaking, Ellen stepped down onto the stone walkway and headed for the street. Just as she reached the gate, Mike called out to her.

"Honey, wait," he called and she waited, not turning to face him, but not pushing the gate open. When he caught up to her, she glanced at him. "You're not staying for a drink? Or an extra dessert?"

She shook her head. "No, I'm tired. I had a long day at the store and I just want to go home and sleep."

"Can I ask what's going on with you and Marty?" He put up a hand when she started to speak. "It's not about the twins. I know that."

Ellen was silent. "I don't want to talk about it."

"Then don't make it an issue when we're all together." She scowled at him, opened her mouth to speak. He touched her lips with his finger and she quieted. "Please, Ellie. I want to make you the happiest woman in the world. I love you. I love the fact that you have your business. But Marty's my sister and I can't change that. I don't want to. What I want is for my wife and my sister to have at the very least a civil relationship."

Ellen smiled tightly, not meeting his gaze. "I know, Mike. I'm sorry." She finally looked at him. "I love you, too."

She opened the gate and stepped through. She had already disappeared around the corner when Mike realized that she had not addressed his concerns. He thought about going after her, then decided not to. Time enough for that later.

Turning back to the house, he saw that his younger sibs had come out to the porch, each carrying another plate of cake and ice cream. Mike made no comment on his wife's abrupt departure as he rejoined the twins on the steps. Cassie and Pete were sitting on the steps and talking quietly, shifting over to make room and leaving Mike free to think his own thoughts, which now centered mostly on their father.

Poor man, alone without his soul twin, fumbling in the dark for the light that is no longer there, he thought and smiled at his own flair for poetry. He remembered going up to the attic days after their mother's funeral with Marty, looking for a box of books he'd stored there. Marty had found a shoebox full of their mother's poetry hidden in a corner, as if she had been ashamed or embarrassed by her output. It seemed as if their mother had sprung back to life and Marty had taken the shoebox to her room, hiding it under her bed and taking it with her when she left town.

Mike watched the twins with some amusement — although they were too young to remember Denise Brye, they loved her as completely as if they did. The twins relied on both his and Marty's memories and old pictures to keep her, if not alive, then fresh and relevant to their own lives.

Cassie was beginning to resemble their mother more every day and Pete, well, Pete was a fine mixture of both their parents, even if he did enjoy taking chances, like now – walking along the porch railing with his eyes closed. He missed a step and Mike thought his heart would stop, but Pete recovered gracefully by leaping to the ground and rolling onto his back. Cassie hurried over to make sure he wasn't seriously hurt, which he wasn't – Pete was like the proverbial cat with nine lives.

Like Mike himself had been, once upon a time....

From inside, they heard Bessie shriek. Pete groaned.

"Can Dad fire her already?" He sat on the porch swing, next to Mike. "It's not like we need a babysitter or anything."

"No kidding," Cassie sighed, sitting on Mike's other side. "Will you or Marty please talk to Dad about her? She's driving us crazy."

Mike nodded. "Tomorrow. It's her day off, which she spends almost exclusively at Nell's beauty shop. Perfect timing. I'll call Marty and we'll do an intervention."

They fell silent, watching as the sky shifted from pale gold to hot pink then to deep royal purple as the sun settled over the horizon. Mike found himself thinking of Marty again – unlike the twins, secrets had not been difficult to keep between them, but he knew she had had a deep crush on Dan Williams, their former pastor.

He wasn't sure of what had gone on, exactly, between them, but he had suspected then that it had been of an intimate nature.

He was more certain of it now, when Marty had discovered that he was now seeing the English teacher, Daria Brennan.

Bessie had been filled with malicious joy over telling Marty that one.

Then Pete was looking at him strangely and Mike stirred uncomfortably.

"I'd better go. Ellen's not going to be happy if I'm not home at a reasonable hour."

"I don't understand why you got married if you can't do what you want."

Mike laughed. "You'll either get it or you won't, but

the fact is, it seemed like a very good idea at the time."

"Maybe you guys should have kids. I bet she's feeling that maternal instinct kicking in," Cassie said. "And it would be nice to have someone to boss around, besides Pete."

"It's on the table, but don't hold your breath." Mike grinned at his younger sister.

Pete looked up, puzzled. "Why would we do that? We'd pass out."

Cassie made a face at him and Mike laughed.

Then Mike was on his feet, hugging the twins and wishing them good night before going down the walk and through the gate, turning left towards Fry.

The twins watched him go, silent – then Bessie came out, murmuring 'good night' to them and avoiding their gazes as she left. They watched her leave as well, then went inside and shut the door.

*****

The dark figure crouched in the shadows on all fours, its scarred, misshapen body hidden in the elongated shadows. Each movement, no matter how slight, sent deep aches to the marrow of its bones, but it couldn't not move, couldn't not behave like the predator it had been made to be. The bright glow of the full moon bathed the town in pale, white light, making the buildings appear flat, without dimension. Lifting its nose, it scented another like it – male, alpha, strong, young.

Whole.

The figure growled low in its throat, desiring nothing more than to bend it to his will, to dominate the youth before killing it.

Slipping from shadow to shadow, it circled the parameter of the town, the desire to overpower and best the young one so strong, it left a sour taste in its mouth. When it had crossed the high school's baseball field, it paused abruptly at third base, scenting the air again, tasting something new and fresh as it floated on the gentle breeze.

It was in the cemetery, it was alone and it was *female*. Hot fury coursing through its veins, the figure changed course, loping easily towards the cemetery.

Somewhere on the south-east side of town, the young one crested a low hill, lifting his nose occasionally to taste the wind. He scented the same information that was both familiar and different and altered his course to make his way to the cemetery, intent on defending the female he knew he had protected once before, but was unable to remember where or when.

Or why.

SIXTEEN

Ordinarily, walking from her father's house back to the house she'd grown up in would have taken maybe twenty minutes, twenty-five tops. At the moment, however, Marty felt a restlessness that was more in her soul than in her body. It would not be satisfied by simply going home, so she wandered the streets of Wolf's Head Bay. Eventually, she realized that her feet had taken her towards the cemetery entrance.

The Wolf's Head Bay Cemetery had been founded in the fall of 1853, not long after the town's founding. The first resident to be laid to rest in the cemetery had been a man with no name – his grave was unmarked and lay hidden under the brush on the north-east side of the cemetery. The only reason the grave was known about at all had been due to a reference in Jonas Brye's journals and letters, now safely locked away in the library, until they could be moved to the historical society's archives at its new location.

The main gate was closed and padlocked, Marty noted as she approached, but the smaller gate, the one for visitors to use after hours, was not. She pushed the wrought-iron gate open wide enough to allow her to slip through.

Behind her, the Wolf's Head Bay church was dark, silent, its steeple a sharp white point in the evening sky. She stared at it, thinking of the lie she had told Mike about the man who had hurt her. There had been a Ben in her life, and he had been a creep, but it was not him that she had been thinking of.

Winding her way through the gravestones, she stopped at her mother's, kneeling so that she was eye-level with the chiseled name.

She touched it, her fingers tracing the letters and numbers carved into the cold, gray granite. *I miss you, Mom. I wish you were still here.* Standing again, she gazed around at the surrounding graves, some as recent as last year, some as old as the original township, and sighed. Loathe as she was to admit it, Bessie was right – her father had to put aside his grief and get on with his life. It would help, Marty supposed, if she did the same. Poring over the past wasn't exactly the best way to do it.

Something blacker than the shadows flickered from the corner of her eye and Marty turned to her left, searching, her eyes straining to pull apart the varying shades of black to see what had caught her attention. It didn't reoccur and she put the incident out of her mind, giving her mother's gravestone a final touch before she turned and left.

She headed down the winding path and soon found herself at the outdoor chapel that had been built near the cliff's edge in 1929, six months before the stock market crashed and plunged the nation into the Depression. Benches ten rows deep curved in a half moon shape, the redwood seats and back supports held in place by stones brought up from the beach below. A protective metal railing curled inward, towards the chapel and with no easy access to their supports.

They stood between the benches and the white wooden fence that former Mayor Thomas Boyle had put in thirty years ago when a teenager had plunged to his death on the unforgiving rocks below. Sitting on the bench closest to her, Marty closed her eyes, listening to the waves as they thundered heavily below, the sharp, salty scent tickling her nose.

She thought of Holly, her oldest friend since kindergarten, the one person who knew her best, outside of family. And just like that, the tears came in a flood. Curling up on her side, the bolts holding the bench seat in place digging into her hip, Marty finally allowed her grief to overwhelm her and she sobbed into the wood, her tears hot and scalding as they slid down her face.

It seemed a long time before they stopped and she was just lying there, looking up into the sky, watching the stars, her face raw, her eyes swollen.

A breeze picked up, caressing her cheek in a lover's touch and she shivered. Next to the forests, this had been her favorite place to be alone and think. No one ever bothered her here and it was at this very bench where she'd decided that she was going to UCLA instead of San Francisco state two hours away.

Shifting into a more comfortable position, dabbing at the stray tears escaping, Marty remembered the excitement that had filled her when she made her final decision. It was the idea of going to a school and city that was as foreign to her as the Amazon jungles of South America that had made it so thrilling.

Her boyfriend at the time had not been overly thrilled with her final decision when she did tell him. It was only three weeks before graduation and she wanted to break it off with him fast before he got too set on her for the rest of his life.

Jimmy Moore was always pushing for something she didn't want and it bewildered her as to how she'd started dating him in the first place. And when she at last mentioned her choice for college casually to him the following night on their date at Myrna's, he argued persistently for her to change her mind.

"Why would you want to live and go to school in a polluted city like Los Angeles?" he demanded, his thin face red. "It's the bottom of a black hole."

"Black holes have no bottom," she said, hoping to lighten the mood.

Judging from the way his expression quickly soured, she had not even come close to succeeding. "You know what I mean, Marty. How can you give up Wolf's Head Bay for Los Angeles?"

"Who says I'm giving anything up?" she shot back, suddenly angry. "I've lived here all my life. I'd like to go away and see the world a bit. That doesn't mean I won't come back here for a visit."

"We'll do it together." Jimmy took her left hand. "After we get married."

Her jaw dropped in surprise. "Excuse me?"

"Not right away, of course," he said easily. "After college."

"Jimmy," she said coldly. "I'm eighteen years old. I'm not going to marry you, not now, not after college, not ever. I don't like you and you don't own me."

His grip on her hand tightened like a vise, grinding the bones together until she wanted to scream, but she did not, never looking away from his suddenly dead eyes. A part of her wanted to scratch at them, but another was very much aware that he could break her hand if he so chose. She wondered, not for the first time, why she had ever agreed to go out with him in the first place.

Then he relaxed as suddenly as he angered and he leaned back in his chair, a grin on his lips that did not reach his eyes. She regarded him warily, wanting to flex the pain out of her hand, but not wanting to give him the satisfaction of knowing he'd hurt her.

"We'll do all right," he said comfortably. "It's you and me all the way, baby."

Anger burned acid in her stomach at his arrogance.

"I'm not going anywhere with you, Jimmy. I'm going to UCLA and that's final."

His eyes narrowed to slits. "No, you aren't."

That was it. Time to go. She stood up fast, almost knocking her chair over in her haste. "Let's get something straight, James Moore. I am not your 'baby', I will *never* be your wife and I *am* going away to Los Angeles. Put that in your pipe and smoke it."

She turned to leave, but the bruising hand caught her by the elbow and pulled her back. Jimmy studied her, his eyes flat and unyielding. She was suddenly aware that he frightened her and that angered her even more.

"Let go of my arm," she said in a low voice.

"Don't make a fuss. People are watching."

"Let go of my arm," she repeated loudly.

A hand descended upon Jimmy's shoulder and they looked up. Reverend Williams had come up to them unobserved and was now gazing mildly at Jimmy. Tall and in his early thirties, he was handsome in a way that contradicted the idea of what a reverend should look like. In spite of the fact that he was married, most of the women who went to church to hear his sermons did not go with the intention of saving their souls.

"Something the matter, Jimmy?" he asked. His tone was pleasant enough, but Marty caught the sharp intent behind the question.

Jimmy was shaking his head, sullen. "No, sir."

The reverend caught the lie easily enough and his lips tightened – Marty saw that as soon as Jimmy opened his big mouth. But the older man didn't press the issue. Instead, he looked at Marty and some of the warmth she'd always associated with Dan Williams came back.

She flushed all the way to her toes, her breath short.

"You all right, Marty?" She nodded, suddenly relieved. "Go on home, then. Jimmy and I have some catching up to do."

It was an easy out, she knew. She also knew that if

Dan Williams had not come in when he did, Jimmy would have followed her and serious trouble soon after. She had told Holly about it the next day and her friend had been both indignant and afraid, urging her to leave the Bay as soon as possible.

Kicking at a loose stone, Marty stood, frowning. She had never run away from a problem before and hated herself for running from Jimmy, in spite of the fact that she'd been ill-equipped at the time to handle him. As for Dan Williams….

Heat flamed her face as she tried to think past *that* humiliating experience. So intent on her thoughts, she did not see the shadow coming up behind her until a strong hand clamped her shoulder.

Startled, she yelled, her hands grabbing hold of the man's wrist. In a quick twist, she had flung him over her shoulder and onto the ground. Then, as the path lights flickered on, she stared at her attacker and gaped.

SEVENTEEN

"Jimmy?"

To the north of the cemetery, heavy, overgrown bushes swayed gently in the night breeze. Marty paid no attention to the rustling of leaves or to the wind as it teased her hair, brushing it out of her eyes impatiently, her incredulous gaze on her ex-boyfriend.

"Aw, God," Jimmy groaned, lying still on his back, his eyes closed. Even though he was older, weather-beaten and had a scraggly beard, he looked much as he did fifteen years ago. "What the hell did you do that for?"

"Why the hell did you sneak up on me?" She glared down at him, breathing heavily, and suddenly the anger she'd been holding inside for the last fifteen years welled up and she kicked him in the side. He groaned. "Goddamn it, Jimmy, you scared the shit out of me. What the hell were you thinking, following me here?"

He sat up slowly, wincing. "I ran into Ellen at the gas station. She told me you were back. Thought we could pick up where we left off." He poked at his ribs. "I think you broke something."

"Are you out of your fucking mind?" She turned and began to walk away, tossing over her shoulder, "We were over long before I left for college. Get it through your thick head, jerk, and go home to your floozy of the month."

He got to his feet, following, trying to be his jocular old self, an act that depressed her. "I heard you got your mom's place, so I went there, looking for you. But you weren't home so I figured you were out here." He glanced around uneasily. "I still think you're fuckin' morbid for hanging around here."

She scowled at him. "They're dead. They can't hurt me. It's the living you have to be careful of."

He grabbed hold of her left arm, quickly turning her until she was facing him. "You know, when your mom died, I figured you going away was put out of your mind for good. I was wrong then, but you're back now."

She tried to wrench away from him, but his grip was too strong. "Let go of my arm, Jimmy," she said through clenched teeth. God, this was surreal – it was like a replay of what had happened in Myrna's Diner. Different setting, but the same words.

He laughed. "Or what? You'll scream? The reverend's not around to help you this time."

In that moment, she hated him more than she thought possible and it infuriated her that he thought he still had a claim on her, even after all this time. Without thinking, she lifted her foot and put all her weight onto his right foot, feeling a cold satisfaction when she heard something pop.

He screamed in pain, pushing her away. "Goddamn bitch!"

Stumbling backwards, Marty struggled to regain her balance by grabbing hold of a marble angel, but her momentum was too strong and she tripped over the base, falling to the ground heavily. Her fingers brushed against something rough and she closed her hand over it, recognizing it as a branch. She shifted her position so that she was facing Jimmy, but the angry words she wanted to throw at him died on her lips when she saw the dark shadow bounding towards him.

She opened her mouth to cry out a warning, but her voice was gone and in one fluid movement, the creature tossed Jimmy to one side.

He gave a startled cry as he hit the ground with a heavy thud, falling silent when his head struck a rock and he grew still.

All conscious thought was driven from her mind as it approached her, growling deep and low in its chest. The only thought remaining to her was that it bore no resemblance to the classic monster she'd grown up with. Unable to move, Marty watched as it advanced towards her, slobber dripping from its massive jaws, its eyes a maddened red.

Now, standing over her, its oppressive, rank scent choked her, its breath hot against her cheek. Closing her eyes, Marty wished she'd said good bye to her father.

Then suddenly, it yelped in pain and, opening her eyes, she saw why. A large, black wolf was standing several feet away, its hackles rising as it growled deep. The monster standing over her snarled, but even she could see that it was unsure. The wolf sprinted forward, barreling into the monster heavily. It howled in pain, snapping at the wolf's tail, but the latter moved away nimbly, ears back, pink tongue lolling easily. They eyed each other warily, circling Marty as if she were the prize.

Then the monster leapt for the wolf, its jaws seeking the other's throat. The wolf ducked and sank its jaws on the monster's right hind leg. Shrieking in pain, the monster kicked at the wolf, sending it to the ground before hobbling a short distance. It turned to find the wolf standing protectively over Marty.

Dark eyes gleaming with the promise of death, the monster howled, frustrated, and disappeared into the shadows.

The wolf remained tense for several minutes and

Marty was afraid to move, lest it turned on her and sank its teeth into her arm. Then it relaxed, satisfied that the monster was gone, and turned to her, nosing her hand, its snuffling noises tickling her skin and her funny bone. She laughed, high and shaky, but it was a relief to do it.

It looked up, blue eyes boring into hers, panting, then licked her palm. Its tongue was rough and she raised her hand cautiously. Immediately, it put its head under it, acting very much like its domesticated cousin. She laughed again, this time sounding less shaky and scratched behind its ears gently. A streak of silvery white fur began at the edge of its right eye, ending in a loop behind its right ear.

"You saved my life," she said softly. It whined anxiously and licked at her face. She laughed. "Stop, that tickles!" After another long minute of concerned snuffling to satisfy himself that she was all right, the black wolf stepped back a couple of feet and sat on his haunches expectantly.

Climbing unsteadily to her feet, she glanced over at Jimmy warily. At first, when he didn't move, she thought he was dead. Then he moaned indistinctly and she turned away, no longer caring.

The wolf barked sharply — three concise sounds that caught her attention.

She met the wolf's intent gaze. "What? You got something to say?"

It glanced over at the dark end of the cemetery and she understood. Whatever that thing was might come back. It would be safer to get home and fast.

Turning, she walked hurriedly to the gate, aware of the large, black wolf padding silently along beside her. She didn't try to kid herself that it was a stray domesticated dog that she had found. Even if it didn't periodically stop to sniff the air, circle her or take point, it was very clearly a wolf.

*****

The creature seethed with the heat of rage and humiliation

at being brought down by one as pure as it was not. Lurking in the shadows of the church, it licked its wounds gingerly, hissing with pain, conflicting emotions coloring its thoughts. Panting, drinking in the cool night air greedily, it scented a place to come to earth.

It loped off into the darkness, ignoring the sharp pain in its leg.

*****

Home was a welcoming sight and she hurried up the walk to the front door. Opening it, she turned to usher the wolf in, but it refused, wagging its tail gently.

"Well, if you're sure," she said. Under the glare of the porch light, its dark blue eyes met hers calmly. Something about it stirred a memory, not old, she knew, but it was not fresh, either, and she could not place it. Seeing that she was safe, it turned and trotted to the front gate, questing the air with its nose. Then, quite deliberately, it lifted its hind leg and urinated, marking her place as its territory.

Ordinarily, such an act would have pissed her off, but after tonight, she understood the wolf's intention. Later, in the bath, she would realize that she had been touched by its concern and mock herself gently for it.

Now, it turned to look at her. Something in those eyes stroked that elusive memory once more; then the wolf barked and disappeared into the night.

She went inside and shut the door.

*****

The monster crouched in the elongated shadows, licking its wounds, its tongue rough on the old scars that ravaged its body, hate flaming in its black heart. It would kill the wolf that had come between it and its prey. That was a certainty.

A plan was needed. Consult with the shadow. *She* would know…..

As it shifted back into human shape, a plan began to formulate within its twisted mind.

*****

129

In the hills just beyond the old Madison place, the black wolf stopped and turned to look back at the town he had left, his dark eyes searching for and finding the house he had been driven to protect. Her scent had been familiar, teasing out a hazy memory of the woods during a cold night when she had gotten lost. She had been gone for what seemed to it an eternity – now she was…..different somehow.

His thoughts then turned to the other, the half-changed wolf, the monster.

It confused him, that misshapen creature. It was full of scents unfamiliar and strong, yet underneath them, he recognized something, knew a scent that he could not readily identify and this bothered him.

The woman was its target for some reason – beyond the obvious fact that she was female, the wolf didn't understand what the monster wanted with her. It would be a wise choice, the wolf decided, to keep a close eye on the woman with the bright green eyes that glowed.

*****

Marty was in the tub, soaking her sore muscles and enjoying the fresh scent of her bubble bath when the telephone rang. She resisted the urge to scramble out of the tub to answer the phone, allowing the answering machine pick up.

"Hey, Marty, it's Mike." He sounded tired. "I was wondering if you could talk to Dad about firing Bessie. Circumstances, as you know, keep me from participating in what would be a fine performance by a housekeeper."

"Sure, Mike," she responded to the silence following his message. "Wouldn't miss it for the world."

The cat strolled in, purring loudly as it sat on its haunches, observing the bubbles in her bath with great curiosity.

"Well, hello, cat." She held out a bubbled hand – it reached out, sniffing the bubbles delicately before walking away, tail in the air.

Snickering to herself, she sat in the tub for another twenty minutes. When the water had cooled considerably, she climbed out and wrapped a large blue towel around herself before going into her room and calling first her brother and then her father.

EIGHTEEN

The woman known simply as Madison amongst the townspeople was sitting quietly on a bench in front of the Rosemont Hotel. At her side was a small carpet bag and a paper sack filled with items from her recent trip to Wickerman Falls, one that she was able to make at least once a month. She did not drive and no bus system connected Wolf's Head Bay to the outlying world.

Her coven's secretary, who lived down in Bodega Bay, would come pick her up and Madison would stay over for at least two days and no more than five. In this last visit, they had spent three days preparing for the solstice ceremonies in the middle of the month and another two creating blessing wards. However, rather than the upcoming festivities, she was thinking of both the past and the present.

She had come to the Bay at five years of age, an orphan being sent to her mother's older sister, between whom there had been no love lost.

Madison didn't learn the reasons why that had been until many years later, after her aunt had become crippled and forced to move from her grand master suite on the third floor to the library renovated to accommodate the older woman's disability. Her duties to her aunt tripled then, but later, after Victoria Madison had had her dinner and retired to bed, the night belonged to her and she embraced that freedom fiercely.

On some of those nights, she would climb into the attic and go through the trunks stored there, careful to replace everything as she found it, even though Victoria Madison was no longer able to walk, let alone climb the stairs. But the girl Madison had learned long ago to never trust her guardian.

And it was on one of those expeditions to the attic that she had found boxes of old letters, dating back to the early part of the nineteenth century.

Many of the letters spoke of mundane events, recording marriages and births, much like the family bible Old Lady Madison had also found, stored in the same crate, among the boxes of letters. Quite a few of the letters came from a respected doctor in an East Coast clinic, commenting on the various treatments being given to Charlotte Madison in 1853 and her lack of improvement. The doctor went into great detail of the treatments that by today's standards would be barbaric, but in 1853 were considered cutting edge. One letter from that clinic stated that the patient had escaped after attacking a night orderly, leaving severe neck wounds. The patient had not been found. The orderly in question died a week later from severe blood loss.

She had read them all, of course. Including the most damning of them all.

Love letters. From Victoria Madison to her fiancé, Julian Edward Turner, and his replies. And then from Julian Turner to Anne Madison that were platonic at first, then clearly reflecting the growing love and admiration between them.

After that, it had not been too difficult to understand Victoria's attitude to her niece – she was the daughter Victoria should have had with Julian Turner. Instead, the girl was a constant reminder of love desired and rejected.

She also looked too much like her mother, Anne.

Satisfied that the secrets she sought were found and laid to rest, the girl turned her prowling to the outside world and, on the next full moon, her bitter aunt snoring into her dreams, the girl ventured out of the mansion.

The Craft came later.

Guided by the glow of the moon and stars, she would steal away down a path she'd discovered on one of those nights that led down to a small cove, where she would strip naked and luxuriate in the salty night air as it bathed her skin, giggling at the sensation of the water as it tickled her ankles.

It was on one such night that she had met Denver Clarke. And it was on such a night many weeks later that they would make love. Not long after, he revealed a secret that she had long suspected belonged to many of the townspeople.

A car driving down the next block backfired – it broke into her deep reverie and she looked around, as if trying to regain her sense of her surroundings. In the distance, she could hear the heavy sounds of the surf as it pounded against the rocks, could smell the salt heavy in the air, but that was not what had her attention at this moment.

With nimble fingers, she sketched a pattern in the air before her – each line glowed a soft blue. It hung there, shimmering, before she crossed a hand through it.

The silver rings on her fingers gleamed brilliantly in the pale street light that even now was being slowly swallowed by the fog and she turned her hands this way and that, feeling a girlish pleasure in her jewelry.

Denver Clarke had given her one of them less than a year after they had met – pure silver with a dark blue sapphire. He had said once that it had matched her eyes, but didn't have half the sparkle. He had been careful handling the ring – it left marks that looked a little like burns on his fingertips.

She thought about him as he was then, as they had been when they were together, the pleasure they shared with each other. Her heart was heavy with the knowledge of his death, her old woman's body aching with a young woman's desire to feel him, touch him, love him once more.

She stood now and started walking north. She liked to keep her visits into town short and rare – she was very much aware that the locals regarded her as an eccentric, perhaps a little crazy and were, subsequently, a little unnerved by her. It was a reputation that she had taken great pains to cultivate. It helped to keep the riff-raff away.

Of the locals that she chose to deal with as of late (and there weren't that many), she enjoyed the company of Reverend Dan Williams best. He had an open, pleasant face and was very much interested in the history of the town his great-great uncle had helped to establish.

She frowned as she passed the movie theater – he had something heavy on his heart, something that had been bothering him for some time now. Knowing he was a widower with a teenage son, Madison pondered the idea that maybe the boy was having problems, either at home or in school for a few minutes, then pushed it away.

The reverend wouldn't soon be confiding any of his secrets to her, whatever they were. He had been seeing Daria Brennan now for several months. If he was to confide in anyone, it would be her.

With the exception of the good reverend and Denver Clarke (may he rest in peace), no one visited her anymore, not since the elder Brye girl had gone off to college fifteen years ago. Her frown lightened into a grin. Except the girl had become a woman and was now back home. Perhaps she would be entertaining again, soon…

The clock tower rang once, sounding the half-hour in a deep, mellifluous voice as she passed the police station. The lights were still on and as she glanced at the building, a shadow passed by a window and she knew that Sheriff Dylan was up late again, worrying over the recent deaths. Then he would turn his thoughts to something more pleasant, such as whether or not he should propose to Elizabeth Phillips.

Smiling, Madison walked on. They made a nice couple – anyone with eyes could see that. As she paused at the corner of Talbot Road and Oak Glen Street, something fluttered at the edge of her peripheral vision and she turned, eyes searching the dark.

Talbot Road was quiet, cars parked and silent, the street lamps glowing orange in the mist. The post office tower stood on the opposite corner, looming above her, one of the oldest and tallest structures in the Bay at three stories.

She held a moment longer, allowing her eyes to become unfocused, before stirring and walking forward, crossing to the other side of Talbot.

The shadow fluttered again – the edge of a long coat or skirt flapping in the breeze.

Madison whispered a spell, casting for illumination.

It didn't work like it should have – it sputtered like a candle against a strong wind – but it held long enough for her to see familiar features set on a deathly white face.

The shadow melted into the dark and Madison could no longer see her. *Yes*, the old woman thought. *That shadow is female. I haven't seen her in awhile. I wonder what she's been up to, lately...*

Madison considered tracking the shadow, to see the lair where she came to earth, but decided against it. Familiar or not, she knew better than to follow. Night was not the time to go hunting, especially alone, even armed with her Craft as she was.

And not knowing what she was up against would add to her danger.

Still, she stood on the corner next to the Rosemont, staring down Talbot. If one kept to Talbot, it dead-ended into Church Lane. Not an original name, perhaps, but a suitable one that served its purpose, for at the end of the lane, was the church and the reverend's modest home. And just south of the lane was the separate entrance to the cemetery and the great Pacific Ocean beyond.

She came back to herself, to the Rosemont. In her mind, she continued her own self-guided tour. *To the north, were the woods, the mountains and her own worn-out home, the Madison House...*

Laughing at herself, Madison turned away from the Rosemont and headed towards Weaver's Garage. Behind it, lay a short cut to Lighthouse Way, the road to the stalled housing site and the main road leading out of town. She made her way behind the garage easily, coming out onto the unnamed road.

She paused, searching the night with all her senses. Except for the occasional rustle of a frightened rodent and calls of an owl, she was very much alone. Satisfied, she began the long walk home.

Twenty-five minutes later, she paused at a fork in the road – to her left, Lighthouse Way continued on to the lighthouse itself. The dirt lane that branched off the road to her right, led to her home.

She stared long and silent at the structure on the cliff.

The lighthouse was black against the night, cold and empty. She stared at it for a long time before continuing on home.

My dear M.,
We weighed anchor just north of our original destination, due to heavy fog and the rocks jutting through the surf spotted just after dawn. The fog lifted an hour or so later, swept away by the strong ocean breeze – I was able to view the coast with a clear eye for the first time, noting the majestic sweep of the cliffs, the crowning beauty of the redwood pines, whilst above….

I gave a start, then caught myself, chiding myself for the strange, boyish fancies that took me. The mountains that rise above the forest are grand and imposing and, for just a moment, resembled three wolves, their heads raised as if towards the moon, howling their grief, their loves, their hunts…..

With a shudder, I looked away and tended to the day's business, the cost of effort of not gazing once more upon those mountains breaking a sweat upon my brow.

Andrews I left in charge of the ship – I had appointed Stevens to the first boat, now loaded down with necessary supplies, and took command of the second, which had been packed securely with belongings. Also joining us on the expedition was Mr. Madison and his wife and child, along with two other members of my crew.

I objected to Mrs. Madison joining us on this first trip, before the area was secure, but Mr. Madison ignored them. I allowed this with great misgivings.

Reverend Williams was extremely vocal in his protests over staying behind, but on this, Mr. Madison and I agreed – the good reverend was to stay behind. He had flounced below decks, almost knocking Billy off his feet as the boy bounded out. I would not see the reverend for twenty-four hours.

It was a refreshing thought.

I conferred with Andrews quietly, awaiting the moment when I would set foot once more onto my craft and sail to the shores of a state not three years old, when I felt a sharp tug at my elbow.

Looking down, I saw that Billy was fairly dancing with excitement. "Sir, may I join you and the others?"

Resisting the urge to ruffle his hair, I gazed steadily into his bright, anxious eyes and shook my head. "Not today, Billy. I am still concerned over the state of your health." At his disappointed sigh, I added casually, "However, should Doctor Kelley find you in exceedingly good health, I may reconsider and have you join us tomorrow."

He shouted with glee and set about proving that his health was no longer in question. I caught Andrews's eye and broke into a grin, which he could not help but answer in kind. Having the boy onboard had been a point of argument between us – I for it, having been one and he against – but Billy Tanner had won his place on the *Bonnie Jane* through hard work and enthusiasm.

At last, the time came for us to board the boats. The small crafts made the dizzying descents to the water, but we departed safely and I turned to look back. Billy was at the rail, waving energetically. I raised my hand in reply and, as I did so, my heart turned over and I was startled to realize that I had come to regard the boy as the son I had all but given up on having.

With great effort, I forced myself to look ahead at the pale, sandy beach below the steep rise of the cliffs, the waves crashing heavily against the shore.

Towering above on the curve of the hillside stretched a forest of great depth and color, somehow warm and inviting, despite the chill of the ocean.

We landed safely and, once the boats were pulled up on shore, everyone pitched in to unpack, sort and carry what they could. What we could not carry was secured under a heavy tarp and left in the company of two of my men. Under Mr. Madison's guidance, we discovered a path leading up the cliff and away from the beach. I kept an eye on Mrs. Madison, concerned that she would exhaust easily. But she held up and the infant she carried made infrequent cries. When we finally reached the top, I paused, allowing the others to go on ahead.

What I saw astounded me – the view of the blue-gray ocean swelling with each new wave, the jutting cliff separating us from an area I now saw was a bay spread out in a wondrous display at my feet. Lush, tall wild grass covered the ground as far as my eyes could see in velvety greens, dotted with the bright orange of poppies. The forest edged the area in thick groves.

I did not notice Mr. Madison's presence beside me until he spoke. "There," he said softly. "Is it not beautiful?"

I did not spare him a look. "It is." But there was something wrong with what he was proposing, I could feel it, but I could not say why. Without another word, I turned and went ahead to help pitch camp.

SATURDAY, JUNE 10, 1978

NINETEEN

Morning dawned cool and gray, fog drifting through the streets like transparent wraiths on the hunt. The old lighthouse rose high and forbidding through the gray shroud, resembling a tower of some medieval past.

Jimmy drifted back towards a consciousness as gray as the fog, wincing at the pain lancing his skull and deep into his neck. The shadow must have stopped whispering in his ear at some point during the night – he knew that only because he had finally passed out into a dreamless sleep.

She had been instructing him on something important, but he was having the devil's own time trying to remember what it was.

He groaned as he struggled up into a sitting position, wincing again when his aching body protested. Gingerly, he felt around his body, looking for any broken bones, hissing sharply when his fingers grazed the large knot on his forehead. His fingers found a knot of flesh on his neck and he pulled his hand away to see blood. He wondered, dully, if maybe he got bit and if he had to go get a shot for rabies or something. Grimacing, he looked around blearily before crawling to the nearest grave, balancing himself against the cold marble.

He took one step forward and yowled when fiery pain shot up from his foot. The one that bitch had stepped on. He gritted his teeth in a death's grimace. He would make her pay for this injury. Pay dearly before he killed her.

Slowly, with an old man's shuffle, he began the long walk back home, memories of the night before teasing him. He remembered clearly the argument with Marty over their relationship, but after…After was just plain nuts. He had been attacked by a big rabid dog that, miracle of miracles, hadn't bit him. He happened to glance down just then and froze, his heart dropping to his boots when he saw the paw print.

Make that a *giant* rabid dog.

And then he remembered what the shadow lady had said to him — *clean your rifle, be ready, watch the woods and you will know.*

Suddenly feeling more energized, he hurried out of the cemetery, his pace picking up from a limping shuffle to a brisk limping half-jog.

*****

Marty awoke with a startled gasp, her muscles protesting with pain. Then the night before hit her with a sudden clarity and she stared out the window, seeing past the trees to the mountains beyond. What, exactly, had happened last night?

After the worst family dinner in history and Jimmy's sudden and most unwelcome appearance at the cemetery, what had followed could only have been a nightmare of the strangest order, a waking dream, maybe, inspired by two wild dogs fighting over some unseen prize. Except that she had been the prize and no matter how hard the logical side of her wanted to believe anything but, she knew that the black wolf with the silver scar had fought and won the battle.

The question she found herself asking of no one in

particular was *why*.

She shoved it aside, threw off the covers and got up, trudging downstairs. Going into the kitchen, she put the kettle on for tea, put a handful of crunchies into the cat's bowl, then browsed through her nearly empty cupboards idly, not really hungry, but wanting to put something in her empty belly.

She grabbed a box of cereal and a bowl and fixed herself a light breakfast, her eyes straying out the kitchen window and to the wooded mountains rising above the town. She hadn't had a good hike in a long time.

And on the way, she would stop at her father's and have a nice chat about his over-bearing housekeeper.

Filled with a fresh purpose, she dumped her unfinished cereal into the trash, put the bowl in the sink and hurried back upstairs to change.

*****

Marty knocked on the front door, grateful that it was Bessie's day off. It was with mixed relief that Ronald Brye opened the door.

"Hey, Dad," she said. "Can I come in?"

He smiled vaguely as he stepped aside, allowing her entry. "On the phone last night, you said you wanted to talk."

"Talk." She said the word carefully, as if she didn't know its meaning. "Talk…Oh, yeah, talk. Yeah, I did." Shutting the door, she followed him into the kitchen, absently noting his slight limp. "You okay, Dad? You're limping."

He glanced down at his leg in mild surprise, then at her. "I guess I stepped wrong when I got out of the shower this morning. You want some tea?"

"That would be nice." She took a chair at the table by the window overlooking the backyard, slinging her small backpack to the floor while he fussed over mugs and put the kettle on.

He cleared his throat. "So, what is it that you wanted

to talk about?"

She took a deep breath. "I think you should let Bessie go. She's irritating the twins and presuming too much on her duties."

He smiled benignly. "You just moved back, Marty. You live in your mother's family home now. How could you possibly know what goes on in this house?"

She faced him, trying not to feel like a twelve-year old. "Just because I haven't lived here for awhile doesn't mean anything. The twins talked to me on the phone, Dad. And to Mike. They aren't blind and they're not stupid. She's got her eye on you, in case you haven't noticed. Which I'm beginning to believe you haven't."

"Marty, Bessie's a good housekeeper. How can I fire her for having a crush on me?"

She tried to keep her temper, but it was difficult. She disliked being made to explain herself to anyone, especially her father, about anything. "Dad. It's not just a crush. She is dead set on having you court her. That's why she's always leaving those awful books at your house. She's hoping you'll get the idea."

"What idea is that?"

Her father was dense. Had to be. Vague and in mourning for his long-dead wife, it was the only answer because she knew he wasn't stupid. "That you'll marry her."

At last that fogged look in his eyes began to lift. "Marry her? Wherever did she get that idea?"

She relaxed her breath. "You've been alone since Mom died, for one thing. She's also been working for you almost as long as that and you haven't been dating. What else is she going to think?" The kettle began to whistle. Ronald Brye seemed so stupefied by her words that he didn't seem to hear it.

So she stood and went to the stove, turning the flame off quickly and pouring the hot water into the mugs. "Which brings up something else that's been on my mind.

We need to get on with our lives. I have to stop protecting you and you have to dig your nose out of your books and start living again."

He blinked, startled by the intensity in her voice. "That's a lot to ask in five minutes, Marty."

She handed him his mug. "I'm not asking you to do it right now, this minute or even tomorrow. I'm just saying that maybe you should get out more, mingle with the people of our town, help out at the library. Just do something. Anything. Make her realize that she hasn't got a chance of marrying a man who doesn't think about her beyond her next paycheck."

He contemplated his tea quietly. "That's awfully cold, Marty."

"It's a fact, Dad. It's the way it is."

"You said 'we'. What about you? What are you going to do?"

She looked at him, smiled wryly. "I'm going to do what I said. I'm going to stop trying to protect you."

They were silent again for several minutes. At last, taking a tentative sip from his mug, he said, "I suppose the twins could start picking up around the house more."

She relaxed, a little surprised and pleased at how well it went. "You know they'll grumble about it."

"As it will be mostly for show, I shouldn't expect anything less from them." He sighed, watching her move about the kitchen, a little startled to realize at how much she resembled her mother. "Marty, what made you come home?"

"Felt like it," she said, flashing him a quick grin. "I liked living in the LA area and my teaching job was great, but the city was way too busy for me."

Oh, but that felt like a lie and she turned away from her father, not wanting to meet his curiously blank gaze. How could she explain to him that something buried deep inside her had yearned to come back to the place of her birth, something beyond the death of her mother?

Something she couldn't even explain to herself?

"Is that all?" The concern in his voice made her smile.

"Yes…no." Marty cleared her throat. "Can I ask you, about the day Mom died?"

"Why? What could you possibly need to know about that day?" Her father looked at her, horrified.

"I just do, all right? She jumped out of a window and hung herself on my birthday. I think I have a right to ask the questions." She took a long, deep breath. "Look, please just humor me, Dad."

Her father gave her a look she couldn't read. "I don't see what good it will do you to rake up old hurts like that."

"The feelings you're talking about are mine," Marty said. "Hurtful or not, I need to know." She paused, waited for him to nod 'yes' or 'no'. When he finally nodded assent, she asked, "Did Mom seem upset to you? Depressed? Unhappy?"

Ronald Brye considered her question carefully. "Not that I recall. She seemed fine to me when she came into the kitchen." At her blank look, he added, "I was slicing up some tri-tip to put on the barbecue."

"You always did make the best tri-tip."

He preened. "It's all in the sauce." He paused. "I didn't really notice anything wrong with your mother, honey. I'm sorry." He looked at her searchingly. "This isn't why you came back, is it?"

"No, of course not." She pushed the doubt aside and sat opposite him. "Nothing was holding me down in LA. I have some money saved. I figured I could do the free spirit thing here."

He nodded, apparently satisfied by her answer.

She cleared her throat. "Um, Dad. I was wondering if you knew where Mom's old jewelry box is."

"I think so. Why?"

Marty squirmed. "Well, she left me some pieces. I only have the one moonstone she gave me for my birthday."

He blinked. "I packed everything of hers up into the attic when we moved here, but I think it's still up there. I'll dig it up tomorrow. Is that okay?"

She smiled, nodded. "That's fine."

They sat in silence for a long time, sipping their tea and thinking of the woman whose shadow still crossed their lives.

TWENTY

cool, inviting, home

The black wolf with the silver scar loped effortlessly through the woods, his paws making next to no sound on the damp earth, drinking in the fog-enhanced air. He came upon a clearing suddenly and stopped at the edge, scenting something strange in the wind, but unable to identify it.

Cautiously, he stepped into the clearing, lifting up his head, his nose tasting the area on the wind. Nothing. Then why did his hackles rise with unease? He suddenly realized that the woods were heavy with quiet and it was that which disturbed him. Backing the way he had come, the wolf started to turn and circle the clearing when the explosion came out of nowhere, striking him in the left shoulder.

Barking with pain and rage, he hit the ground and rolled. Climbing to his feet, he scented the air again, seeking to pinpoint the gunman and failing. He bolted, finding a rarely used, over-grown path and taking it, ignoring the searing hot pain in his shoulder as he sought to escape.

*****

After leaving her father's house, Marty stopped off at the local market, picked up a small bottle of water and a couple of candy bars and drove out to the end of Lighthouse Way, passing the old Madison place. Half a mile later, she parked in a tiny clearing and got out, the Bug's engine ticking as it cooled behind her. Shouldering her pack, she began her long-awaited hike into the surrounding mountains.

Less than twenty minutes later, the weight of her backpack bouncing lightly with each step, she was still thinking of the conversation she'd had with her father when she heard the first shot. She froze, bewildered, scanning the surrounding trees, alert to any sudden movement of the brush. Nothing, not even a flash of color to indicate that the wearer was human and not animal.

Which made sense, Marty supposed. Hunting season wasn't open and wouldn't be officially until August. Someone was breaking the law and, although some part of her was demanding she head back to town and get the sheriff, her feet gained ground on the trail, determined to find the illegal hunter and put a stop to his shooting.

*****

The wolf was losing blood — with each movement, he could feel a fresh spurt from his wound as it oozed down his left foreleg. He would have to come to earth soon and rest — safe or not, he would die if he didn't do it. Going on would soon become impossible and he was growing increasingly lightheaded with each passing moment. He was unable to breathe without pain, his joints ached with cold.

The change would be inevitable.

Something to his right caught his eye, stirring memories in the same way the woman with the bright green eyes did last night. It was a shadowy hollow, sheltered beneath an old tree. As a hiding place, it would do well — he was too exhausted to explore the chaotic tapestry of his memories at this moment. Stiffly, he curled up into the hollow, prepared to die like his ancestors or heal and find the gunman.

He closed his eyes, allowing himself to sort and analyze the scents his nose picked up, intent on knowing who shot him even as his blood pumped from the wound.

*****

Marty scrambled through the brush, twigs slapping at her, leaving behind small scratches on her face, some ensnaring her hair. Lungs burning from exertion, she sought the area for anything unusual and found nothing.

Not paying any attention to her path, she stepped on a loose rock and, with a startled yell, tumbled off the trail, rolling down the slope, hitting several rocks and half-exposed roots along the way. She landed into a tree with a sharp groan, the breath forced out of her lungs.

The second gunshot brought her back to awareness and she remembered that the hunter was still around somewhere, most likely in camouflage that better hid him from her untrained eyes. Climbing slowly to her feet, she started moving again, crouched low and very much aware of the sharp stitch in her side that made her wince with each step she took. Considering that her breath was harsh and her heart was pounding in her ears, she was faintly surprised to hear a deep moan, as if someone in pain had fallen asleep and could not escape it.

Brushing sweat and hair out of her eyes, Marty stumbled to her left, trying to orient herself on that sound. A gnarled old tree sat on top of a small hill – she felt a throb of recognition for it and could not figure out why, even when she trudged around it and found the hollow below.

The vague, half-memories took flight, however, when she saw the man lying naked at her feet, looking for all the world as if he'd just fallen asleep. Dark hair covered his arms, his legs and most especially his chest, the thick hair tapering down his stomach in swirls to a narrow stripe past his belly button.....

Resolutely, she dragged her eyes up to his face, noting the shadow of day-old beard on the strong jaw, the slight cleft in his chin and the grayness around his mouth. A silver scar marked his neck just above the jugular and her lips tingled with a sudden anticipation of kissing it. Her eyes drifted down to his shoulders and all amorous thoughts ceased abruptly. A dark red fluid was oozing down his arm and she realized that he was bleeding profusely from his left shoulder.

Her gaze went back to his face. She knew him. The FBI agent whose glance had made her aware…

Shrugging off her back pack, she unzipped it to pull out her flannel shirt and tried to cover him with it, to keep him warm, vaguely remembering something about shock from loss of blood.

He stirred slightly, as if responding to her touch, but did not open his eyes. Blood soaked the flannel almost at once – searching her pockets, then her pack frantically, she found nothing else to staunch his wound.

In desperation, she tore off her shoes, then her socks, placing them over his wound and pressing down firmly, hoping it would help stop the bleeding.

The heat was coming off his body in waves (she couldn't help but notice that it was a very handsome, well-sculpted body) and, wiping the blood from the palm of one hand on her jeans, she placed it on his forehead, checking for a fever.

She found it damn near impossible to tell if he was running one or if he was just naturally so warm.

Almost of its own volition, Marty's hand crept up from his forehead to brush a thick lock of hair back behind his left ear gently.

At a casual glance, his face seemed to be a carbon copy of the angst-ridden heroes typically plastered on the covers of those stupid bodice rippers Bessie liked to read so much. But as she examined him closely, Marty realized that it had been a shallow judgment on her part. Although he had the haunted, world-weary, mysterious look down pat, she also saw that he had lived hard, as if the years had not been kind to him, leaving deep lines around his mouth and eyes.

Her fingers brushed against the scar hooking from his right eyebrow to his right ear, partially hidden by his hair. She frowned, pushing back the thick, black hair. Where had she seen a scar like that before? Even better - why had he been shot at and who had shot at him? Which brought up another interesting point – what was an FBI agent doing running through the woods naked?

"I'm a nature lover." The voice was soft and gravelly, as if it had not been used for a long period of time. She started, realizing that the man had regained consciousness and was now observing her as closely as she had him.

She supposed she should not even notice his deep blue eyes, but that was impossible to avoid. She was still putting firm pressure on his shoulder and their faces were in close proximity. Electricity arced between them, leaving her breathless and his eyes grew even darker than before.

"I suppose you read minds," she said, more sharply than she'd intended.

The smile he gave her was strained, but it had some humor. "You have a face that's much too easy to read."

She snorted. "That's remarkable, since everyone else thinks I have a poker face." She took his good hand and clamped it over her socks. "Hold it there firmly. You need medical attention and maybe some stitches, which I am not equipped to handle." She reached for her shoes, slipping them on and tying them snugly.

"There's no need, really." Carefully, he sat up, unmindful of her flannel as it slipped down around his hips. He removed her blood-soaked socks and dropped them. They fell to the ground with a soft squelch. Marty paid no mind to them – her eyes were riveted to the area where blood had been pulsing out in a slow stream. Except for the blood drying on his skin, the shoulder looked as if it had never been touched. "See? All better."

She gripped his arm above the elbow, stunned.

Where the open bullet wound had been was a well-muscled shoulder. No scar, no scratch, no shattered bones that indicated that he'd ever been injured. She met his gaze, resenting the amusement coloring his smile and the sudden desire to taste his lips.

"I don't understand," she grumbled when the tree splintered just above her head, wood showering both of them. He pulled her down quickly, shielding her body with his own, ignoring her strangled cry of surprise.

TWENTY-ONE

"Quiet," he whispered into her ear, his breath warm, teasing the hairs on her neck. Her skin prickled – not two seconds later, another bullet whizzed by, embedding itself deeply into the turf beyond the tree. Marty found it difficult to breathe, but wasn't sure if it was due to their perilous situation or the implied intimacy of their position.

He scowled down at her. She blinked up at him, confused. "I can't think why he wants you."

"Me? But, he's shooting at you!" She tried to move, but his weight kept her pinned to the ground. She gave up when she realized that, far from loosening his grip on her, she was actually growing familiar with his shape. "Let me go."

He clamped a hand over her mouth, effectively shutting her up. "Keep absolutely still, woman. Our lives depend on it."

Eyes blazing, she insulted him long and furious – although her words were feathers against the palm of his hand, her intent was obvious. Laughing softly, he buried his face into her shoulder, his body shaking with silent mirth against hers. It was not, she admitted reluctantly to herself, an unpleasant sensation and immediately found herself comparing him with Ben.

Being cradled against Ben's chest, although very brief, had been safe and warm and comforting. Being cradled against this man's chest was intoxicating, holding a hint of danger, and she found herself inhaling his scent – warm and musky and feral, almost like the wilderness around them. The wiry chest hair bristled against her T-shirt, causing her nipples to harden and something akin to heat stirred deep inside her, racing through her body like lightning, sensitizing her skin to his.

No contest. This man out-stripped Ben just by breathing.

At last, he came up for air, laughter still dancing in his eyes, bright with awareness of her, but alert to the heavy, ominous silence that hung over them. Marty found herself staring at the silvery scar on his neck, fascinated, and licked her lips. He felt it under his palm and glanced down at her, his lips curving into a knowing grin. She felt her body flush from her toes up to her crown.

"Mrumph, mph, rf," she said, impatiently.

He removed his hand slowly. "What?"

"Why are they trying to shoot you?" she asked, sounding out of breath. He laid a callused finger across her lips and she repeated the question in softer tones.

He hesitated before answering, in equally soft tones. "You wouldn't believe me if I told you." His breath caressed her ear and she shivered involuntarily. He looked at her sharply. "Cold?"

She glared at him. "Actually, no. I seem to be overdressed for this little," she made a feeble gesture with her hand, her fingers brushing his hip lightly, "whatever."

He glanced down at himself in mild surprise, as if realizing for the first time his nudity. "I'll have to make use of your flannel, then."

"Keep it," she said shortly, closing her eyes. "You bled all over it…" His finger touched her lips again and she fell silent, both of them listening to the oppressive quiet around them. Marty slowly grew aware of how the silence itself was palpable, almost a living thing unto itself. He shifted slightly, as if to find comfort in his limbs, and she was drowsily aware that he had an erection. Far from being offended by it, she wriggled her hips slightly, enjoying the sudden harshness of his breath in her ear. A feather-light touch traced the lids of her eyes, down her nose to her lips, caressing her cheek.

She didn't open her eyes again until she felt his weight vanish – absurdly, she found herself missing him. She cut that train of thought off abruptly by sitting up and watching him. He stood, his movements lithe and graceful as he fashioned the flannel into a kind of skirt by buttoning it as high as he could, then tying the long sleeves securely around his hips – which, she now realized somewhat dazedly, were narrow and tapered into very masculine and sexy legs.

"Are you all right?" She blinked, dragging her eyes up from his ankles and forcing herself to meet his gaze. He seemed aware of the direction her thoughts were going, but thankfully, he didn't pursue it. Instead, his eyes expressed a concern for her welfare that wasn't readily accessible in his face. He held out his hand. After a brief minute, she took it. The electricity crackled between them again as he pulled her to her feet – she jerked away, as if burned, grabbing her pack. He stepped closer, trying to get a better look at her. "I didn't hurt you?"

She shook her head, avoiding his gaze as she slung her pack over her shoulder. "I'm fine. You?"

"The same, thank you." He took her hand again, tugging at her gently. "We have to leave, we're not safe here."

She freed her hand easily. "Fine. Whatever."

She sensed rather than saw the grin he gave her – still, her pulse reacted accordingly. Clenching her hands into fists, she was determined not to let him affect her any more than he already had, aware that she affected him just as much.

She followed him silently when he stepped off the path, leading her deeper into the woods and away from the little hollow.

She tried to keep her eyes focused on the land, the trees, the rocks - *anything* but him, but found her gaze helplessly drawn to the hypnotic movements of his rear, the ends of her flannel swishing around his thighs seductively.

Several times, he would push her down, his body taut as he listened to the woods around them intently, his nostrils quivering. It struck her as strange, his almost animal-like behavior, but it passed from her mind when the trees opened up on a small grove formed over thousands of years by the fast-moving creek. The hollowed-out trunk of a pine lay across the bank, half in the rushing, gurgling water. He left her side and went directly to the dead tree.

"What is this place?" she asked, her voice soft, almost reverential in the face of such beauty.

He tipped her a curious look. "You don't remember?"

"Remember what?" She watched as he reached into the hollowed trunk and pulled out a battered rucksack. Something about his movements struck a chord in her, but the memory was elusive and slipped away when she tried to look at it. "I don't think I've ever been up here before."

He snorted derisively as he pulled out a pair of jeans. "You have curiously bad memories."

"Is that any way to -?" she began, then turned her back on him abruptly, her cheeks scarlet when he began to remove her flannel from around his hips.

He was apologetic, but she could hear the amusement in his voice. "I apologize if I've embarrassed you. I'm very comfortable with my nudity and I forget that others might not be."

"No sweat," she said, her imagination working

overtime, remembering her first look at him. "I just don't make it a habit of looking at strange men in the buff." She heard him zip up and turned, her breath catching in her throat. It was impossible, but he looked even sexier now than he did before. What a little denim could do…. "You just happen to be the exception to my rule, that's all."

She waited for the standard, arrogant male reply – there were many, but they fell into one of two camps; the 'I'm sorry' from those who are either just as embarrassed as you are or filled with a kind of condescending pity (*as Ben had been*, her mind thought spitefully). The other camp was into boozing and screwing and quite willing to fix the situation to their sexual gratification.

Although she already half-suspected he was not the run of the mill kind of man she'd known either in Los Angeles or in Wolf's Head Bay, his reply still caught her by surprise. "Your courtesy is noted and appreciated, but pointless. However, I will keep in mind your sense of propriety."

She regarded him warily. "Thanks. I think."

He pulled on a shirt, his muscles flexing attractively. A throb of anticipation licked at her and she tried to ignore it by looking around. A boulder was lodged at the head of the creek, creating a small waterfall just above from where they stood now. She made her way to it, climbing on top of the smooth, sun-bleached boulder and sat, cross-legged, turning her eyes towards the sea.

A light breeze kicked up, teasing her hair and she turned her face into it, relishing the coolness. It didn't seem right to enjoy the scenery while someone was aiming to kill him, but it drew her, nudged her and she felt an unexpected sense of peace. Her eyes left the horizon to find him watching her expectantly, as if wanting her to recall something she didn't know was buried in her.

"Who are you?"

His answering chuckle as he climbed up beside her was doing unusual things to her pulse. "I thought we covered that.”

“Actually, we didn’t,” she said, her skin aching to touch his once more. “We were being shot at. At least, you were.”

He regarded her silently, drinking her in with an intensity that startled him and tried to look away, failing. She met his deep blue gaze, seeing the warm intimacy in his eyes that was advertised only in hysterical romance novels and was now finding very difficult to breathe.

Almost of its own volition, his hand reached up and traced the outline of her jaw, tucking a loose strand of hair behind one ear. “I’ve missed you,” he murmured softly. “I’ve wondered….”

But she never found out what it was he had wondered about. Instead, she was staring stupidly at the red spot blooming swiftly on his chest. It went from bright red to dark and his face grew ashen as he tried to look. He’d been shot at again and this time, his pursuer had gotten him but good. Casting an anxious look around, she went to his good side and looped his good arm around her shoulders. She slipped her arm behind his back quickly, and braced herself against his weight, knowing he’d need her support, then carefully eased him down from the boulder to the ground, jumping after him.

He was sweating profusely, his skin cold, clammy to the touch.

She was suddenly frightened. “We have to get out of here,” she said, tugging at him. “Come on, stand up.” She grunted under his weight.

He shook his head. “No, not town….”

She glared at him, her fear fueling her anger. “You’re bleeding and it’s not healing like before and right now you look like death. I know someone who might be able to help and she’ll keep mum about it, too.”

“Who?” His voice was a whisper.

It was her turn to smile grimly. “Trust me.”

His answering smile lasted less than a second, but it

still sent her pulses racing. "I'm afraid I'll have to."

She could have cheerfully kicked him, but it seemed more productive to get him out of danger.

She would kick him later.

*****

Jimmy scowled. That damned pup had more lives than a cat. Like the shadow lady had told him, silver was the correct choice if he wanted to kill the man. He hadn't believed her – werewolves? In real life? What a joke! – but it seemed that the joke had been on him, after all.

He watched as the woman helped the man back into the forest and out of sight, a frown darkening his sallow face. It came to him suddenly – it was Marty who helped him, Marty who was looking at him the way she should have been looking at him, Jimmy. A slow, corrosive burn twisted his belly. She wanted the wolf man? Over himself? It was oh, so clear that there was a bond between them – it wasn't fresh and that puzzled him greatly, but it would have to wait.

And he burned with a sudden rage and hate for his ex-girlfriend, wanting revenge against her for spurning him.

Then he shook himself. There would be a moment for hurting her as she humiliated him, but it would have to be good. And for it to be good, he would have to wait.

For now, at any rate.

Moving with an eerie, silent grace, he followed his target.

TWENTY-TWO

The back gate to the Madison place looked rusted shut but, after disengaging herself from her wounded companion, Marty pushed it open easily, smiling grimly. Old Lady M put a lot of stock into appearances, which was why people generally left her alone.

Behind her, he gave a soft moan and fainted into the overgrown ivy at her feet.

"Oh, no, you don't," she grated, grabbing hold of his good arm and giving him a hard yank. "Get up! It's not that bad."

He stirred. "Silver…"

She grunted, swaying unsteadily. "Hell of an allergy, pal."

"Not in the way you think, my dear," a voice crackled low in her ear and she gave a small scream, dropping his hand and jumping back. Old Lady Madison gazed at her with mild gray eyes, her colorful silk blouse not in any way subdued by the heavy, velvet skirt she wore. Her thick hair had been braided and wrapped around her crown neatly. "What happened?"

"Jesus, Lady M," Marty gasped. "You scared the hell out of me." She adjusted her grip on the man. "He's been shot. Didn't you hear the gunshots?"

The older woman frowned. "No, I didn't." Before Marty could question her, she was on her knees beside the man, examining his wound. "Help me get him inside. If I don't get that bullet out soon, he'll die."

Knowing better than to argue and more than a little concerned herself, Marty helped Madison get him to his feet and through the servants' entrance into the house.

*****

Although she could not remember a day without seeing Lady M (barring her years away), Marty had never been inside the old manor that was the subject of the wildest gossip and rumor for over sixty years. It was like passing through a gateway from one world to the next, was Marty's first thought – the exterior of the house was a forgotten and tired façade hiding the texture and warmth of a time decades past.

Between the two of them, they half-carried, half-dragged the bleeding, semi-lucid man into the kitchen and down the dark-paneled, poorly lit hall. They paused in front of a door that, Madison would tell her later, had once been the library before the local doctor ordered it to be converted into a bedroom fifty years before. It had been redesigned for Victoria Madison, Old Lady Madison's aunt, when the old woman had lost the use of her legs. Evidence of its former existence was still present – tall bookcases stretched from the floor to the ceiling, empty now, but waiting, ever hopeful, to fulfill its destiny. Wooden ladders on tracks were in one corner of the room, covered in dust gray sheets.

To her left, in the corner diagonally opposite the ladders was an antique bed-frame with a king-sized mattress, ready-made; with great effort, they managed to get him on it, trying to be as gentle as possible.

Still, he emitted a deep-throated groan that curdled Marty's blood. Lady M began probing his wound, her fingers light and her gaze sharp.

"Go boil some water," she ordered briskly. "And bring the disinfectant and towels. You'll find them in the pantry."

Marty did as she was told, leaving the spacious room and padding down the hall to the kitchen, the thick carpet muffling her steps. Once there, she put the kettle on, went into the walk-in pantry, found the items Madison had asked for and hurried back.

Lady M took the towels and disinfectant and pulled what looked to be the world's largest pair of tweezers out of one pocket, pouring a generous amount of the liquid over its prongs.

Marty swallowed. "I…think I'll go see about the water."

"Put out tea for us, will you dear?" She bent over the unconscious man before Marty could turn her back. When she reached the door, he gave a choked cry.

She fled to the kitchen.

*****

Old Lady Madison returned to the kitchen twenty minutes later, both of her hands stained with blood. Marty was sitting at the table, sipping her tea. The older woman went straight to the sink and washed her hands vigorously, drying them on her skirt. She glanced at the old tea kettle questioningly.

"I turned it off, but it's still hot, I think," Marty said. "Or, at least warm. I put a mug on the counter for you." She paused, asked carefully, "Is he -?"

Madison turned the burner back on. "No worries, dear. He'll need some strong tea of my own recipe, but he'll be fine." Madison turned the kettle off when it began to whistle and poured out the hot liquid, preparing her tea. She joined Marty at the table and slapped a metal object in front of the younger woman.

Marty stared at it, uncomprehendingly while the older woman focused on her tea. It was small, blunted at the tip and silver in color, if not entirely.

She picked it up for a closer look. "What is it?"

Madison sipped her tea. "A silver bullet."

She almost dropped it. "You're kidding."

"I'm not." Madison was silent for a moment, then gestured for Marty's mug. "Let me see your tea leaves."

Marty passed her mug over, still puzzling over the bullet. "Why would anyone shoot him with silver?"

Madison turned the empty mug over, peering into it carefully. "Did he tell you who he is?"

She rolled her eyes. "I saw him at the police station, he's the FBI agent brought in to investigate the mass grave. I don't know his name, though. Funny that he should be allergic to silver. Funnier still that he got pegged by a silver bullet, given the town's history. Almost as if someone thinks he's a -" She stopped abruptly.

Madison looked up and gazed at her, mildly inquiring. "Yes, dear?"

"Nothing," Marty said at last. "I was just going to say that, with the Bay's peculiar history, it's funny someone thinks our guest is a werewolf, but that's ridiculous."

"Whatever you say, dear."

"It's crazy, Lady M. Werewolves are as real as…as vampires."

"Did you know that one lives in Wolf's Head Bay?"

Marty almost dropped her cup. "What?"

Madison sipped her tea, pursed her lips and added more sugar. "You didn't know about her? I saw her for the first time myself a couple of years ago. She's been here for decades." Madison sipped her tea, nodded approvingly, sipped again. "I actually find her quite fascinating."

"Why?"

Madison took a long, satisfied sip of her tea. "Because I don't think she knows that she is a vampire."

Marty found her voice. "You've been in the Bay for decades, but everyone's just calling you crazy, um, I mean, eccentric."

Madison looked surprised. "Because I am, dear."

Marty tried again. "If there is a….vampire, then where does she live? There's not a lot of castles on the market here."

Madison smiled. "Dear, if I knew where she hung her cap, we'd be talking about her in the past tense."

"You'd try and stake her?"

Madison shrugged. "I'd do better than try, but yes."

Marty groaned, covering her face with her hands. "I can't believe that we are even having this conversation about things that don't exist."

"Have you ever met one? A vampire?"

"Well…..no."

"Then you can't say for sure."

Marty persisted. "And, anyway, even if there were such things as werewolves, he's got to be cursed, right? Like Lon Chaney Jr. when he got bit in *The Wolf Man*?"

Madison shook her head. "Not necessarily. There are three very different types of werewolves. Inherited genes mark the true werewolf, the second are the cursed, as poorly represented in the film as it is, and then a bite from a true werewolf when they are in the midst of changing from human into wolf form."

Marty gave up. Clearly, Old Lady Madison had gotten more than a little batty while she had been away at college. "What do my leaves say today?"

Madison didn't answer right away, her nose barely touching the rim of Marty's mug as she studied the tea leaves. At last, she said, "You are going to uncover something that's haunted you for years and come between the light and the dark. The moon will be the light which guides you." She frowned, then shook her head. "That is all they say."

Marty stood, her legs feeling suddenly weak. "I'd better be going."

"Take him some tea, then."

Marty left the kitchen, a second mug of tea in her hand. She hesitated briefly in front of the former library, then quietly turned the knob and opened the door. Madison had left the room dimly lit and from where she stood, he appeared to be sleeping deeply. Crossing the room on tiptoe, she approached his bedside and placed the mug on the nightstand that was in easy reach of him. She noticed that his blanket was slipping down – carefully, she adjusted it, her eyes drinking in his face.

It had softened in his sleep, making him less haunted and more….vulnerable. She frowned slightly, thinking. No, that wasn't it, but she could not think of any other word that might have worked.

With an exasperated sigh, she started to leave.

"Thank you," came his quiet whisper.

She turned back. His eyes were open, watching her, and the expression in those dark velvet orbs made her think of fireplaces and plush carpets. Ignoring the heat the images ignited, she grinned hugely, knowing that it was a tad bit bright.

"No sweat," she said, just as quietly. "I never met anyone who got shot before. It's kind of interesting, especially the bullet."

He eyed her warily. "You know?"

"Know what? That you were shot at? That's a given. That you're running around the woods naked? I think that's against the law or something. Which you should know, being the law. That Lady M pulled a silver bullet out of you? I saw it." She started to say more, then shook her head. "I think that's it."

"But I don't know your name."

"Marty," she said shortly. He quirked a brow. "Marita F. Brye."

His gaze sharpened at her name. "Your name is Brye?"

It was her turn to eye him warily. "Yes. You have a problem with that?"

He smiled, shaking his head. "I knew a Brye once, a long time ago. He, too, saved my life. But you're much prettier than he was." His smile widened at her blush. "What does the 'F' stand for?"

She sniffed. "You have to get to know me better for that."

The look in his eyes warmed her to her toes. "I hope we can remedy that."

"Only if you tell me your name."

"Riley," he said softly. "My name is Riley."

She stared at him, indignant. "Oh, right. Now you tell me. All that had to happen to for you to disclose that information was a near-fatal encounter with a bullet. And, to be really clear, it's not just any kind of bullet, but a silver one. What if I wanted to meet your friends? Would you drive off a cliff or something?"

His answering smile was a long, slow action that made her want to get up close and personal. She consciously chose to take a step backward, despite her own body's desire to do otherwise. His voice was low, amused. "No, not quite."

Then they were silent for a long moment, communing solely with their eyes. When she finally shook herself back to the present, she became aware that the sun was crossing over into afternoon.

"I have to go," she said. "I'll see you."

He said nothing as she backed slowly towards the door. Once there, she turned and left, marveling that she was able to walk sedately to the front door, open it, pass through it, shut it behind her, and then down the overgrown walk to the seldom used road. It was when she reached the end of Madison's drive that she finally broke into a run back to her car, wanting to leave her tumultuous feelings behind and miserably aware that it was useless.

TWENTY-THREE

From his perch in a tree on a hill just above the old house, Jimmy watched Marty run up the lane to her car, then shifted his gaze back to the manse.

He was there, that wolf man, with the crazy witch, Madison, under her protective magic. This impossibly simple mission – to take out the man known as Riley – was now growing increasingly difficult. The shadow hadn't taken into account the possibility of the two crossing paths in the forest while he, Jimmy, was trying to kill the wolf with his father's old rifle. Bad enough that Marty stomped on his foot in the cemetery, which had been painful to say the least, enough so that he thought it was broken. But it was like having Reverend Dan put him in his place all over again.

He had never forgiven Marty for that.

So. New plan. Find a better way to get rid of Marty and kill the wolf-man, Riley. It would have to good.

Easy as pie.

This reference put him in mind of the cold meat pie he had picked up from Myrna's two days before. It was still in his fridge, back in the tiny, single-wide trailer he called home. Which, of course, was on the far south end of town, in the back part of East End Mobile Home Park.

His stomach rumbled.

*****

Marty staggered up the porch steps, her whole body suddenly weak and sore with heavy exhaustion. She glanced at her watch wearily, her left wrist feeling like a dead weight at the end of her arm. Twelve-fifty.

Great.

The door swung open as she reached for the knob – she jumped back with a startled yell. Cassie stood in the doorway, curious.

"Jeez, Marty, it's just us," she said.

"Us?" Marty looked past her sister and saw Pete on the stairs, munching on a candy bar. She stepped into her hallway, hand on the door. "I'm glad to see you, love you both to pieces. Now get out. I've had a really hard day."

"No kidding," Peter said, staring at his sister's disheveled state wonderingly. He pointed at the bloodstain on her jeans. "What happened to you?"

"I fell," she said shortly, motioning them out onto the porch. "And as soon as you guys leave, I'm hitting the shower and bed. Come back when I'm feeling better. Like next week."

"Must've been a hell of a fall," Peter cracked. Marty gave him a sour look. "Sorry."

Cassie handed her a thick manila envelope. "This was in your mailbox. What is it? Did you order a book?"

Marty took it and bit her lip when she saw the sender's name. "No, it's probably just some papers I mailed up here from L.A."

Cassie coughed. "So…thanks for talking to Dad about Bessie."

"No sweat." She gave Cassie a shove. "Now go away. I'm tired." She slammed the door. The teens heard the deadbolt slide shut with finality.

They turned and trotted down the porch steps, Cassie frowning.

176

"What was that all about?" Pete asked as they reached the front gate.

Cassie paused to look back at Marty's house. "She's up to something."

Peter elbowed her, grinning. "I thought that was pretty obvious." He frowned "But what do you think she's up to?"

"One, she's way older than us, so that pretty much eliminates the sibling secrets," Cassie said thoughtfully. "Two, I intend to find out."

*****

Marty watched her siblings leave from the living room window. When they finally turned a corner and disappeared from view, she allowed the curtain to drop back into place, her gaze falling to the manila envelope in her hand.

Holly's familiar, bold script greeted her. Marty bit her lip hard, tasting blood, and wondered what her friend wanted her to know.

She went to the kitchen, wanting a drink, preferably something strong and more than mildly alcoholic. The only thing in her cupboards was coffee or tea. She filled the kettle with water, put it on the burner and turned it on. Grabbing a mug, she found a box of her favorite black tea and pulled out two bags.

As she waited for the water to boil, Marty sat in the nearest seat at the kitchen table, studying the manila envelope in her hands.

"What is this, Holly?" she asked, unaware that she had spoken out loud. She turned it over, sliding one finger under the flap to tear it open, hesitated, then turned it over again to look at the time stamp.

It was postmarked June 7, 1978. The day after Holly had been murdered.

Marty set the envelope down and pushed it as far away from her as she could, cold permeating her entire being, her eyes never leaving it.

177

Was Holly murdered because of what the envelope contained? How did her killer miss it? Did she put it in the outgoing mail for the rest of the paper? Is that why it wasn't on her when she left the newspaper? Was that why it had come to her, Marty?

Behind her, on the stove, the kettle began to whistle as it heated. Almost trance-like, Marty stood and went to the stove, turning it off and pouring the hot water into her mug, watching the steam rise and curl like fingers. She put the kettle back on the stove, but did not pick up her mug, her mind busy and far away.

20 JUNE, 1852

Later.

M.,

I am unsure of the exact time, but suffice it to say that it is quite late. Much has happened and I must apologize for the length of this letter – the pages this one letter spans would fill a book, I daresay. The others are sleeping peacefully and I would not disturb them, so I have taken a lantern and moved some distance from the camp.

I have heard it again – that deep, mournful howling has shaken the sleep from my brain and left me wakeful. I pause now and then to consider the moon, the pale orb now full – it is a brilliant white-blue disc hanging in the night sky. The light it casts on the land is nearly as bright as day, but it has shrouded everything in unusual textures and has flattened the landscape to a degree that it seems an illusion. I try not to think of the night before with some success, but my heart will not and the shadows that cover the land touch the rapid beat within my breast.

After a bit, my eyes grew heavy and I must have slept, for the only explanation for what occurred next could only have been a dream.

Out of the shadows just beyond the circle thrown from my lamp, stepped what I first mistook for a wolf the shade of chestnut, but then reality (as it so often does in the dream-state) rippled and the creature became an elegant woman, her brilliant, fiery hair falling past her hips. She looked as startled to see me as I was her, especially in light of the fact that she wore not one stitch of clothing, except for a pendant that hung on a chain round her neck, dipping between her breasts.

After a frozen moment in which I gazed upon her body with something akin to lust, I immediately turned away, offering her my coat. She took it indifferently, as if it made not one difference whether she was clothed or not. Her eyes, dark gray orbs, studied me intently, an unmistakable air of confidence enveloping her.

When she spoke, something deep within me, something primitive, responded to the richness of her voice and I almost lost her words. I blinked. "I'm sorry?"

"I asked why you have come. What is your purpose here?"

"A man in my care wishes to settle here. He seeks a gold mine."

She barely flicked a glance at my camp, her expression exquisitely disdainful. "They are weak and do not belong here. I ken the one you speak of, and he seeks something that is neither gold nor home. As for you....." Here, she paused, her nostrils quivering lightly as she approached me, leaning in gracefully towards my throat. I felt the faint puffs of her breath against my skin – at once, goose pimples rose and my thoughts once again turned to matters physical. "You smell different. You have both scents on you.....how is that possible?"

Ordinarily, I would have taken offense at such impertinence over perceived stench, but her proximity was affecting me – the intimacy of our closeness was potent and it was all I could do to maintain control. I sensed, rather than saw, her smile and felt her hand trace the outline of my ribs down to my belt and the stiffness growing below.

Heat burned my skin – I desired her. And she knew it.

Then she was standing away from me, her face in shadows, but I fancied I heard her breath quicken when she spoke. "You are not one of us, yet you have our scent. You are not the one I knew before, but his scent hangs over you as well. Why is that?"

I found my tongue, marveling that even in dreams, I could become flustered in the presence of a beautiful woman. "I can't answer that, since I not only don't understand the question, I don't know who you are."

She held out one hand. After a moment, I took it, surprised at the smooth heat of her palm. My skin ached to join hers. "I will show you."

It seemed hours, but was perhaps only minutes, before we crested a rise. Below us, I saw several circular, thatched huts, similar to some of the Pomo Indian structures I had seen in my travels to the northern part of California.

In the center of the village, a small bonfire raged, laughter and subdued conversation wafting in the air softly. Couples were dancing to a rapid beat of drum and violin, groups of twos and threes standing in shadow and watching.

We stopped at the edge of the forest, watching the revelry below for some time.

I must have been entirely too caught up in the obvious nature of the gathering, for I nearly leapt out of my skin when, out of the shadows, stepped three people, presumably those of her kin. They were two men and one woman, clothed in loose-fitting outfits that appeared to serve no other function than to be slipped out of easily, rather than for any modest reasons. They regarded me coldly.

"What is he doing here?" the woman said, her voice

rough in what I perceived to be fury. "And why are you wearing this one's coat? Has so short a time with them shamed you?"

My companion tightened her grip on my hand and addressed the woman. "Peace, Murel. I have brought him to show him what his fellows seek to destroy." She glanced at the tallest of the two males. "He has one of us in his company."

The shorter man scowled. "Has he made a pet of our people?"

"Alban Tanner, there is no fear on him, his or our fellow's." She pushed me towards them a little, smiling when she saw my nervousness. "Do not worry," she whispered in my ear. Her breath tickled and I shivered lightly.

The trio approached me with caution, as if I was an untamed creature of the forest, their noses twitching. Murel's fingers pinched my skin hard – I glared at her sharply, but she merely smiled and stepped away. My companion caught the action and her eyes narrowed with anger.

The tall male stopped before me, our gazes even and unwavering. Cowyn Fraser, I later learned, was his name. He was the village elder, as it were, the leader of the pack and he had brought his people here from the east, to these densely wooded forests, away from those who would persecute them for being different. What that difference was, I gathered, seemed to be of a deeply private and personal nature.

"You're right, Felanna," he said at last. "He is not like that other." She nodded. His next question caught me by surprise. "And how does young Billy fair?"

"Well," I stammered, utterly perplexed. "How do you know him?"

Alban grunted. "He is my son."

Cowyn grinned. "Come. Join us."

They led the way to their village and I remember little

else, except the absurdity of wolves becoming human and back again as Felanna guided me, her hand clasped easily in mine. I observed the strangeness of her people, their ways of greeting each other by sniffing one behind the ear. I turned to ask Felanna about this, but she had left my side and was nowhere to be seen. I felt a moment of panic, but Cowyn appeared, laden with two tankards of ale, one of which he offered to me.

I accepted it gratefully and followed him to the fire, where there appeared to be a sort of wild celebration. Someone pressed a hot, freshly cooked leg of chicken into my left hand and a plate of potatoes and vegetables. The spicy scent of meat and fresh brew awakened my stomach and I ate and drank with relish, not once seeing how they refilled my mug and plate without my knowledge.

We sat on a long wooden bench, away from crush of people, but close enough still to enjoy the music. "How did you come to be here?"

Cowyn appeared to deliberate with his answer, his gaze holding mine with much consideration. At last, he spoke, choosing his words with care. "We settled here some twenty years ago due to….well, I suppose you could say we were being persecuted for our beliefs. Only, it wasn't so much our beliefs…." His words trailed off as he stared into the fire; then, he shook himself aware, grimacing. "We are a different people than what you know or understand, Jonas Brye. And differences, physical or otherwise, can be the cause for unreasoning hatred."

"As it is for the Indian people."

Cowyn nodded. "Indeed, it was a tribe of Cherokee who helped us escape from the east." A good memory seemed to tickle him and he laughed with great amusement. "They called us *waya ayegali.*"

I started at the term, feeling that I had heard or seen it somewhere before. He went on to describe the long journey west with great detail of the hardships they endured, the open hand of friendship of the various Indian tribes and the beauty of the vast and open country that was the Americas, but I was strongly convinced that he was hiding things from me deliberately.

At last, he finished his tale, of how they had found this spot with the help of two California tribes. I was pondering their relations with the native peoples and was about to ask for clarification when the music changed tempo abruptly.

A group began dancing to a seductive, rhythmic beat and I looked over at the fire, addressing Cowyn. "What are you celebrating?"

Cowyn clapped a hand to my shoulder and pointed at a tall youth with thick black hair and dark eyes. He appeared to me to be about ten and, from the expression on his face, wanted to be anywhere but here.

"That's young Tavis Riley. And that," here, Cowyn pointed to a beautiful girl with hair equally as dark, clutching the boy's arm, "is Brianna Dair. It's supposed to be their betrothal, would that Tavis had a mind for it."

I studied the young couple. "Aren't they a little young?"

Cowyn grinned. Once he had been satisfied that I wasn't his enemy, he became quite friendly. "We are very different from you, my friend. Some of your people would say that we are descended from the folk of Shangri-La, but we are much more than people who can live forever."

Puzzling over his enigmatic words, I gazed once more upon the young couple, this time noticing what I hadn't earlier. Although the girl, Brianna, gazed at him, smiling, her hand in his, he stood apart from her, refusing to look or speak with her unless spoken to, his attitude one of reluctance and distrust. Neither seemed to be happy.

A rustle of cloth and movement on my left distracted me and I turned to see Felanna sitting at my side, her hand brushing mine lightly. Balancing my plate on my knee, I took her hand, lacing my fingers with hers. She caressed my fingers slowly and spoke at the same time.

"Has Cowyn treated you well?"

I nodded, glancing at my plate. It held a thick slab of freshly cooked meat, this time pork or beef. In the light, I was not sure which. "I have neither eaten so well nor drank so pleasurably since I gave my crew leave in Santa Barbara."

She smiled, licking her lips lightly. My lips ached to touch hers, but as a gentleman, I could not presume upon her my own desires.

Her eyes turned away, going to the youth and the girl, and she frowned. I looked at them once more as well, but saw nothing unusual.

"It will not go well with them," Felanna said. "Brianna is not for him. He is meant to mate with someone else."

"How can you know that?" Cowyn growled. "You do not have the gift of foresight."

"No," Felanna agreed, "but it is not to be."

"I do not understand you, Felanna." Cowyn shook his head. "She is the only one of age within fifty leagues. He would not find another here. She is the only one suitable for him."

"Suitable, perhaps," Felanna said, her voice cold. "But not for Tavis."

Perhaps it was my imagination, but it seemed to me that the couple heard us – Tavis grinned without humor and Brianna threw the iciest glare at Felanna as any I've ever seen in my life.

It was the only sour note in what was to have been my only peaceful dream. When she at last guided me back to my camp, I found myself reluctant to let her go. It may have been my ego, but I fancied that she was just as equally reluctant to part company with me as I was with her, even after returning to me my coat.

"Morning is not far off," she said at last. "It would be best if you convinced your people to settle elsewhere."

"They are not my people," I said. "It is but one man

and his wife and son who wish to settle here. I am but a hired vessel for them to pursue it."

"Victor Madison," she said and nodded, her face weary. "I knew he would follow."

"You know him, then?" She nodded. "I don't understand," I began when she laid a finger over my lips.

"There is no need for you to understand. Just go. Send Billy home to us and forget all you have seen."

I covered her hand with mine and pressed my lips against her palm. Her breath grew shaky, mingling with my own, but when I sought her mouth, she stepped back.

"No," she said quietly. "Leave this area in the morning."

As suddenly as she had appeared to me, she vanished, leaving only my memories of her and the strange happenings in her village.

How odd dreams are in the blending of reality and fantasy!

Your affectionate friend,
Jonas Brye

SUNDAY, JUNE 11, 1978

TWENTY-FOUR

The Bryes went to church that morning for the first time since the previous fall and sat in the back pew, listening to Reverend Dan Williams as he touched on the lives of Denver Clarke and Holly Prescott-Wyatt. Cassie looked around for her best friend, but there was no sign, either of her or of her father. Then the reverend was turning to the day's sermon and Ronald Brye gave her a look. So Cassie turned forward to listen, but when the choir stood for the hymnals, she couldn't remember a single word Reverend Williams had said in the last twenty minutes.

And then it was at long last over and they came home and after changing out of their Sunday best and into jeans and T-shirts, Ronald Brye sent them to Myrna's for their treat of choice.

Ordinarily, getting Dad to pay for a treat like this was a bit like finding pieces of gold on the beach – possible, but impractical. So, when he pulled his worn leather wallet from his pocket, fingering the bills inside, Cassie eyed him warily. Pete had gone upstairs to grab a couple of sweaters and they were alone in the foyer.

"Here," he said, pulling out a bill and handing it to her. "Go get the biggest soda you can buy."

Cassie took the bill, not bothering to identify the amount. "Why do I get the feeling you're rushing us?"

Her father had the grace to blush. "I'd rather talk to Bessie privately and spare her the humiliation of an audience, if you don't mind, Cassie."

"Small towns have small minds, Dad. With you two alone in the same house, they'll think you're doing the horizontal mambo and with Bessie thinking the way she is, she'll encourage it."

"Not if I hire another housekeeper," Ronald Brye said, but his youngest daughter shook her head sagely.

"Dad, Dad, Dad," she sighed.

Ronald Brye winced at the knowing look in her eyes. He didn't think she was right but, of course, there was the Gaggle Bessie gossiped with every Saturday at the beauty parlor.

He sighed. "I think you are still far too young to know the ways of human nature, Cassie, both good and bad, but I am resigned to the inevitable process."

"Dramatize much, Dad?"

This drew a grin from her dad. "People will gossip and I can't control that. On the other hand, my dear, everyone knew how I felt about your mother. Only the Gaggle will believe anything they're told."

Cassie nodded, looking unconvinced. There was a sudden rumble on the stairs and Pete came bounding down, half-in his sweater and carrying Cassie's, which he tossed to her. She caught it neatly.

"Come on, let's go, let's go!" Pete said excitedly and, flinging open the front door, almost ran into Tommy Williams. Both boys grabbed hold of each other for balance, then just as quickly let go.

Ronald Brye took the opportunity to push his daughter out the door. "Have fun. Hi, Tommy."

"Hello, Mr. Brye," Tommy said formally. The older man smiled briefly and shut the door. Tommy turned to the twins. "Good afternoon, Cassandra. Peter."

"Oh, for cripes sake, knock off the formality." Pete jumped off the porch and landed in a sprawl on the walk below. "Come on! There's a root beer float with my name on it! Maybe two!"

Cassie and Tommy followed. She pulled her sweater on, shivering in the cool air a little and glanced towards the ocean.

"May I come?" Tommy asked, his breath sounding short.

"Sure, if you can keep up." She jammed her hands into her pockets, paper crinkling. Remembering the money her father had given her, she pulled it out.

"Hey, Cass! Did Dad give us enough for seconds?" Pete was fairly dancing on the corner of Main and Oak.

"I was just looking." Stopping at her brother's side, she held it up. Tommy gave a low whistle. Cassie's jaw dropped and Pete dropped to his knees in mock prayer.

In her hand was a fifty-dollar bill.

*****

Ronald Brye spent the next half-hour in his study, poring over old tracking books he had checked out from the library, with help from Mrs. Talbot. He compared them with his own sketches made of tracks in the forests surrounding the town and from his visits to the cemetery. He was not looking forward to the unpleasant task before him (for it was sure to be unpleasant) and put it off for as long as possible.

On the desk beside his books, lay an old jewelry box. It was open and the jewelry inside gleamed in the light.

When Bessie's sharp rap at the door came, he knew that the inevitable, like the fourth horseman of the Apocalypse, had arrived.

Hastily putting down his sketch book and pencil, he tidied up his desk, putting the jewelry box into a drawer, and called for her to enter, only half-aware that he was also looking for an escape.

She came in, wearing a hat that he had always

associated with his grandmother, and was even now fussily pulling on white gloves.

"The kitchen's cleaned up and I put the breakfast things out for tomorrow," she was saying chirpily. He winced. "And on Tuesday, I'll set to and clean this whole house, top to bottom."

"That's really not necessary, Mrs. Mills," he said somewhat nervously, then cleared his throat. "Cassie and Pete will begin doing some chores outside their rooms from now on."

"Oh?" There was a gleam in the woman's eyes, something he had never expected to see in any woman's eyes, other than his wife's. Only, in Bessie's eyes, it seemed almost predatory, somehow. "And what shall I expect my new role to be?"

Oh, hell. His children were right. He was about to become engaged to a woman who looked as if she had stepped out of *The Andy Griffith Show*. But instead of Thelma Lou, it was Aunt Bea's evil twin, at least in spirit.

He twitched nervously, knocking several of his sketches and an old cracked mug full of pencils to the floor. He knelt down, glad of the distraction since it meant he could say the words and not look at her. She killed that idea by kneeling down to help him, purposefully allowing her gloved fingers to touch his longer than necessary as she reached for the pencils.

Her cloying perfume tickled his nose unfavorably and he sneezed repeatedly.

"Bless you," she said digging in her coat pocket. Producing a crisp, white hanky, she pressed it against his nose. He jerked away, falling backwards. Bessie Mills fell on top of him. They regarded each other for a long moment – she with a hopeful, unwelcome ardor, he with something akin to terror.

Her face softened in an imitation of love and she murmured, "Oh, Ronald," before kissing him full on the mouth.

Shocked into temporary paralysis, he came to his senses sharply and pushed her away, rolling to his right and regaining his feet. Wiping the feel of her lips on his mouth with the back of his hand, Ronald could only stare in horrified astonishment. She gazed back at him worshipfully, her chest heaving and her thin, garish lips parted.

In one dizzying moment, she became the badly parodied heroine of her vapid and tasteless romance covers. But instead of feeling overcome with lust, he felt a great need to vomit, for he could not rid himself of the image of Aunt Bea (*grandmother*).

In a dim, remote part of himself, a tiny ember of rage began to glow hotly, clearing his mind of the fog that had been so long a part of him since Denise died. He glared at the housekeeper, seeing her truly for the first time since he had hired her back in nineteen sixty-one.

Scrawny, spiteful and silly, she had presumed to think of herself as his second wife. The idea was not only arrogant, it was ludicrous as well.

He shook his head, suddenly aware that she was talking.

"…..wanted to confess for so long," she was saying. "I ado-"

He cut in coldly. "Stop. Say no more. I can't allow you to believe something that has no basis in reality."

She looked bewildered. "But…."

"Mrs. Mills, I think it would be best if you found employment elsewhere." His heart was pounding in his ears and he found it difficult to think.

"Are you *firing* me?"

"I am. The twins are old enough to start taking on some responsibilities in this house and it's time I started doing the same."

"But you can't fire me!" she burst out. "I love you!"

He tried not to flinch, but it was hard. Turning away and looking out the window, he said only, "I'm sorry, Mrs.

Mills. But I don't love you."

She struggled to her feet, her pale eyes dark with fury and hurt. "But everything was going so well…." Her eyes widened, then narrowed suddenly. "Marita put you up to this, didn't she?"

He refused to be diverted. "What Marty does or does not do has no bearing on this situation, Mrs. Mills. I no longer require your services as a housekeeper and it would be best for all concerned if you kept your distance." He went back to his desk and picked up a check. "This covers what I owe you, plus a little extra. Good night, Mrs. Mills."

Her mouth working jerkily, she approached his desk. He fought the impulse to back away. Reaching for the check with trembling fingers, she tore it in pieces, tossing them in the air like confetti.

"If I don't receive your money, I'm still under your employ," she said icily, turning to leave.

"Mrs. Mills, I'll need my key back." He was surprised at the hard edge in his tone. It seemed that she was, too; she stared at him, stricken. Then, pulling the spare off her key ring, she flung it at him and ran out the door.

Fortunately, she had bad aim. It slapped the wall to his left and clattered to the floor. The front door slammed. Picking up the key, he sat down with a sigh.

"Well, that's over, anyway." He eyed the torn check, then wrote out another, sealing it in an envelope. If necessary, he would have Mr. Jameson, the bank manager, deposit it into her account.

He slumped back into his chair and stared at the ceiling.

TWENTY-FIVE

They trooped down Main Street, laughing over some joke Pete had stumbled over in the telling, passing the library's front entrance, its expanse of lawn dark green from watering and the shade from the maple trees. Cassie saw Reverend Dan sitting on a bench under a tree, reading.

"Hey, I'll catch up with you guys in a minute," she said, breaking off. "I'm gonna go say 'hi' to Reverend Dan."

"Whatever," Pete said.

Tommy hesitated. "Maybe I should go with you. I mean…"

Cassie shook her head. "I know he's your dad, Tommy, but this is private stuff."

Pete grinned. "Yeah, confessional stuff, like should she go out with a preacher's son."

Cassie whacked him in the shoulder and stalked off. Pete gaped after her.

Tommy took him by the arm. "You know, Pete,

sometimes you go too far."

"Yeah, I know. It starts out okay and then goes haywire." He sighed. "Come on."

They walked on as Cassie headed towards the library, hurt still burning. She loved her brother, but sometimes he was such a pain in the ass. She looked up at the old library with fondness, her earliest memories being of Story Hour with Miss Weber every day at four in the afternoon. As she approached the bench, Reverend Dan looked up, smiling warmly as he recognized her.

"Hello, Cassie," he said. "It was good to see you at the service this morning. Going to the movies?"

"Maybe. Definitely one of Myrna's shakes, though."

"Ah, of course. The best in the state." Cassie nodded in agreement. They were silent for a moment, then clearing his throat, he asked, "Am I correct in understanding that your sister has moved back into town?"

"Yeah. Why?"

He made a small gesture with his hand, his ears burning. "No reason. I just – I was just wondering if she's well, that's all."

"She's fine, except that she took a tumble yesterday while hiking."

He looked concerned. "She didn't break anything?"

Cassie shook her head. "Naw, just some scrapes. Nothing that serious." She looked at him curiously. "I know she's been away, but I get the feeling that you guys aren't friends anymore."

He regarded her seriously. "What makes you say that?"

Cassie was silent, but he sensed that she was groping for words to express herself to him clearly. Finally, she met his gaze, her expression just as serious as his. "I know that she admired you a great deal before she left." He winced at that and she pushed on. "And I know that you guys had an argument or something. But she also told me that I could go to you if I had any problems."

He smiled at that, brightening a little, but she sensed that there was something else in his eyes. "Well, she's right, Cassie. You can come to me for anything."

"Even though we only go to church once in a blue moon?"

He nodded. "Even though."

They both fell silent once more. Then Cassie looked at him "You won't tell me, will you?"

He shook his head. "It's between your sister and me." An image of a much younger Marty crossed his mind and he looked down at his book. "If she chooses to tell you, then it is her decision. It's not mine." *But I hope to God she doesn't.*

Cassie seemed to accept that and stood. "I'll see you later, Reverend."

"Enjoy your shake," he said. "And tell my son not to be late for supper." Almost as an afterthought, he added, "Or have too many shakes."

"I will," Cassie promised and hurried on.

He watched her go, not really seeing Cassie, but her older sister. Closing his eyes, he tried to force the image of a younger, willing Marty from his mind and turned desperately for thoughts of Daria.

*****

Finally tackling the security detail and assigning shifts to his officers, John Dylan glanced up briefly, his fingers pausing over the typewriter keys to watch as Eddie Payne entered the station. It concerned him that the younger man's face was still pale.

"You're late," he said amiably, going back to typing up his report. *Next city council meeting, I'm gonna ask them to pony up for more computers. One just isn't enough.*

"I know." Without further explanation, Payne sat at the next table and allowed his face to drop on his desk with a thud.

Dylan looked up. "Sleep well?"

"No." The answer came out muffled.

"Still having dreams?"

"I don't want to talk about it." Eddie raised his head. "When Tavis gets back from his camping trip, I'm gonna pound him."

Dylan grinned. "Sure you are. When you catch him. He's FBI, remember?"

Eddie finally noticed the typewriter. "Why aren't you in your office, using your computer?"

Dylan shrugged. "It's in use."

Eddie sat up a little straighter. "You're the chief of police. Who's using it?"

Elizabeth Phillips poked her head out of Dylan's office. "Your printer ran out of ink, so I'll pick some up at Hallie's Card Shoppe when I go to lunch."

Dylan leaned back in his chair, listening to his spine pop. "Don't forget to keep the receipt for petty cash."

She grinned. "Of course."

Dylan leaned back a little further, tipping the chair back so that he could watch her as she walked down the hall.

"God, John, just marry her already," Eddie moaned.

Dylan ignored him. "Have you got anything more on the Gordon case?"

Eddie shook his head. "I thought about going back down to the spot where I found what was," he gulped, "what remained of Mr. Gordon, see if there was anything else we might have missed."

"Sounds like a good plan."

The younger man perked up. "Really? You think so?"

Eddie's enthusiasm was infectious and Dylan felt himself respond to his deputy's energy. Then his eyes fell on the reports and his grin faded as his gaze traveled from the files to the typewriter. Intuition tingling, Dylan looked up from the report he had been typing. "Actually, I think I've made a connection."

"Really?" Eddie sat up, ready to listen. Dylan was glad to see color come back into the younger man's face. "How do you mean?"

Dylan leaned back into his chair, thoughtful. "Do you remember that Tanner case?"

Eddie looked puzzled. "Jack Tanner? Yeah, a little. Wasn't he found out where they had settled to build the Heights three years ago?"

Dylan nodded. About a week after the city council had announced that the site had been chosen, a contractor had gone out to do some surveying. The corpse of Jack Tanner had been so brutally savaged that the contractor's harsh screams could be heard from the wharf. It had been Deputy Andrews who had responded to the call and then radioed in for the medics to take the hysterical contractor to the hospital. Andrews had also been very specific that they bring restraints – the contractor's hair had turned white and he tried to bite the deputy when Andrews was cuffing him. Jack Tanner's murder was still an open investigation, despite no leads or even a suspect. It was ironic that his widow had become embroiled in the current stand-off with the city council. "Yes."

Eddie thought of Mr. Gordon – his face went green. "So what's the connection? A secret handshake? They were all fishermen?"

Dylan shook his head slowly. "That still doesn't explain Sofia Williams's death. Or Holly Wyatt's, for that matter. Neither of them were interested in fishing."

"I don't understand."

"Think, Eddie. What was it that they all wore, but was not found with their bodies?"

Eddie thought deeply for a long time, his eyes drawn to the black and white photo of Denver Clarke's severed hand, the tan mark on his ring finger stark.

"They all had moonstone jewelry," he said slowly, recalling Mrs. Tanner's dark fury when she found out that her husband's ring was not found among his effects.

Dylan laid a hand on the stack of reports on the chair next to him. "If we go through these reports, I think we'll keep finding more connections." He passed a few to Eddie, who came over and sat across from his chief.

As Dylan typed and Eddie searched, the older man thought he heard Eddie mutter something about pounding Tavis.

In spite of himself, Dylan grinned. *Eddie may be young,* he thought, *but he's a good cop. It's only when he gets behind the wheel of his car that he loses whatever sense he's got.*

The only sound for the next hour or so was the rustling of paper and scratching of pens.

TWENTY-SIX

Pete managed to suck down four root beer floats and had started on his fifth when finally his stomach burbled in protest and he bolted for the restrooms.

Cassie and Tommy looked on in amusement.

"Good ol' Pete," Tommy said. "Eyes always bigger than his stomach."

"Yeah." She stirred her shake with a straw. "So what do you want, Tommy?"

He regarded his sundae intently. "What makes you think I want anything?"

"You're wearing your funeral suit on a Sunday afternoon, when there are no funerals."

He met her gaze then and she was struck by how shy his eyes were.

"I know we've had our differences, Cassie," he began awkwardly, "but I was sorta thinkin…"

She snorted. "That's a start."

He flushed. "I'm being serious."

"Sorry."

He tried again. "I just thought, you know, maybe we could be friends."

"What makes you think we aren't?"

He looked surprised. "You mean we are?"

"Sure." She grinned suddenly. "But any smart-ass remarks and I'll put your lights out, like I did last fall."

"Yes'm," Tommy said humbly. Instead of her usual black the previous fall, Cassie had gone to school wearing fuchsia colored pants and a gray velvet blouse. Tommy had made a flippant remark at recess – neither could remember now what it had been – but the end result was that he had been flat on his back with a bloody nose, Cassie standing over him, rubbing her fist gingerly.

"I'll keep a lid on it, I promise." He grinned back. "I'll be in summer school so I have to toe the line."

"I'll be keeping you company," Cassie said, as her brother slumped back into the booth. "So will Pete."

"Pete'll do anything so long as he lives," Pete groaned.

"That'll teach you to eat four and a half floats at once." Cassie nudged her brother's prone figure with one foot. "You think maybe Dad's done firing the busybody?"

"God, I hope so." Pete propped himself up on one elbow from his prone position in the booth. "Wanna go to the movies?"

"Sure." She went to the register to pay. Tommy and Pete followed a minute later, the latter clutching his stomach and moaning dramatically. "Can the theatrics, Pete. You're getting no sympathy from me."

Pete eyed Tommy hopefully. "How about you?" Tommy shook his head, grinning. With a sigh, Pete dropped his hands. "Well, damn."

They left the diner, chatting amiably.

*****

The Blackwood Movie Theater had been built in 1915 and was owned by the same man who operated it – Richard T. Blackwood, who saw moderate success for a town that, at the time, boasted only fifteen hundred people.

But as time wore on, the world engaged in World War II and the town grew, so did his business. Because the

Blackwood had only one screen, he held double features and started the shows at noon, playing the milder ones during the day and the darker, more adult ones at night.

It was not an uncommon sight to see him in his black slacks and coat, the white shirt and bolo tie walk from his house on Talbot to the diner (then named the Wolf Down) for an early breakfast of eggs, bacon, toast and orange juice.

He would then go on to the theater, where he swept the aisles, vacuumed the rugs, restocked the bathrooms, cleaned the service counters and windows, preparing for the afternoon showings before going to take lunch at the diner. He would then return to the theater and open up, waiting for the crowds.

Blackwood was seventy-nine when he finally decided it was finally time to retire from the movie theater and sold it in 1967 to Edwin Stevens for a tidy profit. He sold his house as well and was preparing to move down to Florida when he suffered a heart attack and dropped dead on his way to the phone. He was duly buried in the cemetery alongside his wife, Pat, who had died ten years earlier.

Edwin Stevens ran the theater pretty much the same way Blackwood did and, except for the subject matter of the films, the structure never changed. In 1972, Stevens hired Stanley Gordon to manage the theater. Up until then, his employees had often heard him mutter, "No wonder Blackwood had a heart attack." Though they wondered at his strange remarks, they never pursued it.

Stanley Gordon, who would be the eventual owner of a mixed dog named Toad, at this point in his life had an infant daughter named Melissa and a desire to work closer to home and watch her grow. When he heard Stevens' usual mutter, he approached him with caution and inquired about a job.

Stevens hired him on the spot, no questions asked.

It was here that the twins and Tommy were headed. It was a strange mix – *The Wolf Man* with Lon Chaney Jr.

as the hapless victim of a gypsy curse and a wolf bite to some vague romantic comedy starring Goldie Hawn. Tommy frowned at the marquee as they got in line behind a pretty blonde.

"What kind of a double feature is this?" he asked, honestly bewildered. "Shouldn't there be two Goldie Hawn films or two creature features?"

"You'd think so," the blonde in front said. "Sometimes, it's just the way Mr. Stevens likes to run it. You know, mix in the old with the new, see if somebody buys."

"It's working," Tommy said. "Hey, Katie."

"Hi, Cassie, hey, Tommy." Katie Blake barely looked at Peter. "Hey, Pete."

"Hey, to you, too," he said, just as curtly. The tension between them was strained, made worse when Katie bestowed an incredibly beautiful smile on Tommy, who blushed a bright red.

They talked of inconsequential things until they got to the ticket booth and saw that Mr. Gordon wasn't selling the tickets. Mrs. Davis was. Katie bought her ticket and waited for the others to do the same.

"Where's Mr. Gordon?" Cassie asked the older woman. Normally, old Mrs. Davis looked like the Scarecrow of Oz's sister, but today she chose to resemble a vampire from some slapstick comedy, with her hair slicked back and bound by a shiny black barrette and the stark colors of her uniform hanging on her bony frame. The heavy mascara and red lipstick did nothing but enhance the image. "Is he sick?"

"Didn't you hear?"

The teens shook their heads. "No," Cassie replied. "What happened?"

"Deputy Payne found him out on Maple Road," here, she dropped her raspy voice to a loud whisper, "torn to shreds."

"How does he know it's Mr. Gordon?"

Mrs. Davis leaned forward. "His shirt was under the Chaney Creek bridge on Maple, torn to shreds. There was a lot of blood." She seemed about to say more, saw Mr. Stevens frowning at them, then straightened, adding a brisk note to her voice. "That'll be six dollars, please."

Cassie forked it over, pondering the gruesome information solemnly, handing them their tickets. Hearing about death was not unknown to them – in a town the size of Wolf's Head Bay, news traveled faster than you could say, "Fire!" But death by means other than natural causes was always news, no matter what the date.

And no matter how hard adults tried to keep any sort of news quiet, kids always found out.

"How many does it make this week?" Peter asked of no one in particular as they went to the snack bar. "Four?"

"Three," Cassie corrected automatically, her mind elsewhere. "Holly Prescott on Tuesday night, Denver Clarke on Wednesday night and now Mr. Gordon." She shook her head abruptly. "I'm going to the library. Wanna go?"

Peter gaped. "And miss the Wolf Man versus Goldie? Not on your life." He elbowed Tommy. "Right?"

"Uh, yeah." Tommy rubbed his side.

"Fine. I'll see you guys after the movies." Cassie went to the ticket booth and got a refund, hurrying across the street to the library. The others watched her go.

"Huh. Wonder what's eating her?"

Katie looked at Peter scornfully. "She's your twin."

"Yeah, but that doesn't mean I know exactly what's on her mind." He paused to order a large tub of popcorn, then added, "Speaking of sisters, Marty took a hell of a tumble….."

And proceeded to tell the tale.

TWENTY-SEVEN

Cassie entered the library, unconsciously walking around on tiptoe as she passed the main billboard, where posters wanting help for after school activities, dog-walking, occasional baby-sitting and local play productions were hung.

Flashing Mrs. Owens, the head librarian, a quick grin, she turned left into the old periodicals room, where thousands of issues of the *Bay News* newspaper awaited transfer to microfiche. Taking the editions that covered the last five days, Cassie slipped into a desk furthest away from the door and began reading.

As she paged through the old issues, she thought of Holly Wyatt. She remembered Holly very well – best friends with Marty since high school, Holly had been a fixture at the house before and after the death of Denise Brye. After Marty's departure for college, Holly had acted as babysitter and then older sister by proxy.

She thought of Patty Wyatt, her best friend, and wondered if she had heard about her mother's death. Even though she was on vacation with her grandparents in Arizona, it was more than likely that word had reached her. She wished she could be there to give Patty a shoulder to lean on when she heard.

Cassie pushed aside the wave of grief and read the article she'd found concerning Holly's death in Friday's edition. Two paragraphs long, it was brief and to the point and said nothing. She put the newspaper down and covered her eyes, wondering what to do next – it seemed as though an eternity had passed before she decided that she didn't have enough information to know what she was looking for.

Instead, she put the newspapers away and went back to the information desk to ask Mrs. Talbot, the head librarian, for access to Jonas Brye's diaries. Two minutes later, a page had arrived to take her to the private room where the original documents pertaining to the history of the Bay were kept.

As long as I'm here, I might as well get started on my history project, she thought, following the page. There were at least twelve known diaries that Jonas Brye had kept before and after the founding of the Bay.

After making sure Cassie had signed out for them and had plenty of blank paper and a pencil, the page left her alone to read.

Taking the diaries to the sitting table in the center of the room, Cassie sank into the stuffed leather chair and opened up the first one. The fine script made her eyes hurt and she turned on the table lamp to read better.

When scribbles stopped swimming, she was able to decipher the year – 1846. Seven years before the founding of the Bay.

She leafed through it, scanning the pages as her eyes adjusted to the script, tapping the pencil lightly on the table. Nothing interesting – just a captain's journal of the daily tasks done onboard his ship, the weather, the feel of the sea as it carried his ship.

Done, she shut it and put it aside, scribbled down some ideas, then reached for the next one, 1847. Then came 1848. By the time she reached 1851, she was six diaries in and the entries were as brief as the definitions in a dictionary.

Even California's admission into the United States in 1850 rated only the briefest of sentences.

"Only six more to go," she muttered without enthusiasm. Picking up the seventh one, she was surprised to find more detailed entries starting in January, reflections on his life, his chosen profession, the growing desire for a wife and children, possibly sons, to leave a legacy to.

"Sons," she sighed. "Always sons. What's the big deal about boys? Can't have 'em without the girls."

She turned pages with a sigh. The diary ended in mid-August of 1851, with Jonas Brye still no closer to resolving his thoughts and feelings. Carefully, she pulled the next one to her and opened it, quickly being drawn back into the thoughts of her paternal ancestor as he picked up where the previous diary ended.

Peppered with observations of his ship and crew, the captain was now detailing his life from childhood, occasionally mocking himself for the dreams of a boy.

By the time she finished reading, Jonas Brye wrote of receiving a letter regarding a charter up to Northern California – a Victor Madison.

Cassie thought of Old Lady Madison as she pushed the diary away and reached for the next. Was she related to this Victor? Couldn't be just a coincidence – the Madisons had lived in the Bay almost as long as the Bryes.

Rubbing her eyes, Cassie opened the diary and started to read. She stopped, a frown crossing her face as she flipped the pages back, looking at the date.

August 1, 1852. Puzzled, she reached for the previous diary and opened it to the last page. The last entry was dated on June 10, 1852.

She sat back in her chair, feeling more confused than ever. Why were there less than two months missing between the diaries? What had happened?

Quickly, she started reading the entries from August

1852 until it ended in January of 1853. There was no reference to the missing weeks.

Stacking the leather-bound books neatly, Cassie slumped down in her chair, troubled by the pointed silence.

*****

After his trip into town, a filling lunch at Myrna's and his subsequent talk with Cassie in front of the library, Dan Williams arrived back at the church to meet with the first of six appointments, which ranged from something as simple as listening to a grievance dating back fifty years to offering counsel.

The church secretary, old Mrs. Bodean, had left the main sanctuary door open and he made a mental note to remind her about locking up, while greeting his first charge and leading them inside. When his final appointment, Mr. Ames and his son, Charley, at last thanked him and went home, it was almost four in the afternoon.

After locking the church door behind them, he walked back through the church, his pace slow, meditative, as he picked up the day's programs and stacked them neatly on his podium at the front of the church.

Then Dan Williams wandered to the back room designated as the office and sat at his desk, contemplating the simple, leather-bound diary he now in his hands.

Cracked with age, it was the same diary in which his great-great grandfather had recorded his thoughts.

Although cramped and plainly furnished, Reverend Dan, as his parishioners called him, found no need to remodel his tiny office. Indeed, he considered the entire church his office, finding that some of the townspeople felt uncomfortable in such close quarters with a man whom they believed held the ear of God.

Hold God's ear he might, but Reverend Dan did not regard himself as anything other than a man approaching his forty-seventh birthday with some trepidation and whose job was to inspire hope, tolerance and charity with his fellows.

He had enjoyed marriage to a woman whose faith in him only empowered his own and her death fifteen years earlier had left him bereft and his son motherless. There had been a few dates, but nothing he had felt inclined to regard as serious.

Until Daria had come into his life.

Turning his chair to the eastward window, he caressed his battle-scarred desk with a light hand, recalling their cautious courtship that had begun perhaps three months after her arrival to town.

They had begun as friends in the easiest of terms, learning each other's personality and had become lovers only a year earlier – through their careful assignations, they had managed to keep a respectable look to their relationship.

It was Daria who had effectively changed his mind about the quality of his office in terms of yielding pleasure. It had been fast and furious and very satisfying. He could not look at the desk without remembering.

But try as he might, the woman whose face he kept trying to visualize wasn't Daria, but Marita Brye.

"Please, God, not now," he sighed. "It's over. Stop thinking about it."

But of course, he couldn't. The more he tried to focus on taking notes on the service request for Holly Wyatt's funeral, the more the dead woman's best friend chose to invade his thoughts.

Not as the woman who returned to the Bay after so many years away, but as the girl of twenty, itching to go off to college.

The girl who came to him as a woman would to a man.

In spite of the guilt that gnawed at his conscience, heat pooled in his groin; he felt himself harden at the memory of her body moving in time with his own, her whimpering cries as he brought her to the brink, his thrusts hard and rhythmic, his breath harsh even to his own ears, barely feeling the rake of her nails on his back.

After, he lay over her, spent, feeling her heart race against his in the aftermath. He raised himself up and looked down at her – she looked up at him, trusting, her eyes moist, her face a rosy pink.

A sudden, horrible thought occurred to him. "Marty. Was this your first time?"

She nodded. "Yes. I lo-"

He clamped a hand over her mouth, hard enough to see the startled pain in her wide eyes. "Don't say it," he said fiercely. "Get your clothes, get dressed and go home. Get out of the Bay, go to college. What you did…it's a rare gift, but I don't deserve it."

The hurt and bewilderment on her face cut him and he stood, grabbing his slacks and pulling them on. She sat up, still naked, still desirable, but so young and vulnerable.

"I don't understand," she said, trembling, trying to sound adult. He could see what it cost her. "I thought," she hiccupped, "I thought…" She covered her face with her hands, forgetting her nudity.

He threw a blanket at her. "You thought what? That now I'm a widower, I can now swoop into your life and save you? Good God, Marty. I'm fifteen years older than you. I don't need a girl, I need a woman. I need *my wife*. Find someone your own age and fall in love with him."

He stormed upstairs, pausing long enough to check on his son, now almost three, reassured to find him fast asleep. From downstairs, he heard her muffled weeping, then the front door quietly opening and closing behind her.

Though he knew, in the end, that he had done the right thing and turned her away, Dan Williams still felt a rush of guilt for the way he had done it, knowing that he could have halted things before they'd even started.

While getting coffee at the bakery, he overheard Ronald Brye talking to his oldest son, Mike, and learned by eavesdropping that Marty had left early that morning without even saying good-bye to her family.

Pulling himself back to the present, Dan was surprised to find tears in his eyes and he wiped them away impatiently. Drying his hands on his slacks, he reached for the diary and opened it, turning the yellowed pages with care until he was once more staring at his great-great grandfather's name.

Reverend Jonathan Williams had been a man of the church, like himself, and who, in the middle of the nineteenth century, traveled to the as yet unfounded town of Wolf's Head Bay with Jonas Brye and confronted an evil man whose heart had been filled with murder.

It was not the subject of evil that troubled him – he sermonized about it both small and large every week – it was the manner in which the good Reverend had written of the incident that unsettled Dan.

Normally meticulous to the point of boredom in his other diaries, the Reverend had merely written of the incident, "We have staved off the full brunt of chaos and the man who let Evil into his heart has been dealt with."

Jonathon Williams had referred to Wolf's Head Bay (although not by that name until 1853) several times leading up to that brief statement, his doubts, worries and fears seared onto the page with more than just a bottle of ink.

Touching the faded, cramped writing with one finger, Dan wished he could speak with old Jonathon and ask him why he wrote so tersely of something that had clearly frightened him so badly.

"Reverend Dan?"

He swiveled his chair around with a jolt, startled, to see Old Lady Madison in the doorway. Rising awkwardly, he was suddenly aware that evening services were only ten minutes away and he was in a miserable state of dishevelment.

The diary slipped to the floor and he stooped to pick

it up.

"What can I do for you, Ms. Madison?"

"I came to invite you to lunch tomorrow," she said cheerfully. "There's someone I'd like you to meet."

Dan sank into his chair with a groan, rubbing his eyes. "Not another one."

She gazed at him with mild curiosity. "Not another one what?"

"Thank you for your kind invitation, Ms. Madison," he said, turning away from her. "But I'm afraid lunch will be out of the question. You know I'm seeing someone, so give your guest my respects and tell her I most humbly apologize."

"Her? There is no her unless you mean Marita, but you already know her." Madison picked her way into the tiny office, pondered an old wooden chair holding stacked books dubiously, then perched on his desk comfortably. He eyed her warily from his chair. "The person I want you to meet knew the man who wrote this."

She touched the cracked spine of the diary with a light finger.

He looked from her to the diary and back again in disbelief. "That's impossible, Ms. Madison. Even if he'd been an infant at the time of the founding, he'd be at least over one hundred twenty years old."

"One hundred thirty-six, to be exact," Madison said easily. "But he doesn't look a day over thirty-nine."

"It's not possible," he repeated stubbornly. "No one lives to see that."

"Come, now, Reverend. In the Old Testament, people have been recorded as having lived over five hundred years." She rose, as if suddenly aware of the time, pausing at the door to add, "I'll expect you tomorrow at one, Dan. And bring that journal. We need to compare notes."

"Ms. Madison!" Dan struggled to get around his desk, but when he finally reached the door, Madison was gone.

TWENTY-EIGHT

"Is it me or are romantic comedies getting worse?" Peter posed the question when they left the theater three hours later, his eyes squinting into the afternoon sun.

"I think they're terrific," Katie said coldly, marching ahead.

Peter blinked. "I didn't say the *concept* was bad. I was saying the *movies* were bad. There's a big difference."

Tommy eyed them warily, not wanting to get in the middle of their dispute. "I think romantic comedies are more about escaping," he offered with some caution. "As for dramas, they make us think and most people don't want to. Think, I mean."

"You're right," Katie said with some surprise, as if the world might come to an end because a friend of Pete's had made a valid point. "*Chinatown* wouldn't have been nearly as good if it were a comedy."

Immediately the conversation turned to movies seen and not seen as they headed for Myrna's, milkshakes tempting their way.

*****

Halfway through her shake, Katie finally warmed up to Pete and they spent a good five minutes spraying each other with whipped ice cream, occasionally hitting some innocent bystander, who would turn and glare over at them. Tommy was laughing so hard that his shake had yet to be touched when Cassie slid in beside him.

"Hey, guys," she said breathlessly. "How were the movies?"

"Wolf Man was fun, as always, but I'm getting really tired of romantic comedies," Peter said slurping his shake. "I mean, they're always the same. Boy meets girl, girl hates boy, boy pursues girl, girl relents, they get together, movie over." He slurped loudly. "It's the sidekicks that save them. This one was cool – you never figured out if it was a guy or a girl."

"Who, the hero or Goldie Hawn?" Cassie sounded puzzled.

Peter leaned over and tapped her forehead with a chocolate finger. "No, the sidekick, silly. Next week's gonna be even better. He's got *Jaws 2* and *Grease*. Man-eating sharks and dancing teens. Totally cool, right?" He slurped some more ice cream. "Find anything useful at the library?"

Cassie frowned at him, brushing his hand aside as she got down to business. Tommy handed her a napkin and she wiped her forehead. "Did you guys know that one of Jonas Brye's diaries is missing?"

They stopped eating and looked at her.

"You're kidding, right?" Katie said at last, her voice hushed.

"Missing?" Peter looked bewildered.

"Doesn't sound too unusual," Tommy said, "I mean, it's probably just pure luck when any documents are found intact. Why?"

Cassie studied him critically. "You're dripping."

"What? Oh, man!" He snatched up several paper napkins from the metal dispenser and mopped up the chocolate drips from his shirt.

"I don't think they even know it's missing," Cassie

went on, trying hard to keep a straight face. "It stops right around June tenth 1852, right after he gets a letter wanting to hire him for a charter to go up north and then jumps to August first, after they return to Los Angeles."

"Did you ask the librarians?" Katie scooped her chocolate ice cream onto the long-handled spoon and ate it.

Cassie nodded. "She and Mrs. Talbot searched high and low in the records room, but no luck. What they got from the Bryes is what they have. If there is a missing diary, then it's either in someone's attic or was burned in a fireplace to keep some numb-nut warm."

Tommy glanced at her. "You wanna milkshake?"

She met his look. "You buying?"

"Sure." Tommy waved a tentative hand. Barry caught it and winked. Three minutes later, he was at their table.

"What else can I get you guys?" Barry held a pen and pad expectantly.

"Strawberry shake, Barry," Cassie said. "Extra strawberries."

"Gotcha." Barry disappeared behind the counter.

The four teens sat in a contemplative silence, Cassie staring out the window. It was Katie who finally broke it.

"So, what are you going to do about it?"

Cassie shrugged. "I don't know. I mean, I'm not sure where I'd start."

"Why not ask your sister?" Tommy suggested. "Wouldn't she help?"

"She just moved back into town," Peter said, stirring his shake. "She doesn't know anything."

"How about asking Old Lady Madison?" Katie spoke softly, but they stared at her as if she'd screamed. She looked directly at Peter. "I mean, she knows everything about this town, stuff not even the town council knows about. Or would admit to knowing about, anyway. They want to keep this place innocent and fun for the tourists. Maybe she knows where it is."

Cassie nodded in agreement. "Yeah, that's right. She'll know what to do." Her shake suddenly appeared before her. She looked up to find Barry presenting her with a straw. "Thanks, Barry."

"No sweat, Cass." He grinned and went off to another customer.

She stuck the straw in her shake and slurped contentedly. *Nothing like a shake to give you brain freeze and pop your ears*, she thought. When she had made a serious dent, she sat back and relaxed. "Hey, do you think Dad's done firing the fusspot?"

*****

At three that afternoon, after spending most of the day unpacking and moving furniture where she wanted it and setting up her childhood bedroom as her office, Marty flopped onto her bed with a huge sigh of relief – it felt more like a hundred years since she'd lain on this bed, not this morning.

Feeling languid and fresh after a hot bubble bath, she stretched out, naked, over the bedspread, burrowed her face deep into her pillow, fumbling for her blanket. She pulled it over her body until even her head was under it, relaxing into the firm mattress with a deep sigh, rolling onto her back.

Paper crinkled under her and she propped herself up on one elbow, pulling the thick file from under her hip. Black and white photos of the house – this house – slipped out, spilling onto her blanket. She picked them up, struggling to disconnect herself from the graphic images, even after so many viewings. In one, the corpse of her mother hung just over the balcony.

Unbidden, Marty found herself gazing at the French windows, beyond which lay the balcony where….

"No," she said out loud, startling herself. "I will stop thinking about this. I'm tired. I have had a long day, I want to sleep."

So saying, she stuffed the photos back into the file,

218

dropped them on the floor and switched off the bedside lamp. She lay flat on her back, breathing deeply, her eyes closed as she sought to relax, the cat purring close to her ear.

Her mind, however, stubbornly flipped through the morning, seeking the cause of her mental discomfort, knowing that she had seen or heard something that demanded her immediate attention.

She sat up so suddenly she flung the cat off the bed. Hissing, it fled down the hall, but she was barely aware of it, remembering what had been bothering her.

The black wolf that had saved her life the night before in the cemetery had had a scar over his right eye that ended behind his ear. The man, Riley, had a scar that bore a strong remarkable resemblance to the wolf's....

Marty lay flat on her back, eyes boring a hole through the ceiling.

*****

Bessie Mills found herself out in front of Marty Brye's house with no memory of how or when she got there. Although it was early, the house was dark.

Probably planning to seduce the good Reverend away from Miss Brennan, after what she did to me, Bessie thought coldly. *Harlot has some nerve turning a good man's head that way.*

The gathering shadows reminded her of another time she had spied on Marty, not long before the girl's abrupt departure from the Bay in 1963. On her way home from a night of cards and gossip with her Gaggle, Bessie had spotted a weeping Marty fleeing down the road, back to the house she then shared with her father and siblings. Curious, Bessie retraced the younger girl's path and soon found herself staring through the living-room window of the good Reverend.

He was sitting on the couch, his shirt partially buttoned, the only light coming from a single lamp on an end table. Although his trousers were pulled up and appeared to be fastened, his belt lay on the floor next to

219

his bare feet. In his hands, he held a red, lacy scrap of fabric, his face a mixture of desire and remorse.

It didn't take much more than that for Bessie to put together the scenario that Marty had seduced her own pastor, especially when the girl stole away early the next morning, perhaps an hour before Bessie was due at the Brye house. She had been walking up to the house and had seen the girl behind the wheel of the tiny car, her face pale, the rattle of her VW bug loud enough to wake the dead.

Now, as she watched, shivering, from the street, a light did go on in the two-story house, then another.

Presumably the slut's bedroom and bath. Bessie snorted. *She could bathe all she wants and never get clean. Most likely reading smutty books picked up in Los Angeles. What kind of name is that, for a city full of half-naked and depraved people?*

Her feet, unbidden, propelled her forward until she was at the gate when something, a deeper instinct perhaps, made her pause, her shoe knocking loose a small rock. Without stopping to think, she picked up the rock, hefted it and then flung it as hard as she could at the house. She felt a sharp sense of glee when she heard glass shatter.

From inside, she heard a startled exclamation and hurried to her tiny home on Shady Lane. She ran up the porch steps to her front door, gasping for breath as she let herself in, a high-pitched noise bouncing off the walls. It took her several minutes to realize that it was the sound of her own hysterical laughter.

As she swept down the narrow hall to her bedroom, she failed to see the shadows behind her gather and separate.

TWENTY-NINE

Hovering in the twilight of sleep and wakefulness, his breathing deep, slow and rhythmic, Riley felt both weighted down by the old, wool blankets and lighter than the feathers in his pillow. His senses, already preternaturally sharp, had heightened their intensity in this in-between state, recording, cataloguing and filing away the scents and sounds of the old mansion automatically. Primary among them was the old woman, who reminded him of the sea after a storm.

More elusive and the one he sought, was of the younger woman, Marty, she who had so gallantly sacrificed her socks.

His lips curved in a soft smile as he shifted minutely, his blankets slipping down and exposing his bare shoulders, the stark white bandage on his chest glowing in the dark. His flesh prickled with the cool air and he struggled to pull the wayward blankets up, with a small degree of success. Pain flared briefly with the movement, then settled to a low burn and he gritted his teeth, knowing that sleep was further away now than before. The scar on his neck itched mildly. He forced himself to relax with some effort.

Footsteps echoed hollowly – he recognized the woman Madison's step easily and placed her as being in the kitchen. Something clinked, metal against porcelain and he guessed she was fixing a meal.

At last, his conscious mind began to drift towards the dark side of twilight once more and he dreamed of a girl whose weeping made her eyes glow.

It seemed as if only seconds had flown by, but when the woman Madison entered the room and flicked on the overhead light, he was startled to see that night had fallen once more.

A few stars, scattered in the black velvet of sky, winked at him merrily through the bay window. Peeking through the trees, its light soft silver, was the pale orb of the moon, its shape not yet a perfect circle. He could see nothing else and turned his eyes to the old woman.

They regarded each other with varying degrees of interest and suspicion.

"We need to talk," she said at last.

He scowled blackly. "We've nothing to talk about. It may be over a hundred years since his death, but I can still smell him in this house."

She surprised him by laughing softly. "Yes, I suppose it would smell that way to you, regardless of whether or not he set foot in it. For me, especially this room, it reeks of Her, no matter how often I scour it clean." Still chuckling, she glanced around. "Which isn't often, these days." She came further into the room, pulling up a heavy, stuffed chair to the bed. "But, as you've said, they've both been gone a long time and it's the present we need to concern ourselves with, not the past."

His frown deepened, the scar puckering severely. "My past is wrapped up in the present. How can I put it aside?"

"You just do it." They held each other's gaze for a moment longer; then he looked away.

"How did you know what I am?"

She nodded, as if expecting this. "There are a great

many things about this town and its history that I know, Tavis Riley." He started at his name. She smiled serenely. "I know that Marita's great-great-grandfather saved a great number of your people," she went on, settling comfortably into the chair. "I know that it is their blood that stains this town and that Victor Madison, your father and my great-grandfather, was responsible for their slaughter." She gestured to the scar on his neck. "And I suspect that that scar didn't come from a knife or brawl. It's vampire-made, isn't it? That's why you've lived for the last century and more?"

He finally found his tongue. "Is that all you know?" he asked, sarcastic, not answering her questions. "Or are you going to read my tea leaves, too?"

"Your hearing's all right, anyway," she said unperturbed. This, more than the hated man scent, irritated him. He could not read her with the same ease with which he had read Marita F. Brye (who insisted on that ridiculously masculine nickname when she was so decidedly *un*-masculine). For a human, Madison masked herself well and the ease with which she could read him left Riley feeling more exposed than when the girl (woman) had found him.

He closed his eyes, suddenly tired. "If you're going to talk, then do so."

She leaned forward, her expression serious. "There is fresh evil afoot in this town and we must stop it."

"I know about the killings," he growled angrily, "and it is a typical human reaction to assume that they were the victims of a sadistic ritual or a maddened animal."

"Whatever killed Holly Wyatt at the newspaper, Denver Clarke at the lighthouse and Stanley Gordon on his nightly walk was not an animal, but it wasn't human, either." She held his gaze.

He thought of the creature that attacked Marita F. Brye in the graveyard and found himself in agreement. Still, he asked, "Why do you think that?"

"Because Holly's head had been nearly torn off her shoulders. Stanley Gordon's remains were scattered. And Denver had been ripped to shreds." Her voice trembled as she spoke and at last he could read the emotions behind the mask.

Already knowing the answer, Riley spoke. "What was he to you?"

Her words were simple. "Someone I loved a long time ago. Someone I still love." She shook herself back into the present.

"So," he drawled, breaking the silence that followed, "a mass grave, three humans killed in four days, someone with silver bullets trying to make me just as dead and a monster wreaking bloody havoc. Any ideas, cousin?"

"No, not one human. Specific humans. This isn't the first rash of killings, boy." She leaned forward, troubled. "Haven't you seen the connection?"

He frowned. "What connection?"

Madison scowled. "Of course you would be that dense. Hiding from your own, only the Goddess knows why." She looked at him sharply. "Your mother taught you to do that, didn't she?"

He scowled back at her, ignoring the question. "Please enlighten me about this link that you seem to think is so important."

"The people who died are connected. They are your people, Tavis Riley." She bent closer to him. "They are being slaughtered for wanting to live. I think I know who is doing this. A rogue. And it has to be stopped."

He shook his head, winced, ignoring the irritating fact that she knew him, knew his people. "I don't believe it. The few of us still left would have known about it, would have sent our Alpha to prevent it from causing this kind of damage."

"Your Alpha is dead and has been for the last fifty years, boy." She smiled without humor at his stricken expression. "Didn't you know that?"

He shook his head, numb. "No, I didn't."

Madison cocked an eyebrow at him. "You don't get news of your people?"

He scowled. "We don't keep a newsletter, which you know."

She snorted. "Well, for an FBI agent, you are very dense. What makes you think they haven't sent anyone?" She reached over and patted his right hand gently. "You're here, aren't you?"

He growled, but they both knew it was only for show.

My dear M.,
I read my pages of letter to you from last night and I know what your words will be — that should I decide to give up life at sea, penning stories of a type that Poe would enjoy may be a profession for me to go into. Even as I write this, I shake my head and chuckle, as I know that you would be right to think so.

It with a start that I woke this morning and for many long moments, I was unsure of my surroundings. Slowly, however, fragments of the night before came back to me and I shook the stiffness out of my muscles. Mr. Madison came up to me as I returned to camp, a jovial expression on his face.

We spoke briefly about the day's plans — he was insistent about pressing onward, to the place of the silent wolf. It seems that this is also where the village in my dreams was located. But that was not the source of my unease. There was a look about him that I did not like.

There was death in his eyes.

Later.

We had just finished breakfast when the boat I had sent back returned with Billy and, I was displeased to note, the good Reverend. He stood apart from Mr. Madison and was, even now, muttering about the presence of evil in our bosom.

We ignored him as best we could.

Billy seemed to thrive on the area, color blooming in his face and his eyes sparkling, scampering from one odd job to the next, often gazing towards the hills with an intent expression. I was struck then by the resemblance between the man Alban in my dream and the young boy he claimed as his son. Was it possible -? No. It was a dream, a damn good dream and nothing more. People do not turn into wolves.

It is not possible.

Half past two.

I am a picture of calm, but inside I am seething with frustration, M. Why I have rules that my crew and charters must follow to the letter in place, I do not know, for there are some do not feel that those same rules apply to them.

It seems Mr. Madison has lost himself in the forest. He had gone for a walk with his wife and child shortly before lunch was called and all three have yet to be found. Several times, the Reverend has tried to get my attention and speak with me over some matter, but I have ignored him, consumed with conflicting emotions – fear, anger, frustration – over two untrained souls and one innocent child lost in such unforgiving surroundings to mind him over much.

My men mutter under their breath over Mr. Madison's foolishness. It appears that young Billy has gone missing, as well, and I have dispatched a team to search for him as well as the missing Madisons. I am frightened for him, my friend – this fear is far bigger than my fear for Mr. Madison, it nearly swallows me with every breath I take.

Since before this voyage began, I have seen how Mr.

Madison looked at the boy – unfathomable, black hate – and wondered at it. Now I fear I am beginning to suspect the answer.

I am uneasy, on edge – there is something so dreadfully wrong that I

Quarter past three.

Reverend Williams had finally forced me into a corner in my tent, demanding that I listen to him. I am now more resigned to this meeting than curious, my thoughts more on Billy than on any sermon.

But what caught my attention was not a discussion of evil or of God's mysterious ways, but the true cause behind Mr. Madison's venture. It seems that the good Reverend was aware of the gentleman's first wife, who had left him some years before under vague circumstances.

"I had not known the woman," Reverend Williams explained to me. "She had left, oh, perhaps nine, ten years ago. And I was only recently assigned to the parish five years ago."

We sat on the edge of the cliff above the camp, close enough so that we could return should my crew need us for any reason. We were, for the most part, in private.

"How did you come to know of her existence?"

Reverend Williams turned his face to the tall redwoods. "I didn't, at first. But you know how stories get around, both exaggerated and untrue. I was pastor for nearly a year before I met Mr. Madison and his intended bride." He turned to me sharply, fumbling for his pockets. I offered him my pipe, but he waved it away, pulling out a silver and glass flask, which he uncorked and took a liberal swallow.

He grinned widely, his face actually softening at my shocked expression and handed me his flask. Whiskey hung in the air as I took it and poured myself a shot. After a brief pause, in which we both savored the fiery liquid, he continued, "It was not so much his desire to come here and make a new life for himself, to take on this gold mine he speaks of so often. Nor was it the thought he wanted to challenge himself against nature, to find his strength and weaknesses, which troubled me. Such a task has merit and I fully support anyone's desire to test one's ability. But there had been reports of skirmishes with the native people and from what I later heard about Mr. Madison, he was not widely regarded as a tolerant man."

He went on to describe the coldness with which he treated his second wife and son, a charge I hotly disputed until he pointed out that the only times I had ever seen such affection displayed was when the family appeared in public. Reverend Williams, who had spent a great deal of time with them before their marriage and now this voyage, knew of their true relationship. Mr. Madison simply took no notice of her and her son except when it seemed politic to do so. Her only source of affection was her son.

In addition to the troubling reports between natives and settlers, the Reverend had also come upon rumors of the true nature of the people who lived over the hill.

I had taken a nip of his whiskey – now I choked, the liquor dribbling down my chin, nearly dropping his flask. He caught it neatly. "It's not true."

The Reverend turned sad eyes to me. "Oh, but it is, Captain. Many people, most especially those of my own profession, would view them as damned souls or even the Devil's children. I do not. How can they be? God created us all equally – the forms, the shapes, even the colors are what He chose for us to live in."

I must have been drunk – my tongue would not work properly. Certainly, my head was spinning. "To speak of werewolves…"

"It seems mad, I grant you, but if you had seen the things I have, and all in the name of God, it wouldn't be so fantastic." He looked down at his hands, a morose expression on his face. "It's a bit like the fairytales coming true, isn't it? Only this time, it's Little Red Riding Hood who is the wolf."

There was nothing to say to that, so we sat in silence.
Waiting.

MONDAY, JUNE 12, 1978

THIRTY

Burnt toast.

Cracking open one eye, Cassie blinked at the sunlight pouring into her room and immediately came to two conclusions: one, that it was Monday morning and, therefore, first day of summer school, and two, that someone was royally burning toast.

Throwing back her covers, she forced herself out of bed, wrapped herself in a robe and padded blearily downstairs, one hand tracing the wall for balance.

At the kitchen door, she stopped, her tired, root beer-soaked mind unable to process what she was seeing.

Her father was standing before the toaster as smoke spiraled upwards, a bewildered expression on his face. He was poking at the burning toast with a fork. One flame shot upwards suddenly, almost singeing his brow.

"Dad," she started to say when the shrill beep of the fire alarm both deafened and cut her off. Upstairs, there was a loud thump as Pete fell out of bed. In a quick movement, Ronald Brye unplugged the toaster and put it by an open window, turning the ceiling fan on to help disperse the smoke.

The alarm cut itself off mid-shriek as Pete appeared,

wild-eyed and hair askew, at the kitchen door.

"What the hell was *that?*" he asked, his eyes darting from his sister to his father.

"Please refrain from swearing in my presence," Ronald Brye said, looking pained. "I'd like to keep some illusions left in my old age."

"Sorry, Dad." Grinning, Pete went straight to the refrigerator, grabbing a glass from the cupboard on the way. Pulling the carton of orange juice out, he poured some of the juice into his glass, adding, "Thanks for firing ol' sticky-fingers and busybody."

"You're entirely welcome, Pete." His father joined him at the table as Cassie fixed fresh toast. "It seems that my children were correct in assessing Bessie's motives. So I owe you, Mike and Marty a vote of thanks as well."

"No sweat, Daddio."

"Since we no longer have a housekeeper, who's going to do the dishes?" Cassie sat down next to her brother and poured a glass of juice for herself.

"Well, now that's something we have to discuss." Ronald Brye smiled pleasantly, but there was something in it that made them both gulp. "Eat your breakfast. You're going over to Mike's. He's walking you to class this morning."

*****

Half an hour later, humming the Bee Gees under his breath, Pete pushed open his sister's gate and hurried up the porch steps, stopping abruptly when he heard glass crunching under his boots.

Mystified, he looked at the glass, then around the porch area for the source. When he found the broken porch light, Marty flung open the door.

"What —" she snarled, stopping when she saw it was Pete. Forcing herself to relax, Marty took a deep breath. "Hi, kid. What's up?"

"Your broken porch light, for one thing."

"Yeah, I know. Some kid, probably."

Pete snorted. "In L.A., maybe. Here, us hicks just t.p. the place, the whole front yard if we've got time." They glanced over at Cassie when the girl whistled sharply. Mike was standing next to her, wearing shorts that exposed the pale scars on his leg and carrying a briefcase. Mike pointed a finger at his watch. Pete turned back. "Speaking of time, we're gonna be late for summer school. Wanna come with?"

Marty shook her head. "No, sorry. I'm still unpacking and then I've got to go have lunch with Madison." She hesitated, then added, "Come by after two. Maybe we can scrounge up some pizza or something. Play some board games."

"Sure. See ya." With a wave, Pete went back to the others.

Marty closed the door, her face grim as she went through the house and into the backyard, her eyes reluctantly drawn to the angry words screaming back at her in red paint on the fence.

"*Bitch!*" screamed one. "*Slut! Whorechild!*" screamed others.

Unlocking her back door, she stepped out onto the back porch and crossed the lawn, unmindful of the still-damp grass on her bare feet. Standing a mere twenty-four inches away, she stretched one hand out, allowing her fingers to trace the bitter, raging words lightly.

She drew her hand back, looked at the smudge of wet paint on her fingertips, then went back into her house.

*****

From behind a gnarled old oak on Shady Lane, Bessie Mills watched as Michael Brye and his younger siblings walked up the street towards the high school. She did not move, even when they disappeared around the corner. She waited patiently, hearing the soft, seductive voice of the shadow in her mind's ear, replaying each word. Her memory of Sunday night was hazy – the mingling of scents, a harsh struggle, the taste of blood – but the shadow's voice had been as clear as glass; here was someone whose hatred of Marty exceeded her own.

Three hours later, she was rewarded – Marty Brye stepped out of her house in jeans and a white shirt, carrying an old blue flannel. Bessie Mills could hear the faint strains of the harlot whistling cheerfully, her mind clearly elsewhere.

Had Marty chosen to look back, she would have seen Bessie stepping into the sun, out of the tree's protection, a large paper sack crackling in her arms.

Bessie didn't know what she would have done had the Bryes seen her – certainly, they might have found her presence on Fry Street curious, since her own little house was six blocks away on Shady Lane – but they hadn't. She was safe.

Now to deal with Marty. The shadow had told her what to do.

Shifting the paper sack, Bessie Mills walked briskly up the street.

*****

Ms. Brennan's English class dragged by that morning. It seemed so unfair – all the fun things flew as if they had wings, while boring stuff (like school) took their own sweet time to finish.

Pete chewed on his pencil, not really seeing the blank pages of his composition book or the dreaded question on the chalkboard. *Using your five senses, describe a place you know well.* Blah. Who really cared about what he knew well? Who cared if he could even write? At this point, he knew he sure didn't. It just didn't seem important.

His eyes fell on the initials carved deep in the old wooden desktop – *MFB*. Marty's initials. Tracing the grooves with his fingers, he looked out the window and saw, not the elementary school, but the expanse of sea grass and the old Sullivan hotel and beyond that, the ocean.

Over a hundred years ago, his paternal great-great

grandfather had weighed anchor just north of where the lighthouse now stood. Jonas Brye had found something here that had warranted his return a year later. For the first time in his life, Pete found himself wondering what it was…..

A shadow fell over him and he looked up into the cool blue eyes of his teacher. She regarded him, amused.

"Something wrong with your pencil, Pete?"

He blushed, feeling the heat rush up his neck and into his face. "No, just my brain. It doesn't want to think."

Daria Brennan smiled. "Try, Pete. You might be surprised." She walked to the front of the class and sat at the table that served as her desk.

At the desk on his left, Davey Tanner snickered, his pencil sketching out a likeness of the old lighthouse and the ocean beyond. Making a face at him, Pete slumped in his seat and chewed on his pencil, his eyes drifting up. From his current position, he could see how Ms. Brennan's skirt rode up her thigh as she crossed her legs. It reminded him vividly of the horror book he'd found at Second Time Around Books. Ironically, it was about werewolves and it had a lot of racy stuff. Pete had just gotten to one such scene when a shadow fell over him and he looked up to see Mr. Wyatt standing there, holding out his hand for the offending book. Pete handed it over, sure that his face was redder than it ever got sunburned, and made tracks for the door. That had been in November and he still hadn't gone back in. Too embarrassing.

Ms. Brennan looked up once to survey her class and caught his gaze. He swallowed with difficulty, trying not to think of what the skirt hid, but unable to distract his mind fast enough. He felt his blush deepen – he felt as if he was burning with fever.

Quickly, he averted his gaze and found himself scribbling about the first time his grandfather, Joseph Fraser, had taken him fishing out on the Bay and the excitement of catching his first fish. Of the fish they had cooked that night for dinner, seasoned by his grandmother's secret recipe.

As if guided by his own thoughts, Pete's pencil flowed over the blank page, filling the lines with words.

THIRTY-ONE

Marty found herself outside the front gates of the Madison property an hour too early, but couldn't turn away. Setting the manila envelope with Holly's neat handwriting on the flat top of the stone pillar to her left, she pushed through the heavy ivy that covered the iron gates. She paused long enough to grab the envelope up again, tucking it under her arm, and walked up the over-grown drive, gravel crunching beneath her shoes. In spite of her curiosity, she had not opened it, though she could feel the hard edges of a book inside. For some reason, she had felt compelled to keep it sealed until her lunch date with Madison.

The mansion loomed over her and she smiled. If there was one thing that told her she was home, it was the old Madison Place, proper pronouns and all.

She walked around to the front porch and walked up the steps, crossing to the front door, about to knock, when it flew open.

"Come in, come in!" the flying velvet rags cried as Madison darted back towards the kitchen. "He's been waiting for you. The fresh bandage and alcohol are on the chair next to the door."

"But..." Marty was talking to an old coat rack. With a

sigh, she picked up the fresh bandage and alcohol and proceeded to the old library.

*****

Riley was standing in the far corner of the room, looking at the few books left standing on a shelf, backlit by the standing lamp. He was dressed in his jeans, but his feet were bare and so was his torso, except for the white bandage over his right breast, stark against his dark chest hair.

Marty gulped, finding it difficult to breathe.

She wasn't sure if she ought to be grateful to Madison or not, but here she was, the fresh bandage, antiseptic, cotton balls and tape clutched tightly in her hands, her manila envelope pressed against her breasts.

Taking a deep breath, she moved into the room, dropping the items onto his bed, then crossing to the nearest window and pulled open the drapes, revealing a sweeping view of the lighthouse, the village and the ocean beyond the bay.

"Last I heard," she said, hating the bright tone in her voice, "it was vampires that turned to dust with the sunlight, not werewolves."

He watched her as she opened another shade, allowing more sunlight into the room, before turning to him. He could see her pulse quicken and felt his own pulse respond. She licked her lips, gestured to the chair by the window.

"Have a seat," she said, sounding breathless. He took the chair offered and sank into it, enjoying her closeness. Her fingers worked at the tape lightly, being careful not to pull on him.

"What's in the envelope?"

His eyes had closed and she felt thankful for that — she honestly did not want to be mesmerized by him at the moment. His presence was intoxicating enough. She blinked, trying to remember what he had just said. "What?"

He gestured. "The envelope. What's in it?"

She shrugged. "Don't know. It was in the mail for me Saturday. Thought it would be better to open it with Madison in attendance." A bead of alcohol slid from the wound in his chest and slid down. Her eyes followed. "So what kind of person suffers from silver poisoning anyway?"

"A werewolf."

She snickered. "Funny, wise guy. Seriously."

"I'm deadly serious."

She snorted. "I can already tell you're a wolf. There's a dangerous look to you."

He smiled. "I won't hurt you, Marty."

"I know." She did know – it was clear in the way he looked at her. "But werewolves – that's something out of the movies. I don't believe in them." He hissed at the antiseptic and she pulled back. "Sorry."

"It's all right." He started to speak, hesitated, then forced himself. "It's what I am, Marty. A wolf."

Her hands paused in their ministrations, but before he could miss it, they continued on. "Don't be ridiculous. I'm not little red riding-hood, so you can't possibly be the big bad wolf."

He covered her hands with his, halting the bandaging process effectively, and met her gaze. "You have Cowyn Fraser's freckles."

"I have my mother's freckles," she corrected automatically. "I don't think he had any."

"I can tell you." He tugged on her – she knelt down so that they were eye-level. He cupped her face with one hand, his thumb caressing her lower lip. "He loved those damn freckles, especially the ones that formed the constellation of Taurus on his back. It was his only vanity."

"My freckles don't do that." She sounded regretful. "They just look like dots."

He touched her mouth and she fell silent. "There was

one freckle – a mole, actually – that he was very proud of. He felt that it was a family symbol, because his father had it, his father's father had it and he had found it went back to his ancestral grandmother." His fingers left her face, tracing the line of her jaw to her right ear. Just behind her lobe, she felt his fingers touch the nub she'd always been half-aware of, but never really thought about. "Right here, just behind the upper lobe."

She was trembling, whether from his touch or from the pieces of her family history he was revealing to her, she did not know. Somewhere, a bell rang and Madison hurried from the kitchen, muttering to herself. The bell rang again and the older woman flew down the hall with a shrill, "I'm coming!"

Neither Marty nor Riley paid any attention. She finished taping him up, her hands tingling and surprisingly heavy.

"How do you know so much about my great-great-grandfather?" she asked softly. "He died maybe twenty-five years before I was born."

Riley held her gaze. "He was my….foster-father, you might say, after my own was killed in a fire in eighteen hundred fifty-two."

"Stop it." The harshness in her voice surprised them both. In the hall, Madison and her guest were talking in low tones. "Stop talking like you're older than this last century. It's crazy."

He was hurt, she saw it, but she couldn't help it. Behind them, the door opened as he said, "It's the truth. I knew Cowyn Fraser, just like I knew Jonas Brye."

"Just like he knew Jonathan Williams." Madison spoke from the door. In her hands, she held an old, dusty shoebox. They looked over, Marty rising to her feet when she saw who was with her.

Dan Williams stepped forward, his expression unreadable. He was conscious of the energy crackling between Marty and the strange man and, despite his own relationship with Daria, felt an immediate, irrational spark of jealousy. The strange man's dark eyes narrowed sharply, as if he scented something both familiar and unexpected.

Marty flicked a glance from Dan to Madison, her mouth suddenly dry. She felt Riley slip his hand into hers, was glad to feel his strength mingling with hers. The world began to level off and she found that she could speak without sounding shaky.

"Who's Jonathan Williams?" she asked, her tone flippant. "The fifth horseman?"

"No." Dan Williams didn't look at the man holding Marty's hand, as if by refusing to acknowledge it, it would not exist. "He was my great-great grandfather. One of the founders of Wolf's Head Bay."

Old Lady Madison coughed gently. "Let's see what Holly sent you, Marty, dear. Then we can pool all the information together."

THIRTY-TWO

Tommy was waiting for them at the school entrance when the last bell shattered the sky, ending the first day of summer school.

He was reading an old comic book, its pages worn and tattered, when Cassie and Pete emerged from the building. Pete was still griping. Tommy shrugged – what else was new?

Cassie looked over and saw him – she waved. He waved back.

"So, what's the plan?" Tommy shoved the comic book in back pocket.

"I'm going over to Katie's for an hour. They just got their TV hooked up with cable last Friday. Maybe I'll join you bozos later." Cassie started walking towards town.

Pete snickered. "Hey, you just called Marty a bozo."

She only laughed. Pete elbowed Tommy as they walked home. "Hey, what are you doing this afternoon?"

Tommy shrugged. "Nothing, I guess. Why?"

"Wanna come over to Marty's? Have some pizza, play cards?"

"Is she home?"

"Naw, she's up at Madison's for lunch. Won't be

home till after two, but she won't mind. She'll make us some pizza."

"Are you sure it would be okay?"

"Sure, I'm sure. Why wouldn't it?"

"Well, as long as she doesn't hate me or anything…."

"Jeez, you're a melodrama king. She doesn't hate you. Where'd you get an idea like that? Now, come on. I need to go the store first."

*****

Marty felt as though she had stopped breathing. At least, the heavy weight on her chest made it harder. She wanted nothing more than to run to the nearest window, push it open and run as fast as she could towards the bay, cast herself in, become part of the foam as waves crashed onto the rocky beach. Her gaze was riveted on the man standing next to the old woman and she felt her face go hot and her heart go cold.

Memories came fast and furious into the forefront of her mind as she stared at him —of her initiation into the complexities of sex, his angry rejection, fumbling for her clothes, tears scalding her face as she ran out into the night, of waiting until dawn cracked the sky before slipping downstairs with her last suitcase and getting into her car, of driving as far as Monterey before stopping at hotel.

Someone touched her hand – warm, calloused, strong – sliding fingers through hers in a gentle grip. As if from another plane of existence, she looked the long distance to her hand, not quite recognizing it as hers. Holding it was another, more masculine hand. Her eyes made a slow progression up the arm attached to the hand to the shoulder, the neck and jaw, then met the eyes of the man that belonged to the arm.

Her wolf.

The heaviness lifted and she could breathe again. She faced the newcomer.

"Hello, Dan," she said and was pleased to hear that her voice was steady, calm.

"Hello, Marty," the man said and dropped his gaze.

"Well." Old Lady Madison put her box on the table and clapped her hands together, delighted. She looked for all the world like a little girl hosting her first tea party. "Shall we get started?"

Dan gratefully volunteered to help set up chairs and a table while Marty helped the man he recognized as the FBI agent into a button-down shirt. After directing where to set things up, Madison disappeared into the kitchen.

After arranging the four chairs around the table, removing the heavy blanket from the table and then wiping them all free of dust, Dan went to the corner bookcase, where the tall standing lamp stood, and perused the titles shelved there, trying very hard not to listen as Marty murmured something to the other man.

He had just finished composing a legitimate excuse to leave when Madison returned, wheeling a tea tray into the room and headed for the table.

"Everyone, please sit," she said cheerfully. "Marty, please bring that package with you."

"Miss Madison," Dan said, wanting nothing more than to leave, "I just realized that I have some important business to attend to. I can't stay."

"Nonsense," Madison said. "Sit down. This concerns you, too."

Marty took one seat, the man Riley sat to her left. Madison took the seat to Riley's right, leaving Dan no other choice than to sit next to Marty. He shifted his chair closer to Madison.

Marty fumbled with the envelope, her finger sliding under the sealed flap. With a jerk, she tore it open. "Cassie found it in my mailbox on Saturday. Holly mailed it to me. She must've put it in the mail-drop the night she…." Marty stopped, swallowed, went on. "Anyway, I haven't looked at it."

A cracked, leather-bound book slipped out of the envelope and into her hands. She put it on the table.

"Open it, dear," Madison urged. "Read it out loud."

Obediently, Marty did so, turning to the first page. Her eyes widened. "It's one of Jonas's diaries. But, I thought the library had them all."

"Apparently not," Dan said. She looked at him. He refused to meet her gaze.

Marty carefully paged through it again. "No, not a diary. Letters to someone named 'M'."

"Read," Riley urged.

Marty cleared her throat. "'13 June, 1852. Dear M., I must thank you for the gift of Mr. Dickens' *David Copperfield* and Mr. Melville's *Moby Dick*. It gladdens me that you have remembered how much I enjoyed the shorter tales of both of them…..'"

As she read, each listener found themselves wrapped in the words of the writer and soon, the only voice they heard was his.

THIRTY-THREE

The first thing that Pete noticed when he and Tommy turned onto Fry Street half an hour later was the dark figure scuttling away from them and towards Shady Lane. Frowning, he shifted the paper bag to his other arm and elbowed Tommy, who was poking through his sack hopefully.

Tommy looked up, blinking. "What?"

"Did you see that?"

"See what?"

Pete rolled his eyes. Tommy was a darn sight brainier than most of his friends, but when he got something on his mind, it took an eight engine freight train to bring him out of it. "I'll take that as a 'no'."

"Huh?"

"I saw someone run out of Marty's yard," he said patiently.

Tommy stared at him, confused. "So? Maybe she's home."

"Then why would she run out?"

Tommy thought about that. "I dunno."

Pete remembered the ugly black look in Bessie's eyes and felt the first tingle of fear. "Come on."

"What for?"

"Just come on."

Clutching his bag, Pete ran up the street, his feet pounding the pavement. Behind him, Tommy huffed along, his face red. When they reached Marty's gate, they stopped and Pete was suddenly, deeply afraid.

The front door stood wide open.

Tommy sucked in a deep breath. "Pete, I don't like this."

Pete didn't either, not by a long shot, but he couldn't say so. Instead, he dropped his bag and walked up to his sister's house with extreme caution, apprehension dragging his pace to a crawl. Drawing closer, he could see that someone had ripped up the flowerbeds the old gardener had just put in over a week ago. He or she had done a real number with them, beheading the buds and stomping on them, their crushed petals littering the porch, stems tossed aside on the walk.

He really didn't want to go inside or even approach the front door to look and see the damage that had surely been done there, but he could smell something sour as it drifted on the breeze. Something foul.

"Pete? You see anything?"

"Tommy, go get my dad!" he shouted, suddenly cold. "Tell him to call the cops and get over here!"

"But….."

"Now!!" he roared.

Tommy went, dropping his bag of groceries at Pete's first cry, his feet scarcely touching the ground as he ran.

Pete backed away from the porch, hardly aware of his friend's departure, his breath coming short and shallow. This was unreal – nothing like this was supposed to happen, not here, in Wolf's Head Bay. In Chico, maybe, or even in Humboldt, where college students thought this kind of stuff was funny, but not here.

Too weird.

Pete blinked, suddenly aware that his vision was

funny, like he was on Mr. Parker's boat and the waves
were a little too choppy for his taste, tossing the boat
higher than was comfortable. He decided that maybe he
should sit down on the lawn and fell over on his back
instead.

"Gaaaa," he muttered thickly, blinking up at the sky.
Heavy, gray clouds shifted above him and for one crazy
minute, one began to take the shape of a wolf.

Too weird.

*****

"Mr. Brye!"

Even over the roar of his lawn mower, Ronald Brye
could hear the panic in the voice and turned to see Tommy
Williams running up the street towards him. He switched
off the mower and eyed the boy with some concern.

"Tommy," he said, as the boy came to a panting halt
in front of him. "Where's the fire?"

"Pete said to tell you to call the police," the boy
wheezed. "Marty's house is messed up something bad."

It wasn't until Tommy cried out in pain that Ronald
realized he had been gripping the boy's shoulders tightly.
He let go. "Is Marty all right?"

"I don't think she's home," Tommy said. "Pete said
she went up to Madison's."

"Thank God," Ronald muttered. "Stay here while I
call the police. Then we'll go back to Marty's."

"Sure thing," Tommy said gratefully and sat heavily
on the curb to wait.

*****

Ten minutes later found Ronald Brye, Pete and Tommy
standing in Marty's front lawn, a crowd of curious
onlookers held back by a couple of deputies.

The call had been answered on the first ring. "Wolf's
Head Bay Police Department. This is Elizabeth Phillips.
How may I direct your call?"

Ronald was tongue-tied, but only for a few seconds.
"This is Ronald Brye. Can you put me through to the

sheriff?"

"Are you all right, sir?"

"I'm fine, but I have reason to believe that my daughter's house has been broken into."

"I'll put you through right now," she said and connected the line.

Now, John Dylan was inside the house with a photographer and a couple of his best detectives.

The house was a mess – whoever had done the damage came in after Marty had left sometime that morning and before Pete and Tommy had arrived an hour earlier. Whoever the perpetrator was, he or she had trashed the place well.

"Hey, John, come take a look at this." The photographer, Sophie Radcliffe, was in the kitchen, looking out the window and into the backyard. Coming up behind her, he flinched at the garish paint and the harsh words it spelled out. "Pete said it was already there, didn't he?"

"Yup." But Marty hadn't reported it, he knew. "Get pictures of it."

"Do you think it's related?"

"Dunno. Couldn't hurt to put this in the file."

"Sure thing." Shifting the camera in her hand, she flicked a glance at Dylan. "We're not going to be on this all day, are we?"

He poked around the cupboards. "Why? You got a hot date?"

She grinned, kicking the linoleum. "Yup. Red pepper chili spicy enough to burn a hole through this floor."

He waved her on. "Go take pictures."

Chuckling softly under her breath, Radcliffe went out the back door while he looked around the kitchen. Whoever had made the house a mess had left the kitchen alone and that bothered him. It was almost eerie, seeing everything put away in its place. Even the cat dishes had been untouched in their corner.

He blinked. Wait a minute. What cat?

"Mrrroooww!!" The angry howl came from a cupboard, accompanied by furious scratching. He followed the sounds until he found the source underneath the sink and, crouching low on his heels, he opened it cautiously.

Fur exploded from the tiny space, hissing, spitting, scratching anything in its path. Even though he was half-expecting it and jumped back, he still managed to get a deep wound on his hand.

The cat paused long enough in the doorway to glare at him, as if it was his fault that it had suffered the indignities of being trapped, then bolted to the front of the house.

There was an astonished yell, an angry howl and something breaking.

Great.

With a sigh, he put a damp paper towel on his wound and went outside to speak with Ronald Brye.

*****

"I'm sure I couldn't say." Ronald Brye sounded troubled. "Marty grew up here. She's a part of this town and she just moved back. You know that, John."

Of course he did. Everyone did. In a town as small as Wolf's Head Bay, it would be hard to hide even the Invisible Man.

Pete tugged at his father's elbow impatiently. "Dad, tell him about Bessie."

John Dylan's senses sharpened. "What about Mrs. Mills?"

Pete drew himself up importantly. "Mike talked Marty into talking Dad into firing Ol' Stickyfingers because she's been snooping around in Mom's things and spying and treating us like babies. And she hates Marty."

"Any reason why?"

Pete shook his head. "Except for the fact that Marty told Dad to fire her, no."

John Dylan looked at Ronald. "Did you fire her?"

Ronald turned red. "I did. It was awkward because she thought that I was, well, about to...."

Pete interrupted. "She thought Dad wanted to marry her."

Dylan and Brye looked at the boy, then at each other.

Dylan spoke. "Why attack Marty?"

"Bessie knew that Marty had suggested I fire her. And Pete's right. There's no love lost between them."

Dylan nodded. "All right. I'll have a talk with her."

Pete was outraged. "You mean you're not going to arrest her?"

The sheriff smiled patiently. "We don't have any evidence directly linking her to the crime, Pete."

Pete scowled, but said nothing. After a while, it was done – the crowd left, then the police. The three of them were left behind.

Ronald Brye clapped his hands together. "What do you say we get the place cleaned up before Marty gets home?"

Pete eyed his father dubiously. "Think we can?"

"Sure." He started down the walk. "I'll go and get supplies. You boys get started."

"You think this might put me on Marty's good side?" Tommy asked as Ronald Brye left, whistling cheerfully.

Pete groaned, shaking his head, exasperated at his friend. "Tommy, for the last time, she doesn't hate you."

They went inside, in search of a broom and a mop.

THIRTY-FOUR

While Pete and Tommy went to the grocery store before going on to Marty's, Cassie was lying on her stomach on pink shag carpet, reading an old issue of *Life* magazine. Katie sat on her canopied bed, painting her toenails a rose pink, an open issue of *Seventeen* lying before her.

After she had left the school grounds, Cassie had gone over to the Blake residence with Katie to check out the new cable TV. Unfortunately, since Mrs. Blake was hosting a knitting circle, the two girls were forced to go to Katie's room.

"Who do you think is cuter?" Katie closed the bottle of polish tightly. "Andy Gibb, Shaun Cassidy or John Travolta?"

"Jeff Bridges, hands down." Cassie closed the magazine and pushed it away, sitting on her heels. Her eyes strayed to the window and she frowned. "How can you sleep with your window facing the old Madison place?"

Katie flopped onto her back, giggling. "You can only see it if you're standing up."

Cassie threw the magazine at her — shrieking with

laughter, Katie flung a pillow.

After several minutes of horseplay – cut short when Mrs. Blake called upstairs to remind them that they need to behave like *ladies* – Cassie lay flat on her back, her sides aching with each fresh spasm of giggles. She finally propped herself up on her elbows and said, "I'm bored. Let's go out."

"Nuh-uh, no more milkshakes," Katie groaned. "I'm all milk-shaked out."

"We could always spy on Pete."

Katie flopped on her side, the mattress shifting with her weight. "No way. He's probably doing something I don't really want to know about."

Cassie sat up, thinking. Her eyes strayed to the window again, to the trees and the tip of Wolf's Peak beyond. Her gaze slipped lower to the Madison place.

"I've got a better idea," she said and, grabbing Katie's hand, led the way out.

*****

Much of Cassie's enthusiasm for the adventure had disappeared by the time they crested the hill two miles outside of town forty minutes later. They stared down the dirt road that branched off of Lighthouse Way, looking as if it hadn't been used in decades. At the end of it, the Madison place waited for them.

It didn't help that the sudden ocean breeze was conspiring with the dirt road to make dust devils. What was left of their enthusiasm suddenly vanished.

The mansion loomed above them – even with the ivy-covered fence surrounding it, they found themselves paralyzed to the spot.

"It's even creepier up close," Katie said softly. Cassie nodded in agreement; then, swallowing hard, she tugged on Katie's arm and they began walking up the road.

Katie stopped abruptly. Cassie almost tripped. They were thirty yards away from the gate. Through the thick ivy, Cassie could see iron spikes at the top.

"I don't know about this, Cassie," Katie said. "Let's not do this, say we did and go to the movies instead."

This sounded very agreeable to Cassie, but she forced herself to roll her eyes in disgust instead. "What are you, chicken?"

Katie clucked noisily, flapping her arms wildly. Cassie burst out laughing and when both girls finally regained control of themselves, they had reached the gate.

Beneath the overgrown ivy, they could see the heavy chain and the padlock that held it secure.

Cassie scowled. "How the hell did she get in if it was locked?" She kicked the fence with a sneakered foot. "Ow!" She leaned against the offending gate, holding her foot with care, unlacing and removing her shoe to see the damage.

Katie looked around uneasily. "They'll hear us if you don't stay quiet."

Cassie rolled her eyes. "Oh, please. What're they gonna do if they do hear us? We're on the outside of the gates. We're not trespassing."

Katie pointed to the bent grass. "Where do you think that goes?"

Cassie led the way, limping. "Let's find out."

They crept alongside the fence, their eyes alert to any break that would allow access inside. They came upon the back gate, propped open with a huge rock and, with Cassie leading the way, slipped through.

Crouching low, they scurried over to the nearest window. Peering through it, Cassie realized that they had found the kitchen. It was empty of life, although someone clearly kept house here – the kitchen was tidy.

Cassie tugged on Katie's arm. "Look, someone lives here. They have tea ready."

Katie rolled her eyes. "Duh, Cassie. Old Lady Madison lives here. You remember, the crazy witch?"

Cassie ignored her. "Come on, let's see what else is here."

She led the way, crawling on hands and knees, unmindful of the stickers and barbs that caught at her. Katie muttered under her breath. They followed the foundation to the west side of the house – the air was saltier, crisper than in back. The sound of the ocean pounding on rocks was a dull roar – Cassie paused, trying to orient the sound, found only the beacon light of the lighthouse instead. The distant cry of seagulls accompanied the surf, complementing the loneliness of the sea.

Shaking her head to free it of such fancy images, Cassie was about to move forward when Katie tapped her shoulder pointedly. Looking back over her shoulder, she saw that her friend was pointing at the window above them. The window was open a few inches, allowing for voices to escape.

With care, they both stood, peering inside with great caution. Once their eyes had adjusted, they were able to make out the shapes that filled the room. It had been a library once, Cassie guessed, to judge by all the empty shelves. A bed had been moved into the room – it looked to have been in that central spot for many years.

At the opposite side of the room, four chairs had been set up around a table and she could see the people sitting around it, talking. There was an intensity that came in loud and clear in their body language. She recognized her sister's back facing the window, Old Lady Madison and a vaguely familiar man in between.

Katie tugged at her elbow. "Who is that?"

"I don't know," Cassie whispered back. "But I'm gonna find out."

There was movement – Old Lady Madison was pouring out tea for four. Cassie's eyes widened and she shared a shocked look with Katie.

What was Reverend Dan doing at Madison's?

THIRTY-FIVE

Reverend Dan, at the moment, was quite convinced that he was in the presence of three lunatics.

At least, that was what his rational mind said. Except, in his heart, where it mattered, he knew they spoke truth. After reading aloud from the letters in Marty's possession, he knew deep in his bones. It so clearly validated his own ancestor's veiled words inked into his last journal.....

Riley watched the reverend closely as the other man listened to the extraordinary history that was being laid out before him. He was well aware of the man's discomfort around Marty, suspected the reasons behind it, took comfort in the knowledge that it was no longer an issue for her, but that was not what troubled him at this moment. The scent he tasted on Dan Williams troubled him and he was unsure how to process it. He knew that scent, knew that he knew it, but he found that he doubted his own nose, his own memories and even his past because it simply could not be.

The owner of that scent no longer lived, he knew that, he saw her die, yet there it was, almost hidden beneath the reverend's after-shave and soap.

Riley closed his eyes, wishing he could close his nose

as well.

Reverend Dan stirred his tea, staring into the dark liquid intently, as if hoping to find his answers there. The tea itself had long since grown cold and he sighed, putting it on the tray before him.

He looked up and found himself locking gazes with Riley. "I know you're a member of the police department," he said, suddenly. "At least, you work for the FBI and you're here because of the mass grave found at the Heights. Does this…..condition affect your position?"

"You mean, is my true nature known?" Riley shook his head. "No. My senses are heightened, of course, which helps, but it is not common knowledge among my fellow officers." The sarcasm was heavy in his voice. "There are others like me, of course, here in the Bay. And we would not betray ourselves to outsiders."

"In what way?" Dan cleared his throat, ignoring the pointed comment. "In what way has it been helpful?"

"Picking up scents, sounds, objects an ordinary man couldn't." Riley's gaze seemed to bore into Dan's – he desperately wanted to look away and couldn't. "Even if it is only a week old."

Dan thought briefly of Daria, of her naked, warm shape in his bed four days earlier. He cleared his throat. "It's been a fascinating lunch," he said, feeling a sharp tightness in his throat. "And I thank you for your confidence. But I must get back to work…"

He stood. Madison did the same.

"You understand the importance of what was said here." It was not a question.

Dan regarded his hostess, a woman thirty years his senior with a reputation in town as a half-baked eccentric at best and a lunatic at worst.

He nodded. "I do. Your secrets are safe with me."

Madison nodded, satisfied. "I'll see you out."

*****

"What's going on?"

Katie looked up at Cassie from her seated position on the ground.

Cassie was still peering through the window. "Well, Reverend Dan is leaving. Old Lady Madison is following him and Marty's getting cozy with the hunk."

"Can we go, then? I'm starving and American Bandstand's on in twenty minutes."

Cassie spared her friend an irritated glance. "You know, you're such a girl. This is exciting stuff – Marty with a gorgeous mystery man, Reverend Dan having tea with the local nutcase and you want to go home and watch Dick Clark introduce the flavor of the week?" Cassie rolled her eyes. "What am I going to do with you?"

A shadow fell over both of them. "It is well within her rights to go, Cassandra."

The two girls shrieked. Madison stood before them, her expression amused.

"Next time, try the front door, if you want to come in. It's far more polite."

"Jeez, ma'am, you scared us," Cassie gasped. "What'd you go and do that for?"

Madison smiled. "Marita, as you may have guessed, was busy." She gestured with impatience. "Come on, then. Inside."

After exchanging uneasy glances, Cassie and Katie reluctantly followed.

*****

Riley had gotten back to the bed and closed his eyes after Madison and Williams left the room, savoring Marty's fresh female scent and the weight of her arm across his chest as she curled up next to him.

He was almost well, thanks to Madison's herbs – tonight, when the moon breached the sky, he would change and slip back to his home. And when the time was right, he and Marty would engage in a far more pleasing act than this…..

For her part, Marty simply enjoyed the intimacy of

the moment. She liked his musky scent, the warmth of his arm around her and snuggled closer. Her eyes flicked to the scar on his temple, suspecting now that he had been in his wolf form while defending her in the cemetery. Her eyes dropped to the scar on his neck and soon, her fingers were tracing it lightly before she realized it. His eyes met hers openly. It was easier, now, to accept what he had told her; the combined weight of Jonas Brye's diaries and Riley's words were hard to ignore and her own heart refused to disbelieve….

When she drew her hand away, he was watching her with an intensity that made her flush deep inside. He caught her hand and pressed her palm to his lips. It suddenly didn't matter that what he claimed to be was more accepted in the realm of fiction than reality, that his eyes weren't the color of the ocean, they were still blue, she was still drowning in them anyway….

The door opened and she sat up sharply. Riley eased himself up. Madison entered, followed by two teenagers.

"We have company," Madison said primly.

Marty crossed her arms, trying to look stern. "Uninvited company."

Cassie ignored her sister, regarding the man beside her with interest. "Hey, aren't you on the police force?"

He grinned, shaking his head. "FBI Special Agent Riley, at your service."

"Is he the reason you got all banged up?" There was suspicion in Cassie's voice – too young to remember her sister dating him, she had seen Jimmy at his best over the years and it wasn't pretty.

Marty understood at once. "He got hurt and when I tried to help him, I got hurt."

"How'd he get hurt?" Katie asked.

Great. Answer a difficult question, get another.

It was Riley who answered. "I was shot."

Cassie eyed the bandage. "You're lucky to be alive."

"So I am. Thanks to your sister."

Marty shot him a glance. "I didn't tell you I had a sister."

He met her gaze. "You didn't have to."

Cassie frowned. There was clearly another conversation going on.

Marty grinned suddenly. "That's right, I forgot, you're a wolf."

Okay, so her sister had gone more than slightly bonkers over the weekend. But then, considering how gorgeous the man involved was, Cassie decided she really couldn't blame her.

"Wolves have fur and tails and walk on four legs," Katie said practically. "You don't, so you're not a wolf."

Riley grinned, clearly enjoying this. "Technically, you're right. I'm not a wolf."

Katie nodded, satisfied. "There you go."

"I don't think Marty meant 'wolf' in the literal sense," Cassie said. "Men can be described as wolves because they're….well, cads."

"I'm not that type, either."

"So what type are you?"

"A werewolf."

THIRTY-SIX

Cassie stared hard at Riley, realized he spoke the truth. Or what he obviously believed to be the truth. The room started to tilt and she sat down hard on the floor, the strength running out of her legs.

"This is absolutely crazy," Katie said matter-of-factly. "I hope you know that. There are no such things as werewolves or vampires or whatever. It just isn't possible."

Madison, Riley and Marty exchanged looks – Cassie caught it, but didn't understand why they seemed amused and uneasy at the same time. At last the old woman spoke, her eyes on Katie.

"It was Shakespeare, was it not, who said that there are more things in heaven and earth than are dreamt of in one's philosophy?" Madison made herself comfortable in the overstuffed chair that was in desperate need of repair.

Katie looked at Riley. "Were you bitten by one?" She blushed hotly. "I mean, that's how it happens, right? To become a werewolf?"

"It is one way," Riley agreed, "but that usually involves a curse invoked by someone with great power."

"Like in *The Wolf Man*," Katie said, remembering the movie.

"Yes."

"And the other way?" Cassie asked.

"What I am. A race of people who have the ability to shift from human to wolf form, which is not entirely controlled by the moon, as some legends would have you believe." He debated silently with himself, then added, "Other than changing into wolf form and highly attuned senses, we are not so different from you."

"There is a third way to become a wolf," Madison murmured from her chair. Riley glanced at her sharply, but she was gazing at the ceiling, a dreamy look on her face. "A true were', like Riley, could, while in the process of shifting his shape from man to wolf, bite and draw the blood of someone else, thus making the victim a werewolf."

Cassie mulled that over. "But…how does that work? I mean, what's in your genes that makes you different?"

Riley shook his head. "I don't know. None of us do, though a few of us went into the sciences to try and find out. As near as I can tell, it is merely a quirk in our genetic structure that makes us who we are. It is a small thing, a marker much like the one that chooses hair color, height or even the number of freckles on one's back…."

For no reason that Cassie could see, Marty blushed a rosy pink.

Amused, his eyes never leaving Marty, Riley added, "I knew your ancestor, Jonas Brye. Your grandfather, Cowyn Fraser, as well. He had a fascination with freckles."

"Whoa, wait a minute. I don't know if you get this," Cassie said, "but…if you knew him, you'd be over a hundred years old."

Riley met Cassie's gaze. "I am one hundred thirty-six years old."

Marty sighed heavily. "Don't remind me." But her hand sought his and held fast.

Cassie looked troubled. "How can you be so old and still be alive?"

Riley considered his words, thoughtful. "I....was bitten by a vampire while helping one of my pack escape the fires of 1852."

"That's impossible," Cassie said with utter conviction.

"Is it?" Madison asked. "Victor Madison didn't think so. That's really what brought him here in 1852. Why he tried to massacre an entire village for what he perceived as not only a betrayal by one of its members, but by what he also called an abomination against God and nature."

"There was a village here in 1852?" Katie looked shocked. "Why isn't it in the town history?"

"Cowyn Fraser, Jonas Brye and Jonathan Williams thought it would be safer that way." Riley studied his hand, observing the lines as it linked with Marty's. "They felt it was the only way to protect what was already here and to live in plain sight, rather than to hide."

"Typical white male thinking," Cassie muttered. "What did Cowyn Fraser have to do with any of this? Bad enough that one great-great grandparent is involved with white-washing history, but two?"

Marty glared at her sister. "Haven't you been listening?"

"To a lot of bullshit, yeah."

Marty held her sister's gaze. "Cowyn Fraser was here in 1852, in 1845, going back to 1834. He was here before Victor Madison, before Jonas Brye." She held up an ancient looking journal. "Jonas wrote all about it."

Cassie was hardly aware of rising to her feet and crossing the short distance to the bed where her sister and the wolf – no, the man – sat. Even when her fingers closed around the cracked leather binding, Cassie felt as if she were in a dream.

Hands trembling, Cassie opened the book, saw the dates inscribed. "Hey, this is the missing diary. Shouldn't this be in the library with the others?" She paged through the book carefully, Jonas Brye's familiar cramped script swimming until her eyes adjusted and a name popped out:

The book fell from her lifeless fingers onto the bed; Cassie met her sister's gaze.

"Is it true?" she whispered. "We're…we're…." She swallowed, tried and could not finish.

Marty crawled to her sister, holding her tightly. "Yes."

"Does Mike know?"

Marty smiled. "I don't know."

"Is it why Mom died?"

Marty sat on her haunches, touched her sister's cheek. "I don't know, honey. I really don't." Cassie suddenly started giggling. "What is it?"

"I was just thinking. I'm a werewolf. How cool is that? I mean…." Cassie groped for words. "Pete's gonna flip when he hears this." She looked at Riley, her eyes sharp. "We aren't evil, are we?"

"We are who we are. Can one person be wholly evil or good? No. It is the same with those who are outside the norm." Riley laughed softly, mocking himself. "Brianna would kill me for saying so — she always held that non-were' folk were outside the norm, that they were nothing more than an unenlightened species not worthy of respect." He shook himself, as if to rid his memory of her.

Cassie thought for a minute. "If Mom was a werewolf, why did she die? Aren't you — we — immortal?"

Riley shook his head. "We are as mortal as Madison, in spite of what we are. We can survive most injuries, but silver is our weakness." He hesitated. "And a broken neck is just as fatal to us."

"Why haven't we changed?"

Riley glanced at Marty — she shrugged. He took that as assent. "It is only my opinion and I could be wrong, but even among pure werewolves, it has happened that the gene skips a generation or two, only to show up in a later generation."

Observing the chemistry between her sister and Riley, Cassie rolled her eyes and said, "Well, I can safely say that it won't be my kids."

"As for your mother, that is something I cannot answer."

"You're a big help."

"Cassie."

"Sorry."

"I don't understand," Katie said. "How does Jonas Brye fit into all of this? I mean, what was in it for him to come back?"

Riley caressed the cracked leather. "He fell in love with my mother. She wouldn't have him. And he came back, hoping. But he never saw her again."

The former library fell silent as each occupant considered what had been said.

THIRTY-SEVEN

John Dylan was going over Fletcher's preliminary report on Denver Clarke's autopsy when a knock sounded on his door.

"Come in." Dylan felt a familiar surge of pleasure when he saw Elizabeth.

She stopped just inside the door, her dark cheeks rosy. "Ronald Brye is here."

Dylan glanced at his desk clock – two-fifteen. Right on the dot.

"Send him in," he said, adding impulsively, "would you care to join me for dinner?"

She raised a brow. "That would be lovely. When?"

"Tonight at seven?"

She considered his invitation seriously, but the light in her eyes only teased him. "I believe that seven-thirty might work better for me."

"That's fine," he said quickly and she laughed.

Ronald Brye walked in just then, bemused. "What's the joke?"

"Work-related," Dylan said. "Thank you, Elizabeth."

She nodded and left, a smile curving her lips.

"Have a seat." Dylan gestured to the scarred wooden

chair closest to Ronald, who did so with a sigh.

"I brought something I know Bessie handled recently." He leaned forward, placing a brown paper sack onto Dylan's desk. Dylan took the sack, holding the edges carefully as he opened it, peering inside. The scantily clad heroine on the lurid cover of a historical romance novel greeted him, promising sensual desires fulfilled after a certain amount of conflict. He looked at Ronald, who shrugged. "I used barbecue tongs to pick it up. I don't know how useful it will be to you."

Dylan grinned. "Watching old episodes of *Perry Mason*, right?"

Ronald Brye had the grace to blush. "Well, yes. In between my collecting tracks and studying books on the local wildlife, it was one way to pass the time."

"Whatever the case, I'm sure this'll help." Dylan closed the paper sack, rose to his feet and started for the door. "I'll get this to the lab, see what they come up with." He paused, recalling Jena Fletcher's recommendation of Ronald Brye. "You study tracks as, what? A hobby?"

Ronald looked puzzled by the question. "Yes."

Dylan hesitated, weighing his options carefully. "I have an animal paw print that Fletcher's having a hard time with. Care to take a look?"

An eagerness filled Ronald Brye's face – the years fell away from him and Dylan could almost swear he was in the presence of a ten-year old boy rather than a man on the dark side of sixty-five.

*****

They left Madison's place twenty minutes later, having enjoyed the strong tea and overly sweet cookies the older woman had served.

Marty had almost choked on one cookie when she realized the time. "Oh, God, I was supposed to meet Pete at my place!"

"I'm sure he'll understand," Cassie said pointedly. The energy crackling between Marty and Riley was strong,

274

almost physically so. Although she had never seen anyone in the throes of lust before, she was pretty sure she was seeing it now. Except it wasn't lust, not exactly.

"No, I promised him," Marty was saying. "We were going to watch TV and eat junk food."

"We can tell him you got held up," Katie offered.

Marty shook her head. "No, it's okay." She stood reluctantly away from Riley, her fingers still entangled with his, their gazes locked.

Cassie sighed. "We'll be outside."

Marty looked up at that, but Madison and the teens were gone.

"Madison will give me a clean bill of health," he said softly, "which means I can leave tonight."

"And move in with me? Whatever will the neighbors say?" The thought of him in her house, in her bed, thrilled her nevertheless. "Okay, forget the neighbors. Just a bunch of gossipmongers, anyway. Besides, don't you have a house of your own to go back to?"

"Tavis," he said in reply and grinned at her puzzled expression.

"What?"

"My name is Tavis Riley."

"Tavis Riley," she repeated slowly, sounding out the syllables on her tongue. "I like it. It's got a bite to it."

"Like me?"

She colored. "We haven't tried that yet, so I wouldn't know."

He pulled her down beside him, holding her close, his breath tickling her ear as he nuzzled it. "Care to try now?"

She allowed herself to drown in the moment, aware that he was doing the same, inhaling his scent. "I want to, but I have to go." She started to move, paused. "But I'll give you something to remember me by."

He started to say that he was physically incapable of forgetting her when her lips, feather-light, touched his, her tongue tracing the outline of his mouth, his teeth, then teasing his tongue. Quickly, his pleasantly shocked instincts responded and he answered her kiss with one of his own, growling low in his throat, burying his fingers in her thick, auburn hair.

Reluctantly, she pulled away, breathless, her eyes bright, cheeks flushed. "I really have to go. We can finish this…conversation later."

"Tonight, if you wish."

She had kissed him again, a soft taste and then she was gone, her throaty laughter soothing to his ears.

Now, as the two girls lead the way to the end of Lighthouse Way, Marty's fingers traced the cracked leather of the bound journal and the thick packet of letters Madison had pressed into her hands. Wondering what to do with them once she got home, Marty spoke up. "Why don't you two join me and Pete for lunch?"

For the first time, the two girls realized it was almost three in the afternoon and that they were starving.

Marty grinned. "Last one to my house has to clean up."

She broke into a run. They followed close behind.

*****

Pete and Tommy were waiting for them on Marty's front porch, eating ice cream. Only ten minutes earlier, the two boys had finished cleaning up the house before Ronald Brye took his leave. The orange cat had disappeared upstairs and refused to come out.

Now they watched as first Cassie, then Katie and last Marty stumbled into the yard.

"Well, it's about friggin' time," Pete said, indignant. "Where the hell have you guys been?"

"Up at Madison's place," Marty panted, sucking in air to fill her lungs. She scented something in the air, frowned. "Pete…"

"While you guys were having all the fun," Pete went on dramatically, oblivious to his older sister's glare, "Tommy and I not only went grocery shopping, we defended your home against ants, cleaned it from top to bottom, called the police, painted the back fence, ordered pizza and…"

"Pete." The growl in his sister's voice was unmistakable, but what made him take a step back was the look in her eyes.

"Whoa, baby," he said, startled.

Marty took a deep breath. "What happened?"

Pete gulped, tried to speak and found that his voice wouldn't work. Tommy spoke for him

"Your house was broken into," he said. "It was pretty bad, ma'am."

She sighed. "I used to baby-sit you, Tommy. You can call me 'Marty'."

"Yes, ma'am, I mean, Marty." He turned pink. "Anyway, I ran and got your dad and he called the police and…"

"To make a long story short," Pete interrupted, "we think it was Bessie."

*****

The post office's bell tower rang out the fifth hour as Jimmy Moore took the steps up to the door of Olson's Bar with care, one dirt-grimed hand on the knob, the other scratching behind his ear.

His blood-shot gaze swept the empty streets, the street lights strange, hooded aliens in the gathering mist from the ocean. Just up the street, Weaver's Garage had its lights on – it would stay open for another half hour or so. He could hear the surf pounding against the rocks, taste the salt in the air. He could hear something else pounding in a steady beat under the surf. Several steady beats.

He shook his head, his gaze moving to the thickly wooded hills that surrounded the town, a frown crossing his face.

When he had been unable to take a clear shot at the wolf-man, he had gone home to his tiny single-wide home in the trailer park in the south end of the Bay. His plan was to find a way to monitor the Madison place, but the shadow had ix-nayed that idea. She had a better idea and they stayed up until dawn, going over it.

His body flushed, heat pooling deep below his belt, stiffening, as he recalled what else they had……discussed.

His gaze shifted, passing over the ocean, the tiny harbor and wharf, registering only the thick forests above the town. There were mountains behind the forests, hidden from his sight from this perspective. But go out on a boat, and the range would reveal itself, slowly, like an angry god rising from the bowels of hell…..

He blinked, snorted at his own fanciful ideas. He could not see Wolf's Head Peak from this perspective, for which the town had been named, but he knew it was there; he could almost feel its presence.

But it was not a god, angry or not – just rocks, silt and dirt.

He opened the door and went inside, the smoky atmosphere swallowing him up. At the bar, the owner, Jack Olson, set him with a wave and a heady beer at the counter. The two regulars, Clayton and Ross, sat at the far end of the bar counter.

They mumbled greetings before returning to an argument over some strange noises they'd heard the night before. In the far corner to Jimmy's left, a skinny woman in tight jeans and a loose tank top had draped herself over the jukebox, feeding it loose change and punching in her music choices. He had never seen her prior to this night, but Jimmy thought it very likely that they would soon be making acquaintance with each other before the third song was over.

In the back, the hack reporter Dan Burman was slumped over his table, snoring, his right hand clasped loosely around his half-empty mug.

Warren Zevon came on, howling over the speakers.

Jimmy took a seat at the far end of the bar, only half-listening to the conversation.

"I'm tellin you it was comin from the forest," Clayton was saying over the music, waving his cigar to make a point. "Up behind the Madison place. Howlin."

Jimmy felt his skin prickle at the name, his thoughts going to the woman who lived there alone and he shivered. Crazy old woman gave him the creeps.

"It was dogs." Even over the music, Jimmy heard Ross's low drone. The old man sounded uninterested in the subject. "It was dogs you heard, y'old cuss."

"I know dogs when I hear em, boy." Ross and Clayton had been in grade school together over eighty years ago. "Didn't sound like dogs."

"Coyote, then. Have lots of those around, too."

"Maybe…" Clayton sounded unsure of himself. "Coulda been, but they must've been big ones."

"Why do you say that, Clay?" Jimmy spoke before he realized he'd even opened his mouth and for a minute, he thought the other man would clam up.

But, after considering him silently for several seconds, Clayton replied, "Sounded to me like wolves."

Ross laughed scornfully. "Must've been drunk, Clay. There hasn't been any wolves here in over a hundred years."

Clayton scowled at Ross. "I know my own ears. Drunk or not, I know wolves when I hear em." He eyed Jimmy, daring him to disbelieve.

But Jimmy was not interested in insulting the old man.

THIRTY-EIGHT

Mike turned down Fry Street, his limp a little more pronounced than usual as he walked home. He felt some pain, but nothing a couple of aspirins and a hot shower wouldn't take care of. Maybe he wouldn't work out at the gym tomorrow, or at least not so hard. His leg twinged and he grimaced. Maybe he'd skip the gym altogether.

Thinking this, he glanced over at the old homestead – Marty's home now. The lights were on in the living room and for just a moment, he could almost see his mother calling her family to dinner, laughing when his father caught her round the waist and planting a loud kiss on her cheek… He shook his head, clearing his mind of the past.

Then Pete popped up, an expression of utter surprise on his face, and Mike almost laughed out loud.

He saw the Williams boy and the Blake girl watch as Cassie and Marty debated with Pete. It looked to be very serious. Must be over pepperoni pizza.

Grinning, Mike turned away from his childhood home and entered his yard. His leg twinged again as he climbed the steps, his briefcase feeling heavier than usual. Ignoring it, he opened his front door and went inside, dropping the briefcase next to the umbrella stand.

"Ellen, I'm home!"

No answer. Glancing at the old grandfather clock Ellen had painstakingly restored, he took a moment to admire her work. Recalling her enthusiasm when she dug it out from under a pile of clothes at the old Hallens place thirty miles away, he felt his heart skip a beat – she came alive with her work.

The clock's ticking brought him back to the present – he saw that it was almost five and realized she was most likely still at her shop

Well, good. He had time to clean up and start planning dinner. Maybe this time, he could find a way to unlock the reason or reasons behind his wife's animosity towards his sister.

He wanted to understand, was desperate to. It hurt that the two women he valued most in his life could not at least be civil. He hoped to make Ellen understand his hurt, or at least try.

Thinking this, he went down the hall to the master bedroom and a hot shower.

*****

Ellen Brye was, indeed, at her shop, doing the final sweep in the preparations for closing up her antique repair and restoration shop. Around her were various artifacts, large and small, from people in town, hoping to rediscover a treasure that lay hidden underneath the grit of time.

But it was not on these time-travelers that consumed her thoughts – it was her life with her husband and his sister. Her sister-in-law.

It was a question she had asked herself a number of times, on different occasions – why did she so resent Marty for pursuing her dream when it had been her, Ellen's, choice to stay behind? Did she, like Marty, dream of one day leaving the Bay, bound for some grand trip that would change her life?

Instead, she had stayed behind, with Mike. Watching him raise his younger siblings while his father mourned.

The courses she took that paved the way for her shop weren't the same as it might have been had she left. And, if she were honest with herself, it really wasn't so much Mike's taking on the role of raising of the twins that had held him here, in the Bay, as it was the accident that had shattered both his leg and his dreams.

Unaware that she was doing it, having done it so many times it had become habit, she surveyed her shop, proud of her skills in the art of restoring the past and the doors it had opened for her. She fingered the moonstone ring Mike had given her as a birthday gift absently.

She had liked watching him with Pete and Cassie, liked the way he fathered them, watched out for them. Found herself wondering if he would raise his own children the same way, sometimes. Okay, a LOT.

They married in August of 1968 – Marty had been there, holding the twins' hands, joy for her brother tempered by…..something.

It occurred to Ellen, as she moved around her shop in 1978, that Marty had avoided the reverend Williams at their wedding. Then she dismissed the thought.

Because, truth be told, it was the children that made her so angry. The lack of them, to be more accurate. Ten years, and no children.

She and Mike had never been shy about sex. The first years of their marriage, they had been at it like bunnies, never worrying when she didn't catch.

Turning the sign in her window from *Open* to *Closed*, she frowned, her thoughts itching to turn back to Marty.

She knew it hurt Mike that she hated Marty and it grieved her that she hurt him, but the feeling seemed so much out of her control that she felt both frightened and helpless to stop it. She didn't think she'd always felt this way – in high school, while not the best of friends, they'd been at least friendly and hung out with the same crowd.

And then Denise Brye had died at Marty's eighteenth birthday party.

Ellen shut off the overhead lights and locked the door behind her. She took a deep breath, aware of the sun's golden hues as it began its slow descent for the night, then began walking the ten blocks home, her thoughts twisting like black snakes.

Her eyes went to the hills east of the Madison place, where Wolf Heights was now currently stalled because of the graves found there.

For a brief moment her footsteps slowed, then stopped, a vague memory nagging at her. She tried not to look too closely at it, tried to relax her mind and let it surface on its own, but the memory wouldn't come.

Shaking her head, she resolved to talk to her husband about her feelings towards his sister as best she could.

Hopefully, there might be a way to work through this.

Feeling lighter, she continued to make her way home.

*****

Myrna Kowolsky sat in the leather chair and tried not to glare at the heavy-set man sitting across from her.

She succeeded only marginally.

Mayor Franklin Marlowe looked like an over-ripe pear — it didn't help that his suit, now wrinkled with the day's exertions, was a pale green. It was made even worse by the fact that the man's sweat was beginning to role off of him in waves and the day hadn't even topped 80 degrees.

She tried hard to focus on his words, but her nose kept twitching at his stench. Her favorite bracelet — a simple affair with moonstones — felt suddenly uncomfortably tight on her wrist, but she refused to allow the mayor see anything that he would perceive as a weakness.

"…understand your concern," he was saying, "but with the discovery of the graves, I'm afraid the development of the Heights and the opening ceremonies are unavoidably delayed."

By that damn Tanner boy and his nosy-parker

mother, Myrna thought sourly, but did not say aloud.

Instead, she said, "And what about the Bay's upcoming anniversary?"

Mayor Marlowe shrugged. "That's a separate matter. I don't recall it being a part of the festivities with the Heights. There is no need for concern."

Myrna Kowolsky held on to her temper by the barest of margins. "I am concerned over my contract with the city, Mayor. Whether or not the Heights is ever finished and the ceremonies for it go forward as planned is beside the point. My contract also includes the Bay's anniversary, which I had made a point of adding and to which you signed off on."

Mayor Marlowe frowned. "And your point?"

She smiled. "I expect to be paid in full. I have already spent a considerable amount of money on orders for foods that you, yourself, specified for the event. There is no refund."

"Myrna, please." Marlowe tried to look pained, but managed to look piggish instead. "Your contract for both events will be honored. Now, if you'll excuse me, I must stop by the sheriff's office for an update on the Wyatt and Clarke murders."

Myrna could not help it – the glare she'd held onto for so long won out and Marlowe flinched.

"You had best be sure that it is," she said, her voice cold. Rising, she left, anxious to be away from the close quarters of his office…and his stench.

THIRTY-NINE

"So what are you going to do about Bessie?"

Pete posed the question as he helped himself to another slice of double pepperoni pizza. Marty didn't answer right away, her expression thoughtful.

They were in the living room, sitting on over-sized cushions on the floor or lounging on the couch. With all the food on the coffee table, the orange cat ought to have been all over the place, demanding expected treats. But it had fled upstairs in an orange streak when the police had freed it earlier in the day. Now it had taken refuge under Marty's bed and growled low in its throat when she tried to coax him out.

He refused to make amends with Marty, even when the human had done what John Dylan did not and put a scrambled egg in its kitty crunchies.

Apparently, the cat blamed her for the indignities he had suffered.

So, she left the cat alone, hiding the journal in her underwear drawer before going back downstairs to her younger sibs and their friends.

Now, amused by the antics of Abbott and Costello as they fled Bela Lugosi and Lon Chaney Jr. on the TV,

Marty said, "Nothing."

Pete was outraged. "Christ, Marty, she broke into your house and trashed the place."

"Circumstantial evidence."

All four teens regarded her suspiciously, but Marty was absorbed in the movie and didn't see.

Pete eyed the situation and decided to change the subject. "So, what were you all doing up at Madison's?"

Marty waved a hand. "Spying on me."

Pete perked up. "Really? Any dirty secrets you care to share with me, your brother?"

"We weren't spying," Cassie said firmly. She felt Marty's gaze heavy on her and flushed. "Okay, so we were spying. But only because there was nothing else to do and it looked like they wouldn't have shared what we found out."

"Like what?"

"Werewolves."

Tommy gaped. "What?"

Pete blinked. "Come again?"

So Marty explained everything to them, beginning with her encounter with Riley in the woods on Saturday and the wound that led them to Madison's. She spoke of the silver bullet the old woman had pulled out of Riley. Of the diary Holly Wyatt had mailed to Marty before her death. Of the revelations that a community had lived here prior to the date listed as the Bay's founding.

Of those within that community, one had been Riley as a boy and the other had been Cowyn Fraser, maternal great-great grandfather to the Brye children. That this unknown community that was thriving before the arrival of Jonas Brye had been one peopled with werewolves. Marty said nothing of the vampire that Madison claimed to be hiding within the Bay — it was just too much, even for her.

Pete sat up suddenly, his face open with shock. "Mom was a werewolf?"

"Damn," Tommy said softly. He looked at Marty. "And my dad knows all of this?"

"Yes," Marty said. "His own great-great grandfather was there, helped save those people."

"Wow." Tommy fell silent.

Pete shook his head. "Man, I don't believe this. Mysterious gunmen, werewolves, silver bullets, and murder. Has Barnabas Collins decided to relocate to Wolf's Head Bay or what?"

They all laughed.

*****

When they left, Marty's, instead of breaking off and heading to their separate homes, the four teens headed out for the cliffs just south of the cemetery, overlooking the bay.

Perched on a protruding rock, they watched the surf as it pounded the beach below, rocks clattering in sharp cracks as the water pulled back.

"So what now?" Katie asked.

"We should split up," Cassie said.

Pete picked up a small rock and hurled it over the cliff. "Why?"

Cassie sighed. "Someone's got to keep an eye on Bessie and someone's got to do research."

"I'll do the research," Pete volunteered and frowned when Cassie shook her head in the negative. "Why not?"

"Because you're no good at it. That's why you're in summer school, dummy. You and Tommy do the spying." Cassie indicated Katie. "We'll do the research."

Pete sighed heavily. "Oh, all right. When do we start?"

"No time like the present."

"Fine. Come on, Tommy." The two boys began walking towards town.

Katie watched them go. Cassie, in the meantime, had picked up a handful of good-sized pebbles and began chucking them, one by one, over the cliff and into the surf below.

"What interests me," she said slowly, "is the silver bullet. Who knew that Riley was a werewolf? And why shoot him?"

Katie shrugged. "I don't know."

Cassie hurled the rest of her pebbles over, suddenly impatient. "Well, that's what we've got to find out. Maybe the diary has some clues."

"What about Reverend Dan?"

Cassie waved that aside. "Riley was shot on Sunday. I don't think Reverend Dan even met him until today."

"Doesn't mean anything."

She nodded, her eyes troubled. "I guess you're right."

Katie kicked a rock. "Besides, I don't see what the diary has to do with anything. It's over a hundred years old."

Cassie started walking back towards town. "Who says that what's going on now is based on the present?"

FORTY

Reverend Dan sat alone in his living room, the shades pulled down, a single lamp on to chase away the shadows. In his hand was a glass, ice melting, the sharp bite of whiskey rising from it.

He thought of Tommy, his only son, and wondered where he was, then shook his head. Most likely he was with Pete Brye, at the movies or Myrna's. He would call around and ask. Later. Soon, he would have company.

He had tried hard to dismiss what he'd learned earlier in the day, aided by more than a few drinks, but couldn't — it had only cemented his own fears inspired by his ancestor's diaries. The whiskey only made his mind slip towards that dark truth faster than had he been sober.

He heard the key turn in the front door and felt the unbearably black weight lift from his heart.

"Good evening, Dan," Daria Brennan said softly from behind him. He stood, a bit unsteady on his feet, and turned. She was before him, her dress in a soft heap on the floor, her body gloriously naked. The scars on her back were cast in shadow and he could not see them, but he would feel them before long. The scar on her neck remained hidden, both by shadow and the curl of her hair.

He knew that and became suddenly aware of his own hard desire.

She closed the distance, bringing her mouth to his in a deep kiss – he buried his fingers in her thick black hair, kissing her back, rediscovering her body with his own, his mouth, his hands.

When they parted, breathing heavy, she nuzzled his left ear, whispered, "Take me upstairs and I'll show you what you want to know."

In moments, they were upstairs, in his bed, naked, sweating, the sheets kicked back, the only sounds their cries of release as they engaged in the most primitive and intimate of acts.

And when it was over, his throat hoarse, he surprised himself by weeping.

*****

Pete and Tommy found Bessie with no trouble – she was at home, fussing in her garden over which roses to pick.

They ducked behind a neighbor's hedges, concealing themselves well.

Bessie tramped towards the backyard, passing close to the boys, then came back, dragging a hose. She was muttering to herself, but neither boy could make out what she was saying.

There was a rumble of pressure – water suddenly rained on them when she turned the hose on the hedges. By the time she moved to another section both boys were soaked to the skin.

"Man, spying is the pits," Tommy whispered.

"No kidding," Pete agreed.

A car pulled up and parked on the curb. Peering through the hedge, the two boys saw Eddie Payne step out of his police cruiser and approach Bessie with caution. The water finally stopped.

"Deputy Payne, this is a pleasant surprise," they heard her say.

"Evening, ma'am," he said. "I was wondering if I

could talk to you for a minute?"

"Why, of course." She dropped the hose and stepped closer to Eddie. "What's the problem?"

"Well, it seems that there was a break-in over at Marty Brye's place," he said. "I was wondering if you had any information that might help?"

"I don't see how I could," she said, sounding doubtful. "We aren't especially close and I only see her in relation to her father."

"The reason why I'm asking," Eddie said slowly, "is that you were seen in the area."

From their hiding place in the hedge, Pete and Tommy could see the woman's face harden. Either Eddie didn't see or he chose not to.

Then she was all smiles, gushing over the embarrassed policeman. "There must be some mistake. I've been in town shopping, that's for sure, otherwise I've been here, in my garden."

They went around in circles like that for several minutes – then, letting it go, Eddie took his leave, not seeing Bessie Mills' cold expression.

After he had left, Bessie stomped up the front porch, slamming the front door shut behind her.

Cautiously, trying to disturb the hedge as little as possible, the two boys emerged from behind it and peered into Bessie's yard. Nothing. A light went on in one window – they crept into the yard and peered in.

Bessie was in the kitchen, surrounded by an over-abundance of porcelain bric-a-brac, fixing herself a light supper of a sandwich, fruit cup and tea. On the counter lay several napkins neatly folded into triangles.

She placed all these items onto a tray, which she carried out to the living room and set onto the coffee table. Turning on the TV, she settled into a hideous chair and began to eat, her eyes glued to the screen.

After watching several minutes of this, Pete nudged Tommy. "What say we pick this up tomorrow? I don't think she's going to do anything."

"Sure."

They crept back the way they came – upon reaching the street corner, they heaved a sigh of relief and headed their separate ways home.

*****

She sat in her chair, her eyes glued to the game show and its brightly colored panels, but she wasn't paying attention to it. Nor, as was her usual habit, did she make disparaging remarks regarding the glazed-over expressions of the contestants.

Her attention was elsewhere, heightened, she knew, by the visits the shadow that had made to her on several occasions since…since *he* had fired her…

She turned her mind away from that – this new thing was better, better than what she had wanted. Seeing, smelling, even her sense of taste was different. Unbidden, her gaze fell on the ring that circled the forefinger of her right hand and she sighed, her small eyes dreamy. It was hers now, not *his*, and she prized it above all her possessions. The shadow had understood that.

It was a woman, after all. Who could understand better?

She listened as the two boys crept away from her window, planning to come back at a later date. She smiled – let them. They would not have enough time to regret such an action, but they would.

Sipping her tea, she allowed her attention to be drawn into the game show, sure now that her little followers were gone and that she was quite alone.

It did not take long for the shadow to descend upon her and rip her head from her shoulders as easily as plucking a grape. The shadow carried her still-warm and twitching corpse from her home and into the gathering darkness.

*****

To go by the furious Polish coming from Myrna's office,

294

one would think that the woman was being mugged or abusing the mugger.

Barry paused in the middle of making himself a shake to glance over at the office door, worried. He had been working at the diner for a little more than six months now, and Myrna's behavior bewildered him. Tonight, it flat out scared him.

Annie caught his look and grinned. "Don't worry. She's always like this right before a big catering job. Usually it's the grand old Fourth of July breakfast that puts her into such a snit. It's a creative thing."

Barry turned back to his shake. "So what's the gig that's driving her buggy now?"

"The Wolf Heights project." Elise handed him a glass and straw.

Barry looked confused. "I thought the big to-do over at the site put it on hold."

Annie snorted, her hands deep in soapy water as she began washing dishes. "You mean the bones they dug up? Won't amount to much, if you want my opinion. Not like it's some Indian burial ground up there. They settled further north, didn't even come down this way." She waved a soapy hand, indicating her meaning. "No, some poor travelers that took sick or worse, is what's making all this fuss, guaranteed. That and Cory Tanner's nosy parker mother."

The office door opened. "Too much talking is going on! I can see Mr. Clayton walking up the street!"

The door slammed shut. A picture fell, glass cracking.

Elise picked up a pad and began writing. Done, she tore off the ticket and handed it to Barry.

He looked at it. "Ham and cheese on rye, heavy on the onions, no tomatoes and a little hot sauce on the side."

Annie looked at Elise with approval. "You're getting good."

Elise shrugged, but it was clear that she was pleased. "Well, he orders the same thing every day, so how could I not remember?"

Annie looked at Barry. "Fix Clay a coffee shake."
Then she went to clean up the frame and glass.

FORTY-ONE

That evening, Ronald Brye sat at a quiet table deep in the local library, surrounded by books on tracks and the animals that made them. Sitting prominently before him was the photo of the track that John Dylan had given him.

A shadow fell over him and he started.

Mrs. Talbot was gazing down at him, a curious smile on her face. "Mr. Brye, the library is getting ready to close."

"What?" Ronald looked at his watch – it was reading five minutes before eight. He blinked. "Time does go by."

"It does, indeed." She led the way forward, pausing to wait while he gathered his books. "Your book came in today, Mr. Brye. Did you want to check it out now?"

"Hmm? Oh, no, I can come back in the morning."

Mrs. Talbot's smile deepened – he found himself liking it very much. He studied her closely. She couldn't be more than fifty, he thought. Not much older than Denise when she died. He struggled to remember Mrs. Talbot's first name – it was something decidedly old-fashioned. Lavinia? No, Letitia. She was a divorcee, no children. He couldn't recall what the reasons were behind the divorce.

She caught his glance, blushed. He stared, fascinated.

Thoughts of her past faded and he wondered about her future.

She held the door open, waiting for him to pass through so that she could lock it behind him. He paused.

"Mrs. Talbot, I mean, Letitia," he stammered. She looked at him expectantly. With a sudden impulse, he asked, "Would you consider going out to dinner with me tomorrow night?" She only stared at him, surprised. He reddened. "I realize that it's short notice, so I don't expect you to say yes…."

She interrupted him, smiling, her face softening into its youthful past. "I would very much like to have dinner with you, Ronald."

They stood in the doorway of the library for a moment more, each consumed by his or her own thoughts of possibilities; then Ronal Brye left, clutching his papers and books tightly, feeling as though he was floating on air.

Behind him, Letitia Talbot disappeared back into the library as it began to shut down for the night.

*****

Mike found himself standing outside the cemetery with no clear memory of how he got there. His feet were sore and he spared them a glance – he has taken off his sneakers at home, just before his shower, and had put on something else not so comfortable. Leather shoes met his gaze, partially hidden by the cuff of his khaki trousers. So much for making a little effort and looking nice for Ellen at dinner. The way the meal had ended, he may as well have stuck to jeans and sneakers.

He shook his head, turning his gaze up to look at the old, ornate, wrought iron arch-way. The cemetery's original name was a series of curved bits of metal – close up, it was hard to disentangle, but stand back far enough, it would spell out *Wolf Peak Cemetery*.

He was distantly aware of the pounding surf, of the mist coming off the bay and the chill in the air.

Shaking his head, he looked at his watch. Eight-fifteen. Only forty-five minutes since he'd left the house to think, forty-five minutes since the fight that had spurred an irrational fury forced him to leave before he'd said or done something he could not take back.

Dinner had been pleasant – he remembered that, pleased that he had been the one to inspire the soft expression of love to his wife's eyes when she saw the roses in the vase they'd received as a wedding gift and the lit candles on the table. They had spoken of her day at the shop, of his classes, each aware that what they were really doing was circling another, bigger subject, neither quite sure how to breach it. Equally apparent was that neither wanted to be the first to address the subject.

Marty. Even now, Mike couldn't remember what had been said, how it started. But he remembered the look in her eyes when she spoke first. Fear, he realized now. She had been afraid – of his reaction, of what he'd do.

"I don't understand them," she'd said, her voice quiet. She reached across the table, taking his hand in hers, squeezing. The candlelight glistened in her eyes. "My feelings scare me. I know that it's irrational, for me to feel about Marty as I do, but they feel bigger than me, too. Like they're going to swallow me up."

He'd gripped her hand, bringing it to his lips, brushing her knuckles lightly. She'd reddened and looked away.

"I know it's hard for you," she went on, her voice even lower than before. "And I wish it would go away. Because the last thing I want to do is hurt you, Mike."

That, he realized now, was the last quiet moment. He had opened his mouth and, instead of being what he should have been – her husband – he'd instead become what he'd hated most about his father when his mother had been alive. He'd seen it in Ellen's eyes, the way she had shut down and grew cold.

"I think you're putting way to much importance on how helpless you feel," he had said, recoiling from the words even as he spoke them. "You have a choice, Ellen. All you need to do is decide."

It disintegrated from there – she flung the bowl of hot tomato sauce at him, scalding his chest and stormed down the hall to their bedroom. Before she locked the door on him, she threw out his high school football trophy. It hit the wall and clattered to the floor, intact. The wall would need patching and painting.

Mike screamed through the door until he was hoarse, his rage a hot, living creature inside his chest. Then, grabbing his coat from the hall closet, he stormed outside into the fading twilight, unwilling to stay and find out if things would get worse.

And now, here he was, in front of the last place he'd expected to be. He hesitated, then pushed the heavy gate open and went inside.

He hadn't been inside since the day his mother had been buried here. He wondered if that meant something, then dismissed it. Lots of people didn't visit graveyards, even if they had relatives in them. Didn't mean a darn thing.

He walked down the well-kept paths, turning this way and that until he came to his mother's grave. He knelt beside it, his leg stiff.

"Hi, Mom," he said, feeling – well, face it. Stupid. He knew Marty did this, had done this, but it still felt stupid. All the same, he found comfort in saying her name, a word that had not truly passed his lips after she had died. "I suppose you know Marty's back in town, so I won't bore you with those details." God, he sounded so dumb. What was he doing here? And then he heard himself say, "I got in a really bad fight with Ellen, Mom. You know Ellen. She's Hank Farley's daughter? Anyway, she was trying to be honest with me and I blew it. I pulled a Dad on her and it just fell apart. How do I fix this? I love her. I – "

He broke off, suddenly alert. He'd sensed something out of the corner of his eye, a shadow of some kind. A big one. Slowly, he rose to his feet, trying to ignore the uneasy feeling ticking the pit of his stomach.

"I have to go," he said, his voice sounding tight to his own ears. "I'll try to come back more often. Maybe with Marty and the twins."

Touching her gravestone, Mike began to walk back the way he came, struggling to remain calm. That sense of the shadow was growing stronger – he heard a rustling in the bushes that he knew wasn't caused by the wind. He could see the gate ahead of him – only twenty yards away. It seemed further. He quickened his pace – the shadow matched his stride.

By the time he'd reached the gate, he was almost running, his bad leg hitching every other step. And when he reached Chaney Street, the police station in sight, he felt a sense of relief.

Until the roar from behind and the sharp raking of claws down his back, he hadn't known the shadow was still with him.

He screamed, louder than he'd thought possible. The last thing he saw before the darkness took him was a large, inhuman claw.

FORTY-TWO

She was standing in the backyard of her home, as it had been fifteen years earlier, her friends crowding around her, wishing her well on her birthday – Tavis was behind them, his eyes connecting with hers, as if they were the only two in existence. It didn't puzzle her dreaming self that he could not have possibly been there at the time. Her mother was standing on the back porch, one hand shading her eyes against the sun before she went back into the house, ostensibly to fetch something. Another gift? Never mind, Tavis was here...

And that had been the last time she had thought of her mother until she heard glass cracking, heard deafening silence before the screams began, saw her mother swinging by a rope from the attic window, only inches above the balcony off the master bedroom. The dark shade of blue had begun to give way to purple – her mother was dead.

A shadowy movement from the attic caught her gaze and she stepped forward, the light reflecting off the windows almost blinding. Then the screams did begin, but she did not recognize the voice at first. Only when she passed into darkness did she realize it was her own.

Then she found herself in the forest, her path illuminated by the full moon. She was no longer the scared and unhappy girl, running from the horror of death, but a woman on the precipice of discovering her true nature. Her bare feet glided over the warm, damp earth, her hair soft about her face. The light cotton dress she wore flowed over her hips, caressing her legs sensuously as she climbed the hill, her eyes searching, following a trail she had trod upon before.

Her senses heightened, she picked up his scent easily — her pulse quickened, heat raced through her like lightning.

She looked at the tree before her — it curved slightly, as if protecting the tiny hollow where she'd come upon him twice now. Climbing down into the hollow, she kneeled to touch the flattened grass, her skin tingling as she recalled his nudity.

Then she stood, knowing where he would be if she could not find him here. She walked on until the small boulder where he had been shot by the silver bullet came into view. She went to the boulder, standing close, her hand caressing its smooth-rough contours.

The tiny hairs on the back of her neck prickled, as if responding to the electricity in the air and she knew, without turning, that he was standing behind her. When his hand touched her, tracing small circles on the back of her neck, she shivered, feeling delicious, aroused, warm. Her hand covered his — he stood beside her, drawing her into his arms as they stretched out on the grass.

The heat of his body enveloped her in waves and she felt alive, exhilarated, her lips parting slightly when she looked into his eyes and saw herself reflected there. She could feel-hear his heart beating restlessly against his chest and was not surprised to realize that her own heart was beating in sync.

He began raining gentle kisses on her hair — she turned her face up so that he could shower those kisses elsewhere. When he finally lowered his head to claim her mouth, her body responded with such fierce hunger that she almost tore his slacks at the seams in an effort to free him.

"Easy, little wolf," he murmured against her lips. "I've waited for you, now you wait for me."

She only moaned in reply, savoring the shape of his mouth, his teeth and delighting in his inquisitive tongue. His leg resting between hers, they continued to kiss slow and deep, her right hand, now resting above her head, linked with his left. His free hand traced the outer swell of her breast down to the curve of her hip and she shifted against him, restless and aware of the stiffening bulge in his slacks, the answering heat in her loins, wanting it.

Somehow, their clothes had come off — she had no memory of yanking her cotton dress over her head nor of how Tavis managed to divest himself of his own clothes while they were still touching, teasing each other. Naked, they explored their bodies and when he finally lay between her legs, his cock at her entrance, his mouth on one breast, she wrapped her legs around him, lifted her hips and took him into her.

It was long and slow, pleasurable. Each stroke lifted them to new heights and when she felt her orgasm rip through her, he followed close behind. Then they simply lay together, entangled.

Her body shuddered unpleasantly — she gasped, felt her joints grind together in painful unison and she gripped his arm tightly, her nails digging into his skin, drawing blood.

She looked to him, feeling helpless. He gazed back at her, his eyes sorrowful and wise. "It is beginning." He kissed her brow, a light touch. "I am here, but you must go through it."

Thick patches of silky chestnut fur covered her forearms — pain ripped through her and she screamed, arching her back, seeking to escape what she knew she could not. Her bones cramped — she could feel them shift into some new shape. Her vision seemed to be able to pick out shadows she had not noticed before. She could smell the musky odor of their sex intermingling with the scents of the forest. Below, almost ten miles away, she could hear the townspeople mutter in their sleep.

Her body wracked with pain, she could only curl up on her side and watch as her skin and bones rippled, her hands reshaping themselves into paws, fur pelt growing fast and thick. She could feel her tail grow out and her face — oh, God her face! She looked over at Riley — he had already shifted into wolf form. Now he stood over her, whining in sympathy, licking her new ears, but unable to do more than offer support.

Her body shuddered one last time and then it was over. She was wolf now, weak and tired, but wolf.

He licked her ear once more — she rolled her eyes at him, panting, too tired to resent his playful air as he stood over her. He had been doing this forever — it was not new to him.

Second nature.

At last, she found the strength to sit up on her haunches, carefully taking stock of her new form. She was surprised to find that she still retained her human intelligence, though it was now tempered by her new nature. Whatever that might be.

She looked at him. Even in his wolf eyes, she could see his heart. It was hers. She nestled up to him, wanting him to show her more...

She woke up abruptly, her joints and body aching as if she'd been running. There was a pleasant heaviness to her limbs as well, as if she had actually made love with Riley instead of dreaming, before....

She shifted on her side, gazing at the moonlight spilling through her window.

Her hand caressed the empty pillow next to hers and she almost saw his image lying there.

"I wish it hadn't been a dream." Her own voice startled her and she laughed, pulling the blanket over her head.

*****

At home once more, Riley stood in his darkened bedroom, naked, drinking in the night's air and sounds. The open window next to his bed faced the south-west side of town, which was now hidden by the marine layer. Only the line of orange smudges of light told him where the harbor lay. On the east wall of the room, another open window looked out onto the forest and he inhaled its perfume every night, as he did now.

He had left the Madison place at sundown in his wolf form, keeping to the forest and the trails that wound their way around and into the town below. The route he chose took him directly past the Heights construction area, void of activity until later in the week, the bright yellow Caution tape flapping in the breeze, tied securely to wooden stakes. He was well aware of his surroundings, the sounds and smells of the forest, even more so now in case his mysterious shooter decided to make his presence known.

He arrived at the back door of his single-storey home without incident, shifted back into human form, then went inside to shower and change into fresh clothing. By half past seven, he had fixed a dinner of half a dozen burgers, toasted up the buns and ate leisurely, each burger fortified with pickles, lettuce, tomatoes, ketchup and mayonnaise. He washed each one down with a beer, ignoring the loneliness as he would a gnat. He went over his notes regarding the mass grave at the Heights for an hour, making notations of questions to ask as he read. It was early when he decided to turn in for the night and he fell asleep quickly and easily.

He woke with a start from a dream in which he and Marty had at last made love before her first transformation into wolf. Heat stirred in his loins at the memory, but he ignored it, wanting peace and finding only marginal success.

"I wish it hadn't been a dream."

It was only a whisper, carried on the wind, but he knew it was her, recognized her voice's timber.

"Neither do I," he replied softly.

1 JULY, 1852

My dearest friend,

Ten days have passed. I can barely see to write, but I must put down what happened that dreadful day when — no. Be calm. One word at a time.

At half past three on the twenty-first of June, with Mr. Madison and his wife gone missing, the Reverend revealing the true nature of the voyage, my crew uneasy and Billy still unaccounted for, I went from uneasy myself to a high state of panic when I scented smoke. With Stevens and Jones right behind me, I retraced my steps from the dream and led the way to the fire.

It wasn't until we crested the hill that I was finally forced to realize that my unusual dream hadn't been a dream at all, that what Reverend Williams had been speaking of was indeed a reality. Below us, the village where I had been made welcome and had scarcely noticed, being too caught up by the woman at my side, was now engulfed in a ring of flames.

With a torch in one hand and a gleaming knife in the other was Mr. Madison, his voice hoarse. I froze, my eyes caught in the purity of the blade's reflection — and if my dreams were true, that people do indeed change into wolves, then what he held was pure silver. He was fighting off a woman – she bit him savagely on the arm, drawing blood, and he screamed shrilly, slashing at her throat with his blade. It slid in easily and as he drew it out, blood spewed forth and she slumped to the ground, dead. I recognized her as Murel, one of the three from my dream and it was this, more than anything else on that black afternoon, which galvanized me.

Felanna. Where was she?

Ignoring their shouts, I left my men behind. Armed with only my pistol, I ran into the burning village, shouting her name. At one point, Mr. Madison and I abruptly came face to face – blood spattered his visage in a grotesque pattern, his unnaturally pale face wild and resembling nothing human.

In one hand, he still held his torch, its fire out.

"You will stop," I said coldly. "You will not harm these people any longer."

"They are the devil's spawn," he hissed, his eyes feral. "She must die and the land must be cleansed with their blood." He flicked a glance at my pistol. "Kill me, if you can. Others will come to finish what I've started."

Too furious to speak, I raised my weapon and aimed for his heart, but something struck me from behind. Unable to keep my balance, I stumbled to my knees, my head reeling from the blow.

Everything after is a blur – all I see now are faces. Cowyn, young Billy, Tavis Riley, several others. In the midst of the chaos, the Reverend rushed in, brandishing a gun and sword, managing to aid the people with whom I had shared bread. I was not conscious to see this – Alban and Cowyn, with me now in my quarters, have just finished telling me what had happened.

Victor Madison's silver bladed dagger lies on my desk, a seemingly innocent tool until picked up. Its handle is an intricately carved piece of pure white ivory, not yet yellowed with age, its shape of a wolf howling.

I have seriously misjudged the two men who had bought passage on my ship and this, as much as the needless slaughter I have witnessed, weighs heavily upon me.

Victor Madison is dead. The Reverend Williams killed him with a single gunshot to the heart. While the dead villagers were buried in a single, large grave on the hill close to the forest, Mr. Madison's body was put to rest apart from them, on the jutting cliff, face down, head pointing towards the water. According to the myths of Billy's people, water kept the unworthy from seeking salvation.

Mrs. Madison had been found tied and gagged in a small clearing a few yards from the decimated village, her infant son lying nearby. She collapsed into a dead faint upon learning of her husband's evil deeds and it was then we discovered two deep and bloody wounds in her neck, just beginning to clot.

One of the villagers had medical experience – it was Alban, of course – and tended to her, though his expression was troubled. Back aboard my ship, Mrs. Madison began to scream at the top of her lugs and thrash about wildly – it took four members of my crew to subdue and physically restrain her, before carrying her to the cabin she had shared with her husband.

Along with my ship's doctor, she remains sedated and is currently sequestered in her cabin. Her son had been taken in by her companion, who was even now being aided by one of the village ladies, who refused to be ignored. It is hoped that Mrs. Madison will forgive herself and accept the help offered.

The village, of course, burned to the ground. The remaining survivors have either fled into the forest for parts unknown with the help of one of the Miwok tribes or have joined me, my crew and are on my ship for the safety of the cities – they are trading in the beauty of nature for the anonymity of a major metropolis. We are only hours away from Portland, Oregon.

My injuries, surprisingly, were slight – scratches, a minor burn and a large bump on the head. It is my heart that hurts the most, however – I never found out what happened to Felanna.

Neither of the two men will tell me – I noticed how easily the subject was changed whenever I tried to glean any information from them regarding her. In the end, I decided not to pursue it and soon bade them good evening.

I sit here at my desk, wondering.......

TUESDAY, JUNE 13, 1978

FORTY-THREE

Driving in the fog had been a big mistake.

Slowing his cruiser to a crawl, Eddie Payne flicked the high beams on, but that made things worse, so he flicked them off and contented himself with squinting. For the life of him, he couldn't understand why he always forgot the yearly June fog and the diminished vision. The distance from his apartment to the station was only three miles, but, as usual, it seemed to take forever.

He'd heard of June Gloom, but this was ridiculous.

Maybe he should have walked…..

Glancing at his watch, he saw that it was four-fifty. Great. He was going to be late again, the fourth time this week. Blaming it on sleepless nights caused by finding a dead, mutilated man was beginning to sound weak, even to him.

A stop sign loomed out of the fog with a suddenness that made his heart skip a beat and he hit the brakes, squinting into the watery light, barely able to see through the thick mist to read the street sign next to it. Clifton Street. He was at the corner of Clifton and Cooper and still had two more blocks to go.

With a sigh, tapping his horn lightly to let others

know he was there, he proceeded with caution. Myrna's diner gleamed at him, the neon sign mysterious in the fog.

He had a sudden craving for pancakes and sausage.

Five minutes later, he was pulling into the police station parking lot, searching for his marked spot, relief heavy in his limbs. Switching off the engine, he let out a huge sigh, glad to be at work finally and not driving. He had just reached the front steps when a dark shadow stumbled out of the fog and collapsed at his feet, groaning.

Eddie jumped back, suddenly aware that he was sweating bullets, his heart pounding in his ears, his hand instinctively reaching for his gun, staring at the dark shape. Even in the dim, gray light he could see it was a man who, by the looks of it, was the loser of a very bad brawl.

The man mumbled something – leaning closer, Eddie thought it sounded something like "wolf".

He sighed. He hated packing the over-inebriated into the drunk tank. Sometimes they cried or sang horribly off-key. One actually threatened to kill him – Eddie recalled with a shudder that it had been Jimmy Moore who had done that.

The smell of liquor would hang over them like a cloud of invisible smoke – Eddie liked the occasional beer, but that was too much.

And it was just last week that Dick Burman threw up all over Eddie's uniform when Eddie tried to help him into the back of the cruiser. He wasn't likely to forget that one very soon.

So what if Burman had been a top reporter who used to work for a San Francisco paper? His love affair with the bottle had derailed his twenty-year career and he had to settle for the *Bay*.

The stench took days to wear off.

The man on the steps groaned again – after a quick look to ascertain that there were no weapons, Eddie knelt beside him. The alcoholic fumes he expected did not assault his nose.

"Come on, buddy," he said, reaching over to shake the man's shoulder. "Time to get up."

The man rolled over easily – Eddie sat back on his heels in shock, staring at Mike Brye's bruised and battered face. Without further thought, Eddie stripped off his jacket and draped it over Mike before bolting into the station, where he told Amelia to call the ambulance and get them the hell over here quick.

And when he finally sat down, the faint sounds of sirens reaching his ears, Eddie decided that next time he would walk.

*****

After breakfast was over, Pete gave their dishes a quick wash in the sink and put them away in the cupboard while Cassie gathered up their back packs and Ronald Brye went into his study.

Done, Pete met Cassie by the front door.

"Later, Dad," he yelled as they sailed out. Their father's soft reply was cut off by the door slamming shut.

"Can you slam the door a little harder, next time?" Cassie asked. "I think you could actually crack it."

"That's my goal in life," Pete said. "Cracking doors."

Cassie laughed. Tommy was waiting for them at the corner.

"What's so funny?" Tommy asked.

"Well –" Pete started to explain, but, as with all jokes, the humor vanished with the telling. Pete gave up when he saw the glazed expression in Tommy's eyes. "Never mind, it wasn't that great anyway."

"Had to be there, huh?"

"Yeah."

"Hey, do you think Ms. Brennan is going to be easier on you now that she's been dating your dad?" Cassie asked.

Tommy blushed, looking away. "Not really. I think she's going to be harder on me *because* she's dating Dad."

Pete stopped abruptly on the sidewalk, slapping a

317

hand to his forehead. "Omigod! And I forgot my homework!"

Cassie looked at him, amused. "Too late to do it now."

"No, I mean, it's done, I just left it at home." Pete turned, began retracing his steps back to the house. "Seriously, it's summer school, it's the second day and already I have homework due. What gives?"

His sister snorted. "It's a condensed version of the regular school year."

Pete sighed. "I guess. I'll catch up with you guys later."

He hurried up the sidewalk, disappearing around the corner. Cassie and Tommy watched, then continued on towards the high school, their pace slow, easy.

After a minute, their hands linked together.

*****

Pete hurried up the walk to his house, whistling softly under his breath. Not wanting to catch hell for not being at school (even if it was to get his homework), he slipped in through the front door, closing it quietly behind him.

He listened for a moment – except for his breathing and the faint cries of the gulls, the house was quiet. No father to pounce on him and demand explanations, awkward or otherwise. Quick and light on his feet, he hurried upstairs to his room, pausing in the doorway briefly. He scanned his room – spotting his notebook on his desk, he went in, grabbed it and hurried back downstairs. He was at the front door, his hand on the knob when a high-pitched whine stopped him.

Ears straining, Pete was rewarded when the noise repeated itself. High-pitched, one note, it sounded mechanical. And it was coming from the garage.

He hesitated, not wanting to get caught, but wanting to know what the sound was, all the same.

The garage won.

Stashing his pack and notebook behind the couch,

Pete went through the house and out the back door, crouching down and creeping around to the far side of the garage. He didn't question the impulse to do this – it just seemed safer to remain hidden. He pulled himself up to the window cautiously, shading the sun's glare from his eyes.

Ronald Brye was at his work station, goggles perched high on his head and wearing a leather apron over his faded jeans. He wore no shirt underneath the apron, and his back, marked with deep and twisted scars, was visible to his hidden son.

Pete frowned – how did his father get those scars?

And when?

Ronald Brye was studying a tiny object that glinted in the pale light emanating from the lamp above him.

Curious, Pete pressed his face close against the glass, trying not fog the window with his breath, wanting a better look at what his father held in his hands. What he saw made his mouth dry and he swallowed hard – what was his father doing with his mother's jewelry?

Ronald Brye dropped two pairs of earrings into a thick metal cup, pulled his goggles down and flipped a switch. The high-pitched whine he'd heard earlier filled Pete's ears and he tried to plug out the sound. His father picked something up, shifting his position at the same time. It was a blow torch, its blue flame a tiny, bright spot that could singe his eyebrows off.

Pete frowned as his father held the flame underneath the cup. Why was he melting down Mom's jewelry like that? And for what?

A hand touched his arm – he barely managed to cover the yell in time with both hands. Katie stood before him, arms crossed, brows quirked.

"What do you think you're doing? You're going to be late for mmmph!" She glared at him furiously, eyes blazing.

Pete was unrepentant, firming his grip over her mouth. "I'll let go," he whispered, "but you gotta promise to be quiet."

She slapped his hand. "I'll be quiet, Peter Brye," she hissed, "but you keep your hands to yourself."

Pete nodded, no longer listening, his attention back to the window. Curious, her own fright melting away, Katie also peered through the garage window, frowning. "What's going on? What's he doing?"

Pete shook his head. "I don't know. But it looks like he's using Mom's old silver jewelry to make it."

Katie looked at Pete. "Silver?"

Ronald Brye began melting down the silver earrings as Pete looked back at Katie, the same thought crossing their minds at the same time. But before they could voice it, another voice, gravelly, hoarse, not quite right, spoke behind them.

"Hello, Pete. Hello, Katie."

They screamed.

FORTY-FOUR

The distant sounds of sirens penetrated her sleep and Marty woke with a start, her heart pounding wildly.

Then, recalling her dream, she smiled lazily, stretching her sore muscles and feeling her joints pop as she turned onto her side. She blinked. The orange cat sat on the pillow next to her, regarding her with the detached curiosity of a scientist. Then, with a great delicacy, it lifted one forepaw and placed it on her mouth. Marty propped herself up on one elbow – the paw fell away.

"Good morning to you, too." She glanced at the bedside clock. Seven-thirty AM. "I take it you're an early riser." The cat yawned, revealing sharp teeth. "Well, I'm not. I'm going back to sleep."

She flopped back down and pulled the covers over her head. The doorbell rang. She burrowed deeper under the covers. The doorbell rang again, more insistent.

Marty sighed, threw back the covers. "What now?"

She sat up quickly – bone-deep pain raced through her and she fell back against the pillows, barely aware of her own nakedness. The memory of her dream came back again, stronger now, more vivid. Tavis. Heat raced through her, pooling deep within her – she could feel the hot blush as her face turned red. Aching, flushed, Marty rose from her bed a bit slower this time, gazing at her skin, her hands, recalling the patches of fur, how her hands became paws….

Giving herself a quick shake, she slipped on an old blue Wolf's Head Bay High School sweatshirt and jeans and trotted downstairs, a pair of old canvas sneakers in one hand. The cat followed close behind her, pausing on the last step as the doorbell rang once more.

She opened the door with a hard yank. "This had better be good…" she began and stopped.

Ellen stood before her on the front stoop, her face pale, eyes red and swollen from weeping.

Marty found her voice. "Hey, what's up?"

"May I come in?" Ellen asked, her voice straining to remain calm.

"Sure." Puzzled, Marty stepped aside to allow her sister-in-law entrance. Ignoring the questions that begged to be asked, Marty led the way down the hall to the kitchen, wondering at Ellen's presence. "Can I get you something to drink? Coffee, juice, tea? I don't have any creamer but I do have some milk in the fridge."

Her sister-in-law followed, uncertainty and discomfort in her every step. "Tea would be fine, thank you."

Marty had gone to the cupboard, pulling out mugs and setting them on the counter.

"Is Mike here?" Ellen asked, hesitating in the doorway.

Marty filled the kettle. "No, why?"

Ellen started to speak, hesitated, then said, "He didn't come home last night."

Marty stared at her sister-in-law, surprised, but before she could say anything, the telephone rang. Both women jumped – then, shutting off the water and setting the kettle in the sink, Marty hurried down the hall to the phone stand, picking up in mid-ring.

"Hello? Who is this?"

Sounding as if he were leagues away, Eddie spoke. "It's me, Marty. Eddie."

"Eddie, I hope you know it's not even eight in the morning yet. Whatever it is you have to say had better be really, really important."

"I'm really sorry to bother you, but I'm looking for Ellen. I tried calling over at her and Mike's, but there was no answer."

Marty glanced at Ellen, who now stood beside her. "She's standing right here with me, Eddie. Why?" A cold thread touched her heart. "What's going on?"

"It's Mike." Eddie sounded unhappy. "I found him in front of the station when I got there at five this morning. He'd been beat up pretty bad."

"Where is he?" Marty snapped out her words. Ellen looked at her sharply.

"Over at Memorial. I'm there now. He —" Eddie never finished. Marty had hung up on him.

Grabbing her purse, Marty steered Ellen back towards the front door, pausing long enough to grab the shoes she'd dropped by the front door earlier.

"What's going on? Where are we going?"

"To Mike."

The front door slammed shut behind them. The orange cat yawned delicately and padded silently towards the kitchen.

*****

They stood outside Mr. Wilson's Algebra class, not talking, only listening to the low hum of conversations floating around them as they waited for the first bell to ring, their hands still linked together.

The first bell shattered the air — conversations stilled, then resumed, this time in disgruntled tones regarding class. Cassie stepped back, aware of her reluctance, and grinned. "Gotta go. See you after class?"

"Sure." Tommy caught her hand again. "Myrna's. My

treat."

She gave him a brilliant smile that made his stomach flutter before disappearing into the sea of shifting bodies. She reappeared only once – at the top of the stairwell leading to the second floor. Then she was gone. Tommy stumbled into Mr. Wilson's classroom and sat at his desk, dreaming.

*****

Cassie made her way to Mrs. Snyder's art class, a subject she'd discovered a talent for earlier in the year and took great pleasure in.

The door was propped open, but neither her classmates nor her teacher were in the room – Cassie entered anyway and shrugged off her pack, setting it on a desk nearest the window. Facing east and overlooking the parking lot, Cassie thought it also held a great view of some of the surrounding woods. On a good day and from an extreme angle, she thought she could catch a glimpse of the Peak.

A flash of movement caught her eye as she turned away – leaning forward until her nose was pressed flat against the cool window pane, Cassie recognized Ms. Brennan as the teacher hurried towards her car.

Frowning, wondering why the older woman was leaving, Cassie watched as Daria Brennan got into her car and drove away, disappearing out of her view.

Cassie was out the door before she realized it, almost running into her classmates and knocking Mrs. Snyder's coffee mug out of her hands.

Ignoring their startled cries, Cassie flew downstairs.

FORTY-FIVE

Eddie met them at the ER entrance fifteen minutes later. He looked lost, twisting his cap nervously.

Ellen had grown steadily paler on the short drive to the hospital to the point where Marty was secretly alarmed. Now, under the harsh fluorescent lights of Memorial's main entrance, Ellen looked ghostly.

"How is Mike?" Ellen's voice was thin, reedy.

Eddie swallowed, then gestured for them to sit. Marty immediately began to adjust her shoes, securing them properly on her feet. "Conscious and not happy about it. Doctor Jackson thinks he's got a mild concussion, so they're going to keep him for twenty-four hours. He's got several deep wounds that they've stitched up, among other things, but he's in otherwise good shape. He'll recover in time."

Ellen closed her eyes, heaving a sigh of relief. "Oh, thank God."

Marty took her hand, squeezing gently. "When can we go see him?"

"Now, but only for a few minutes. They said he's still a little groggy." Eddie then led them into the hospital, down the long corridor, turned right and went into the second door on the left. Marty's sneakered feet squeaked against the cold linoleum floor, her left hand holding tight to Ellen's right hand.

Mike was awake when they came in, still sounding a little slurred as he groused at the candy-striper. She ignored him pointedly as she went about her business. When she saw Eddie, she gave a huge sigh of relief.

"He's all yours if you want him," she said, leaving the room.

Marty looked after the girl. "What was that all about?"

Mike scowled, yawned. "She won't let me leave."

Marty looked at her brother. "Looking like that, why would you want to?"

Clean and bandaged, Mike was almost unrecognizable. Dark bruises were forming in patches along his jaw, arms, on almost every exposed inch of skin. Both hands were wrapped in temporary casts. His right foot was also in a cast, his left, wrapped in thick gauze. Only his right eye bore any resemblance to his previous condition.

Ellen gasped.

Mike tried to smile, his battered lips twisting gruesomely. "Eddie. Marty. Nice to see you both." He glanced at Ellen, looked away. "Ellen."

Eddie swallowed, sensing the tension. "I'll, uh, be over at the station if you need me for anything." He left, his footsteps echoing back.

Marty frowned, looking first at her brother, then her sister-in-law. "All right. What gives?"

"Nothing," Mike said shortly.

"It is not nothing. Even Eddie could see that. Whatever's going on with you two, get over it." She approached Mike, her gaze intent. "Who attacked you last night?"

Mike looked away from her. "I don't know."

"You don't know." Flat, disbelieving.

He met her gaze, furious. "Christ, Marty, it was dark. All I remember is some huge dog trying to rip me apart after I left the cemetery."

"What kind of dog? St. Bernard? Great Dane?"

Mike scowled, or at least tried to. It was very clear in his voice. "All I know is that it was big and had teeth. The rest is a blank. Next thing I know, I'm waking up in this room and Doctor Jackson is telling me that the fingers of both my hands were either broken or dislocated. Same with my toes. I have stitches going every which way and I know they're gonna itch like crazy when the painkillers wear off and I won't be able to do a damn thing about it." He breathed deep, exhaled. "They had to test me for rabies and I think I've gotta have shots."

Marty sat on the edge of his bed. "What were you doing in the cemetery?"

Mike cleared his throat, not meeting his sister's eyes. Even through the bruises, he looked ashamed. "After we had dinner, I took a walk. I ended up there, so I decided to pay Mom a visit." He glanced over at Ellen. "I got the feeling I was being watched, so I left in a hurry. I got attacked right outside the gate." He shrank back from the strange light in his sister's eyes. "I don't remember much else, just that it was big and hairy."

"Did it have scars?"

"Marty…"

"Never mind, I know, it was dark." She gave him a light kiss on the forehead. "I'm glad you're okay. I can't imagine why she is, but your wife is glad, too. Make up with her right now. I've gotta go."

Marty flew out the door, her sneakers slapping the linoleum.

FORTY-SIX

John Dylan stared at the report, his eyes swimming, not really comprehending what it spelled out. Although written in simple, concise English, it was as alien to him as most legal documents were to civilians.

Sitting across from him, Ronald Brye shifted uncomfortably in his chair, clutching his animal tracks book tightly in one hand.

"No," he said flatly. "I can't accept this."

Ronald Brye looked pained. "But this is what I came up with. I'm not lying to you."

Dylan waved a hand. "I'm not saying you are. I just think it's ridiculous to suspect a bear of coming out of the woods and killing a man for no apparent reason."

Ronald Brye shrugged. "Bears are animals, predators. Why do we need to accord them any reason? It's always in the news of some bear climbing up a tree in someone's backyard or bathing in their swimming pool."

Dylan met Brye's gaze. "Bears have not been sighted in this town for more than twenty years. They prefer to stay away from humans unless there's a drought or their food supply is low. It doesn't make any sense to think that, all of a sudden, they would come into town and deliberately maul people to death."

Ronald Brye sighed and settled back into his chair, giving the appearance of a man shrinking. "I suppose so." He sounded reluctant to accept Dylan's opinion.

A knock rapped against the door – without waiting for permission to enter, Fletcher stepped inside the office, a file folder in her hand. She held it up. "You wanted the report on Denver Clarke?"

Dylan stood – Brye accepted this for what it was (an end to their meeting) and stood as well, moving unobtrusively towards the door. "Thank you for your time, John."

"Yours, as well, Ronald." He waited for the other man to leave the office, watching as the other man wove his way around to the front. Then Dylan motioned Fletcher to the chair Brye had recently vacated, holding out his hand for the file. "So, what really killed him? An angry fisherman and his dog?"

Fletcher shook her head. "No, and I'm afraid you aren't going to like it. Those tracks do not belong to any type of dog, domesticated or otherwise."

Dylan half-sighed, half-chuckled. "So what are we looking at? Wolves?" He looked up when Fletcher didn't reply. "You're kidding, right?"

"They're too big to be wolf prints, but…they look the same. Even the bite radius I pulled from one of the wounds is very similar to a wolf bite."

Dylan groaned. "Great. Just what this town needs, given its history." His face grew thoughtful. "This print….this is the same one I gave Ronald Brye, right?"

Fletcher nodded. "It is. Why?"

Dylan leaned back in his chair, stared up at the ceiling. "If those are the same prints, why would you come up with wolf? And why did Ronald Brye come up with bear?"

Fletcher grinned, stood, made her way to the door with a wave. "That's why you're the cop, John. Your job is to find out why, mine is to find out when and how."

*****

Tavis looked up from a crossword puzzle, amused, when Eddie walked into the break room and flopped facedown onto the old, gray couch.

"Tough morning, huh?" he asked.

Eddie waved a hand. When he spoke his voice was muffled against the cushions. "I told you once there are days when I hate the fact that the Bay is a small town? This is not one of those days."

Tavis pushed the crossword away, leaned back in his chair. It groaned in protest of his weight. "So what happened?"

Eddie turned his head so that he could see Tavis and breathe easier. "Michael Brye collapsed on the steps this morning. Did Amelia tell you?"

Tavis shook his head slowly. "No. Is he all right?"

Eddie considered. "The doc wants to keep him overnight, but Mike thinks they're being silly."

"Was he ill?"

"Naw. Someone just worked him over like a punching bag. Ellen's with him right now. So's Marty — say, have you met her yet?"

Tavis felt his face grow hot — his skin tingled and his clothes felt too tight. He was glad that their positions were such that Eddie couldn't see. He cleared his throat, found his voice, was glad to hear it was steady. "Yeah. Ran into her over the weekend while I was camping."

Eddie sat up. "How was it? I was thinking maybe going camping over at the lake, do some fishing. You wanna go?"

Tavis opened his mouth to reply when the door opened. He felt his face go white when he saw the woman standing there — all the smells he'd scented, that teased his memory flooded through him and he felt ill.

Daria Brennan regarded him thoughtfully. "I thought I recognized your scent."

Eddie stared, his gaze swinging back to Tavis. "What?"

Tavis finally found his voice, but it sounded far away. "You were killed…in the fire…after the vampire attacked you."

She shook her head, smiling. "Surprise."

*****

Marty had had every intention of driving over to the police station, wanting to see *him*, to talk with him about her family history, of the wolves……Instead, she found herself at the cemetery, where Mike had said he'd been attacked.

Odd, that it would be in the same place….

Resolutely, she climbed out of the Bug, aware for the first time of her back as it sent a sharp twinge through her spine. Ignoring the pain, she went to the cemetery's gate and pushed it open gently, going inside.

Following the path, she made her way back to Denise Brye's grave, where she stood for several minutes, regarding the marker, her expression both thoughtful and grim. She barely paid attention to the screaming gulls, or the lonely bell of the buoy as it bounced in the ocean. Turning in a wide circle, she observed the lighthouse, dark and quiet now that its keeper was gone; the pointed steeple of the church; the Madison place.

All seemed dark and quiet – given what had happened at the lighthouse, she wasn't sure that the goose-bumps on her flesh were from the ocean breeze.

She walked out of the cemetery, hesitated at her car and decided to walk, in spite of the aches that were reminding her of every muscle and joint she had. It was cool still, not yet even nine. Her feet began to cramp and she stopped long enough to unlace the canvas sneakers and pull them off, tying the laces together and draping the shoes over her right shoulder. The paved sidewalks leading away from the old church were relatively new and smooth as she followed Cemetery Road east – they felt good against the soles of her feet, a rough massage. She passed the Williams house without looking at it, a wood-frame building with gables looking north.

Her eyes roamed, seeing nothing and everything. They passed over the construction site, with its dark-colored tarps flapping in the breeze.....

Movement there arrested her gaze and she stopped abruptly, not quite sure of what she was seeing. Then the movement repeated itself and she knew.

Someone was up at the Heights. She started running, unmindful of the gravel biting her bare feet.

FORTY-SEVEN

Cassie hid in the alley behind Myrna's, her eyes never leaving the entrance to the police station.

She had followed Ms. Brennan from the high school, stealing Dave Tanner's bicycle and cutting through several alleys in order to keep up. Now, as she leaned back against the diner wall, she rubbed her aching legs and wondered what the teacher wanted from the police.

When the front door opened, Cassie gaped – Daria Brennan stepped out, followed closely by Tavis Riley. They trotted down the steps, talking in an earnest fashion – about what, Cassie didn't know, but was determined to find out.

She watched as they walked hurriedly up to his car and got in – furious with Riley and at her sister for trusting him, Cassie got back on the bike and peddled as fast as she could after them.

*****

Katie swam back to consciousness in a slow, circuitous motion, dimly aware of the sharp sounds of metal striking earth only a few feet away. She couldn't place the noise – each strike was in synch with the throbbing in her head. She tried to rub her temples, found she couldn't move her hands – they had been tied behind her back.

Lifting her head, she saw Pete lying next to her, unconscious. A thin trickle of blood had dried on his forehead. Wincing at the effort, she shifted her position, her eyes taking in the piles of freshly turned dirt only a few inches from her nose. Something struck the piles, scattering some of the dirt into her face. Spitting, Katie rolled her eyes as far as she could – and saw the shovel. Saw the dirt it scooped up. Saw the shallow ditch that was taking shape.

Saw Jimmy Moore's scruffy smile as he dug with grim determination.

Struggling against the waves of panic that threatened to overwhelm her, Katie tried wriggling her hands, testing her bonds. The rope was snug, but not tight. Biting her lip, she began working her hands together, trying to slip them free, her eyes on Jimmy only a few feet away.

"Pete," she whispered, her voice rough. "Pete, wake up." He didn't stir. She tried inching towards him, but the effort was too much and she concentrated on her bonds instead. The digging was a constant, sharp noise in her ears, mingling with the strain of trying to breathe in shallow, noiseless breaths.

"What are you doing here?"

The voice was male, she knew it, but couldn't place it. Another shovelful of dirt went flying – this one held a rock and it struck Katie on the forehead. She flinched back, dazed, and felt the blood trickle in a slow track into her left eye – she tried to look at the new arrival, but couldn't make her eyes focus. The newly forming bump hurt when she tried to tilt her head to the left, hoping to see the newcomer.

Her vision swam – before she could breathe in to cry out, she tumbled into blackness and fell still, unconscious.

*****

They sat in silence as Tavis drove, his face grim, hands tight on the steering wheel as he navigated the car through town.

Daria touched his arm. "I realize it's a shock to see me now, when you thought I was dead, but that's no reason to drive so fast."

He didn't reply, only pushed the gas pedal more.

She regarded him, amused. "Why are you so angry?"

He didn't reply at once. "I'm not angry. I'm….perturbed. At a loss." He glanced at her. "I thought you were dead. That vampire took a lot of blood. And then the fire…."

She studied her hands, thoughtful. "I knew how you felt, Tavis, back in the day. It wasn't easy for you, nor was it easy for me, our betrothal. When Victor Madison came, it seemed the wiser choice for me to set you free by dying. It was the only way the elders would have accepted it."

Tavis considered her words, nodded. "You're right, of course. Mother would have appreciated it."

Daria smiled. "Who do you think gave me the idea?"

He snorted at the thought. "Why did you come back?"

She gazed out the window, at the buildings streaking by. "You know that not all of us that left stayed away. Like Cowyn and Albon and you and I, some have returned over the years. We know each other, we just prefer to….let the past rest."

He repeated the question. "Why did you come back?"

She didn't look at him. "I came back because it's home."

They were silent for a minute. Tavis cleared his throat. "Why didn't you contact me? Who are you protecting? And are you Brianna or Daria?"

She didn't answer right away. He could see that she was searching for words and left her alone until she was ready. At last, she spoke. "For the longest time, I thought I was protecting you. And then I realized, when I came back here three years ago, that it was to protect someone else. That's why I never contacted you."

"Reverend Dan."

She glanced at him sharply, her eyes narrow, then relaxed into soft laughter. "You know, then. But no, not him."

"Who?"

"Cowyn's children. And Jonas's heart."

FORTY-EIGHT

On that same Tuesday morning, as Tommy and Cassie walked to school and Pete spied on his father in the garage, Dan Williams did as he did every morning when his schedule would allow – he took a walk.

He did this often, more so now than in his youth, finding the trails snaking through the woods surrounding the Bay peaceful, particularly when the fog had rolled in, giving his surroundings a fresh and mysterious beauty.

He always began his walks in the early mornings, the woods behind the Madison house his starting point – it was a short trip from his house on Cemetery Lane to the church, then to Lighthouse Way and the great rambling house beyond.

When he first began his long walks twelve years earlier, he took a more roundabout way to get to the same destination – the hill overlooking the town and the bay.

It wasn't until Old Lady Madison had finally cornered him in the produce section at Wilson's Market and demanded a good explanation as to why he wasn't using the many perfectly good trails up behind her home that he realized she would not shoot him on sight as a trespasser.

So he continued his walks to the hill, even when the

construction began. It angered him that this view, this wonderful hill he'd come to know as an old friend, would soon hold the weight of twenty new homes, with more to be built in the years to come.

He hoped fervently that Mrs. Tanner would succeed in her attempts to block it, but a bleaker voice whispered in his heart that she may fail, that no one could stop the march of time, that as small as the Bay still was, it now held more people than he remembered even ten years ago.

They will come and they will feast off the land. It is the way of all mankind, even if some are kinder to the earth than others.

He did not like this voice very much and so the walks became more than just a way to ease his soul and his heart – they became a way to ward off the bleakness he felt every Sunday morning when he saw more faces he did not know than those he did listening to his sermons.

Shaking his head, trying to rid himself of unpleasant thoughts, he saw that he had stopped on the trail above the hill. He couldn't see it, but heard a tarp flapping noisily in the breeze. He smiled faintly, remembering Mrs. Tanner's passionate speech at the city council meeting two weeks earlier, how adamant she had been in her conviction that the grave which had been dug up belonged to a previous settlement.

She was not far wrong. He wondered if Mrs. Tanner knew of the Bay's hidden and dark history, then shrugged. It didn't matter – he couldn't think of anyone better suited to be the guardian of the Bay's history or of its future.

Breathing the air deeply, he smelled the tang of salt, heard the distant cries of gulls as the breeze picked up, the tarp now snapping loudly.

Dan Williams took in another deep breath and exhaled, his thoughts turning to the archeology crew now currently finishing up their duties as teachers at both Humboldt and UC San Francisco. They would be issuing finals to their students now. He wondered when they would be returning to finish the job that the construction crew had begun by unearthing the graves.

Now he found that he was deeply curious by what had been done so far.

So he walked off the path and headed towards the construction site, where he found himself only a few feet from a disheveled and filthy man striking the earth aggressively with a shovel. He recoiled in shock when he realized he was staring at Jimmy Moore.

"What are you doing here?"

Jimmy's eyes burned red in their sockets, as if he hadn't slept in days or weeks. He glanced down at his hands, then met Dan's gaze. "Digging."

Dan blinked. "I can see that, but why?"

"I have my reasons." He sniffed loudly, swiped his nose with a sleeve. "Have a good day, Reverend."

Dan Williams nodded automatically, wanting badly to get away when some noise, at odds with what his eyes saw, reached his ears and he turned away from Jimmy, trying to orient on the sound. At first, he couldn't make sense of what he was seeing – two bodies, hands and feet bound, young people he knew, knew very well. He started towards them, heart pounding in his ears.

"Jimmy?" Dan felt relieved to hear his voice sound calm as he knelt beside the two figures. He recognized Pete and Katie almost immediately, frowning at the dried blood on the girl's cheek. "They're hurt, we need to get them to a doctor…."

He started to turn, heard the whistling of air almost too late and ducked. The shovel struck him high in the shoulder – there was a crack, the pain whipped through him and he screamed, falling onto his back. When the pain began to subside into a steady throb, a shadow fell over him and Dan looked up, squinting against the glare of the sun. "For God's sake, Jimmy, what are you doing?"

Jimmy Moore stood over him, the shovel fitting his dirty hands easily, his dark and reddened eyes blank. "Jus' followin' orders, Rev. Sorry."

"Whose orders, Jimmy?" he gasped, struggling to keep the pain at bay. "Who asked you to do this?"

Jimmy gazed down at him. His expression, under any other circumstances, might have been one of sorrow.

"She doesn't know who she is anymore," Jimmy sighed. "I s'pose it don't matter, in the long run. But she has secrets."

Dan Williams kept his eyes on the shovel in Jimmy's hands. "What kind of secrets?"

Jimmy cackled. "Damned if I know, Rev."

The shovel went up high.

FORTY-NINE

Cassie stopped at Weaver's Gas Station and Garage and walked around back, leaning the bike against the wall near the restrooms. She had lost sight of her teacher and her sister's boyfriend almost as soon as they left the police station and had spent the last hour or so bicycling around, hoping to find them again. No such luck, which was why she ended up at Weaver's.

Digging in her pocket, she pulled out thirty-five cents and wandered out front. The gas station had a soda machine and she was dying for a root beer.

A mechanic was bending over the open hood of a car when she came around, a radio on the ground next to him, the d.j. announcing the next line-up. Warren Zevon came on, howling out his words.

Dropping her change into the machine, she pushed a button and the root beer can dropped down. Picking it up, she pulled back the tab, tossed it into the nearby trash bin and drank deep, feeling the bubbles slide thickly down her throat.

A shadow fell over her. "Fancy meeting you here,

Cassandra."

Cassie choked, spitting up root beer and staining her shirt, her eyes wide when she turned around. "Ms. Brennan, I can explain…."

Daria Brennan smiled, her eyes amused. "I'm sure you can." She glanced at Tavis, standing a foot behind her. He had hooked his thumbs through his belt loops. "Shall we take her with us?"

He shook his head. "No. It's not for young eyes."

Daria looked amused. "She is one of us."

"Brianna, it's not like how we were brought up. She's too old to gain this by instinct and too young to follow."

The woman considered. "Then what of your mate? Is she not older than this one, to gain by instinct?"

Tavis met her gaze, then looked away. Cassie looked from one to the other, her brow wrinkling in confusion. "Who's Brianna?" Her eyes widened suddenly, remembering the missing diary Marty had read at Madison's. "Ms. Brennan, are you a….?" She gulped, unable to say it and turned to Tavis. "Is she a….?"

"Yes." Tavis's reply was curt.

"My name is Daria, now, Tavis."

"I'll try to remember that." He turned and walked back to the squad car, running his fingers through his hair, clearly frustrated.

Just as he opened the door, Daria stiffened, her whole being quivering with tension, her eyes wide with shock. Cassie eyed them, suddenly afraid. Whatever was bothering her teacher, also seemed to affect Tavis, for his face went white.

"Did you hear?" he asked Daria.

She nodded. "I did. I'll go. Watch her." The woman began to walk away, her usual graceful strides becoming jerky and uncoordinated. But when she passed the garage, she seemed to catch herself and her movements became…..*fluid*, Cassie thought. Almost like running water tumbling over rocks in a stream. Then the woman was running, her thick, dark hair falling from the tightly braided bun and fanning out behind her like a horse's mane. As Daria Brennan disappeared around the corner, Cassie thought she saw her teacher shimmer, become wolf-like.

And then she was gone.

A hand dropped on her shoulder and she jumped. Tavis stared down at her. "Come on. I know where she's going."

He escorted her to the squad car, put her in the back seat. It was a little too warm for her liking – wanting some fresh air, she automatically tried the handle to roll the window down. Her hand fell against nothing. "Hey, how do I roll the window down?" Then she took a closer look. "More importantly, how do I get out of here?"

In the driver's seat, Tavis looked at her through the rearview mirror. "You don't."

He put the car into gear and drove.

FIFTY

Marty reached the bottom of the hill, panting, her hand pressed deep into her ribs, cursing her lack of fitness as the stitch seized her side. She had lost her shoes somewhere along the way, but was in no mood to go back after them. She paused, trying to breathe and ignoring the deep ache in her joints when the scream rose up in the air. Scents teased her nostrils as she picked up her pace, running, the ache in her joints now unbearable as she struggled with the hill….until she tripped, stumbled and fell.

A mass of trembling limbs and confusing thoughts, Marty lay back at the bottom of the hill, curled into a fetal position and watched, her mind disconnected from her physical self as the bones in her left hand cramped, then ground themselves together, shifting into a new shape.

Dreaming, she thought, her mind swirling with new, sharper scents, new shadows and light. *I'm dreaming again…oh, Riley, this HURTS!!!!*

Above her, on the other side of the hill, the scream shrilled again. Rolling onto her stomach, she struggled to regain her feet and fell, discovering that her feet had begun to change as well. Clawing the earth with rapidly changing limbs, Marty dragged herself up the remaining few feet, barely aware of the thick pelt growing over her forearms. All that she was aware of was the consuming fire in her bones as they endured a final grinding, cramping pain. Then it was over.

Another scream rent the air – a younger voice, a male voice. She knew that voice, oh, so well. Snarling with rage, with pain, the wolf leapt to her feet, finding new energy, and bounded up the short distance to the top. A low growl emanated from deep within her throat as she took in the scene before her.

Katie and Pete had somehow managed to untie themselves – Pete looked dazed, as if unsure of his surroundings. Hovering in front of them, trying to shield them with his own battered and injured body, was Dan Williams. His arm hung at an odd angle – somewhere in her wolf's mind, she knew it was broken.

Even in her non-human state, the wolf that was Marty recognized the dark male figure towering above them not by his clothes or features but by his scent – drunk, arrogant, stale, cruel. Another, more familiar scent hung over him, but it eluded her, teased her. Shaking her head, the wolf pinned her ears back, bared her teeth, growling. This one scent was enough.

Jimmy blinked, as if not quite believing what he was seeing. "A wolf," he said, as if tasting the word for the first time. "Hey, wolfie. You don't belong here. They killed you off, oh, 'long time ago." He moved towards Pete and Katie, ignoring the reverend, chuckling. "Wolves in Wolf's Head Bay. Makes a kind of sense."

He uttered a shrill cackle as he raised his shovel.

The wolf leapt without warning, jaws open, teeth bared as she tackled him to the ground, snapping at his leg, tasting blood, relishing it. Jimmy screamed, a deep, guttural sound as he tried to block her razor-sharp teeth with the handle of his shovel. Powerful jaws grabbed hold of the old wood, snapped it in two with ease; then, placing her massive forepaws on either side of his chest, sought his soft throat.

Dan Williams shifted, trying to keep Pete and Katie from seeing.

Something big barreled into her, knocking her off of Jimmy, forcing the breath out of her in painful rush – she was on her feet in the time it took for her to draw new breath and facing her attacker.

A silver-gray wolf stared back at her, old scars striping her back, her hackles raised, but not in reaction to the younger she-wolf. Marty/wolf growled low in her throat, baring her teeth, feinting left. She wanted the blood of the dark man, the one who tried to kill one of her own.

The scarred silver-gray countered every move, her eyes never leaving Marty/wolf, then barked – short, sharp sounds that the new wolf understood clearly.

He is not the one you seek to destroy. He is but a servant.

Unseen by the two wolves in stand-off, Jimmy had risen to his feet, fishing in his pocket for the buck knife he always kept there. Opening it, he started for the wolves, intent on killing one or both, not caring that he himself might die in the process.

Dan Williams saw him move, felt his heart stop at sight of the huge knife – then, unmindful of his broken arm, he found himself on his feet and launching himself at the unkempt man. Cursing his broken arm freely, the reverend managed to get a lock on Jimmy's neck with his good arm. The wolves turned as one at the new conflict, now on the same side but before they could act, Jimmy had shifted, bringing his hand up – the knife gleamed cruelly for one brief second – then it plunged down, burying itself in Dan Williams's chest. The reverend's face bleached white, his mouth a shocked "oh!"

Then the two wolves were on Jimmy – he screamed, tried to get away and tripped on his own feet. He fell, hit his head against the shovel and lay still.

The she-wolf that was Marty scented his blood, fresh and bright like a new coin – excited, she started forward, but her legs began trembling and she collapsed suddenly, pain shocking itself throughout her body.

The silver-gray hesitated, concerned, but a deep moan caught her attention and she trotted over to the bleeding man, the knife still in his ribs. Dan Williams looked up at her, smiled faintly, no longer surprised by anything when the wolf blurred, shifted, became the human woman he loved, unmindful of her nudity. Surprisingly, he found he had the beginnings of an erection.

"I don't understand…," he whispered as she took his hand.

She regarded him, folding her hand around his, ignoring the encroaching coolness of his skin, love suffusing her face with a softness he rarely saw. "I am what you think I am, my love. No more, no less. My heart beats for you just the same as before."

He touched her cheek with a trembling hand. "I never thought you were ordinary, Daria."

She closed her eyes, nuzzling his hand gently before it dropped away, listening for his breath as it came and went, slower and longer each time. She thought she heard him whisper her name and she leaned closer to his mouth. His eyes held hers, but she doubted it was herself he was seeing.

"I love you," she whispered in his ear. She thought she heard him whisper it back – *I love you.*

Then his breath stopped, his lids drooped and his body seemed to settle deep into the earth.

Dan Williams died.

FIFTY-ONE

Sorely tempted to simply vanish into the surrounding woods to cry out her grief, Daria forced herself to stand and went to Marty. The young woman had reverted to her human form and was now shivering.

"How are you feeling?" Daria was dismayed to hear her voice sound so steady, so normal.

Marty grimaced. "Sore, cold. Like every bone in my body wants to implode. Does it get any easier?"

"In time." Daria held out a hand – Marty took it, gained her feet and found that she wasn't as light-headed as she'd feared. Then she saw Dan Williams's body and her hand tightened around Daria's in sympathy.

"I'm sorry, Brianna," she said quietly.

Daria nodded, no longer surprised. "How did you know?"

Marty met her gaze. "To be honest? I didn't. It just…..made a kind of sense. Tavis couldn't have been the only one to return."

Daria smiled and Marty was glad. There would be time for friendship, if that, later. Now, there was only grief.

Gravel crunching under tires caused both women to turn. Tavis parked the car and got out, going to the back and letting Cassie out as well. The girl ran the distance to her sister.

"Where's Pete? Is he okay? What happened? And where the hell are your clothes?" Then she was kneeling by her brother, not yet seeing the body of Reverend Dan or the unconscious form of Jimmy Moore.

In the meantime, Tavis had gone through the trunk of his car and pulled out two blankets. Approaching the two women, he handed the blankets off.

As they wrapped themselves in warmth, Tavis cuffed and dragged Jimmy to his car, pushing him into the back seat. Daria went to fetch Marty's clothing – Marty didn't try to stop her, only because she sensed that the other woman needed time to herself.

So she went to Pete, who lay shivering under Cassie's right arm. Katie was hugged close in Cassie's left. What struck her was their eyes – wide, moist, haunted. *Huge, for their faces*, she thought then recalled what they had been through and hugged them both fiercely.

"Pete," she managed eons later. "Did Jimmy hurt you? Did he -?"

Pete was shaking his head. "No. Just grabbed us, tied us and gagged us. But…." He swallowed hard. "Show me how to be a wolf."

He burst into tears. Marty hugged him hard, unmindful of the blanket when it began to slip, soothing her brother with words.

Daria came over, holding Marty's clothes. Somehow, she had managed to tie the blanket off, making it look like the gown of an ancient Greek. "Let me take them over to Madison's. She'll have something that will help."

Marty nodded, pulling on first her jeans, then her shirt, stuffing her undies in a back pocket. Tavis emerged from his car, his face grim. "That was the chief of police. Bessie Mills' place was broken into and Eddie found blood in the living room. I think Jimmy here knows something about it." He gestured to the corpse. "I need to stay here until the coroner comes to take him away. Can you make it home on your own?"

Marty nodded. "I left my car back at the cemetery, but I can walk." She glanced at her siblings. "I'll come for them."

Daria nodded. "I will look after them."

Tavis looked at Marty, his heart evident in his gaze. "Shall I see you later at home?"

Marty met his gaze, suddenly shy. "Only if it's on your way."

His grin warmed her as she started walking back towards town.

FIFTY-TWO

While Marty hurriedly got dressed, Daria took her blanket, walked the short distance to Dan's body and draped it carefully over him.

She wondered who would tell Tommy that his father was dead, that he was now an orphan, wondered if he had any other family and if he would want them to come.

Half-tuned in to the numb tones of Pete and Katie and Cassie's worried one, Daria finally took in the construction site, her memories of another time overlapping with the here and now. If she closed her eyes and listened to the ocean, she could almost be back when the graves were first dug, the aftermath of the fire that had nearly killed her, the unexpected gift of life from Felanna…..

She saw it, then, the path leading back into the woods, that connected with a dozen more, one that would eventually track behind the Madison place.

She turned back to the three teens. Marty was kneeling next to Cassie, talking in low tones. Daria didn't need to strain too hard to understand what Marty was saying – that she would be along at Madison's in an hour or so, to take them all home. In the meantime, they would be safer there.

Cassie looked over at the blanket-draped corpse and Daria knew she realized at once who lay there – the comprehension flooded the girl's face as swiftly as the blood drained from it. She gulped back the tears that shimmered in her eyes and turned away.

Daria's throat tightened and she looked away, back towards the forest that stretched into the mountains beyond. Her deepest instinct was to shift, change into her wolf form and flee, baying out her broken heart to the sky before coming to earth and hiding from the world as she allowed her grief to consume her alive. She sucked in the cold air, shook her head, trying to clear her mind of dark thoughts. She had responsibilities to tend to and any self-indulgent moping would have to wait.

Daria glanced back over her shoulder at the others and saw that Marty had begun to walk back the way she'd come. Marty was heading back to the cemetery, where her car sat, waiting. Daria went to Cassie – the two of them helped Pete and Katie to their feet and started walking towards the path.

Daria turned back once, to find Tavis watching her. "Yes?"

He started to turn away, looked back, shrugged. "Call if you need me."

For the first time, she found a smile. "Making contact with your own at last. She'll make you our alpha yet."

He looked startled, opened his mouth to object – *being alpha is for someone else* – then shut it, his expression thoughtful.

With Cassie leading, the silent foursome made their way to the path – it seemed like hours before they reached the clearing where the waterfall fed the creek into the ocean, but it was only an hour, maybe a little less.

Pete and Katie were still in a state of shock, responding monosyllabically, seemingly unaware of their surroundings, stumbling over a root or loose rock on the way, but while they rested at the clearing, the sound of the waterfall as it passed over rocks and back into the creek soothing in the background, their words began to string into sentences and soon they were asking questions, not about the woods, but about the village before.

Daria hesitated in her answers, thinking she would find it difficult to talk of the past, and was pleasantly surprised at the pleasure she took in talking about her old life, telling of the people who had lived here with her before, their journey for sanctuary and hope in another time.

It did not entirely take away the ache in her heart, but it eased it, and she found she was able to see the next few hours with some clarity.

And when Madison found them some twenty minutes later, carrying an old carpet bag filled with a loose skirt and blouse, the three teens had surrounded their teacher and held her while she sobbed out her grief.

FIFTY-THREE

Ellen hesitated at the bottom of the porch steps leading up to her father-in-law's house and stared.

In spite of the brilliant light cast by the sun, the house seemed dark, full of shadows and secrets. Not sure she wanted to go up to the front door, Ellen toyed briefly with the grand idea of simply turning around and going back home, of calling Ronald Brye and informing him of Mike's injuries.

Instead, she forced herself up the steps and knocked sharply on the front door. No answer. Relief swept over her and she began to turn away when her treacherous hand reached for the door knob and turned. The door gave way easily, swinging open, the hall before her as dark as any cavern.

She swallowed, heard the dry click in her mouth.

"Ronald?" she called, leaning into the door frame. Silence answered her. She tried again. "Ronald, it's me, Ellen. Are you here?"

Still no reply. Worried now, Ellen stepped inside, flipping on a switch, flooding the living room with light.

Although nothing appeared to be out of place, she couldn't help but felt that there was something terribly amiss, that her father-in-law had left in some kind of hurry to avoid missing some important date.

She turned to leave when a sound – a low sound, like something scraping wood – caught her ears and she turned, peering down the long hallway. At the end, a door swung open slowly, allowing dim light to escape.

"Ronald?" Suddenly, her voice sounded huge, echoing off the walls and she wanted very badly to get out of the house. Every instinct she had was screaming for her to run, to flee the seductively quiet house, to go back to the safety of Mike's hospital bedside and forget, but something deeper compelled her forward.

She found herself in front of her father-in-law's study – giving herself a shake, she knocked. The door swung open, revealing the room within. The small desk lamp was on, throwing more shadows than light. She went in, her hand sliding on the wall to her right, searching for the overhead light switch. Flipping it on, her eyes adjusting to the new light, she blinked, taking in the room carefully. Books, maps, trail guides – these stacked every flat surface in the room.

An old shotgun hung from pegs on a wall behind the desk – she remembered Mike telling her about it, that it had belonged to his grandfather, Carl Brye. Her eyes fell on the cluttered desk. In its center, holding down a small stack of papers, was a wooden box, just under two feet long and ten inches wide. Its latches were undone. She was at the desk before she realized she had even crossed the room. She touched the wooden box, the skin on her finders recoiling at its feel. She opened it – empty, save for the faded black velvet lining.

To the left of it, lay a small, tan, rectangular box. This one was made of cardboard and was unmarked – it appeared to be quite unremarkable. She picked it up, hefting its startling weight, and opened it, frowning in confusion as her brain processed the unusual information her eyes took in. Bullets gleamed back at her. But they were not ordinary bullets.

The bullets in the box were silver.

She stuffed the box into her coat pocket, still hesitating. There was a scent in the air that teased her – she sniffed, wrinkling her nose in distaste at the sickeningly sweet and metallic smell. Her eyes rested on the bundle that had been set on the old stuffed chair behind the desk. It held something that seemed to be leaking. Ignoring the impulse to run, she stepped around the desk, leaning forward, her hand shaking as she grasped the dark swath of material and pulled. Bessie Mills' head stared back at her.

All her original instincts came screaming back and she turned, fleeing the house, slamming the front door behind her.

All that mattered now was getting to her husband.

FIFTY-FOUR

Marty turned in at her gate, hurried up the walk and trotted up the porch steps. She had found her shoes on the way back to her car, lying askew on the west side of Lighthouse Way and picked them up in one fluid movement, barely faltering in her stride as she did so. Now, she searched her pockets for her house key, debating on what to do first – hot tea or hot bubble bath?

The hot bubble bath won out – the tea could wait until Riley got there later. If she was thinking clearly.

She stood inside the entry way, the door closed, her face warm with the blush she knew was covering it. With a soft whistle, she trotted upstairs, dismissing her sudden jitters as anticipation for Riley's presence.

She entered her room and went directly to the bathroom, not bothering to turn on the lights, not noticing the shadows that had grown. Turning on the water, she put in the plug, poured in a healthy amount of bubbles, then padded back into her room, going to her dresser and rummaging for sexy under things, not seeing her father sitting in the shadows until he snapped on a light.

She jumped back with a yelp, her heart pounding. "Dad! You scared me. What are you doing here?"

He looked distressed. "I'm sorry, I didn't mean to……"

Marty waved it away, irritation replacing fright. "How did you get in?"

"I still had a key." He had the grace to blush under her startled gaze. "I wanted to talk to you." His eyes never left hers – Marty met his gaze, uneasy. "About your mother. She had secrets, you know. Dark secrets."

"Is that all? I didn't think she just sprang into being." Marty was relieved her voice sounded calm, because her heart was pounding wildly against her ribs. *What is this fear? It's my father, not a ghost.* "So what kind of secrets did she have? An illicit affair? I'm not your daughter?"

In the bathroom, the water continued to pour out.

"No, nothing so dramatic like that." He smiled at her – vacant, quiet, not-there. He moved closer to her – without thinking, Marty countered his move. "May I have some tea?"

"Sure. Let me turn off the bath." She turned and went into the bathroom, reaching over to turn off the water.

The blow came without warning, catching her high between the shoulder blades – shocked breathless, she stumbled to the floor, sliding on the bath rug. Pain sung through her – collapsing to the floor, she sucked in as much air as she could, barely aware of her father as he stepped over her and turned off the bathwater.

She stared up, squinting against the overhead light as her father towered over.

No, not her father. A stranger with her father's face.

Her eyes flickered to his hands as she fought the coming grayness – in one hand, he held a sock weighted with heavy stones. In the other was an old, cracked, leather-bound book. Understanding flooded her, leaving her weak, and she knew at once who had been behind Jimmy's attempt to kill Riley. Who it was that had tried to kill her, then Mike, in the cemetery.

Who had killed her mother.

Ronald Brye watched as his eldest daughter's expression shifted from pain to horrified comprehension. His own blank face did not change.

"Dad, what did you do?" she croaked.

He looked puzzled. "Do? I did nothing."

"You killed Mom. Is that nothing?"

His eyes were empty. "I killed a monster."

The grief she'd held for so long fell away and hot rage burned in its place. Without thinking, she lunged forward, unmindful of her pain. Her father swung the weighted sock effortlessly – it hissed through the air and cracked against her skull. She slumped forward into darkness, only dimly aware of her father grabbing under her arms and dragging her out of the room and into the hall.

When the darkness finally cleared, Marty found herself in the attic, hanging by her rope-bound hands from the over head beam. Her body weight pulled on her arms with a bone-aching heaviness. In front of her, a table had been set up. Spilled over it were pieces of jewelry, all of them fitted with moonstones.

Somewhere behind her, she could hear her father moving.

"Mom loved you," she croaked out. "How could you kill her?"

"Because I knew then what you know now," he said with a calmness that scared her. "It was revealed to me."

"How?" she asked, her throat clearing.

He came around to her front – she flinched back from his black, blank gaze, barely taking in the fact that he removed his t-shirt, revealing a soft, pudgy white torso. "She told me."

Marty shook her head, wincing when the razor-sharp pain lanced through her skull. "I don't understand. Who told you?"

He regarded her. The absent curiosity set her on edge. "She did. The pale woman in black who lives with the witch. She told me to follow your mother when she went out one night. So I did, all the way out to the edge of the woods, beyond the clearing above where that old witch lives. And I saw."

"What did you see?"

He leaned close to her ear. "I saw the creature pretending to be my human wife take its true form as a wolf."

Marty strained at the ropes. "Who told you, Dad? Who told you to go spy on Mom?"

He didn't reply, merely regarded her for a long moment, then turned to the table and she saw what had been hidden under his long-sleeved shirts all these years.

Pink scars twisted themselves over his shoulders. Her eyes followed the scars down his arms and for the first time in her life, she saw the deep, ragged scars that puckered his forearms. Teeth marks.

"What did you do, Dad?" she whispered.

He turned to face her, a tired smile on his face. "I confronted her over it. And then I killed her. She wasn't a true human and she tainted the rest of us with her filth."

He frowned, fell silent and stared at the window opposite them. Marty realized, with growing horror, that it was the same window her mother had fallen out of. He gestured to it vaguely. "She wasn't expecting it, of course, didn't realize what I intended until I put the noose around her neck. Then she knew. She bit me, as I pushed her out. Half woman, half wolf, that bitch bit me, cursed me even as she died."

He smiled then, his half-closed eyes soft with memory. "I keep seeing more of them, you know. They keep coming back here, like they own this town, coming back to whelp more monsters." He looked at her. "It was very easy to manipulate an angry, bitter, jilted man like your ex-boyfriend to do the dirty work. It was easier than it should have been, but then, he does have a rather high opinion of himself."

A part of Marty wanted to close her own eyes, to run and hide and be sick, but her life in this moment depended on no one but herself.

Resolute, she drew in breath, finding her feet at last, standing, relieving the ache in her arms. "You might as well have killed Mom for having red hair. She was human – this were' aspect is genetic, not demon."

"Which made it worse," her father said agreeably. He held up an object wrapped in black velvet – with a soft rustle, the rich fabric fell away to reveal a simple, yet deadly-looking knife. Its handle was ivory, yellowing with age now, but at one time had been pure white. It was carved in the shape of a wolf.

Marty's blood ran cold – she knew without a doubt that the blade was silver. And, that it had belonged, thanks to Jonas Brye's detailed description in his letters, once upon a time, to Victor Madison. Another thought struck her and she blurted out, "You killed them all, didn't you, Dad. Mr. Palmer. Mr. Tanner. Ellen's dad. Denver Clarke. Stanley Gordon. Mrs. Williams. Holly." Her voice cracked. "How many more, Dad?"

He stared at her, saying nothing.

It tickled her again, that sense of something not quite right. The heightened senses of her other self suddenly shifted and she knew what stood before her. "Monster."

"Not quite," he said. "Human."

Rage boiled in her blood, coursing through her body in hot lightning streaks – her vision browned out as she pulled at the ropes that bound her. In some dim part of her mind, she noted the sheer terror on her father's face.

She liked it.

At the table, Ronald Brye stood frozen, disbelieving, as he watched his daughter shift shape.

Thick chestnut fur began to cover her face, her body, her limbs in patches. Her skull, jaw and muscles began molding themselves into new shapes – the pronounced canine muzzle and snout, a flattened forehead with eyes that held an unearthly glow. This gaze she turned on him – he fell back a step, felt his bowels loosen, the silver dagger suddenly a dead weight in his trembling hand. When the ropes snapped, freeing the wolf that was Marty, he voided himself. He knew.

She opened her mouth to scream – a rich, full howl issued forth instead. The ropes that bound her fell to the floor.

Ronald Brye's body suddenly shuddered violently – the familiar sensations were far more intense than any previous change he'd experienced even as he fought it, his fear, his hate, his self-loathing flooding every cell, emanating from every pore of his body.

Before Marty's change to wolf was complete and he lost his human mind, Ronald Brye bolted forward.

A small furry body landed on his head, clawing at him fiercely, small teeth digging into his right ear – the orange cat made a slicing movement with one paw – blood gushed out from his left eye.

Screaming shrilly, infuriated by the pain, he swiped at the cat, his hand connecting solidly with the small body and he threw the cat against the wall. It landed on the floor and lay still.

Tightening his grip on the ivory handled knife, he lashed out at the wolf that had been his daughter – she snapped her jaws around his wrist and bore down. Bones cracked and broke easily under the crushing weight of her teeth – he shrieked in agony, the knife falling from his hand to the floor. He struck her repeatedly with his good hand, raining blows around her eyes and ears.

Growling low in her throat, the wolf/Marty whipped her head to the right, then snapped back to the left, releasing Ronald Brye at the last minute.

He stumbled backwards, struggling to maintain his balance as he fell hard against the window; the glass groaned, but did not break – the brunt of his weight had landed on the frame. He caught his breath, feeling the deep ache within his own bones as his body began the process in shifting back towards human.

Cradling his broken wrist, Ronald Brye stared with uncomprehending horror at the creature that was once his daughter. The wolf had planted herself between him and any chance of escape – the look in her eyes spoke of death.

Only three feet away, the knife beckoned, enticing in its smooth, clean lines – he broke for it, desperation flowing from his every pore, his internal struggle with his other self-evident in his every painful move. A low, deep-throated growl stopped him – the orange cat, fur puffed out, stood over the knife, eyes blazing. Although it clearly hurt from the force of his blow that sent it into a wall, the cat seemed equally determined to keep Ronal Brye from reclaiming the knife as the man was to grab it.

Then the she-wolf leapt, tackling him from the side – in a single, fluid motion, they crashed through the window, tumbled down the raked angle of the roof and onto the grassy lawn below.

The wolf/Marty twisted her body, instinctively following her fall and rolling so that when her paws hit the roof's edge, she pushed forward, leaping gracefully to the ground, gravity causing her to stumble and fall when she hit the ground.

Ronald Brye felt/heard the shuddering crack when he landed on his back – the pain pierced him, so sharp and consuming that he could not find the breath to scream. He felt the change slow, then ebb away, slipping past his conscious self, following what had been his soul into the dark.

Beside him, breathless, stunned, but unhurt, the wolf staggered to her feet, glancing briefly at the dying man beside her, then turned away.

"Marita."

She turned, saw the gate creaking open and a man walk through. He had spoken her human name, he was like her, wolf-kind, older. She knew him, was glad to see him as he stood patiently before her. She walked towards him, legs trembling, feeling his heart beat through the air, sensing his smile. Then the world grayed out; the next thing she knew, Riley was holding her close, his jacket wrapped around her shoulders to cover her nakedness.

In the distance, she could hear the familiar cries of the gulls, the lonely keening of the harbor buoy's bell and something new – howling.

Wolves.

Tavis Riley heard them, too – lifting his head, he closed his eyes, basking in their music, hearing them reach the sky in chorus for the first time in more than a hundred twenty years.

Soon, he knew, he would join their music as pack leader. But not now. Not just yet.

She turned luminous eyes on him. "It was my father. How could he…?"

He touched her lips with his – heat coursed through them, leaving them both shaken and desiring more. She touched his jaw with gentle, tired fingers, felt him tremble at her touch. She had never felt so powerful as she did in this moment – knowing that she held his heart, that he held hers, that it was for life.

"Because hate is easy to hide when it's someone you love and trust," he murmured against her fingers. "Just as it is difficult to recognize friendship in one you distrust."

She held him close. "How did you know to come here?"

He glanced at the corpse that had been her father. "Mike called. Ellen had gone over to see your father, to tell him about Mike. He wasn't there, so she went in. She found an empty wooden box and a case of silver bullets on his desk and Bessie Mills's head. And I knew." He hesitated – she felt his unease.

"What is it?"

He shook his head. "It doesn't matter."

"Tavis."

"I saw that box. It held *his* knife." She didn't have to ask him who 'he' was. Tavis Riley was quivering with rage. "How he got it, I want to know."

"The vampire Madison spoke of," she said quietly, voicing his own suspicions. "She must have something to do with this. My father wasn't acting alone, Tavis. *He* said as much, up there, in the attic…" Her voice trailed off, then firmed. "My father…he killed them all."

Tavis held her close. "I was wondering the same thing, Marita." At her questioning look, he added, "If Madison's vampire fed on your father's mind, his own fears, and then influenced him to commit these killings."

Marty was silent, her mind sluggish with fatigue from the day's events. She forced herself to focus, to bring clarity to her thoughts. "I think his desire to kill was there, all the time. Even before he knew my mother was a werewolf."

He nodded. "Madison will want to see us, to plan our next move."

Marty nodded, her thoughts turning, not to the old woman, but to Daria and the grief she now bore. Daria was in Madison's care now – no one better could give her the help and care she needed. Madison would insist that the woman who had lost her mate stay and take shelter in the old manse. Madison would also go with Daria and help break the news to his son that Reverend Daniel Williams was dead.

Marty wondered briefly what would become of Tommy, who would take care of him now. She didn't think he had any family left other than his father. Sorrow swept over her – this time, the grief came easily and she embraced it.

Sirens sounded in the distance, getting louder. Aware of her nudity for the second time that afternoon, she struggled to her feet. Tavis helped, giving her his strength as she needed it as they walked from the backyard to the kitchen entrance and through the main part of the house.

Climbing the stairs, they paused at the second floor landing. The big orange cat lay by the door of her room, resting stiffly, mouth open, teeth exposed.

Pulling Tavis's jacket closer, she knelt down and checked him – her untrained eye saw no outer injuries, but she had the good sense to leave him for the moment until she could get him to the vet.

Tavis knelt down beside her, holding his hand out for the cat to sniff. "What's his name?"

"Jonas," she said without thinking. She met his gaze. "Help me find my clothes."

He began to laugh as they entered her room.

*****

At the intersection of Fry Street and Shady Lane, completely hidden in the darkness of the surrounding trees and the rapidly descending twilight, the shadow watched the gongs on at Number 17. The wolf and his mate were upstairs, while in the backyard, another lay still, death cooling the corpse.

Soon, more would arrive, in their flashing lights and metal boxes on wheels. Others would observe, as she was doing, from the shadows, in their true form, howling as they were at this very minute to the silver moon as it rose high above the mountains that had given this town its name.

She did not want to stay, she did not understand why she could not go home, feared the strange hungers that consumed her until she tasted the coppery tang in her mouth as she drank, why she felt tied to this place that so long ago had been a site for nightmares and grief, that held her to it as fast and sure as her love for her son tied her to him, why she couldn't leave. She could not understand why she had been unable to find him, even though she felt his presence so strongly.

Turning away from Number 17 Fry Street, the shadow, her hunger satisfied from an earlier feeding, followed her son's presence as she did every night, and soon found herself at the end of the drive to the Madison House. It was here that she felt her son's presence the most. But only the old woman, the witch, lived there now.

She did not understand anything, least of all who she was, why she was, and what it was that she most needed to finally leave. None of those that she had recruited to help her find her way home again were willing to do so, even when she eventually gave them what they wanted – the taste of their blood mixing together like a rich and delicate sauce that slid down their throats in silken waves of red.

She found herself at the main gate of the old house with no memory of how she got there. This happened a lot, arriving somewhere without her being consciously aware of actually traveling. She reached for the gate to push it open, jerking her hand back as though it had been shocked. She hissed, staring at her hand, remembering shocks of a different kind, screams not her own echoing in the haunted halls of a remote building. Standing mere inches away, she stared through the ivy-covered gates and up at the old, dark house, sniffing the air hungrily, seeking any sign of her son and not finding any.

The witch was in there, however, with three young ones and another wolf.

They would help her find her son.

Even if it meant their own deaths.

EPILOGUE

1 July, 1852, late evening

He sits at his desk, his left arm bound securely and held in place with a sling. He frowns at the loose sheets of paper that curl at the edges as he tries to write and, after a few failed attempts, he finally places a book at the top edge, holding them down. He dips his quill in the inkwell and writes.

Dear M.,

I have recorded the events of the last few days with as much detail as I can recall, which seems considerable, given the knock on the head I received. I regret to say that poor Mrs. Madison had to be put in restraints when she tried to bite Andrews' neck. Even now, one can hear her howls from the decks below. She sounds quite mad. Doctor Kelley has given me his full report and has just left me to return to the infirmary. He seems to think that Mrs. Madison will recover from her neck wounds, but is at a loss as to her lethargy and nightly mood swings. I will have to talk to the Reverend about getting in touch with her family, perhaps connect her to a specialist's care.

There is a brisk knock at his door. He pauses in his writing, rests his pen and calls for his unknown visitor to enter. His eyes remain on the paper and his own, unmistakable writing, unseeing. The door to his cabin creaks open, but instead of the boy he had grown to think of as his own son or even a member of his own crew, he is rather surprised to see the Reverend Williams poke his head in, a sheepish smile softening the harsh lines of his old face. They had begun to speak of other things since the fire, other than the reverend's main purpose in following the late Mr. Madison. The captain is bemused once more by his own mistaken ideas of both men's hearts.

He moves to stand in greeting, but the reverend motions him to remain seated. "It is not that I don't enjoy your company, but I haven't come here to go over what has already discussed, Captain," he says, his eyes twinkling merrily (*how*, the captain wonders, *did I ever think that those eyes were so cold, so unfeeling?*). He stands in such a way that the captain wonders if he is not alone.

The reverend's next words confirm this suspicion. "There is someone here with me who wishes to speak with you." He steps back, gesturing for his companion to enter the cabin.

The captain stands, all pain forgotten, his eyes solely on the one person he thought he would never see again.

Felanna stands before him, clad in a simple, almost shapeless dress, her hair tied back in a long, thick braid. Her eyes meet his and he is struck once more at how open her soul is to him. *Windows*, he thinks, *the damn poet was right, eyes are truly windows to one's soul...*

The reverend, unnoticed by either of them, steps back into the passageway, closing the door just enough for privacy's sake, but cracked open a foot so that propriety was met as well.

They continue to stare at each other – he, speechless, she, amused. The silence that fell between them was not uncomfortable; indeed, rather, it was electric with unspoken feeling.

"I had grown used to the idea that you were dead," he says at last. His voice sounds rough to his own ears and coughs, clearing his throat.

"It would be better for both of us if you continued to think so," she says.

He holds out his hand, aching for her to take it, to feel the touch of her skin against his once more, but she refuses. Instead, she takes a step backward, holding herself tall, austere.

He allows his hand to fall to his side. "Why must I think so?"

She stands firm on her thought. "I am not of your world, Jonas. We cannot mix."

"Just because we are different......."

She will not bend, but he can see the regret in her eyes. "You are human, I am not. You have seen what happens when our worlds mix. My culture, my people, do not belong in the world you live in. I tried to live as a human, tried to have a son in your world and be true to my people. Victor saw only the wolf, he did not see what we truly are. It does not work."

He tries to sway her. "I am not Victor Madison, Felanna. I would not ask you to be what you are not."

She wills herself not to be tempted by this thought. "It cannot be, Jonas. You must find someone else to have a family with, someone who is not so different than you, as I am. You must forget me."

He tries to engage her in a conversation about her wolf nature, thinking that perhaps it would ease some of her concerns if he showed an open mind. But she does not answer his questions, only turns it around on him until at last, he gives up. And when she finally takes leave of him and his cabin, he fancies that he can taste her scent on the air – fresh pine mixed with earth.

He suspects that she is right, that his desire for family would dictate that the woman he ultimately married would be human. *But she is wrong to think that I would ever forget her.*

He moves to shut the door securely, notices that the reverend had the grace to vanish without a word being said upon Felanna's departure. Something bright against the worn wood planking catches his eye – bending carefully, he reaches down to pick the item up from the floor.

It is the pendant Felanna wore the night they had first met – the moonstone glowing in the pale moonlight as it crowned her neck.

The heat of tears pricks his eyes as his hand closes over the pendant. She owned his heart and soul, just as he owned hers.

Seating himself back at his desk, he decides to return to the bay. The idea comes to him with such fierceness that he knows it will be the only goal he has until it comes to fruition. He thinks of Cowyn, wonders what the pack leader would think if he knew of the idea forming in the captain's head.

His eyes fall on the letter he had been writing before Felanna made her good-byes to him. Picking up his pen, he dips it into the inkwell again and begins to write.

I will go back to that place and wait. Perhaps I will rebuild and honor her people in the way they should be honored. The story of the people – the werewolves – will have to be altered. I dislike hiding the truth, as it seems a cowardly thing to do, but it may be for their safety and for the safety of others like them. At the very least, they will have a haven to return to, if they so choose. To live life without fear of persecution. Is that not what our Founding Fathers sought when they stood against King George V?

I am hopeful that Cowyn would understand, if he would appreciate such a plan. He is a practical man, their pack alpha and for their survival, he would do everything in his power to protect them.

Perhaps there is a way to help them identify one another, beyond their powerful sense of smell, without giving away their true nature.

Perhaps using the moonstones.... An excellent idea there, my friend. I am not a wolf, but already I seem to be thinking as they do.

I'll speak with him tonight and see if he's willing to return, to start fresh in the same place, and mask the past with an eye to the future.

It would be interesting, to see what would happen in a hundred years...

ABOUT THE AUTHOR

J.J. Brown lives in Southern California, surrounded by an eclectic assortment of books, two cats and several horses.

She is currently at work on several projects.

You can follow her at J.J. Brown, Wordslinger on Twitter, Facebook, and Instagram.

You can also follow her blog: jjbrownwordslinger.com.

www.ingramcontent.com/pod-product-compliance
Lightning Source LLC
Chambersburg PA
CBHW060616100726

47907CB00006B/1643